I0592705

Blood of Heirs

Book One of The Coraidic Sagas

Alicia Wanstall-Burke

Cover Art by Pen Astridge

ISBN: 978-0-6484478-0-1
Imprint: Independently published

First edition: October 2018
Reprint: May 2020

For Hadrian
Of all the things I have ever created,
you are the most spectacular

In loving memory of Percy Wheatcroft and Keith Bickley
— I wish you were both here to see this

Dorfa

Redona City

Lake Lith

The Woacler

Burd

Shartridor

Fort Dawa

Bata

Isord

Grey Cliff

Arinn

Ravens

River Arrus

Port Hadeen

Syod Archipelago

Wolban

Nan

Marsaw

Daylin

The High Tund

Marlow

Harben

Orhia

pire

Godwin

Usmein

eleanor

Visorcrest

Laliva

The Ruken

ja

Kederen

The Altipa

The Malapa

Fradure Pass

Jungle Meridian

Tolak

The South Lands

Jaggu River

The Black Teeth

CHAPTER ONE

The Caine, Tolak Range, the South Lands

The thunder of hooves hammered in Lidan's ears and she ran.

Her feet pounded the earth; hard, rocky soil slipping under the soles of her boots, her bow and quiver bouncing against her back. She pumped her arms and sucked in ragged breaths, racing, stretching out her stride. Long leaves on low hanging branches slapped against her arms, and she ducked around the trunk of a soaring ghost bark.

She had to clear the bush before the riders, had to be there when they reached the valley.

The deafening thunder grew until it was closer, more insistent, louder and deeper, vibrating in her chest, drumming against her bones.

She ran: harder, faster, leaping over a dry creek bed and clearing the gully. She slammed into the ground on the far side and stumbled, scrambling to regain her footing and her speed.

They're here. They're back. They're coming.

Her thoughts repeated, faster and faster, until the words ran together into incomprehensible babble.

They're here they're back they're coming.

She broke through the tree line and staggered to a stop, her hand coming up to shield against the blinding sunlight. The tablelands loomed to the north, a dark line of cliffs rising in the distance from the valley floor. The shallow valley between here and there waved with pale, wind-swept grass, parched and suffering in the dry season. Several hundred feet away to her left, the thunder of hooves emerged from the bush, dozens of mounted rangers teeming from the trees towards the foot of the Caine.

Lidan's breath caught in her throat. *They're back.*

She set off at a jog, mirroring the rangers eastward advance as they hurried their horses from the bush. It had been weeks since they left the village of Hummel, working their way west to scour the border between Tolak and Namjin, hunting for raiders too stupid to heed her father's warnings.

Her father should be there, somewhere among the crush of trail-weary horses and rangers. She scanned the crowd, her gaze darting across faces and features. She recognised many, but could not see her da anywhere.

The rangers followed a wide creek into the lowest reach of the valley, fording the trickle of water where the track cut south towards her and the village at her back. She could see their faces clearly now; men and women with their hair pulled back in tails or cut short to their heads, their shirts, jerkins and trousers filthy with dust, grime and blood. Sacks hung from the saddles, surrounded by swarming flies, darkened from within by foul stains.

Heads.

Lidan smirked. Had they found the raiders who attacked Malmerrin before last moon? Or perhaps they stumbled across some other pack of fools who'd been in the wrong place at the wrong time. She stopped on the incline beside the trackway and watched the riders approach, her chest rising and falling as she fought to catch her breath, horses filing past on their way up to the village gate. Her legs shivered and her skin tingled, blood rushing in nervous anticipation. Surely they would not all look so damn calm if something had happened to her father.

Rangers nodded at her as they passed. They knew her face—knew who she was. Daari Erlon Tolak's eldest daughter. His heir.

Some frowned, probably wondering what she was doing out here, beyond the confines of the village walls. Some shook their heads, no doubt imagining the rage Dana Sellan would fly into if she discovered her daughter had once again slipped away to explore the Caine—the massive stone monolith behind the village—and the valley at its foot, painted faded green and brown, orange and gold, drained of its brilliance by the dry season.

Lidan didn't care.

She'd been out here every day for a week waiting for the ranging party to return—watching the trees, the place where the western track snaked off into the bush along the face of the tablelands, listening for the thunder of hooves and the shouts of riders returning home. One day she would be allowed to go with them. One day…

The daari's face appeared within the crush of rangers and horses, and Lidan darted forwards. Erlon Tolak was a mountain of a man who filled every hall and hut with his presence from the moment he entered to the second he departed. With his words, he commanded the ear of every man, the eye of every woman and the rapt attention of every child. And at this very moment, he was painted head to foot in several weeks' worth of trail dirt and a decent amount of old blood.

'Da!' she shouted over the clamour of horses, the creaking of leather tack and the rumble of conversation coursing up towards the village gate.

'Liddy?' Her father frowned down from Titon's saddle. His boots strained in the leather stirrups as he guided his huge black horse out of the stream of mounted rangers and towards his daughter. 'Does your mother know you're out here?'

Her excitement at seeing him staggered, punched out by the thought of her mother scouring the village under a raging storm cloud. She glanced over her shoulder at the wall of the village. 'Probably not, but I wanted to talk to you before she had a chance to…'

She turned back as the enormous Titon snuffled his soft nose into her hand. Her father raised a brow and she sighed.

'You know she has the final say, Lidan,' Erlon said, anticipating her question, and the air of resignation in his voice blew out the last spark of hope she'd been sheltering in her chest. It was the same answer he'd given her when he left with the border patrol.

'Da, please talk to her? She doesn't understand!'

'Liddy, she's your mother. She decides what skills you learn. It was only through the sheer power of nagging that she let you learn to shoot. I can't see that she's ever going to relent and let you train as a ranger.'

'But the other girls—'

Her protest died when he pressed his lips into a thin line. 'The other girls have their mothers' permission to train. You don't.'

Lidan scowled down at the long blades of grass dancing in the chill wind. At twelve years old, she was well and truly of an age to begin her training, but her mother had other ideas. 'She said she would let me if the horse was broken in…'

Erlon's gaze softened despite the glare of the afternoon. 'Only the rider can break the horse, Lidan. It's clan Law and it's to keep you safe. Until she lets you break him in yourself, you can't ride him.'

Lidan sighed through her nose. She'd be a hundred summers old before she was allowed to even sit in a saddle by herself.

'Come on, we'll take Titon back together, eh?'

If anything could brighten an afternoon, it was a ride on the back of her father's saddle. She put her foot on his boot and he pulled her up to sit behind him, arrows bouncing quietly in the saddle-quiver as he guided Titon up the hill towards the gate.

The sun began to slip behind the tablelands in the west and cold shadows crept out to strangle the valley. The only warmth lay in the village, Hummel; the centre of her world. A horn blew from Hummel's wall to signal the end of another day, calling the clan's people in from foraging and grazing their stock in the valley. They wandered back to the gates in clusters, women carrying tired children on one hip and their day's gathering or weaving on the other, men with braces of birds or hoppers slung over their shoulders. Lidan scanned for her mother's auburn hair and milk pale face in the crowd that had gathered to watch the rangers from the top of the wall, but she was nowhere to be seen.

Lucky... she thought.

It would be a quieter evening if she wasn't seen on Titon's back. Learning to ride was the very last thing her mother planned for her and she was certain to cop a tongue-lashing if discovered even sitting on Titon.

According to her mother, she wasn't going to do *anything* with her life except match to another daari's son and make babies, and leading the clan when the day came that her father passed into the realm of the ancestors. She was a girl, and the first daughter of a daari. She knew it now at twelve-years-old, and she would know it for sure when she was eighteen and old enough to match. She just didn't understand why it meant she couldn't train as a ranger like everyone else. Training was important—something she had to learn if she had any hope of earning her people's respect and loyalty. But her mother said such pursuits were far too dangerous for so precious a child.

Behind the village, the Caine loomed high, carved by wind and rain to the shape of a wild dog's tooth, glowing orange in the light of the setting sun. Hummel lay at its base, a settlement where grassland met rock in a collection of a hundred or so grey and brown buildings, stone and timber, most with lilac smoke rising from their thatched roofs.

Only one small building stood apart, a few hundred feet away from the village proper at the very foot of the Caine. It appeared to be such an unkempt hovel neither man nor beast could stomach living in it, but Lidan knew better. The hut's single occupant stood concealed in shadow by the woodpile, perfectly hidden unless you knew what to look for; a pair of sharp grey eyes watching Lidan with unwavering intensity while the rest of the body remained still.

Lidan hated those eyes. Sometimes they tracked her from dawn 'til dusk for no reason at all, then vanished for days at a time. They watched her as if they knew her intimately while they'd never come within spitting distance of each other. She ignored them but they remained, always present, never truly gone though they might be out of sight.

She shivered and buried her face in her father's back. One day she hoped to wake and know those eyes weren't watching from the shadows of the hut, because the old woman they called the Crone had done everyone the favour of dropping dead.

As the high timber wall of Hummel rose before them, its gates yawning wide, a tall, fair-haired ranger rode up beside them and broke her thoughts with a smile. Her father slapped the man's shoulder in the silent greeting men often preferred and they continued on. Siman Jarrah, the leader of the daari's rangers and her father's close confidant, was so familiar he could almost be her uncle. His light hair and skin hinted at the northern heritage in his blood, but he was neither as pale as Lidan, nor as dark as her father. He spent his time guarding the daari's back or discussing whatever clan leaders discuss over ale and meat, hardly leaving the daari's side, much less his sight.

'You get any raiders this time, Siman? Or just lose more arrows?' A gateman called from the wall with his bow resting casually in his crossed arms. He was a wide lump of a man, old muscle turned to fat with an ale belly hidden behind the parapet.

'Got more than you ever did, old man!' Siman gestured to the collection of bulging sacks tied to his saddle. The heads inside would soon decorate a line of pikes beyond the wall—a reminder to any outsiders of the price paid for encroaching on Tolak land.

The gateman dismissed Siman's sourness with a wave and vanished from sight as Erlon urged Titon under the lintel of the gate and into Hummel's common. An enormous cheer erupted as they entered, clan's people waving and shouting their congratulations to the daari and the rangers for a successful patrol.

Lidan couldn't help grinning, a rush of pride coursing down her limbs. But she didn't dare linger. She jumped from behind the saddle before anyone could alert her mother and ran into the crowd. She owed her unbroken horse his dinner and he was likely to be unimpressed if she turned up late. Again.

By the time she finished cleaning out her colt's wide stall and dragging in a fresh bag of feed, the night's first stars sparkled in the eastern sky. The horse, who she had named Theus, baulked at the clunk of the closing timber gate and threw his head. Lidan stood where he could see her face and shrugged in the dim light of the wall torches.

'I know it's not the high country, but isn't this better than running from wild dogs all night?' The horse pawed the ground. Lidan chuckled and waved a handful of feed under the animal's nose. 'Eat your food.'

A few sniffs had him eating happily from the bag, the confinement of the pen forgotten. In his distraction, she reached tentative fingers towards his nose and he tossed his black head to flick her away. Undeterred, she reached for him again and the horse threw his head higher.

'Don't be a fool!' Lidan slapped his neck and cursed. 'Do that again and I'll boil your bones for dog food.' She jerked the bag away to hang it on a peg and the horse snorted. Two steps forwards and he had his head back in in the feedbag, chomping and snuffling like a bush-boar gouging a root from the ground. 'You're a smart one; I'll give you that.'

Lidan left the wild-born animal to settle for the night, easing the side door shut to trap some of the day's warmth behind the clay and timber walls. Dinner waited in her father's hall and if she dallied, she'd be left with nothing but scraps.

'It might be kinder to let the poor beast go,' a voice spoke from the darkness and Lidan squealed with fright.

'Oh, petal!' Her mother darted forwards and pulled her into a suffocating embrace against her breasts. More than ample for an otherwise slender woman, it was like being shoved between two fleshy, pale pillows. Sellan knew well enough that her daughter spent each evening in the stable, but Lidan wondered why the woman had sought her out. Had she heard about Lidan's earlier adventure around the Caine? Or was it something else? 'Don't fret. I'm sure your father will let you ride it one day.'

'He said *you* said I couldn't!' Her words were lost in the depths of her mam's cleavage. Confusion and hope warred in Lidan's chest. Would the dana relent and let her break the horse in, if she had her father's permission?

Her mother withdrew slowly and held Lidan's arms tight, her emerald eyes narrowed, scanning her daughter's face. Lidan felt herself shrink under the glare. 'Your father likes to twist the truth, Lidan.'

'But Mam, he says it's up to you if I start my training—'

Fingernails bit into her arm and she jammed her lip between her teeth to stifle a scream. Stupid girl! She knew better than to talk back to her mother.

'Lidan, you were born of a dana and a daari.' Her voice was calm, even kind, but the pressure of her fine hands and her unflinching scowl left Lidan in no doubt. Sellan never made threats—she made promises. 'You are not some shit-flecked horse herder. You are not a scrub digger. You are not a rider or a fighter. No daughter of mine will *ever* be a ranger, be they a first or minor daughter.'

'Mam, please,' Lidan wheezed, wincing away from the pain. 'You said you want me to lead one day. Da said ranging is—'

'There are other ways, Lidan,' Sellan growled between clenched teeth. 'There are safer ways. Ways that don't end up with you trampled under the hooves of one of those beasts or gutted by a Namjin axe. Your position is too precarious, too important to risk.'

'But they won't let me lead if I haven't trained!' Lidan tried to twist out of her mother's clawing grip, but the dana held tight. Why couldn't she understand? She just wanted to—

'Oi, Sellan! Lidan!' Erlon's voice boomed across the darkened common from the door that led to the hall's kitchen and he waved. It was time to eat.

ALICIA WANSTALL-BURKE

A dazzling smile instantly broke across Dana Sellan's face and she returned the gesture enthusiastically. As Erlon returned inside Lidan jerked away but her mother snatched her arm and yanked down, her features hard in the fractured light from the torches on the outside of the stable walls.

'They will let you lead, child, but you must let me guide you. No more talk of ranging, do you understand? Or that precious horse of yours might find his next meal to be his last.'

Lidan froze.

Would she truly do it? Would she kill Theus if she thought it would stop Lidan's persistant pursuit of training and riding? Of course she would. She hated the horse. She only let Lidan keep it because it was a coming of age gift from her father. Perhaps the dana was right—ranging was dangerous. Perhaps Lidan just needed to listen more, then her mother wouldn't be so angry all the time.

'Yes, Mam,' she whispered, conceding the point.

Sellan gave a nod and one more pinch for good measure before releasing her grip. 'Go to supper.'

Rubbing her forearm, Lidan hurried towards the hall.

Stupid, stupid, stupid girl...

While she might disappear into the hubbub of the family meal, Sellan would find her later to make sure her point had stuck and Lidan didn't plan on disappointing her. She'd suffered for disobeying her mother before. The cruelty was etched on her skin in places people couldn't see. She knew better than to push the point and her mother's decision was clear: no training—ever.

CHAPTER TWO

Hummel, Tolak Range, the South Lands

Laughter echoed in the daari's hall, warm light and the scent of cooked meat and flat bread radiated from the doors. Lidan ducked into the kitchen, breathless, and a tine-woman of middle years glanced up at the intrusion. Of all the tine-women in the long, busy kitchen, she alone noticed Lidan cutting through, but when their eyes met the woman did not speak, staying silent just like a slave ought to. Lidan left her to the business of yanking the skins from a pair of bouncers and slipped into the hall.

From the kitchen, a screened corridor ran the perimeter of her father's hall, allowing the tine-women to move unseen with trays and urns of ale and wine. In the light filtering through the woven reed screen, Lidan paused and caught her breath. She rolled her embroidered shirt sleeves down over the marks of her mother's nails and straightened her trousers and over-skirt until she looked presentable. She was in no mood to field questions about bruises and cuts she'd rather not explain.

Regaining some composure, Lidan spied an empty seat at the table occupied by her nine sisters and ducked through the gathering to sit with them. Mess and chaos filled the hall to brimming, the returned rangers and their families were dining with the daari and several trade masters in celebration of the patrol's success. Many were linked by blood or matching, everyone related to someone else in some manner. Tomorrow the hall would once again become Lidan's family home; but tonight, it was a heaving mass of humanity crammed within four walls to the point it seemed the hall might burst.

Men shouted across the room at their children to sit down, eat, and listen to their mothers, and children screamed when their siblings or cousins knocked over cups of milk, or stole the last baked potato from a platter. Mothers scolded and cursed, wiped and sighed as the collection of children ran rings around them; meat, bread and sauces hitting the earth floor in an endless shower.

Daari Erlon's burly hunting dogs strategically positioned themselves under the tables and inhaled scraps as they fell, tails wagging as though a better feast had never been seen. At the head of the long fire pit cut deep in the floor, the daari sat with his seconds, talking and laughing, picking roast meat from platters and slathering flat bread with pickled preserves.

It was chaotic, dirty and exhausting and Lidan clenched her jaw, forced a smile and dropped down beside her full-sister, Marrit. She and Marrit were the only daughters of Dana Sellan and Erlon and had both inherited their northern mother's distinct pale skin. They stood out like beacons among their half-sisters, all of them darker and cut from the same cloth as most of the clan. Erlon's next wife, Raeh, fussed over her four daughters while bouncing baby Lucija on her knee. Lucija was the last of Erlon's ten daughters, and his only child with the fourth and youngest wife, Farah. His third wife Kelill sat opposite, her brown hair tied in a tight knot on her head. Her three girls all sported the same style, as well as Erlon's smiling blue eyes.

Lidan thanked the ancestors daily that four wives were the legal limit for a daari. More wives meant more children, and she really did think her father had his fair share of offspring. All he was missing was a son, and she knew that niggled at him like a buried splinter. Many wives also meant many mouths to feed, and the number any man could acquire relied solely on his role and his ability to support them all.

Lidan filled her cup with spiced milk as one of her smallest and favourite sisters, Abbi, crawled silently into her lap. She enjoyed the company of her tiny sister, because little Abbi was the quietest of all the Tolak girls. While the rest of their half-sisters chatted and giggled, and Bridie and Elva squabbled over the heads of the smaller girls, Lidan and Abbi ate together in a comfortable silence.

'Don't be stupid, Elva,' Bridie snapped. 'Everyone knows yawks don't really exist.' The nine-year-old rolled her eyes as though her eight-year-old half-sister was so very immature.

'They do so! Mam said they do!' Elva insisted, undeterred by Bridie's disbelief. 'And the pankars and the namorras. *They* catch you and suck your brains out.'

'Not your brains—your soul,' Bridie corrected. 'They fly on the wind and steal your soul. That's how they turn you into one of them.'

'Your soul is *in* your brain!' Elva's voice rose higher, attracting the narrowed eyes of her mother.

'It's in your belly, you idiot!'

The argument would likely continue for hours if someone didn't intervene, but Lidan had neither the energy or the will so she let their words flow past her like water over stones. Kelill placed a board of meat and bread in front of Lidan and cut across Bridie and Elva's argument.

'If you two don't stop bickering, I'll put you both out in the wind for the namorras to take. Now, be quiet and eat!'

As if to emphasise her point, a strong gust moaned through the thatch above and the girls fell silent. Kelill moved to separate her other girls, Iscah and Hanne, who were wrestling over the ownership of a cup.

Silenced but not defeated, Bridie and Elva stuck their tongues out at each other—a clear signal that the battle was not over.

Famished from a day in the valley, Lidan tucked into her food and let the noise melt the memory of her mother's threats, even though it did nothing to ease the pain of her bruises, while Abbi nibbled at some flat bread and ignored the roasted vegetables her mother pushed across the table. Lidan glanced at the assembled crowd. Around the hall, rangers debated and gestured, discussing plans for hunts and flinging crass jibes at any available chance. Was Sellan planning on showing her face in the hall tonight, or would she take her meal in her private quarters, as she was wont to do when the daari hosted a party of rangers?

Farah appeared, directing tine-women with boards of sweet treats towards the daari's table, twisting to avoid children and dogs on the way.

Shouts of disagreement angrily cut the happy murmur of eating and drinking.

The attention of the hall swivelled to focus on a dim corner and a bench tucked behind a pillar where two men glared at each other with clenched fists and set jaws.

Lidan squinted and craned her neck to see.

The same men had been at the last open Hearing, airing a dispute settled by her father according to the Law. Hender stood almost a head higher than his adversary, Poll, and sported a full head of dark hair despite his years. Poll made up for his lack of height with his broad barrel of a chest, fit from wielding timber-cutting axes.

They silenced the hall with the scowls they traded across the table, all except a few children too young to sense the tension in the air. In the unusual quiet, Erlon rose from his bench and tapped the base of his horn cup on the table, drawing the eyes of the gathered clan to him.

'Kinsmen, what brings you to shout in my hall?' Her father eyed the men and Lidan stretched up to see over the heads blocking her view. Would they return to their seats or voice their dispute? It would be a welcome distraction from her mother's ruling on her training.

Poll hadn't been impressed with the daari's decision at the last Hearing, spitting at Hender's feet and storming off into the night. Was this the same problem, the same fight? To Lidan's left a shape retreated into the shadows behind the reed screens and she guessed it was Hender's daughter, Neilly, making a quick exit to escape the embarrassment of her father's feuding.

Erlon gestured with his cup. 'Come forwards if you won't sit, and let's settle this… *again*.'

He glared at Hender and Poll in turn, fire in his eyes and a muscle twitching in his jaw as he climbed the hall's dais to his audience chair. It was a huge thing, carved from the stump of a Red Core tree and draped with furs. On the wall above the chair hung the longest knife Lidan had ever seen. Her father called it a sword—the only one of its kind south of the Malapa, and the profit of a trade with a wealthy Arinnian for the finest wild-born and stable-bred horses of the season, broken in and trained by the Tolak clan. Erlon never carried the blade though, complaining that it fooled with his balance and Titon fussed when it hung from the saddle.

Hender and Poll wove between the benches and tables, exchanging dark glares as the assembled rangers silently fell back to eating. It wasn't often food came with such good entertainment. Lidan shifted Abbi onto the bench beside her and shuffled onto her knees, her feet tucked beneath her, so she had a better view.

'What is it this time?' Erlon asked, a tine-woman appearing at his shoulder to refill his cup while Hender and Poll arranged themselves in the space at the foot of the dais. Neither man spoke and Erlon narrowed his eyes. 'Is this about the daughter, again?'

Lidan winced.

Neilly, she thought. *Her name is Neilly...*

'Oh yes, sir, the daughter is at the heart of the matter.' Poll nodded fiercely and stabbed a finger towards Hender. 'And the promises her father made!'

'If memory serves, this was dealt with at the last Hearing.' Erlon kept his voice even, but the low, menacing edge of his voice was hard to ignore. 'Hender's first daughter may match with whomever he decides is best.'

'Not after she was promised and said to be matching to my son!' Poll's balding head turned dark red from front to back. He tended to become a tomato when angered.

'The promise was never certified,' Hender interjected, folding his arms across his chest. 'And I paid you handsomely in skins and hides, as the Daari ordered.'

'Hender speaks true.' Erlon leaned forwards slowly. 'Can either of you explain why this is still a problem?'

'Because, sir,' Hender turned so his voice carried across the hall. 'This man has been raiding my plot and fouling my stock's drinking water with dead things. Can't afford to foul water and kill beasts in the dry season for no good reason, and he has no reason!'

Men and women in the hall nodded in agreement, filling their cups and settling in for the resolution.

Erlon raised a brow at Poll, who shuffled his feet a little. 'Does he speak true?'

'I've nothing to do with dead things ending up in his water!'

'And the plot raiding?' pressed Erlon, seeing through the bluster. He always picked the liars from the crowd. When Poll failed to answer, the daari worked his jaw. 'Poll, it is unwise to bicker among kin and neighbours when we all face the same enemies outside our gates. The seasons and the other clans make enough trouble without us causing more. But I see you are unhappy with my judgement. What must be done to calm you?'

Lidan shuddered. This was like watching horse-trading, except instead of well-trained animals, they were bartering with the life of an eighteen-year-old girl who had no say in any of it unless her father deemed otherwise. A small fire ignited in Lidan. That would not be her fate. At least, not if she had anything to do with it.

Erlon drank deep and waited. He always waited. He watched and waited, and Lidan knew there was wisdom in that, though she couldn't work out how he decided to act or what to do. It seemed like magic; the ancestors whispering in his ear, showing him the way forwards in words no other could hear.

Poll's frustration burst out in a flurry of words.

'My son and my family were *shamed* when his daughter matched to another, certified promise or not. I've now got to find the boy another wife and we all know the time and cost that takes!'

Again, the gathered crowd nodded and Lidan's mother slowly approached from behind the reed screen to stand near her husband. How long had she been there, listening to the Hearing before revealing herself with the languid grace of a snake. Lidan's gaze fixed on Sellan as the woman watched the disputing men with calm interest, calculations whirring behind her sharp eyes.

Poll opened his hands to the daari. 'I deserve more than skins as repayment for my trouble.'

Sellan cleared her throat before Erlon could reply, and Lidan froze.

'You're a tradesman, aren't you, Poll?'

Her question jolted the shorter man, and Erlon's glare settled on his first wife. He took another drink and gestured to the tine-woman for more. Lidan grimaced and sank back to her seat, untucked her legs and slipped below the adults' eye-line. Her ears and cheeks burned with embarrassment. Trust her mother to interrupt a Hearing, of all things!

'Yes, Dana, I am a man of the trades.' Poll inclined his head and returned his attention to Erlon as if the fact was of little consequence.

Lidan's heart started to race.

Undaunted by Poll's dismissive tone, the dana smirked.

'So, what under the sun and sky made you think this man would match his first daughter—his prize child, second only to his first son—to your offspring?' Her words carried high in the stifling air and even the children fell silent. 'Did you offer a great dower for her, or perhaps your first son as an equal match? No, if I recall, your first son is already matched, with a child in his wife's belly. So, if not him, then who? What did you offer Hender as sufficient *repayment* for matching his first daughter to the son of a tradesman?'

Poll stared at the dana, redder than Lidan had ever seen him, the veins in his neck throbbing.

Beside him, Hender cleared his throat to interrupt. 'He offered his third son, an unskilled labourer in his timber works.'

A smile twitched at the edges of Sellan's mouth and she nodded as if finally understanding, every movement mocking Poll. 'You offered your third, unskilled son, to match to Hender's *first daughter*? You might as well have asked him to match her to a pig!' The hall erupted with laughter. If Poll got any redder, Lidan was sure he'd burst. 'Hender, have you minor daughters of matching age?'

The taller man nodded. 'Only one of matching age.'

'She's fifteen, then? And how old is your second son, Poll?' Sellan asked, easing down to sit on the edge of the dais, her fine woollen dress pooling around her.

'He is closer to twenty,' Poll replied, somehow managing to keep most of his anger behind his teeth.

'Ah! Perfect. All is settled; a son will marry a daughter and that will be the end of it.' Sellan glanced at Erlon and smiled, but his lips didn't return the expression. Her back straightened and eyes narrowed. 'Are you not pleased, husband?'

'Oh no, wife, please continue…' He saluted her with his cup, his voice thick with sarcasm. 'Soon you'll have me out of a job.'

Some of the rangers chortled nervously, but most remained still and averted their gazes to their plates or the floor.

'I have found you a solution, have I not? An amicable arrangement that need not result in blood?' Her mother's hand opened towards Poll and Hender, both motionless and surely regretting allowing their dispute to come before the daari again so publicly.

With a groan, Lidan hid her face behind her hands and waited. She was good at waiting—almost as good as her father. While she had inherited her mother's stubbornness, she hardly held a candle to the woman at over-stepping what was proper. Sellan was a veritable expert at taking things too far, a disregard her half-mothers claimed she brought from the north. Lidan imagined Sellan's boldness had once entranced the daari, but by the look on her father's face, she wondered if the novelty had begun to wear off.

'Wife, as always I appreciate your… *counsel.*' He seemed to swallow a mouthful of words and turned to the feuding men, frustration and fatigue etched in the lines of his face. 'Poll, your third son is not a sufficient match for a first daughter in her matching year. We keep our first daughters un-matched until they are eighteen because they are precious to us. Expecting Hender to prefer your third son over a proposal from a ranger like Lucus Hoofmar is foolish and I'm sure you wouldn't accept the same arrangement for your first children. A fair resolution has been found, if you agree to it?'

Poll puffed out his chest as if trying to make himself larger, or at least taller. 'A second daughter is of lesser value than a first.'

He was right, Lidan had to concede. A minor daughter came with a much smaller dowry and fewer tine-women and livestock. Still, the endless references to value began to eat at her, as if Neilly were nothing more than a broodmare fit for foaling.

Poll continued, 'I require something further to repay the insult of the—'

'You've already killed *four* of my goats, old man!' Hender snarled, leaving Lidan quite sure it took all his strength not to punch the balding man in the face. 'You've taken enough payment.'

The shorter man's fists shook, balled tight at the ends of thickly muscled arms. Short and round he might be, but the timber cutter was strong and well built. Only a fool would underestimate him, and Lidan doubted Hender to be such a man. His younger children spoke of him as wise and fair, not easily angered but deeply wounded by any slight on his honour.

Daari Erlon placed his cup aside and rested a casual hand on the hilt of his bronze knife. 'Do we have a resolution?'

Lidan's heartbeat quickened and her breathing laboured in the palpable tension of the hall. What if Poll refused? Hearings could turn bloody if one party could not accept the ruling of the daari.

Poll's head twitched in a nod and the hall breathed a collective sigh of relief. Erlon clapped his hands down on the arm rests of his audience chair.

'Very well then. The second son of Poll Timmith and the second daughter of Hender Hide are to be matched. Consider this confirmation of the promise and see to it the matter of this dispute ends here, now, and is never spoken of again. If I hear reports of this rearing its head again, I'll deal with the matter more severely.' Her father looked pointedly at Poll. 'This is your final warning and my final word.'

The bald man's head inclined again and Erlon waved them away. Lidan tried to swallow the hot ball of embarrassment in her throat and refused to look up at the faces around her as the hall fell into chatter once more and eating resumed. Were all mothers as humiliating as hers?

Chapter Three

A fortnight after the Hearing, after a short ceremony that promised the two children of Poll and Hender, Hummel seemed a lighter place. By the time the clan recovered from the ale headaches and the effects of nights spent in celebration, it seemed most of Hummel's residents had forgotten that it was the dana who cut across her father's authority and made the ruling for him.

Lidan, however, had not.

She tried to avoid her mother, and to quell the unrelenting embarrassment roiling in her gut, disappearing into the stables at any opportunity, but she could not escape every lesson her mother forced her to sit through. She was atrociously inept at sewing, much to her mother's disgust, and failed miserably at some odd little tea ceremony her half-mothers made her practice at the dana's insistence. She struggled to weave a serviceable basket when asked and had no patience for planning meals and arranging significant clan events. She couldn't grasp how any of these mundane tasks would make her a more capable or respected clan leader, and she itched to escape to the ranger's barracks and training yard, even just to watch.

The only lesson she relished was taught by her father, while she sat beside him and learned to read and draw maps. Today they worked outside in the sunny warmth of the common, drawing symbols with sharpened white chalk on a flat slate; her father sketching a symbol while she watched then copied it.

'No, that needs to curve up and down more. Otherwise it looks like the line of a track, not a bank of hills. Here,' he scrubbed the markings away with the ball of his hand and drew the symbol again. She bit her lip and concentrated, winding the line up and down to mimic the symbol above it. 'Much better—do ten and then we'll—'

'Surprise!' Farah's voice sang out behind them and they both started at the sound. Erlon grinned when she emerged, chestnut curls dancing around her smiling face. He wrapped a muscled arm around Farah's waist and dragged her into his lap, her half-mother's laughter peeling across the common as his unshaven jaw nuzzled her neck. He whispered something and Farah blushed a deep red.

'Stop it, husband!' Farah joked with a playful slap to his shoulder and regarded Lidan with a warm smile. 'You're making poor Lidan awkward! Oh, your symbols are coming along so nicely, Liddy. You have a calm hand for drawing pictures as well as bows.'

It was Lidan's turn to blush and her face flushed at the praise. 'I'm lucky Da takes time to teach me.'

'My father didn't teach me symbols,' Farah said and leaned closer to study the slate. A daughter of the Namjin, Farah's matching to Erlon had been an attempt at forging peace several years ago. That peace had since failed spectacularly, crushed under the weight of sparse resources and the harsh southern climate. 'Looks like gibberish to me!'

Her husband nodded. 'Lidan is no ordinary girl, my love.'

He tousled Lidan's hair and she immediately swatted his hand and corrected it before anyone could see the black bird's nest it became if set free from its braid. In truth, he only agreed to teach Lidan her symbols as consolation for her mother's refusal to let her break in her horse. Map reading was a rare skill reserved for rangers, and map drawing was rarer still, so she tried to take to her lessons with enthusiasm, knowing all the while it was but a tiny sliver of the full training she yearned for.

A pile of buckets crashed to the ground across the common in an echoing clatter and Lidan's eyes darted to the source. A tine-woman with flaxen hair scrambled to collect her dislodged load of washing buckets, which, thankfully for her, were empty when she ran full-tilt into the dana. Sellan stood unmoved at the bottom of the kitchen stairs, with her arms crossed and a sour twist to her lips, glaring at Erlon, Lidan and Farah as though they'd been plotting murder.

Lidan glanced at her father in time to see the light in his eyes fade and his smile straighten to a thin line. Her heart skipped a beat then hammered back into rhythm, shocked by how quickly the darkness in her mother's gaze sucked the happiness from her father's face. Lidan had little memory of Raeh and Kelill's arrival at Hummel, too young to care or remember, but she did recall Farah's no more than a year or two before. She remembered how Sellan had smiled her best smile and welcomed the daari's fourth wife into her new home. And she remembered how every day since that smile had become tighter, more forced, until it dissolved into an undisguised scowl, born of the blatantly obvious regard Erlon held for Farah over his other wives.

'Afternoon, wife,' Erlon called a cool greeting to Sellan and tapped his finger on the slate. Lidan turned quickly back to her symbols and tried to ignore the strain vibrating between her parents. Apparently, her mother's intrusion into the Hearing had not been forgotten or forgiven.

'Husband,' Sellan replied without moving. Farah shifted and tried to stand, but the muscles in Erlon's arms flexed and held her firmly in place. After a moment, Lidan peeked up, not daring to lift her head more than an inch to glimpse her mother's narrowed eyes and the dark shadows deepening above her cheekbones, as though a cloud above her blocked out the sun. Sellan's eye twitched, a tiny movement that would be missed by anyone not staring as rudely as Lidan, then the dana spun away. She spat at the tine-woman and stormed up the stairs into the hall, her auburn hair vanishing into the dim interior like a trail of angry flame.

'What did I do?' Farah murmured.

'Nothing, my love. She angers quicker than a summer storm and leaves a wake of confusion just as wide.' Erlon kissed his wife and let her go. 'Pay her no mind.'

Lidan found no solace in the overheard words and her blood thumped through her veins. Why was her mother scowling so ferociously? Surely it was her father who had grounds to be cross and not the other way around?

'Liddy?' Farah's voice reached through the flurry of her thoughts. She knew her panic was as plain as the nose on her face so there was little point trying to hide it. Lidan stared at the scrawled symbols, infantile compared to her father's. 'Lidan?' Farah whispered in her ear. 'Are you all right, blossom?'

'I...' Lidan didn't know what to say. She was *not* all right but she couldn't explain why. Her gut churned and twisted as though she'd swallowed a basket of snakes, her skin beading with anxious sweat, dread creeping up her spine. 'Yes. Just tired.'

Her lie took a moment to take hold. The youngest of her father's wives laid a cool hand on the nape of Lidan's neck and frowned back at the door. Lidan chewed the inside of her lip bloody, half expecting Farah to take off and follow the dana, but instead she pursed her lips and gave Lidan a gentle pat. 'If you say so... Early to bed after supper. We'll all be up at dawn to see off the hunt.'

A cold shiver rippled from Lidan's scalp to her fingertips, her eyes glued to her drawings as Farah moved away. She felt numb, empty and heavy all at once, the hectic noise of the common replaced by a high-pitched ringing in her ears. Her mother's angry glare filled her vision and the pinch marks on her arms burned as if the dana held her where she sat. Why was her mother so angry?

Perhaps Sellan had been looking at *Lidan*, still furious about their argument outside the stable and her insistence on continuing to learn things only a ranger should know. She probably blamed the daari for continuing to indulge their daughter.

Lidan squeezed the lump of drawing chalk until it crumbled and decided that tomorrow she would tell her father to take Theus back. Without the horse, all this animosity would surely end. Before her father left to lead the rangers on another hunt, she would ask him to give the colt to one of the apprentice rangers, or perhaps to Poll's son as a matching gift, and be done with it. Yes, that would please her mother and no one would be angry anymore.

Sunlight cut through the window shades and dragged Lidan from a heavy sleep. Marrit's bed stood empty across the room, a mess of furs and blankets piled on the floor. In the corner, a bowl of washing water stood on a table beside a basket of clean under linens and fine clothing their mother insisted they wear. Lidan splashed her face with the water and slipped a creamy embroidered shirt over her head before climbing into a pair of her favourite trousers.

A skirt wrapped over the trousers, the fabric split from the ankles to the hip on both sides, then an apron fell over the front of that. Her boots stood by the door, scrubbed clean and ready for another day. Too impatient to sit and lace them properly, she shoved her feet in and hopped clumsily down the corridor, glancing behind door curtains as she passed. It was already late morning and each room stood empty, her family already in the common to farewell the departing hunt.

The journey along the border of the Tolak range took several weeks and the rangers wouldn't return until they'd caught enough game to smoke for the dry season stores. The dry season drove the game closer to the peaks of the Malapa, seeking the greener grass that sheltered in the damp foothills, taking them closer to the territories of the ice dragons who dwelt above the snow line. There weren't many dragons left in Coraidin, the largest of them hunted to extinction while the rest were either too small to warrant any attention or kept themselves hidden in places men dared not tread. With the migrating mobs came the clan's neighbours, eager to see what food could be found in land that was not their own. The rangers scouted not only for game, but for signs of the neighbouring Namjin and Wolban clans crossing their borders, answering each slight with anger and blood.

Lidan hurried from the living quarters, hoping to find her father in the hall finalising his business. If he stood with the rangers, she wouldn't dare try and return the colt to him—the shame would be intolerable! If she spoke to him alone, away from the others, he might understand. There was no way to avoid giving back the horse, as much as it broke her heart, but it had to be done quietly; no one could know.

At the kitchen's entrance to the main hall, she heard the deep rumble of Erlon's voice, his words obscured by the thick walls. With a lump of sadness in her throat, Lidan stepped through to confront him.

A rough hand caught her wrist and pulled her behind the woven screen, another slapped over her mouth. She hit the floor and winced, then spun to free herself from the grip of the unseen hand. The owner relented, demanding silence with his finger across his lips. It took a moment to recognise his face in the gloom, and when Lidan nodded her understanding, his hand fell away from her mouth.

'Behn?' asked Lidan with a scowl.

'Shh!' The forge apprentice pressed his finger harder to his lips as if she had misunderstood the gesture.

'What in the name of the ancestors are you doing here?' she hissed.

'You don't want to go in there,' Behn replied. A year or so older than Lidan and apprenticed to the forge master, his already tan skin was so stained with soot it looked black as night in the dim corridor; his straight teeth and the whites of his eyes were ridiculously bright by comparison. This morning his brows furrowed into grimy creases across his forehead and his eyes scanned around.

Lidan recoiled at the thick collection of filth under the boy's nails. 'When was your last bath?'

Behn ignored her, his attention fixed on the muted conversation beyond the screen. 'I've got a message for the daari from Master Rick, an important one he needs before the hunt…' He paused and glanced around. 'I nearly went straight in!'

Lidan didn't understand the problem; all he needed to do was rap a knuckle on the doorframe before entering. Why was he squatting in the corridor like a kicked dog? A voice echoed from the hall and her blood ran cold.

Dana Sellan's words shattered the silence. 'I've tried to advise you and you ignore me time and time again!'

'Told you,' Behn muttered and sat down heavily. 'You don't want to go in there.'

Lidan scrambled to her knees and peered through the screen's weave. Her parents faced each other over a table near the hall's fire pit, the surface covered with parchment sheets, scrolls, quills and ink cups. Sellan had interrupted Erlon's preparations and it appeared serious enough that he'd dismissed his rangers and emptied the hall.

'For the sake of the ancestors, woman!' Daari Erlon's tone held an anger that made Lidan shiver. He threw his quill down and spread his arms wide. 'I've things to see to, a clan to feed, and you choose now to saunter in here and tell me what I can and can't do with my own wives?'

Sellan leaned forward, palms down on the papers, and lowered her voice to a growl. 'I am your dana! It's my *job* to tell you what to do with them and when. If you ignore the signs—'

'What bloody signs?' Erlon spat.

'The auguries! Only a fool would ignore signs from the ancestors.'

'You've been casting auguries about me?' He stepped towards his wife but she didn't flinch. 'I don't recall ordering auguries to be thrown, and if I had, it would be about the dry season, or our hunts, or our enemies, not *my* wives.'

'The reason for casting the blood doesn't matter—it only matters that you heed the message!' Sellan's words came out as sharp as knives but the daari dismissed the comment out of hand and turned away. Lidan knew when he waved his hand like that the conversation was over. She knew when he turned his back, it was the end of it, but her mother didn't care. She jabbed an accusing finger in the direction of the living quarters. 'Ever since *she* came, you've ignored every—'

'Since who came?' growled Erlon, deep as a wild dog defending its kill. Lidan's pulse thundered so loud she could hardly hear her parent's snarled words.

'You know who, Erl,' Sellan retorted, swift as a whip crack. 'Don't make like you haven't changed your ways since she flounced down from the Namjin range. You've had her twice as often as the rest of us—and with a hundred times the hunger!'

The pain in her mother's jealous face was unlike anything Lidan had seen. Genuine anguish creased the corners of her eyes, the line of her lips held tight lest they betray a single tremor of emotion. The daari didn't respond and Lidan's mind flew into panic.

She didn't want to hear this.

She didn't want to know the private conversations of her parents, or see them bickering and spitting venom at each other. Fixed to the spot, there was nothing to do except struggle to understand their furious words.

Sellan continued in the offered silence. 'Thanie has advised me—'

Her husband turned and hurled the table out from between them. '*Fuck* that bent old woman! What has the Crone ever done to justify my feeding her toothless hole of a mouth?' Erlon's rage set the air to crackling, his face burning red and broad chest heaving.

'Her name is Thanie, and she is your *only* hope of conceiving a son, Erlon Tolak, and you know it!' Sellan snapped.

Lidan started and glanced at Behn. He shouldn't be seeing this. Neither of them should. Only the ancestors knew the punishment they'd get if they were found spying, but they had no way to escape without being seen or heard. They were stuck, pinned to the spot, unable to look away and unable to leave.

'Is that right?' The daari's boots scuffed the dried grasses spread across the hall's bare floor. He paced slowly towards the dana even though his temper was well and truly lost. 'So why, in all the years since you and the wrinkled bitch came here in that trading caravan, have none of my girls been boys?'

Silence filled the hall like icy water. Only the breeze whistling through the thatch roof and Behn's breathing reached Lidan through her fear. The daari was right—after more than thirteen years and four wives, he had not one son.

'Well?' Erlon pressed, stepping closer. Sellan didn't reply, her fierce eyes trained on his face in a defiant glare. 'I thought so. I've done things your way for long enough with nothing to show for it. Now I'll do what I like, when I like, *how* I like. As for the hag, she's to be gone from my lands before the hunt returns.'

'No! You can't turn her out!'

Erlon's arm flew and the back of his wide hand connected with the side of Sellan's face with a sharp crack that echoed against the ceiling. Lidan stifled a cry and Behn winced away. Lidan knew her parents fought, she knew things hadn't been right between them for a long time—her mother's distain for Farah and her father's disregard of Sellan's wishes cutting a rift between them that had been yawing open with each passing season. But Lidan had never seen her father, the biggest, strongest man she knew, strike her mother. The shock of it ripped through Lidan, vomit burning at the back of her mouth.

'How dare you...' Sellan snarled, undeterred and shivering with rage. She didn't lift a hand to the brilliant red mark from her jaw to her eyebrow but her fingers clenched and unfurled as if she'd like to wrap them around his throat.

'Oh, I *dare*. I'm the master of this hall and it's about time you recognised it.'

'I will not allow you to turn her out. I will not allow—'

'That is not your decision!' Erlon's roar vibrated through Lidan's chest and brought terrified tears to her eyes. 'I don't know how she does it, but she's got hold of your mind and you're dancing to her tune. I won't stand for it! She'll be gone before the hunt returns, or I'll deal with you both like the disobedient tine-women you are. Do you want that?'

For the first time, his threats struck a chord. After a long, charged silence, Sellan gave a single, stiff shake of her head. 'As you wish. She will be gone.'

'Good. I won't hear another word about when I can or can't lie with my wives, or which ones I choose.' Erlon straightened his belt and jerkin and left the hall with the echo of his heavy steps trailing behind.

Lidan didn't move. She couldn't. Her face burned like a flame and her heart beat fast and hard. Behn's rough metalworking hand reached over and closed tight around hers, offering some small reassurance, but a tear fell down her cheek despite it. She cursed herself. She should have left as soon as she realised her parents were alone in the hall, before the fight, and not continued to sit here eavesdropping like a tine.

Dana Sellan stood alone in the middle of the hall, her eyes on the door Erlon had vanished through. The muscles in the woman's jaw tensed and relaxed, grinding her teeth as she stood perfectly still. Not one tear marked her face; no sobs shook her lips. After a moment of utter silence, Sellan swept from the hall, leaving Lidan and Behn to stare at the empty space left behind.

'Come on,' muttered Behn, standing and pulling her with him. Despite the shivers of cold fear across her skin, Lidan managed to find her feet.

What in the world had possessed her mother to challenge the daari like that? Her status as dana leant her a lot of influence and a significant amount of authority, so much so that she could speak her mind to the daari without fear of the consequences others might face, but not to that extent. As Lidan stared at the abandoned table in the middle of the hall, she sensed her mother's protective façade rapidly thinning.

'Come with me.' Behn dragged her by the hand and they hurried towards the cold stores at the southern end of the kitchen. They burst through the storeroom door and down a timber ramp to sunlight and freedom. Beside them, the Caine rose high in the morning, the sky bright and duck-egg blue for as far as the eye could see. Chests heaving, they paused in the lee of the building, out of sight. 'I still have to give my message to your father.'

'Wait!' Lidan snatched at Behn's arm as he stepped away. 'Don't say anything. Please... to anyone?'

'Liddy...' Behn shook his head in disbelief. 'As if I would.'

She released him and he jogged around the corner of the hall, his thick leather apron flapping loudly against his legs. Lidan groaned and took off in the opposite direction. The stables offered the best hiding place—her mother hated the horses and even if her life depended on it, she wouldn't set foot there. In the stables, Lidan could shelter from Sellan's rage and muddle through the mess of thoughts and emotions filling up her head.

CHAPTER FOUR

The Disputed Territory, Western Orthia

If a place existed in Coraidin where the Underworld realm of the Dark Rider broke the surface and sucked all the joy and light from the world, Ranoth Olseta stood at the edge of its yawning maw.

The screams of the injured and dying tore at his ears, arrows whistling overhead as he ducked behind a crumbling wall and ran. His breath rasped, acrid smoke stinging his throat and eyes.

A ragged shout echoed over the battle and Ran hit the ground, his hands clasping the back of his head in a feeble shield. A boulder smashed into the tallest wall of the Signal Hill ruins and sent a cascade of stones and ancient mortar crashing down on the soldiers sheltering at its base.

Their screams, garbled and incoherent, cut the air and he gasped, rolling over to stare at where the remains of the old tower had been. Soldiers limped and crawled away, but too many were trapped under the rubble—some silent and still, crushed into bloody puddles—others writhing and twitching as their bodies fought the inevitable pull of death.

Bile surged into Ran's mouth and he forced it back down.

Now was not the time.

He had to find his lieutenant, if she hadn't already been punched full of Woaden arrows or crushed by a flying boulder, and get the fuck out of here. The Hill wouldn't last long under this barrage. It was some sort of gods-given miracle that they'd held it for this long at all, and now those very same gods had decided the Orthian's luck had run out.

He scrambled to his feet, put the gruesome scene at the base of the tower at his back, and sprinted.

Lieutenant Pallent and what remained of her fifty soldiers had arranged themselves around the ruins of the south tower. It was hardly an ideal defensive position, but it was the best they had.

Arrows sailed out from behind the shattered wall, some finding their marks among the Woaden advance, most falling short or missing entirely. Ran slid to a breathless halt beside the lieutenant and caught her arm.

'We have to go,' he croaked over the melee. 'Send runners to the others. We need to retreat.'

The words caught in his throat like a fish bone. His father would have his skin for calling a retreat, but he had no choice. The Hill was lost. He'd lost it, and there was nothing to be done for it.

'What others?' Lieutenant Pallent frowned at Ranoth, her face contorting in confusion.

'Norris and his—'

'Norris is dead, your Grace.'

The news hit Ran like a kick to the guts and he all but staggered under the force of it. *'What? When?'*

Pallent pointed a shaking finger at the slight incline leading away from the ruins to the west. 'Wiped out by artillery about an hour ago.'

Ran followed the lieutenant's gesture and bit the inside of his lip.

Arrayed across the face of the Hill was the remains of Bray Norris's half of the company. There hadn't been more than twenty of them left to defend the trenches when dawn broke, but now the position was completely overrun, Woaden soldiers and archers were teeming across it like ants on a picnic. Beyond that, a line of creaking mobile catapults rolled forwards under the power of enormous draught horses, pausing at intervals to launch boulders at the Hill, shattering what remained of an ancient castle that had, many years ago, been abandoned to the war.

The Hill had a commanding, if foul, view of the carnage spread through the valley below. Trenches and artillery lines snaked off to the north and south, across blackened, barren fields that had not seen sprouting grain or a grazing beast in generations.

'Fuck...' Ran breathed.

'Fuck indeed, your Grace.' Pallent turned back to her soldiers and Ran glanced around, counting the heads of the infantry and archers.

Eighteen...

Was this it? Was this all that remained of the hundred souls he'd led out to reinforce the Hill?

His hand began to shake beside the hilt of his sword.

He'd begged for this command. Begged his father, Duke Ronart, to make his fifteen-year-old over-eager son a captain so he might whet his blade in battle. And Ran had been convinced they could hold the position, too—convinced that all they needed to do was repel the Woaden from the Orthian line until the first snow of winter arrived and the annual ceasefire was called across the Disputed Territory.

But the snow hadn't come, and the Woaden had advanced.

Months of trench warfare in the icy northern winds had been broken when a mage arrived in the Woaden lines and used their cursed magic to boil two dozen of Ran's infantry in their boots. Despite a squad of cutters taking the mage out of action, the Woaden had surged forwards in the aftermath, pushing this portion of the Orthian line back, day by day, until they clung to the ruins of Signal Hill with desperate fingers.

Today their grip slipped, and there was nothing left to do but run or die.

Ran didn't really fancy dying today, so he opted to run, dismissing the venomous rage his father would fly into as a necessary evil.

They could come back.

They could take the Hill again.

Maybe…

'Your Grace!' Pallent's shout in his ear snapped him from his thoughts. 'Orders? Do you still want to go?'

He nodded once and the lieutenant started screaming orders.

Bile rose again in his throat, burning away his resolve as the soldiers around him abandoned their positions and scurried away.

It would be a fighting retreat, but a retreat nonetheless, and he doubted very much that his father would care to know the difference.

The Disputed Territory was a desolate swathe of scarred land to the east of the Morgen Ranges, defended by Orthians against the Woaden Empire for generations before Ran had been born. But despite the blood and the danger, the place had called to Ran like a siren's song, luring out a boy who was desperate to prove himself a man. He'd waited with bated breath for his fifteenth birthday and the chance to finally stand with his father and learn the business of war, yet as he beat a retreat to the command centre a day's ride from Signal Hill, he wondered silently if he'd been utterly insane to desire such a thing.

He and Pallent left the surviving soldiers under the command of another captain resting his troops behind the lines, warning them of the Woaden advance, then rode as hard as they dared for Duke Ronart's command post to the south.

When the duke had announced that he'd finally given in to Ran's badgering and would allow his son to take a command, his commanders had frowned, but stopped short of voicing their concern in Ran's presence. Even Ran's tutor, Perce, thought fifteen was too young for a prince of Orthia to lead troops in battle, and had made his thoughts very clear to the duke. Yet, for all his grand plans and bravado, his lessons on strategy and military leadership, Ranoth had lost his company, lost his position, and very likely lost his father's respect.

The reality of it galled him as they approached the duke's camp, their horses shivering with fatigue and blowing jets of clouding breath from their nostrils. Night fell hard and fast this time of year, and he and the lieutenant were lucky to arrive only a few hours after dark.

The echo of battle had long since faded to the dull rumble of a camp at rest. Archers had stowed their bows, and catapults had ceased their barrage of the Woaden lines. Infantry were beginning to settle into their night watches and healers set about doing what they could for those who made it back from the trenches alive.

Lieutenant Pallent regarded Ran as a pair of grooms led their weary horses away and they stood at a distance from the duke's pavilion. She was a short woman, somewhere in her thirties, with a sharp wit and keen eyes that never missed a trick. Even at fifteen Ran towered over her, a head taller and much broader in the shoulders, but her presence on the field and the regard her troops held her in outstripped him ten-fold. Ran liked her, and the pained expression on her face cut him to his core.

She and Norris had been good to him, keeping any reservations they had about his leadership to themselves, following his orders and offering solid advice when they thought he needed it. He already missed Norris' acerbic humour and penchant for using curse words as punctuation marks. And he knew he would miss Pallent's cool head and honesty when she inevitably returned to the front.

'I can do the talking, if you like?' she offered in a hoarse whisper.

Ran shook his head and rubbed road dust from his eye with the ball of his gloved palm. Despite the soft kid-skin leather, his fingers were frozen solid. 'I think it's best he hears it from me. It was my command, after all.'

Pallent shrugged. 'As you wish, your Grace.'

She gestured towards the pavilion, the perimeter of the tent lit with a circle of staked torches that threw dancing orange light on the canvas walls. 'Lead on.'

Ran stepped past her and clenched his jaw, preparing for the onslaught of his father's anger even before they crossed the threshold.

'Ran?' Duke Ronart's voice erupted in front of him and Ranoth started.

The older man stood tall and broad in the shadows beside the tent door, hands on his hips, the whipping north wind tousling his greying brown hair. He had his armour on, and as dulled and dented as it was, it still held a little lustre in the light of the torches. The duke eyed his son as Ran gave him a quick bow and Lieutenant Pallent snapped a salute.

'At ease, Lieutenant.' The instruction came out as a low growl. 'What are you two doing here?'

'W-we have news, sir,' Ran began, his voice squeaking as though he were a six-year-old. It was always worse when he was nervous. He cleared his throat to try again. 'We have news, sir. From Signal Hill.'

Ronart cocked his eyebrow and folded his arms. 'Do you now? And why is it *you* bring this news, and not a messenger? I recall giving you command of a company, not appointing you as an errand boy.'

The duke's hard eyes wandered over Lieutenant Pallent, who stood with her feet apart and her hands clasped behind her back. She made no move to speak. The duke's questions were not for her.

'You did, sir,' Ran acknowledged. 'And the news concerns the company and the Hill.'

The duke's eyes narrowed slightly. It was a gaze Ran never felt entirely comfortable under. It burned away every layer of his confidence until he stood naked and raw, diminished and reduced to a state of infancy. Perhaps that was how his father saw him— still a vulnerable child, hardly strong enough to lift a sword let alone lead troops in action. He'd hoped to prove the man wrong in that regard, but it appeared he had only lived up to his low expectations. The weight of the realisation pressed down on Ran's chest and he fought for breath, lifting his chin, determined to keep his emotions in check.

'Had enough of it, have you? Got the Lieutenant to escort you back to safety?' Ronart gave a dismissive sigh and shook his head. 'I did try to tell you war isn't all victory and glory. There's glory to be found, certainly, but it's in a muddy trench, under the rotting corpses of a hundred soldiers who've spilled their blood before—.'

'We lost Signal Hill, Father.'

The duke glared at his son and Ran's throat contracted. Ronart turned to Pallent. 'Tell me he's joking.'

She shook her head. 'No, sir, Prince Ranoth speaks the truth. We were over run, and the Hill was lost.'

'When?' The low growl deepened.

'This morning, a few hours past dawn.' The Lieutenant continued while the duke's gaze bored through Ran's skin. He clenched his hands into fists and held them tight, pushing all his fear into the skin of his gloves lest he betray a sliver of it in his face.

'And the company?'

Pallent cleared her throat. 'In the end only twenty or so were able to retreat back to the Ford. We left them with Denover who sent messengers up the line. They should be able to hold the Empire at the river.'

'They fucking better,' Ronart snapped. He stepped back and jerked his head towards the doorway to the pavilion, his gaze never leaving Ran's face. 'Get in there. You can account for this debacle like a real soldier, seeing as you're so intent on playing at one.'

Chapter Five

The duke's pavilion was packed with marshals in various states of cleanliness—some covered head to toe in drying mud while others had little more than a clump of horse shit on their boots. As Ran ducked into the tent, servants were setting a long table with bowls of bread and trays of meat, but none of the men sat to eat as they might in their homes. They remained standing and picked at their food as it arrived, frowning over maps and scratching on them with quills and charcoal.

Ran shuffled into a corner at one end, hungry beyond reckoning but too anxious to touch a morsel. He'd find something to eat later, away from the glare of watchful eyes. Pallent saluted the marshals and accepted two cups of ale, shoving one at Ran as he stared blankly at the maps and papers strewn across the table. He wasn't sure anyone had even noticed his entry. He drained his cup before he realised what he was doing, and a servant appeared beside him, refilling it without preamble.

The duke did not immediately follow his son and the lieutenant into the pavilion, and by the time he did appear, Ran had lost count of his refills. A boozy warmth flushed his cheeks, the alcohol hitting his empty stomach and going straight to his head. Lieutenant Pallent slipped his cup from his grasp as the duke entered and the murmur of conversation eased to silence.

'Right, have any of you got some good news, or did they hammer us again?' Ronart asked the assembled marshals.

He collected a roll of bread from a nearby basket and slumped into a chair at the far end of the table. Evening was the only time Ran saw his father's weariness and impatience manifest. Usually, the man kept a tight check on his appearance, despite the toll of the unending defence of Orthia's border against the Empire's advances. For a moment, the marshals glanced at each other.

'Well,' Ronart addressed the marshals, 'get on with it.'

'We regained our trenches in the south, sir, but we think the northern companies have been held up near Sadef's Crossing. The reports are still coming in from the camps,' said Tenner, a tall marshal with bushy brown brows. 'If we push them back from the Crossing, we can recover most of the ground we lost last month.'

When no one else offered a report, the duke's eyes fell on Ranoth and his mouth ran dry. 'Have you something to report, Captain Olseta?'

Ronart used Ran's military title, souring the words with a sarcastic twist that left Ran under no illusions. He had fucked himself good and proper by retreating from the Hill, and his father was going to make him own every moment of it.

'Signal Hill is lost, sir,' Ran replied in the most even tone he could manage.

A murmur rolled through the assembled marshals as Ronart funnelled his anger into ripping apart the bread in his hand.

'Signal Hill had the ruins on it, yes?' Marshal Tenner regarded Ran with an expression gentler than he thought he deserved.

'Yes, Marshal. It was the site of Eddafore Castle,' Ran replied.

'That's the highest ground other than the ridge for a few miles.' Tenner looked at the duke. 'We need to retake it before the snow sets in. If the Empire holds the Hill over winter they'll be too dug in to weed out in the thaw.'

The duke's eyes wandered over the length of the map, the ripping of the bread crust the only sound in the confines of the tent.

'We'll take it back in two days' time,' said Ronart finally.

Another marshal choked on his food and coughed to clear his throat. 'With what troops, my Lord?'

Ran froze and the gathered marshals paused. The duke studied the man across the pavilion. 'That's for the marshals and commanders to decide, isn't it, Callide?'

'Of course, sir, but that doesn't change the fact we haven't got the men to spare on an offensive.'

'You think we'll have enough by spring, when the snow thaws and they're perched up on those ruins raining arrows on us?' Ronart's retort cracked through the pavilion's silence and Marshal Callide's face paled. 'You think I should march the battalion reserves out here and line them up for Woaden target practice? Because I fucking don't!'

He stood and stabbed a meat knife into the lines indicating where the Woaden held their portion of the Territory. 'No one has troops to spare, neither the Woaden, nor us, so we hit them now and hang the expense. You think our soldiers are the only ones exhausted by this campaign? The enemy are suffering just as badly, so we kick them where it hurts and take the spoils!'

Ran watched, awed and terrified by his father. The desperation feeding the duke's anger was evident in the darkness under his eyes and the pale skin around his knuckles. He held his remaining bread so tightly the stuff crumbled in his hand and fell to pieces on the floor. The duke tossed the mangled crusts on the table and put his hands on his hips, glaring at the marshals as if daring them to disagree.

Marshal Callide dipped his head in a slow bow. 'I apologise, sir. I spoke from the edge of my weariness.'

'*You're* weary? We're all fucking weary, but it's no excuse for giving up and chucking it in.' The duke took an angry gulp of wine then stabbed at the map with his finger. 'We have a few weeks left before the snow comes. Every year these dark, dragging days are the hardest we ever fight. Every year they push hard and we push back, because we both know the other is at the end of their resilience. They know, and we know. We're all just waiting for the snow so we can go home. We don't have time to be fucking weary. We need the Hill back.'

'Which companies will attack Signal Hill then?' Marshal Tenner put himself between Callide and the duke to break the tension. As far as Ran could tell, it didn't work. It simmered in the air, rising like heat from a brush fire, fanned by fatigue and wounded pride.

Ronart's gaze slipped to his son's face and fixed there, hazel eyes darkened by shadow and intent. Ran swallowed hard, not daring to guess at his father's next move.

'Captain Olseta's company falls under Marshal Callide's command, so it stands to reason that Callide should take over from here. Wouldn't you agree, Captain?' The duke's tone cut through Ran like the icy north wind and he suppressed a shiver. The duke did not look away from his son as he continued, 'And the Marshal shall stand in the vanguard, a demonstration to the troops on how to belay their weariness and do what must be done.'

A wave of pale dread washed over Callide's face and more than a few of the assembled marshals cleared their throats awkwardly. The duke didn't seem to notice, instead focussing his attention on a leg of roast fowl as an attendant refilled his cup. Ran's heart raced, hammering against his ribs, and he risked a glance at Pallent, who stood rigid beside him, her face ashen and drawn.

'Of course, sir,' Callide whispered with a nod and bowed again. 'I shall inform the troops and have them prepared.'

Ran tore his eyes away from Pallent, unable to stand the sight of her terror. She knew what this meant. They all did. The odds of taking the Hill this late in the campaign, even with a reinforced company, were insurmountable. If they did manage it, it would be at such an enormous cost that Ran doubted he'd ever see a single one of his surviving company again, and that number included Pallent.

Marshal Callide strode from the tent and Ran stared at the empty space left behind, swallowing a lump of fear. What was his father thinking? Surely the Hill wasn't worth such a price?

Duke Ronart yanked the meat knife from the table and propped his feet up on the boards as if nothing had happened to disturb the gathering. Slowly the marshals filled the air with their low chatter but none spoke too loudly nor disagreed with one another. No one dared draw the duke's attention, or his ire, for what remained of the evening.

Ran found an empty chair at the back of the pavilion and remained there until the marshals begged leave of the duke and headed for their beds. The depths of the fire in the brazier were hypnotising, snaring his gaze with the glowing dance of the flames along the surface of the coals.

Images of the battle Callide and Pallent would face flickered before his eyes. He wanted to be there, wanted to lead and fight, but he knew his father would never allow it. Not now, not after his failure to hold the Hill in the first place, and certainly not now that retaking the position had become a suicide mission dropped in Marshal Callide's lap. He brushed the pads of his shaking fingers across his lips and tried to comprehend the madness that drove his father to order one of his best marshals, a veteran of many campaigns at the front, to sacrifice himself for a defensive position on a hill.

He didn't realise he was alone with his father until the older man dropped down into a chair across the fire. Startled, Ran blinked the swirling thoughts from his head and shook away the picture of Callide charging Signal Hill under a hail of falling arrows.

The duke did not speak for a good while, instead staring at the flames and draining cup after cup of wine. If Ran blocked out the murmured sounds of the camp, he could almost imagine they sat alone in the palace at Usmein after the war was over...

'We've taken a beating in the last month and lost ground we couldn't afford to lose,' said Ronart suddenly, rubbing his rough hand over his eyes. 'It's a mess out there, Ran. The end of the autumn always is. It's not so bad in the spring, when the companies have rested over winter and the snow clears away most of the shit.'

'I'm sorry...' began Ranoth.

'Not your fault,' the duke said, draining his cup and refilling it immediately. Ran gulped his own drink for want of something to do. 'Should never have sent you out there. Should have listened to that tutor of yours when he wrote his official objection. If my father had heeded such warnings, your uncle would still be alive...'

Ran sighed and looked into the fire. He knew a little of the fate of the uncle he'd never met—his father's older brother, pushed too soon into battle and lost to the Empire well before his prime. His father rarely spoke of it in detail, but he still carried the wound deep in his soul, and Ran saw it in his hesitance to set his son loose on the Territory. But he'd fought and he'd badgered, and the duke had given in. And his performance, or lack of, on the field of battle had proven both his father and tutor right.

The old tutor was more the "negotiation and diplomacy" type, determined that if Orthia and the other Free Nations of Coraidin simply talked with the Woaden Empire, some accommodation could be made. Ran had wondered the same until he'd seen the battle raging across the Territory. He'd known then that the Empire were not for talking, or listening, nor for negotiating or being diplomatic. They were for killing and taking, and that was the end of that.

Ranoth looked at his hands, then at the fire. His thoughts settled back on Callide and Pallent and the hill they would die on in a few days. 'I wanted to help…'

'Aye…' The duke had clearly had too much to drink. He was a quiet and sullen man when he was deep in his cups.

Equally liquored, Ran shrugged. 'I was fucking terrified at first.'

Ronart shook his head. 'The only soldiers not shivering in their boots the first time they hit the battlefield, or losing their bowels when a charge is called, are those who would be locked up if it wasn't for war. They aren't right in the head. A man without fear is a man without half his mind. This place won't kick the fear *out* of you, it'll only teach you how to hide it.'

'What about the marshals? They're so relaxed about it. They hardly flinch…'

'The things they've seen would make any boy of fifteen, or man of fifty, drop their guts right here.' The duke paused to slosh some more wine into his cup. 'Not a one of them has seen less than twenty years of this war. The Woaden have been swarming over those mountains long before they were even a dirty thought in their fathers' minds. Some started out as runners; some were pickers, out after the horns collecting the dead and wounded. To a man, they've been in the thick of that fight and bled on that soil. The only reason I have the right to command them is because I've earned it.'

'Yes, Father,' replied Ranoth, his eyes trained on the glow of the fire. How had he ever thought he could earn the respect of such men? It seemed an impossible mountain for his inebriated mind to summit, so it switched to another question burning to be asked. 'Do you think the war will ever end?'

Ronart cleared his throat, crossed his arms and leaned into his chair as though he saw the whole of Coraidin sketched on the tent wall above Ran's head. The duke frowned. He liked to think his words over and let them stew before speaking, much to the frustration of Ran's mother.

'I doubt it. Not while we have resources they need to finance their push south. They're getting desperate, Ran. They need what we have so they can take Isord and Arinnia. If I cut them a road from here to the gold mines, another through to the gem fields, and built them a weigh station to sift the minerals from the dirt, then they might sheath their blades and agree to peace. Of course, I'd also have to provide half our population as slave labour for the mines.'

'They don't want much do they?' Ran muttered dryly. It was ever the Woaden way—if they didn't have it, they'd happily kill for it. Expansion was central to the Woaden identity and Ran suspected from everything Perce taught him, they *needed* to extend the Empire to keep it alive.

'Orthia is a coveted prize, son, full of precious minerals and gems, fertile farms and healthy trade—everything the Woaden want and more besides.' Ronart waved his cup in a wide arc, the fire hissing as wine splashed down among the coals. 'Without all that, we'd never be able to pay for reinforcements from the other Free Nations. As soon as they get a foothold in our lands, we're fucked. Understand? We cannot lose ground—not now not ever.'

The duke stood suddenly, wavering on his feet and glancing around.

'Best you get some rest, boy. The Empire will be up with the birds and ready to go again before the day is fully bright.'

'Aye, Father.' Ran watched his father leave the pavilion, then slipped behind a partition to find the cot and personal effects he'd left behind when he rode out for the Hill.

Sleep didn't come easily, despite the alcoholic haze over his eyes. The sounds of the camp amplified in the cold air, drawing pictures of things he tried hard to ignore. Winter was blowing in from Marlow in the north, but it would be weeks until the noise of war was silenced by falling snow.

Beyond the tent walls and the comfort of furs and cushions, the wails of the injured and dying echoed through the trees and against the inside of Ran's skull. He'd heard this chorus before, and no amount of time at the front had rendered it comfortably familiar or easily shut out.

Each night, a voice rose above the others, unhindered by the distance between the pavilion and the healers' tents. Cries for a mother, or a wife, or for the soft thighs of a favourite whore. The voice groaned, gasped, moaned and wept, and inevitably faded as time passed, until it vanished altogether. Then another voice rose in its place, howling curses at the night as though fury alone could ease the pain.

The voices never returned; none of them ever called out a second time. Not here in the central command camp, or out on the Hill. Ran hoped they found comfort and relief in sleep, but he knew in the churning depths of his stomach that the soldier, weakened by wounds and wracked with fever, was dead. No healer could ease the kind of pain that caused people to wail like that. Only death ended that sort of suffering.

Four more cups of strong drink finally muffled the cries and erased the images dancing bloody steps across his mind. They would return again tomorrow, but for now, the numb ignorance of drink gave him peace.

CHAPTER SIX

The Disputed Territory, Western Orthia

Morning broke with a shattering horn blast and screaming headache. Barely able to peel his eyes open, Ran groaned and pulled a blanket over his head to block out the cold light of day. His breath stank and his stomach rolled uneasily, not helped by the thought of what waited outside. He was due his traditional morning vomit, but this time it was not only fuelled by the overpowering stench of death and excrement, but a roaring hangover. The thought did him no favours and he fought the heave of his stomach.

Another furious blast of horns cut through Ran's head with the grace of a blunt axe and his eyes tore themselves open, heedless of the protests from his headache. There was something wrong with that call. It wasn't the standard rouse played to wake the troops at sunrise—it was a desperate and hurried call to arms.

Ran sat up fast and the tent spun around him. Frantic shouts and the clash of steel banished the fog in his mind and he scrambled to pull his boots over yesterday's socks.

'Ranoth! Up, now!' Duke Ronart bellowed and threw back the dividing curtain. 'Get your blade, boy!'

'What's going on?' Ran stumbled to his sword belt as his father's massive hand collected him by the arm and shoved him through the tent's rear door.

The grey light of an overcast day blinded him and he collided with an unseen soldier rushing past. Ronart's grip tightened and dragged him into a run. Ran pumped his legs hard to keep up, blinking to clear his reluctant eyes and shift the dizziness from his vision.

His father charged on like an enraged bull, roaring orders and shoving soldiers aside as if they weighed nothing. There was nothing Ran could do but follow and hope his father didn't lose hold of his arm.

'Father, what's happening?' he shouted into the storm of men and horses tearing through the camp.

'They mounted an attack! A fucking dawn attack! I'll have their general's guts for breakfast when I'm done, then I'll ride across the bloody border and raze Wodurin to the fucking *ground*!'

'The Woaden are attacking? How did they get this close?' Ran couldn't believe it. It made no sense. How had they crossed the lines without anyone noticing?

Cold realisation washed through him and he shivered.

The Hill...

Had Captain Denover failed to hold the advance at the Ford? Had the lines broken because Ran had lost the Hill?

The duke stopped and rounded on Ran, his hands squeezing his son's shoulders so hard he thought the bones might pop from the joints. 'I don't know. Look Ran, you have to get out of here. I can't have you here if this goes to shit. You understand me? I should never have brought you here, not this late in the campaign. You have to go...'

'But I can stay, I can—'

A howl of rage filled the air and the duke stabbed his sword into the space beside Ran's head. Ran spun away as a spray of blood hit the side of his face and he staggered back from the gurgling corpse of a Woaden soldier. Ronart's sword had skewered the attacker's throat, and blood flooded down the front of the man's armour as his sword arm fell limp at his side.

Ran's meagre challenge of his father's decision died in his throat. With a flick, Ronart freed the body from his blade and resumed his grasp on Ran's arm. He didn't argue or resist. Instead he found himself silently praying to whatever gods were listening that he and his father might make it through this alive.

A vanguard of Orthian soldiers swarmed them as they hurried forwards, dirt and blood muting the shining silver shield etched on their armour; the crown, scythe and pickaxe of his father's arms completely covered in muck.

'Sir, this way!' A marshal shouted and the group veered right, following the marshal and cutting a path through the chaos to the rear of the Orthian camp.

Ran glanced back at the battle and his breath caught in his throat. Imperial soldiers teemed through the encampment, swooping on it like ravenous vultures on a carcass.

The Orthian troops struggled to form a counter attack under the assault, scrambling to retreat and conserve their strength and numbers. Duke Ronart was right—the end of a campaign was a mess. The tired, battle-worn soldiers caught in the onslaught dropped quickly and without much of a fight. Many glanced his way before turning on their heels and bolting into the woods and Ran's heart skipped a beat.

The men looked at him, at his father, and saw their leaders not simply retreating, but fleeing. They didn't see a duke taking his son to the rear of the fight—they saw a duke making a break for safety while leaving his troops for dead.

'Father, stop!' Ran snapped away from his father's grip and the duke shuddered to a halt, keen eyes scanning the fight. 'They're fleeing because *we're* running!'

Through the mud and blood, soldiers deserted in droves, scrambling to the relative safety of other camps dotted along the ridge. The controlled retreat formations, drilled endlessly in the fields near Usmein, collapsed into frantic sprinting. If they had any hope of forcing the Woaden back into the Disputed Territory, they had to bring the retreat under control, and quickly. They *had* to, or the Imperial Army would spread into Orthia and devour it from within.

'Fuck me, Tenner sound the retreat horns and get them to pull back like soldiers, not piss-weak children!' The duke seethed and cursed furiously at the failure of his troops to hold their composure.

Ran tightened his belt and pushed his dark, tangled hair from his eyes. 'We can turn them back, Father, we just need to form the lines again.' His study of hundreds of years of battle tactics and wars across Coraidin bubbled to the surface of his mind amidst the disaster of the attack.

'No, Ran. You have to go.'

'No, Father, you need—'

Duke Ronart shook his son violently and Ran swallowed his objection. '*You* can't be here, son. Not my heir; not here, not today. I won't do to you what was done to my brother. You need to get back to Usmein and raise the alarm. Get the court in order and sort out your mother and sisters. I'll turn this herd of cats around, but you have to get home.'

Ronart glanced around as if searching for his next move in the chaos and blood. Soldiers roared around them, the deafening crash of blades shattering the morning amongst the screams of horses. The stench of voided bowels hit Ran like a punch in the face, his eyes watering and his stomach lurching.

'Fuck's sake, I haven't a squad to spare.' Ronart whistled and waved at a soldier, aged in his twenties, holding the reins of a few wide-eyed horses. 'You! Report!'

'Brit Doon, sir!' The soldier gave a sharp salute. 'Watcher, Duke's Guard.'

Ronart propelled Ran towards the soldier and the waiting horses. 'Take him to Usmein as quick as these beasts will carry you. Do not stop, not for anyone or anything. By the gods, I'll use your skull as an ale mug if he doesn't make it.'

The soldier gave another salute and without a word, grabbed Ran by the knee and hoisted him into the saddle. The mount shied and threw its head, the chaos too much for it to abide. Despite his terror, Ran's blood ran cold at the idea of leaving his father in the thick of a battle. The Empire had never broken the lines like this, not in all the decades since the war began. And sons weren't meant to abandon their fathers when things turned sour and the fate of the duchy hung in the balance.

'Aye there lad, let's do as the duke orders, eh?' Brit Doon said and Ran jerked from staring at the fight to see him already atop another of the horses. Brit gave him a quick, reassuring smile and snatched the reins of Ran's horse. 'I don't fancy my skull filled with ale I'm not alive to drink.'

The watcher kicked his steed and shouted above the battle's roar. The horses didn't need any extra encouragement and flew into a barely controlled eastward gallop. The last Ran heard of the fight was the hiss of an arrow over his head and the thwack of several more hitting the dirt beside the horse's flashing hooves. After that, there was nothing but his breath and the hammering beat of his frenzied heart.

Brit forced Ran to ride until he thought his body would collapse in on itself, pushing the horses to the edge of what was considered a reasonable pace if you wanted the beasts to survive. They kept off the road, travelling the quiet lanes and tracks that farmers used to move between their fields and villages. At nightfall, Ran hoped they might rest awhile, but Brit wasn't interested. He led the horses onward, leaving Ran to doze in the saddle.

'We should stop,' Ran suggested for the fourteenth time since sunset. The hard ride from Signal Hill the previous day had left him saddle-sore and extraordinarily fatigued, and he ached to rest, even for a moment. His backside had gone numb, along with the insides of his thighs. His ankles burned from holding the same angle in the stirrups and he hadn't felt his toes in a long while.

'You heard the duke. No stopping.' Brit spat in the dirt and ducked under a low hanging branch.

Ran screwed his face into a frown. Surely his father hadn't meant for them to ride through the night! 'The horses need a break. If they snap an ankle in the shadows–'

'They're fine at a walk,' Brit cut him off without even turning his head.

This time Ran swallowed his dissent and glared into the evening. The cold bit into his hands despite the gloves he found in the saddlebags and the north wind had begun to cut through the fabric of his trousers. If he did eventually convince Brit to stop for the night, there was no guarantee he could actually climb down or walk away from the horse. He might manage it at a crawl, but only with his elbows—there was no sensation left in any of his fingers. They would stop soon, even if Ran had to order the soldier to do so.

'Here, this is a decent place to camp. There's probably a stream nearby,' Ran suggested, taking one last stab at subtlety before he had to resort to pulling rank and issuing an outright order. He was a prince of the realm and a captain, after all.

The watcher coughed and spat. 'Can't stop here. No one stops here. Besides, duke's orders. No stopping.'

Ranoth narrowed his eyes at Brit's swaying back in the dim moonlight. 'What are you talking about? There's nothing here but trees and hills.'

'Why'd you reckon that is?' Brit glanced back at the prince. 'Not bad land around here. Not too rocky even though we're near the quarries and the gold mines are off to the south there. Not bad here at all, but there's nothin'. Just these trackways and the road to the Territory.'

Passing through the area on his way to the front, Ran hadn't taken much notice of the surrounding countryside. To him, one farm seemed identical to the next, and for miles and miles, that's all he'd thought there was to see. Now it was dark and the only faint light fell from the moon, filtered through bands of high cloud and treetops. If anyone lived nearby, their location would be marked by the glow from a farmhouse hearth, or the soft sounds of grazing animals, or working dogs barking in the distance. A bird or two, owls by their screeching, lifted off from nearby branches. Besides the whisper of their wings in the cool air, there was nothing.

Except...

'There's a house!' Ran pointed at a shadowy structure of large square stones on a cleared hill crest a few hundred yards from the road. He jerked on the reins and kicked his horse harder than the animal deserved. Why spend a freezing night in the saddle when succour was so close?

'Oi!' Brit's curse echoed in the silent valley. 'What're you doing?'

'Getting us a bed!' Ran shouted back without looking. Even a pile of hay in the barn would be enough. The tenants would surely lend the duke's son some hospitality, especially on such a frigid night. A chill in the air promised the road would be icy by morning.

At a short stone fence before the house, he swung down and stumbled through a weathered gate jammed open on the path. No light shone from the uncovered window, and Ran reasoned the owner was likely preparing for bed in another room. He rubbed his numb hands together and reached to bang on the door.

'No!' cried Brit.

Ranoth's fist hit the timber panel with a boom.

The door fell inward, splintering on the flagstone floor and the air in his lungs vanished. The impact should have echoed with an almighty crash, but Ran heard nothing. Stunned and wide eyed, he dropped to his knees and stared.

Human skeletons filled the room beyond from floor to ceiling.

There was no telling if a hearth or more rooms lay further in. Mounds of bones and skulls clogged up every available space, brilliant white and dull, dusty grey in the moonlight.

'Shit…' whispered Ran.

'Come back towards me, lad.' Brit's hushed command reached him and he obliged, shuffling backwards.

'What is this place?' His voice broke.

'Come *on*! This is no place to have a chat!'

Deep in the shadows of the house, the hollow eyes of a thousand skulls scrutinised his retreat. Did they wonder where he was going? Did they think he'd come to join them in their lonely countryside tomb? Ran knew the souls once dancing in those black voids were with the Dark Rider in the Underworld, but the fact didn't ease his hammering heart or settle his quivering lips. The eyes of the dead glared, unmoved by his fear, and Ran gave a startled squeak when the gate pressed into his back, barring his way.

He blinked and she appeared—white blonde hair and skin as pale as the moon, translucent enough to see through to the heaps of skeletons. She lay unmoving across the doorway, between the threshold and the bones, long naked limbs pressed against the floor, her back exposed to the bitterly cold air through the fabric of a shredded shift. Her dead eyes stared into the space between them, unseeing, empty.

A shiver prickled across Ran's skin. His heart hammered against the wall of his chest and his throat contracted around a scream, choking him as his mouth gaped at the body in the house.

He squeezed his eyes shut.

She's in my imagination… She's not real… Get a grip on yourself…

His eyes opened and hers blinked, now clear and blue. She paid no attention to Brit, the soldier was close to losing his wits as he screamed at Ran to get out of the yard. He had seen the ghost and the bones and was howling curses, promising to feed Ran his sword if he didn't move. But his voice sounded far away, as if he were shouting across a yawning abyss.

'Go,' said the dead girl, blue lips moving in a whisper.

A cold hand reached inside Ran's head and wrapped bony fingers around his mind. He shuddered and winced, pain lancing through his eye sockets.

'Go, before they find you. They take all they find. Run…. Run! RUN!'

Ran's jaw and body tensed then the grip on his consciousness eased and the girl's eyes faded back to stone dead. Without warning her body lurched to the right, jerking and scraping across the floor as if dragged by some unholy beast, before disappearing into the house.

Ran finally found his voice and screamed.

His legs scrabbled against the cold dirt of the pathway and a pair of hands snagged the back of his coat. He struggled but the grip was tighter, stronger, and his arms were unfit to fight the doom waiting in the house of bones.

'Stop flapping about and get over the fence! By the Dark Rider's balls, let's go!' The hands heaved him over the low wall and dumped him on the ground. He looked up and Brit gripped his jacket by the collar. 'Up, now!'

Ran didn't need to be told twice. He sprinted wildly for his unimpressed horse and collected the reins, his weariness banished by fear. Brit sprang into the saddle and spurred his mount, not waiting to see if Ran followed.

CHAPTER SEVEN

West of Usmein, Orthia

Two days of riding brought Ran within a stone's throw of the city of Usmein, his home and the seat of his father's duchy. Unless asking for the water bladder or suggesting a camp for the night, barely a word passed between the prince and the watcher, and Ran wasn't inclined to change the situation. He spent the remainder of the journey trapped in his head, replaying the scene from the house.

In his memory, it seemed more like a tumbledown old shack than the sturdy farmhouse he thought he saw from the road. Perhaps his eyes played a trick that night, or perhaps something called from within the dim structure with an ulterior motive. No matter how hard he tried, he couldn't shake the image of the bones and the skulls; hundreds, possibly thousands stacked one upon another. Only the gods knew how deep they went into the house.

Questions cascaded through his mind. Had they died all at once in a bloody massacre, or been picked off one by one? And how long had the bones been there? Who had taken the time to put them inside the house, instead of leaving them for the birds or burning them in a pyre to remove the evidence? *Someone* had gone to a great deal of effort for that little house of horror and it turned Ran's stomach to think what kind of person could do such a thing.

Then there was the girl—porcelain pale and as dead as midwinter. She stuck in his mind, so clearly she might as well lie before him; her neck torn open by a gruesome, gaping wound. Her arms stretched languidly across the floor, chest down, her hips turned away and her legs wound around each other. Ran hadn't seen a lot of the world in his short life, but he knew that girl had suffered at the hands of a monster.

Beside a gurgling stream he managed to wash most of the gore and grime from his face but his tunic and leathers needed boiling to remove the stains of the Woaden attack. He didn't want to ride into the palace courtyard and greet his mother covered in another man's blood, but he didn't have much choice. His father was relying on him to prepare the city for, at best, the return of weary, retreating Orthian soldiers, or at worst, an invading Imperial Army, hungry for the spoils of a generations-long war.

But what in the name of the gods was he going to say to his mother? She'd been hard pressed to let Ran go to the front in the first place, but she'd had no say in the matter once the duke had made his decision.

Late on the third day, the hills flattened and the road dipped into one final valley before crossing the farmland surrounding Usmein's walls. Concentrating on staying in his saddle despite his weary body, Ran started when Brit pulled his horse to a halt and blocked the road. The man's eyes settled on Ran for a moment as they sat in uneasy silence. Brit seemed to chew his words over before he let them out, as if unsure he wanted them said.

'What happened... At that house... I'd rather it wasn't spoken of.' The older man glanced at the fields and lowered his voice as if someone might be eavesdropping from the hedgerows. 'I'm not proud of how I reacted, and I'd rather this little *episode* didn't make the rounds of the city taverns, if you get my meanin'?'

'Brit, I'm fifteen and the duke's heir—I don't go to city taverns.'

'Aye, but all the same...'

Ranoth nodded and wondered why Brit needed to be so explicit. 'I don't know if anyone would believe such a story anyway.'

The shadows over Brit's face, the fingerprints of fatigue and stress, suggested he thought otherwise. The watcher shook his head. 'Did you ever hear of Lackmah? I'd guess not, given that you trotted up to that house all bright and cheery without a care in the world... If all goes well and we're not bending a knee to the Empire by the time the snows hit, ask your old man about Lackmah. If he won't tell you, ask around 'til someone will.'

A chill clutched at Ran's heart and an uncomfortable, hot tingling burned in his fingers. He tightened his grip on the reins and wished it away, not convinced he wanted to hear about Lackmah or what it had to do with the house of bones. 'I'll have to tell my father what we found, though. I can't keep it from him.'

'Oh, by all means, Highness. By all means…' The watcher turned his horse towards the city and they continued in silence.

***

Brit vanished in the commotion of their arrival at the duke's palace before Ranoth had a chance to climb from the saddle. A runner from the gatehouse heralded his return and, as expected, his fraught mother dashed from the garden's hothouses, abandoning her inspections of the season's crops. She oversaw Usmein's supply of fresh food during winter, and without the hothouses dotted across the city's common greens and lining the palace's western wall, there was no chance of that.

'Ranoth, where, in the name of the White Woman, is your father? Have the snows come early?' She slowed her approach and scanned the gathered crowd of curious palace staff, squaring her slight shoulders and straightening the apron she wore over her deep green gown. Girls peered from the doors and windows of the kitchen and laundry sheds, men and apprentices in the forges holding their tools still, intensifying the silence. Duchess Merideth frowned at her son. 'Ran, where are the marshals?'

'Only one escort could be spared, Mother.' He climbed unsteadily down, helped by a farrier, and relinquished the reins. The news he carried was hardly appropriate to discuss in public, but the onlookers' expectant gazes bored into him like a carpenter's hole saw. Equally, he couldn't refuse his mother's question without sparking a wildfire of rumours. He had no choice but to make some sort of statement, as ugly as the truth was.

The highest vantage in the palace's cobbled forecourt was atop the entryway stairs, so he gave his mother's hand a gentle squeeze and took the steps two at a time, then climbed onto the wide stone balustrade. Nerves set his heart thumping wildly and blood rushed in his ears. An uncomfortable tingling rippled through his fingers and his neck began to ache as his stamina waned. With any luck, he'd finish without fainting and pitching over the side from exhaustion.

The duke's chancellor, Lithor, slipped through the crowd and stood breathless beside the duchess. He was a weathered old soldier with sandy blond hair who had reluctantly retired to the palace after losing his hand at the front. Chancellor Lithor panted as though he'd run full speed from the garrison in the south of the palace grounds, but squared his shoulders and tried not to let it show. He fixed Ran with deep brown eyes under his permanently furrowed brow, and Ran felt the weight of the man's regard as he prepared to address the crowd. Anticipating an announcement, the gathered staff and officials closed in around the base of the stairs.

Ran cleared his throat and tried to throw his voice. 'Three days ago, the central Orthian camp was attacked in a dawn raid.'

A buzz of muttering rose and he held out his hands to plead for quiet.

'When I left at the duke's order, our troops were regrouping to stage a counter-attack. I returned to bring word and prepare the reserves; however, I must urge calm. The Empire attacks our lines daily, and never come further into our lands than they can spit. Rest assured, Duke Ronart and his men will return when the first snow halts the battle and all will be as it should.'

Even as his voice echoed across the courtyard, greeted by cheers and applause, Ran doubted his words. The gathered staff took them at face value, not having any reason to doubt him, but the chancellor and the duchess stood motionless, staring at Ran with barely disguised horror. They knew what this meant. They knew the fate that would befall the city if his father failed to halt the advance.

He met their gaze and jerked his head towards the door. Any further discussion could not happen in the public courtyard—they needed to call the government's ministers for an emergency council. Duchess Merideth met her son at the top of the stairs, her hands balled into fists as Ran climbed down off the balustrade and the gathering dispersed. He already stood equal with his mother's height, but he had a long way to go before he matched the duke.

His mother put a gentle hand on his arm. 'Come, let's go inside and you can tell us what happened.'

Chancellor Lithor snapped a sharp salute to Ran. 'Sir, I've sent word to the duke's advisors, garrison marshals, and ministers to meet us in the Blue Room.'

'Oh,' Ran said and awkwardly returned the salute. The chancellor didn't offer him the chance to reply, spinning on his heel and striding through the yawning palace entry.

A long portrait gallery dotted with formal receiving rooms stretched to the central atrium of the palace and a soaring dome of carefully carved stone and glass. Daylight filtered through the panels to illuminate several floors and galleries, and wide hearths lined the walls of each floor, distributing heat through the palace as a heart pumps blood to the limbs.

Ran and his mother followed the chancellor as he turned left along the north wing towards a platform lift. When they were inside, Lithor closed the iron screen across the lift's entry and pulled three times at a cord hanging from the roof of the lift compartment. The platform began to slowly ascend as a counterweight dropped towards the bowels of the palace on a complex system of pulleys and ropes.

Between the first and third floors, Lithor turned to Ran and lowered his voice. 'Your Grace, I should warn you. This meeting will be long and difficult. It will be your final chance to withdraw, but you must appoint a delegate to your authority if you do.'

'I'm sorry, Chancellor; I don't understand,' said Ran, frowning.

'The circumstances here are… unusual. The Imperial Army have never pushed any further into our lands than the Disputed Territory, and if their advance is not halted, someone must be appointed to act in your father's stead until he returns. The palace and city must move to a heightened state of readiness. As the duke's heir, you hold his authority in his absence. As we speak, the banner of the Palace Command is replacing the Olseta house standard at the gates.'

Ran's blood turned to ice at the mention of the Palace Command; a term he'd only ever read about in the endless books Perce forced him to study. It was a power enacted only in the direst of emergencies, when the city faced an extreme threat and the duke was unable to lead his government or the garrison.

Lithor went on in his low, careful tone. 'This is not the usual state of play, and a far more serious situation than when your father is commanding the army at the front. It is important people see the palace in control, especially if anything, er… *happens* to the duke. You're the Palace Commander, by right. However, if you wish to defer the role, then you must do so swiftly and without hesitation.'

A quick glance at his mother told Ranoth everything he needed to know. He'd seen that face many times as a child, and as recently as when his father finally agreed to let him take a command at the front; worry tinged with disappointment. But there was something different now.

Something more in how she looked at him. Necessity warred with frustration like a sailor bailing out a boat with a leaky bucket. She did not think him ready, but knew she had little choice but to accept what was about to happen.

He hardened himself against the anxiety creeping up his spine. Now was not the time to allow fear to take over his heart. Now was a time for decision and strength. He'd failed in the Territory. He'd lost the Hill and close to a hundred good soldiers, but he couldn't turn away from this. The cold reality was that he *had* to be capable and willing, even if his heart quailed at the responsibility.

'No, Chancellor. I will not defer.' Ran lifted his chin and steadied his voice. 'I accept the Palace Command.'

Chancellor Lithor slapped Ran on the back and it took all his strength not to topple forwards. For all his eagerness to prove his worth, the news stunned him and he held his silence for the remaining journey to the Blue Room. Events were moving at such a pace he hardly had time to grasp one before the next was thrust his way. Lithor opened the screen when the lift arrived at the third floor, bowed to the duchess, and disappeared across the corridor to the Blue Room.

Ran stopped his mother before she could follow.

'Ma…' He wanted to ask her opinion, to ask if she thought he was making the right decision, but the words failed to form. All he could see was the concern etched in the lines of her face. 'I don't want you to worry…'

For a moment his fingers felt as though they were on fire, then the sensation faded as he squeezed his hand into a fist. He must have sprained his wrist a little at the house of bones.

'Oh, Ran…' Merideth let out a long sigh through her nose and gently pressed her hand to his chest just above his heart, covering the Olseta house crest embroidered in thick silver thread on his filthy black tunic. 'I'm your mother. Worrying about you is my job. And while I have my reservations, there will never be a more opportune moment to prove to these people what you are capable of. You'll be fine, Ran. You've got your father's blood in your veins; all you need do is remember your lessons.'

Ran took a deep, shaking breath. The idea of commanding his father's advisors made him significantly queasier than commanding a company of soldiers, and he couldn't for the life of him understand why. He tried to shrug it off as he crossed to the Blue Room, and hoped his confidence would last the day.

'We've got no one to send, Lithor!' Palace Marshal Gregon slammed his fist into the table and glared at the chancellor. 'If you can find a few thousand men in this city fit enough to wield a sword or bow without killing themselves, then you have my blessing to ride to the Territory and save the day. But mark my words, I've scoured these streets down to the gutters, slums, and prisons and there's no one left. And there's not nearly enough time to call next year's divisions back from the villages.'

'Shall we lock the gates and hope for the best then?' Lithor countered, arms wide as though inviting the Empire to do their worst.

'We *cannot* sacrifice the garrison by sending them to the front,' the marshal repeated, pushing his dark auburn hair behind his ears to reveal a long scar on his neck. 'They've trained to defend the city, not scamper about in ranks on a field. Put them in streets and alleys, rooftops and plazas and they're as deadly as mountain lions, but on flat ground they'll die as quickly as new recruits.'

Two hours of back and forth arguing and shouting had the gathered government ministers and advisors no closer to a plan and succeeded only in grinding the remaining functioning parts of Ran's tired brain to a pulp. The argument went around and around the same points, never straying far from the kernel at its centre; there simply weren't enough soldiers in the city to send reinforcements to the front without leaving the capital undefended.

'Could we survive a siege?' Ran asked. 'If they push through Father's forces and make it as far as the city, could we survive a siege?'

He shifted in his seat and tried to ease the ache in his knotted muscles. He needed a bath and a meal and decent sleep to make any sense of the situation, but none of them seemed likely in the immediate future. This would go on for hours more unless he found a way through the thorny briar of the problem.

Alber Frain, the country's finance minister, licked the tip of his finger and leafed through the pages of a wide ledger open on the table before him.

'With the winter stores full and the livestock penned for the season, we're in a good position. However, if the Empire severs our trade routes to Marlow and Isord, then things become tight. We have enough food to last until spring.' Frain looked over his wire-rimmed spectacles; his frank, steady gaze dropping the weight of decision squarely on Ran's shoulders. 'After that...'

The finance minister's eyes shifted to Lithor, who nodded.

'We can't let them set a siege. Once the snow thins in the Morgen passes, the Woaden will reinforce their supply lines and send fresh troops to the city. Even if we last through the winter, they will break us in the spring.'

At the opposite end of the table the privy secretary, Iiana Frain, listened carefully to her father and recorded the meeting minutes with a swift hand in a code only the duke's administrators could decipher. Ran stared into the coils of steam rising from his mug of tea and wished heartily that it was a huge tankard of ale. It was the same tea Perce made for him in his library, assuring him its bitter aftertaste was worth enduring for the focussing effect it had on the mind. Chewing at the inside of his lip, he let their words and warnings sink in, and let the tea do its work.

'So,' he began slowly, 'we can't ride out to meet them and we can't let them set a siege. Somehow we have to find the middle ground...'

His weary mind began to turn the problem over, examining it from all sides, rolling it to the light to reveal as many angles as he could. The tea took hold and his mind began to fizz, trawling through memories and snatches of thought to find the solution he needed. It was in there, somewhere; hidden in shadow and obscured by time, but the answer was there. There was a way through all this, a plan caught up in the cobwebs of his fatigue, waiting to reveal itself, he just had to reach in and shake it out of hiding.

Never is a battle won on an unprepared field...

A half-remembered image flickered to life; hazy at the edges, blurred and stuttered. Perce mumbling to himself in a dusty corner of the palace library, warm shafts of summer sun cutting through the shadows to lay across piles of old papers and velvet bound volumes.

'Never is a battle won on an unprepared field, young Ranoth.' Perce dropped a long folio of maps in front of Ran, who lifted the cover and sneezed at the dislodged dust. 'Every fight, every skirmish, every negotiation ever undertaken in the history of Coraidin, was won by he who fixed the field to his advantage.'

'Negotiations?' Ran asked, wiping his nose on his sleeve and readying his notebook of bound blank pages. 'Don't they usually happen in a hall or a tent somewhere?' He was only twelve at the time, so Perce gave him some leeway for stupid questions. He was less accommodating now.

'Ah, they may, but even a war of words must be planned and strategised. Failure to prepare the field for even the most benign confrontation will, without doubt, lead to defeat.' Perce wagged his finger and settled in a high-back chair with worn red cushions. 'You tell me, from those battle maps, who won and how they prepared. No supper until it's done.'

Prepare the field...

A plan, once buried in the shadows of his mind, unfurled in the light of the memory. Suddenly, the blackened fields of the Disputed Territory gained an entirely new purpose. They weren't empty and ruined because soldiers enjoyed the sport of destruction. They were in such a state because both sides sought to prepare the field of battle to their advantage. Removing trees and houses, digging trenches and foxholes, had warped the ground of the battlefield as the warring forces tried to outwit their enemy and preserve their troops.

Ran sat back and let a knowing smile spread across his lips. Lithor frowned and Iiana prepared her nib, poised ready for the word of the newly minted palace commander.

'We have no choice but to prepare for the worst with what resources we have,' he told the gathering. 'We've got troops trained to fight in the city but we can't wait for the Woaden to breach the walls before we mount a defence. We need to take the fight *to* them, but we can't send the garrison soldiers to the front. We have to find a middle ground, somewhere that allows our forces to do what they know best without risking the city.'

Across the room, his mother sat sewing by the fire, the twin of his smile dancing on her lips.

He continued on as Lithor and Gregon shared a glance and their eyes widened with understanding. 'We need to prepare the field to advantage our troops and cripple theirs. We need to *cut* the field. We have a little time and a city of citizens to help. We might just be able to do it, if we start now.'

CHAPTER EIGHT

Hummel, Tolak Range, the South Lands

The squeal of children and the thump of running feet reached Lidan across the cold morning and the sound of excited birds in the trees. The trees didn't seem to mind the cold lingering in the shadows of the common, hardy branches that were waving bright yellow and red cage blossoms at the sky in defiance of the dry season and the plummeting temperatures.

'They should be back by now…' Lidan said to Master Rick as he emerged from the back of the forge with a barrow of tin ore. In the neighbouring workshop, potters worked lumps of clay into urns and bowls for firing in an earthen kiln, while Lidan practiced her symbols without her father's guidance.

'Hunts take time, First Daughter. They'll return when they're ready.'

While the frigid cold of the dry season closed around Hummel like an eagle's talons, a turning of the moon had come and gone, and Erlon's hunt party still hadn't returned. Scouts came back to the village each evening, shaking their heads with deepening frowns and shrugged shoulders, and after two weeks the stocky gateman, Jac, doubled the watch on the wall on the dana's order. It made Lidan begin to wonder if something was wrong, but no one seemed willing to speak of it.

She sat by the forge fire wrapped tight in a shawl, unable to concentrate, watching the tine-women hang damp clothing in the lazy wind blowing down from the snowy high country. Built from plans traded by a north-man, the forge made metal not seen south of the Malapa. Rick called it bronze and said in the south the two ores needed were as rare as hen's teeth. The castings didn't always work, but the forge master had managed to find enough to make knives for the rangers and a huge axe for the daari.

Lidan liked to watch the rock turn to liquid then pour like thick, glowing water into the moulds, certain as the sun shone that Rick worked magic, not metal, in those flames. On bad days, when the moulds cracked and the casting failed, Rick cursed the earth and kicked his workbench, muttering about what he'd give for a few barrows of iron instead of tin and copper.

Iron was some northern thing, a secret her people had yet to unravel from the earth, even with Rick's help, and the only iron Lidan had ever seen was in the sword above her father's audience chair. The forge was the undoubted envy of the other South Lands clans, unrivalled, and its workings a mystery to them. Even if the other clans discovered an ore deposit, they wouldn't have the slightest clue what to do with it. The Tolak rangers' arrows were still tipped with flint, despite the arrival of the metal-working magic, which kept the knappers busy in the training yard; Rick unwilling to waste ore on a weapon so easily lost.

While she laboured at her symbols, four of her sisters played in the kitchen garden. Iscah and Hanne were digging holes in places they probably shouldn't, uncovering bugs and earthworms from deep in the soil where moisture could still be found. Beside them, Cerise squealed and Abbi cackled, throwing a worm that dared wriggle too enthusiastically against her fingers. A craw swooped and snatched the worm mid-air, not fool enough to miss a free meal.

'Have you taken that horse out yet?' Rick asked, inspecting the length of a ranger's knife blade and preparing to sharpen and polish it.

Lidan rolled her eyes. 'Not a chance… Mam won't hear of it.' She'd done nothing but feed and brush Theus since her father left and she felt sure if she brushed him anymore his hair would fall out completely and she'd rub his skin raw. 'I'd break my own fingers to get out of weaving another basket.'

'So, you're hiding here with us?' Rick's brow rose and she shrugged with a smile.

'You're the only ones who'll have me. The knappers say I get under their feet!'

'Where is everyone today?' Behn dumped an armload of clean tools on his master's workbench and wiped sweat away with a sooty hand. The only apprentice of five boys to last more than a year working by the furnace, Behn never complained about the heat. Lidan was fairly sure he enjoyed the sweltering forge and its smoky shed, even in the humidity of summer.

'Farah isn't well,' Lidan nodded at the living quarters at the back of the hall. 'All the women are seeing to her and the children. Even Mam has to muck in and help.'

'What kind of sick?' He waved his hand as if to mimic vomiting and Lidan nodded, scrunching her nose. Their quarters stank of bile, hence her perch beside the forge, well away from the stink and risk of being corralled into chores. 'Ugh, yuck...'

'I know... I was trying to eat my breakfast—'

'Open the gate!' A gateman on the wall shouted. 'Damn it, get the *gate!*'

Lidan's words vanished and her mouth ran dry at the audible alarm in Jac's voice. She found her feet as Rick took off, rushing to help the people swarming into the common from inside huts and pens. Together they lent their shoulders to lifting the locking beam faster than the winches could shift it and women rushed to string bows and nock arrows, snatching spears and waving for anyone untrained to seek shelter indoors.

The gate groaned open and Lidan's knees buckled at what she saw on the other side.

By some blessing of the ancestors, Behn caught her before she hit the ground, then ran after Rick. She wouldn't have noticed if he hadn't crossed her line of sight. Her senses were completely overwhelmed by the blood. It was dry and dark, caked on torn cloth and ruined leather armour, clumped in hair and around festering wounds. It was everywhere, and under it all, her father hung limp from Titon's saddle.

'No...' A watery veil of tears blurred her vision.

Titon came through the gate and waited on shivering legs. His foam-flecked flanks and frothing mouth vanished behind a wall of shoulders and Lidan lost sight of her father as he slipped from the saddle to the waiting arms of those rushing to help. Her eyes flicked to the gate behind him and the rangers following on their worn horses. Siman rode among them, his arm strapped against his chest and a man sat behind him sharing the saddle. Their horse staggered and collapsed and the common erupted into panic.

Jac bellowed and pointed, Rick sprinted off and Behn followed two steps behind. Four men lifted Erlon on a stretcher and Lidan's stomach clenched. He wore a black stain across his chest and the thick armour of lacquered wood and leather hung in splinters from his neck to waist, the shirt and skin beneath was torn and covered in old blood and flies. The flies lifted away in a buzzing swarm, revealing a gaping wound and exposed muscle.

'Father!' Lidan screamed and suddenly her feet were running. She shoved at the people blocking her way as if they were reeds by the creek. 'Da!'

A pair of strong arms caught her waist and pulled her from the path of the stretcher-bearers.

'Oi, Liddy, stay back now, eh?' Jac held her and she gave in to the force of his hands. Her father's skin was pale and slick with sweat, his lips cracked and bloodied. He looked close enough to death to hear the ancestors calling, though his chest still rose and fell with breath. The sight turned Lidan's blood to ice. The stretcher-bearers reached the top of the hall's stairs and Jac whispered, 'Get your mothers.'

'Mam! Kelill! Da's back, come quick!' Her cries echoed down the corridor at the rear of the hall. Heads peered out from doorways, brows furrowed with concern. 'Where's Raeh?' Lidan demanded, ripping aside curtains and searching each room. No one was ever where she needed them to be!

'By the ancestors, Lidan, what's happened?' Kelill emerged from a doorway. 'You're so pale...'

Lidan didn't stop to answer. She spun back to the kitchens and saw Raeh dash across the corridor and into the hall quick as a namorra on the wind. She stumbled after her half-mother and greeted chaos with no idea what to do.

The hall, usually brimming with laughing women, drinking men and playing children, stank like the butcher's slaughter shed and sounded just as bad. The rangers staggered in from the grasslands in varying states of injury and consciousness, their groans and screams shaking the ceiling beams, while others lay as still as stones on tables built for feasting, not bleeding.

Grent, the clan's bonesetter, hurried between the tables with a board and a thin sheet of parchment, marking it as he went and shouting orders. She'd never heard Grent say as many words in an entire month, let alone in five short minutes, and he was as loud as a thunderclap. At Lidan's back her mother gasped and Kelill swore. The gravity and horrified awe in their voices brought tears to her eyes, suppressed sobs catching in her tightening throat.

This was bad.

'Grent, how many?' called Dana Sellan.

'Five, Dana, and two dead in the common,' Grent didn't look up or stop moving. 'Seven from a party of twenty...'

Only five survivors? Lidan pressed her hand to her mouth to steady her quivering lips. Her mother couldn't abide weeping.

Raeh turned and buried her face against Kelill's shoulder, but the fabric of Kelill's shirt did little to muffle Raeh's sobs as they rose to join the rest of the noise echoing between the rafters. Lidan couldn't stand the sound a moment longer and fled deeper into the commotion to escape her half-mother's grief. Her father's stretcher appeared between rushing attendants, perched atop his massive ash-wood feasting table and her body slowed.

No one noticed her.

She was barely tall enough to see over their shoulders and so svelte she slipped through the smallest fissures in the crowd without bother. She blocked her ears to the adults, their yelling and rushed conversations. Her father filled her vision, still and pale, laid low by a wound greater than any she'd ever seen.

An arrow hadn't done it, nor a spear or a flint axe or knife. Rangers never bore such wounds. It was too big, and too deep, stretching from his right shoulder across the thick muscle of his chest down to the bone, carving to the left and halting just shy of the soft tissue of the belly. His armour, built to stop stone arrowheads and spear tips, hadn't stood a chance. At his side, Lidan sank to a stool and stared.

Rangers survived battle wounds. They grew strong again, despite the damage, but this was different. This was something altogether more horrific than anything rangers usually suffered, even when the border disputes were at their worst. Was it the work of a neighbouring clan? Surely not the Namjin... They didn't have the weapons to cause such carnage...

By the mercy of the ancestors, Erlon's chest still rose and fell and Lidan sighed with cautious relief. He was alive, albeit barely, his heart still beating in his barrel chest and shallow rasping breaths filled his lungs. He had hope, if only a sliver against the mounting odds of death. While the daari lived, nothing changed. The clan wasn't ready for their leader to die. Lidan wasn't ready.

Grent strode over, big hands scribbling deftly across the paper, recording what he saw for each of the wounded. The midwife, Moyra, appeared and they exchanged hushed words before she hurried again into the press of anxious relatives and attendants.

'Search me what could've done this... None of them remember. They keep muttering about screaming shadows,' the bonesetter murmured. He pressed his fingers on the angry flesh beside the darkened tear of Erlon's wound and clicked his tongue. He didn't like what he saw.

'*I* know,' Lidan replied, blinking away the fog of grief. Grent's brown eyes met hers and Lidan nodded to the wall behind her father's empty audience chair. 'One of those could rip a gash this deep.'

Hanging above the audience chair for all the clan to see, was the fire-forged blade of iron. The long edges shone with sharp intent, and carried enough weight to split flesh from bone in one swing.

'Shit... But, who...?' whispered Grent, frowning as his hand fell away from the daari's chest.

Lidan held tight to her father's calloused hand and shrugged. Forged blades came from the north, but the Malapa was impassable except for a very small window of time every few years in the height of summer. None of it made sense. Moyra called for Grent and he rushed to oblige, his brow furrowed.

Thankfully the commotion died away as Grent and his helpers moved the injured to the treatment rooms behind his home. One by one they carried the prone bodies, calmed with a tonic to ease their pain and dull their senses, until the only man remaining in the hall was the daari. Lidan didn't move from his side, her small hand wrapped around his filthy fingers, his dogs curled at her feet, the brindle one whimpering whenever she stopped rubbing his back with her foot.

Her mothers scurried back and forth, organising the family's tine-women to assist Grent and Moyra, and sending the small children to play with the older girls away from the mess and blood. The last thing anyone needed was a sleepless night with little ones who had nightmares of bloodied monsters and screaming corpses. At one point, Raeh hurried in, searching the hall for Abbi.

Lidan shrugged and shook her head—she had no idea where the little girl had gone. Abbi was known to vanish into a quiet corner when the chaos and noise became too much to bear, but she never wandered far. Raeh did not linger, and went to search the stables, leaving Lidan with her whirling thoughts.

She didn't want to think on what might happen if her father succumbed to his wounds. She didn't want to think what it might mean, given that she was only twelve and far too young to inherit in her own right. The power would likely fall to her mother, and the idea made Lidan shudder. The woman wielded enough authority in the clan as it was, and swung it around like a blunt instrument at the best of times. What she might do given full reign over the place made Lidan's stomach clench.

As if summoned by the very thought, her solitude ended with the rustling of fine woven skirts and the scent of the flowers the dana sprinkled in her washing water. For a time, her mother did not speak and Lidan did not turn. She didn't want to invite her into this moment alone with her father; she wasn't ready to give it up.

'What is Grent going to do with this?' Sellan muttered. Lidan heard her sigh as one might over spilt ale or a broken pot. 'I'm going to get Thanie.'

The statement snapped through Lidan's daze and she scrambled to follow the dana.

'Mam, no!' She caught her mother in the corridor and ducked around her. She spread her arms wide and pressed a palm on either wall to block the way. Her father had ordered the Crone gone from Hummel by the time he returned. She was the last person whose help he would appreciate or accept. She braced for the violence of her mother's reaction.

'*What?*' Sellan's face twisted with indignation, her voice a low hiss. 'You want him to die?'

'No, he'd want Grent to treat him, not the Crone. He said he wanted her gone!'

The words were out before Lidan realised what she'd said. The bitter argument she and Behn had overhead echoed in her head and she shuddered. What had she done? Her mother leaned forwards and narrowed her eyes, her pristine hands with their perfectly shaped nails cupping Lidan's face as she made a soft tsk sound.

'How could you possibly know he said that?' The dana's fingers stroked her daughter's cheek and curled a loose strand of hair behind her ear.

Understanding rippled across Sellan's features and her hand grew still.

Lidan knew the Crone was still in her decrepit hut, defying the order given by the daari before he departed for the hunt. Lidan knew her mother hadn't made any effort to remove the woman. What she didn't know was how to explain how *she* knew of her father's order. She flinched away from her mother's touch on instinct, but too slowly.

Sellan snatched a handful of Lidan's hair and pulled her close with savage force. '*How* in the name of the Dead Sisters could you know he said *that*?'

'I don't!' Lidan squealed her denial and staggered as her mother twisted her hair around her arm and dragged her to the door. She bit down on a pained cry as her scalp ignited with stinging fire, tearing until blood dribbled across her eyes. 'Mam, I don't know *anything*! I just thought—'

Sellan ignored Lidan's begging and forced her up the stony path from the base of the Caine, unmoved by the whimpering and struggling. Lidan cursed her stupid mouth for speaking such ill-thought words. She knew better. Her mother never made threats...

Chapter Nine

Hummel, Tolak Range, the South Lands

There was no pause to knock on the Crone's door, no standing on ceremony. The dana shouldered the rickety timber panel and shoved Lidan through the tiny dark entry. Lidan's boot caught on a step and she toppled forwards to hit the floor, scraping her hands and arms as she slid into the opposite wall.

'You've brought her, finally,' a disembodied voice observed from the hut's gloomy interior. Despite the sun passing noon, the room encased in packed earth and stone was nearly as black as night. Lidan curled into a ball, too afraid to glance at the shadows. 'I'm surprised it took you so long…'

'The little trollop has been *spying* on me! Weren't you, you little cunt? What did you hear?' The dana kicked and slapped at her daughter. Lidan waved her hands wildly in defence, and yelped as boots hit her ribs but it did nothing to deter Sellan. She was in a rage, eyes wide and wild, teeth bared in a snarl.

'Sellan, calm yourself,' the voice commanded and Lidan's mother paced away reluctantly to collect her composure and correct her hair. 'Remember your lessons. Keep your head.'

Lidan's chest burned, desperate for air and her head spun, dots dancing before her eyes. She blinked to clear them and peered over her bloodied arm and torn sleeve to see Dana Sellan glaring from beside the door.

Sellan rushed forwards again and Lidan scrambled back against an unlit hearth. Her mother's face came within an inch of hers and she shuddered at the proximity of such rage, the woman's full lips curled in an ugly sneer. 'I won't ask you again, Lidan Tolak. What did you hear?'

She knew the punishment for lying. Her mother never made threats, only promises. If she told the truth, she might gain some mercy. Her mother raised a hand to hit her again and Lidan surrendered.

'Father said you were to send the Crone away! That's all! I swear, I didn't hear anything else.'

Sellan slapped Lidan harder than she'd ever been struck. Pain exploded across her face and she cried out, the metallic tang of blood filling her mouth, her lip burst and bleeding. Her ears rang so loudly she didn't hear her mother stalk away.

'Is that true, Daughter Lidan?' the Crone's question floated from the darkest corner of the hut.

Unable to stand the sight of her mother, Lidan locked her gaze on the gloom and nodded. 'He did, before he went ranging.'

'Did he say anything else?' the voice asked with casual curiosity.

Lidan shook her head and swallowed bloody saliva. 'No, just that he wanted you off his range before he returned.'

For a moment, there was no reply. Blood dripped from her scalp to her cheek and beat a steady rhythm while she stared at the darkness and waited for its judgement.

'What do you want done with her?' the Crone asked Sellan.

Her mother approached and a shiver of fear rolled across Lidan's skin. She recoiled as Sellan crouched and tenderly stroked her tangled hair, a gesture in complete opposition to her mood a moment before. The shift rocked Lidan as if she'd been kicked, such tenderness so soon after a frenzy shifting the ground beneath her feet. But it was too perfect, too *pleasant* to be real. Backed against a wall, in the most avoided and reviled corner of Hummel, Lidan knew there was no one to save her from what was coming.

Sellan smiled, but it did not reach her eyes. They remained steady and cold in the dim light of the hut. 'The pit.'

Lidan's heart thumped to a stop, paralysed by fear. The pit? What was the pit?

'Very well…'

Lidan screamed, but it was a waste of breath. Her mother dragged her through the hut's rear door, past a stinking midden to a small timber trap door set in the ground beside an enormous cluster of boulders. When the door swung up, Lidan staggered back as far as her mother's cold hands allowed. Below the door was a pit of utter darkness, its depth lost in an ink black abyss. Sellan did not hesitate. She shoved Lidan into the gloom and slammed the door.

Something sharp tore Lidan's hand from knuckles to wrist as she fell, and she cried out, gripping the wound as she hit the floor of the pit and the light of the world above vanished. Stunned, she scrambled backwards until her back hit a hard earth wall and she froze at the sound of a heavy locking bolt scraping home.

A lock?

She'd been locked down here?

She curled into a tiny ball on the floor, blood seeping through her fingers, and cursed her foolishness through her shuddering sobs.

She prayed in the darkness, begging her ancestors for help, but received no answer. If they didn't see fit to rescue her, what chance was there of anyone else coming to her aid? In the commotion and anxiety of the village, it was unlikely anyone noticed her absence. It was not unusual for her mother to keep her indoors for days at a time, forcing her through lessons she hated. But she would have taken a hundred days of tedious sewing over this. She knew better than to challenge her mother. There was no one to save her; no one at all.

Hours crawled past and, in the distance, a wild dog howled to announce nightfall with its drawn-out call, echoing answers rippling along the valley and raising bumps on Lidan's skin. The chill of the night seeped through the soil and coiled around her, squeezing hard like an icy snake. Her arms and legs cramped after hours in the same position, her feet completely numb, the temperature and the confines of the pit conspiring in tandem to cripple her small body.

If fortune saw to grant her some mercy, frost would not creep through the valley tonight and she might make it to morning intact. At least in the dark she was spared the sight of her wounded hand. It would turn foul if not seen to soon, and then the cold would be the least of her worries.

She lay in the inky blackness and wondered about her father. She wondered if anyone had noticed she was gone or if anyone thought to ask. She wondered what excuse her mother gave them and how easily they accepted it as the truth. Sellan could fabricate a story that no one would question for days, maybe weeks. No one was coming for her, and she was utterly alone.

Lidan shivered and tried to hold in another sob. Her eyes burned from the tears and her bones ached, but there was nothing to do but hold still and hope. She hoped her mother might find some sympathy for her and come back to save her from the cold. She hoped her father might recover and break apart the door above her head with his bare hands, but she cried because she knew neither of those things would happen and it crushed her heart.

The door to the pit creaked open.

She didn't know how long she'd been there. Long enough to soil herself from fear and need, long enough to wonder if her fingers and toes would survive the chill. Her eyes and nose streamed and her lips cracked, burnt by the dry air and lack of water. It might have been a night, or perhaps two, and she had passed the threshold of desperate hunger to resigned sorrow some time ago.

'Get out and walk,' ordered the Crone. Above the old woman's head, stars sparkled in the night sky.

What?

Lidan tried to shrink into the ground, sure she'd heard the husky command incorrectly. Perhaps the woman was insensible. Lidan couldn't walk. She couldn't move at all. She couldn't feel her limbs, let alone animate them in an action that even *resembled* walking. She twitched her head from side to side; she wasn't getting up and she wasn't walking anywhere. She'd rather stay here and die.

A wrinkled hand appeared from within layers of furs and woven shawls and thin fingers flexed. A crack of lightning snapped through the air and slammed into Lidan's shoulder, shuddering her bones and searing flesh. Her jaw locked tight and, unable to scream, her body jerked against the hard stone and earth with the force of the lightning.

The lightning stopped and left a breathless silence in its wake.

The Crone has magic… She has magic? Father forbids magic, all the clans do… Oh fuck, she has magic!

'Walk,' the Crone repeated.

'I… can't…' Lidan ground out through clenched teeth, the pain in her hand extinguished by the agony of the power crackling across the surface of her skin.

The Crone has magic! Her inner voice screamed with no one to hear it. Not simply a wise woman from Sellan's homeland, the old bitch was a spell-weaver! People like her were the stuff of fireside tales warning children not to wander off! But here she was, hunched in the starlight at the edge of this miserable storage pit.

'Then crawl,' the Crone said flatly and flexed her gnarled fingers as if to suggest another crack of lightning wasn't out of the question. Grey eyes glared down at her from a wrinkled face, half in shadow, half illuminated by the wane light of the moon.

Unwilling and unable to endure another burning jolt of energy, Lidan pulled herself out of the hole and began to drag herself towards the hut with her elbows, her legs trailing behind like tattered ropes. Rocks on the path cut her clothes with the cruelty of knives, paring away cloth and stitching to expose her soft belly and thighs. She didn't look back to see if she left a trail of blood on the stones. She knew she did. The Crone followed with small, purposeful steps, the light taps of a walking stick beating the time of the torturous march.

The door seemed miles away, paved with painful inches between here and there. Lidan put her head down and glared at the ground. If she focussed on the distance and how far she had left to crawl, she would give in and lie sobbing until she died. She wondered if she would be forced to crawl up to reach the door latch as well, but the Crone slid through the opening, her shadowy figure enveloped by the darkness within. Some sensation returned to Lidan's legs, burning pain licking up her thighs from a hundred cuts. She dragged herself through the door, her last ounce of strength dedicated to flinging the thing shut to keep the seeping cold at bay.

A click of bony fingers echoed in the dark and Lidan jerked back against a crude cabinet, heat stinging her face and eyes. A fire roared to life in the hearth, the single room of the dank hut suddenly awash with warmth and light. She brought her hand up instinctively and immediately regretted it, the barely healed skin tearing. Blood dribbled down her wrist to soak her sleeve afresh and the fine bones of her hand throbbed to the beat of her heart. Despite the torn skin and aching muscles, Lidan stared at the Crone while the old woman gazed into the fire as though its appearance was nothing out of the ordinary.

The Crone's magic stunned her. No one in the clan had magic. No one even dared speak of it. Her father said it was a force of evil, responsible for nothing but death and madness and hunted from the bloodlines of the South Land Clans generations ago. It could only be found north of the mountains and, some said, along the Rinay Coast.

What would her father do if he knew the Crone was more than a wizened old potion brewer and a companion to the dana? Lidan's instincts told her to be revolted and afraid, but an unhealthy curiosity midwifed questions she didn't want to ask, nor hear the answers to.

'You'll need a dressing on that,' the Crone nodded at Lidan's gaping hand wound while absently poking the fire.

Don't you fucking touch me, Lidan snarled to herself. But instead of screaming at her captor, the only thing she could manage was a single tear and a quivering chin. She wasn't sad—she was broken, furious, afraid and sickened by what she saw in the glow of the fire.

The Crone was a bent old thing with lice riddled fur and weaves piled across her shoulders, draping to cover her feet. Only her hands and head were exposed, all filthy and unkempt. Long nails curled from the tips of her stiff, swollen fingers, stained yellow and caked with muck. Her hair was either a wig fashioned from a bouncer pelt, or it hid under some sort of rude, ill-sewn hat. And from her smell, the Crone was every bit as ancient as people gossiped she was beyond the dana's hearing.

Clear grey eyes fixed on Lidan and she shivered under their unwavering scrutiny. The entirety of her body was rotting away, yet the Crone's eyes still held the sole remaining piece of who she once was. They belonged to someone much younger, fierce and unmarred by age and time. There was no doubting the power behind them, a force contained through sheer will alone.

Lidan noticed the slight shake to the Crone, hardly discernible and easily mistaken for the trembling the elderly often suffer as they lose their wits.

But she realised this was not the shivering of a mind losing control of its body, but the strain of a body struggling to control the immense power of its mind.

'Not wise talking back to your Mam like that, is it girlie?' the Crone barked and snapped Lidan from her thoughts. There weren't any words she could muster in response, so she nodded. It certainly *was* unwise.

'Did you leave your tongue in the pit, girlie? You've nothing to say now, no words or lies to spit at me? No pearls of childish wisdom to justify what you did?'

Lidan shook her head.

The Crone smiled with her grey teeth and allowed silence to fill the hut. 'You know I came here with your mother before she matched to Erlon. She had to fight hard to keep me so she's not likely to turn me out. She's from another place; a place so far from these borders your tiny little mind would pop just trying to comprehend the distance. She had a hard past, your mother. Not fit for speaking, so I'll get to the point...'

Lidan turned away. I don't want to hear this... I don't care... I just want to go home...

'I'm not going to leave you in the pit for as long as she wants me to.'

Lidan glanced at the Crone from the corner of her eye. She hadn't expected that.

The Crone went on in her harsh, throaty voice, 'She's being unreasonable and I'll bear her rage if she fires up about it. I've done it before, but not that you'd know. This time I'll decide what to do with you. But by the stars, girlie, step from the line again and you'll wear whatever punishment she sees fit. I won't stop her, even if it kills you.' The Crone stood and set a pot on the low flames at the edge of the fire. 'So, you're staying here for a while.'

'Why?' murmured Lidan, her voice hoarse from hours of sobbing. Tears pooled anew in her eyes.

The Crone shrugged her hunched shoulders and settled back to poking the fire she sparked with her own fingers. 'Need someone to chop wood and plug the holes in the roof before the cold truly sets its teeth in. You think that might be punishment enough, after a night in the pit?'

'I meant, why does my mother do this to me?' It was something she never understood—not truly. She was a wilful, stubborn child, as were a number of her sisters, but their mothers never beat them. Not as far as she knew. She'd been convinced for the longest time the fault lay in her, but perhaps there was something deeper, something she had yet to uncover about her mother that fuelled her rage.

'Pain is the only language your mother understands, girlie. I said she had a hard past. What she does to you in't but a sliver of what she's endured in her own skin. She sees this,' she gestured to Lidan's cut and bloodied body, 'as the only way you'll learn the lessons she has to teach. You get a chance, just one, to save yourself from the wrath she'll bring down if you keep this behaviour up. You act up again and I promise you, not a word of a lie, her past will become your future. You hear me?'

'People will come looking for me...' Lidan insisted, feeling the tiny flare of defiance in her chest flare for a moment.

The Crone shook her head. 'No, they won't. Your mother has a story woven just for those who might ask, and they won't dare to ask more than once. And at this moment, they have more pressing concerns than where you are.'

The lump of fear lodged in Lidan's throat choked her response. She was a fool to underestimate Sellan, a fool to think she could confront the woman and not suffer her wrath. In all the days she had left, she would never, *ever* do so again.

CHAPTER TEN

The bird soared past and Lidan loosed the arrow from her aching hand. It sailed straight up and struck, the bird plummeting into some bushes perched on a cliff edge above the Crone's walled yard. She slid down from the rocks she used as a blind and scrambled amongst the shrubs and trees, disturbing a cluster of small beaded rock dragons as she searched for her kill. It would be their supper and the base of the stew she and the Crone would eat for a few days. A bird that size would keep her belly full even if her heart was empty.

She'd been hollow and listless since her mother dumped her in the Crone's hut. She hadn't returned once to check to see if she was still alive, or to demand more punishment for that matter. Lidan had no idea what was going on in Hummel or how her father and his injured rangers fared, and she'd pushed such thoughts away, recoiling from the pain of the memories. She couldn't tell, from her short excursions onto the Caine, if more rangers had returned or left in search of who had attacked her father's party. She wasn't allowed to show her face in the front yard at all, so she saw nothing of the stables or the back of the forge, nor of her wild-born horse or her friend, Behn. Had Behn asked after her? Had anyone noticed her missing?

The whole experience left her feeling isolated and alone. She watched the clan go about their business, the little she could discern from the crevices of the Caine while remaining unseen. She saw them feeding stock and repairing houses, watched scouts traversing the valley. No one left to hunt or gather in the bush at the foot of the tablelands, and it appeared the majority of folk remained inside Hummel's walls. No one ever looked towards the hut. Not once did a head turn her way, or eyes linger on the Crone's shack. It was as if the place didn't exist at all.

Lidan yanked the dead bird from a leafy bush by its wing and fancied the feathers. They'd be nice to keep back to fletch arrows, if the Crone let her, and she tucked her prize under her arm. She might be young but Lidan wasn't stupid—she didn't dare try to escape and the Crone knew it, so the old woman happily allowed her out to hunt for their supper. Where would she go? Without a trained horse and the help of a ranger, escaping across the range on her own was a death sentence in the frigid cold of the dry season, even without the threat of what was lingering out in the bush.

She emerged from the stand of trees and made ready to climb down the Caine's western face when she spied Sellan striding up the track to the Crone's hut, her unblemished apron reflecting the blinding sunlight, her auburn hair caught in the cold wind. Lidan crouched low behind a twisted bush growing between two massive boulders, but Sellan didn't glance at the Caine, her eyes trained on the uneven ground at her feet. Lidan scurried down the rocky slope and as Sellan crested the rise in the track and came around a collection of huge red boulders at the entry to the Crone's yard, Lidan dumped her bow, arrows and the bird behind a timber box by the rear door and slipped inside.

The Crone's ice-grey eyes caught her instantly and blinked once.

Lidan didn't speak. She slid her left wrist through a leather cuff and strap bound to the hut's back wall and slumped to lie still on a mangy pallet of hay and sacks. Two sharp knocks hit the door and it swung open, the Crone unmoved from her seat by the fire.

'Are you done with her?' Sellan asked, not bothering to utter a word of greeting.

'Afternoon to you, too,' the Crone muttered and spat a wad of phlegm in the fire. It hissed and bubbled and though she did it daily, Lidan couldn't help gagging in disgust.

'I said, are you done with her?'

'Almost,' the Crone replied with a subtle air of disobedience. She was either incredibly brave or monstrously stupid. If Sellan was willing to beat her daughter for speaking out of turn, she doubted the dana would stay her hand with the Crone. Lidan bit her lip and braced for the inevitable scathing retort.

'How much longer, then? They all think she's up here because she took ill with shock after Erlon came back. You best not have killed or crippled her. You'll be explaining it to her father if you have!' Sellan's voice rose with furious panic and relief flooded Lidan's chest. Was her father asking for her? Were her half-mothers or sisters demanding to see her?

'Don't be stupid, Sellan. I'm old, not an idiot. She will be well enough to return in two days. You don't want them seeing any wounds, do you?'

'Good,' Sellan began to pace the small room, her boots softly scuffing the floor. 'Good...'

'Why the rush?' the Crone probed.

'Never you mind—' Sellan dismissed the question out of hand.

'While it's my life under threat from that husband of yours, I'll mind all I like!'

Lidan stiffened in the dark corner of the hut, suddenly terrified. She didn't want to be here if they were going to have it out with each other! The Crone had magic, but what about her mother? Did Sellan know about the magic? Was she party to the secret?

'What are you going on about, you mad old bat? *Your* life!' Sellan snorted, half laughing. 'What threat is there to your life?'

'You heard what she said, what her father ordered you to do. Has he woken and demanded to search my hut, demanded to see if I'm gone? And when he does, where will I go? I can't stay here—he'll have me pegged out as craw bait sooner than look at me!' The end of the Crone's weathered walking stick struck the floor with a sharp crack, emphasising her point.

'Don't be foolish—' Sellan waved the claims away, but the Crone lashed out and whacked the stick on the table where they took their meals. Plates and cups rattled and Sellan fell silent.

'If I go,' the Crone continued, 'and there is every chance I will, what happens to you?'

The question hung in the air like smoke. Lidan held her breath, too afraid to let it out in case she missed her mother's response, scrambling to unravel the meaning of the words.

'You're not going anywhere,' answered Sellan.

'Perhaps not today, but the question stands—what happens if I'm gone? You can't survive here on your own. There's no way they'll let you up here again and that's if they don't tear this place down. Where will you go to finish what we started?'

For a long while there was no reply. The pacing stopped and the air in the hut grew unnaturally still and warm for such a cool afternoon. Lidan's brow furrowed.

Finish what they started?

'Thanie, they won't do that; I swear, I won't let them…' Sellan suddenly sounded like a beaten child, like Lidan, swearing to her elder that she wouldn't break the rules again. It sent a cold shiver through Lidan and she put every ounce of energy into remaining perfectly still. They could never know she heard the secrets in their conversation.

But the Crone knows I'm awake…

The cold shiver froze hard on her skin and she clenched her jaw to stop it trembling. The Crone *knew* Lidan wasn't asleep or unconscious on the floor. The ruse was for the dana alone, so what was the old woman playing at? Lidan wished she could crawl away and block her ears with mud. This was worse than the fight between her father and mother—she didn't want to be privy to their secrets or party to their conspiracies and plots!

After a long, heavy silence, the Crone cleared her throat. 'Sellan, the girl will be ready when I say so and not before. You knew as much when you brought her here and she will return sorry for her mistakes. In the meantime, you best keep yourself in check. What's happened to bring you up here in such a flap?'

'Farah is with child.'

Lidan's heart swelled with joy—her half-mother was pregnant again! She smiled to herself and wondered what her new sister would be called, then felt her smile fade. What if the child wasn't a sister, but a brother—the long-awaited son—the reason her parents had bickered so furiously the day the hunt departed? It was all her father wanted; a son to inherit the clan lands and lead their people. As far as she knew, the daaris of the other clans all had at least one son to their name, and the Law clearly stated that a son would always inherit over a daughter, no matter when the boy was born. Lidan shivered, a chill creeping through her bones. What if the child was a boy?

The Crone cursed in a language Lidan didn't understand. She didn't need to know the meaning of the words to hear the hatred in them.

'Did she fall on this last moon?' the Crone pressed.

'No, at least three cycles have passed since she conceived,' Sellan muttered and the Crone cursed again and spat in the fire. 'It was before he left on the hunt.'

'Get back down there and keep them occupied for another two days, then you can have her back.'

'What about Farah?' The dana's low, careful words rolled across the room, full of promise and intent.

'Do nothing… for now. Go,' ordered the Crone.

Lidan's stomach flipped and her eyes grew wide as she waited in the silence for her mother to answer, but there was no reply.

Do nothing? What could they do? Farah was pregnant. There was nothing that could be done. Unless…

The door creaked and slammed in the wind and the dana was gone. Lidan rolled over slowly to stare at the Crone and found a cold pair of eyes watching her.

'What do you think of all that?'

'I… You…' Lidan crawled to her feet and yanked the cuff from her arm. 'I don't understand… What are you going to do to Farah?'

'I've not decided yet,' the Crone settled back in her chair and raised her unkempt brows at Lidan. 'Not good news for you, though…'

'Me?' she faltered, her concern for her half-mother forgotten.

'If that child is a boy, you best watch your back, girlie.' The Crone nodded sagely. 'You're your father's heir, for now. According to your mother, unless he has a son, you'll be matched in your eighteenth year and the man *you* bring home will be the next daari of the clan. You'll be the dana of your own people, the first woman to ever inherit her father's range.'

The old woman came to her feet and limped to stand over Lidan in the golden light.

The fire might as well have been a pile of steaming dung for all the warmth it gave Lidan's fearful, freezing body. There was no flame in the world hot enough to thaw the dread crawling up her spine.

'If that girl-wife births a boy, he will instantly usurp you. You're nothing if she has a boy. You will cease to exist.'

'That's not true! Mam *wants* Da to have more children! She plans the days—'

'Pah!' The old woman spat and shook a swollen finger at Lidan. 'Your mother spends an inordinate amount of time planning and advising your father when to lie with his wives under the *guise* of helping him put boys in their bellies. She's trying to stop them! She's trying to protect you and your future, you stupid girl!

'Do you see the mistake you made in angering her? In constantly defying her? The enemy you've made in the only woman who cares for your interests?' The Crone jabbed Lidan's shoulder with her bony, twisted finger. It stabbed below her collarbone like a hot knife and Lidan cried out, clutching where it burned. '*You* need to figure out where you stand, girlie. Do you want the future your mother works tirelessly to build, or do you want to vanish into obscurity? Nothing—you'll be nothing.'

Pain throbbed up the bone into Lidan's neck and she shuffled back, staring at the Crone in fearful awe. What *was* the future her mother wanted for her? The life of a subservient wife to a daari? Or something else? A position of power in the clan that no woman had ever achieved? But if Farah's child was a boy...

Her parents' quarrel replayed in her mind. Sellan warning Erlon to beware the nights he lay with his wives, especially Farah. If Lidan lost her place as heir, what did that mean for the dana? No longer the mother of the heir, she would have to concede some authority to Farah. And when Lidan was matched away to another clan, which she surely would be, then her mother would be left behind. Was that what Sellan feared? A time when her position in the clan became so diminished that she might cease to matter?

Her back hit the wall and she slid down to the meagre pile of sacks and hay she called a bed. When the dana warned Erlon against ignoring her advice, she implied he risked not conceiving sons, when in fact she was making sure *none* of his wives bore one and interrupted Lidan's place as heir. She worked on Lidan's behalf, and Lidan had fought against her mother's decisions. It was no wonder Sellan was so furious with her behaviour.

The Crone set a water pot on the heat Lidan no longer felt and resumed her seat. 'So now you see—everything she does is for you and Marrit. *Everything*, and you throw it back in her face with all this talk of horses and becoming a ranger... She's a hard woman, girlie, but her eyes are only for you and your future. If that's the only lesson you learn here, see you keep it in mind from now on.'

Lidan's shameful heart thumped hard and she hugged her knees to her chest. She was near-sighted and stupid—a daughter who didn't deserve her mother's effort and sacrifice. Her mother was trying to secure a future where Lidan didn't have to leave Hummel—a future that granted her more power and authority than any clan woman could dream of. But if her father conceived a son with Farah as the Crone suspected, and her mother turned her back on Lidan for lack of respect and gratitude, what future did she have?

'How can I fix this?' she asked and the old woman looked at her with brows raised in surprise.

'There might not be any fixing to be done, girlie.' She pointed one of those gnarled old fingers at Lidan again. 'You can't fix anythin' once it's shattered.'

Sellan didn't speak to Lidan the day she collected her from the hut. Instead, she tilted her head towards the gate and waited in the doorway as Lidan collected a ragged old shawl the Crone had given her for the colder nights.

She shuffled past her mother and flinched as the woman's sharp nails stung her arm, snatched the shawl and tossed it back into the hut before slamming the door. The dana offered no words to the Crone, nor did she address Lidan as they picked their way down the track and came into the village from behind the stables.

Sellan grabbed her daughter before she could emerge into the common, still quiet in the cold, misty morning. 'Not a word, you hear me? Not. A. Word.'

Lidan nodded. She didn't need further explanation or instruction. She knew exactly what her mother meant and the consequences if she failed to meet the dana's expectations. After more than a fortnight cutting the Crone's wood with bleeding hands and sleeping on a pile of lice-riddled furs with only her thoughts for company, Lidan had turned herself inside out with worry. She better understood her mother, in the new light of the Crone's words, but the revelations were driving her to distraction.

The scheme her mother had underway to inhibit the birth of a male heir was extraordinary. Yet for all her effort, it might have failed. If Farah was pregnant, there was no telling the child's sex until it was born. Would Sellan wait to see if her sister-wife had another daughter, or act to prevent the birth altogether? Lidan shivered and hugged her chest, ignoring Behn's wave and confused frown as they passed the forge on the way to the hall. The Crone had told the dana to stay her hand, but Lidan doubted the old woman's word would count for much if Sellan got an idea in her head.

For now, Lidan planned to keep her mouth shut, especially when her mother was near. If the dana discovered she'd been listening to the conversation with the Crone, she had no doubt what her punishment would be. Some things were best kept behind tightly sealed lips.

She followed her mother into the hall and through the corridors to her parents' chambers—a collection of rooms reserved for the private business of the daari and only ever seen by the most trusted of the family's advisors. Beyond a heavy curtain of wool, Lidan heard the gentle murmuring of men's voices, and her mother held it aside and pushed her through without announcing their arrival.

She stumbled in and Grent looked up from her father's chest wound, his hands poised to fit a clean linen dressing as the daari lay on a wide timber bed covered in furs. The bonesetter smiled and quickly finished, collecting his things and leaving them alone. Lidan grinned and her father smiled despite the dark smudges of fatigue around his eyes, lifting his arm and beckoning her closer.

In a few steps she was beside him, curled under the arm opposite the wound and snuggling against the uninjured side of his bare chest. She refused to cry in case it enraged her mother and made her father think something was amiss, so she focused on the needle-etched tattana lines marked across his chest and down his ribs, tracing them with a finger as she'd done since she was small.

Daari Erlon shifted a lock of her hair to unveil her face. 'Where have you been, Liddy?'

'I told you she took ill,' Sellan answered quickly. 'She was so devastated by your injury...'

For a moment, Lidan considered correcting her mother, but instead she nodded and hugged him closer. She didn't want him to see deceit in her eyes, even if her mother's lie was for the best. No one needed to know the truth of why she'd gone, and they wouldn't believe her if she told them.

'Come, child, leave your father to rest.' The dana's hand pressed on her shoulder and she allowed herself to be led to the door.

'Sellan, where is Farah?' Erlon asked suddenly, casually picking up a parchment page from beside the sickbed and feigning interest in the symbols scrawled across it. The hand on Lidan's shoulder tensed to a hard claw, right above the aching collarbone injured by the Crone, and it took all her determination not to scream at the pain.

Sellan's face remained an expressionless mask until finally her lips curved with a slight smile that did not reach her eyes. She bowed slightly to her husband. 'Your fourth wife is ill with a flux.'

'Kelill came yesterday but wouldn't say what ails her sister-wife...' Erlon's steady gaze settled on Sellan and the grip on Lidan's shoulder intensified, the talons of the claw driving deeper. As much as she tried to hold still, she began to squirm.

'Farah is very ill and must rest—'

'My wife will be brought to me, ill or not. I want to see her for myself.' He waved his hand to dismiss them and Sellan guided Lidan from the room. He hadn't forgotten their disagreement over Farah. The moment of tender happiness shrivelled to a hard kernel of hopeless fear.

Nothing had changed between her parents in the time she had spent confined in the Crone's shack. If anything, their regard for each other had grown darker and more poisonous. Lidan tried to ignore the quiver in her muscles, and the drive to run and hide. Her mother held her tightly, in ways that ran deeper than the hand on her shoulder, leading her from the daari's chamber. She would not escape that grip without a fight.

Chapter Eleven

Usmein, Orthia

For more than three weeks Ranoth watched dark grey clouds loom in the north and west, and read the signs foretelling the arrival of the first snow. Those steely clouds announced the turn in the season and they would blow across the Territory leaving a thick blanket of ice in their wake. The days grew short and dark, yet no word came of the duke and the army, despite the gathering storms—not one sentry had made a sighting, nor had any of Ran's scouts arrived with news of victory or defeat.

The best view of the fields to the west of Usmein was from the top of the palace, where the roofs of the four wings met and the dome curved into the sky. A long walkway frequented by patrolling guards skirted the dome's base and offered a commanding perspective of the city and the farmland Ranoth's people relied on for food. So close to the winter snows, the crops had been harvested and the grain silos under the city stood full and ready, all of it recorded with precision in Alber Frain's ledgers.

Ran had ordered the city's common areas prepared with tents and food stores for the arrival of refugees from nearby towns, if for any reason the advancing Woaden swung away from the main road between the capital and the front. The land between Usmein and the Territory created a natural funnel any advancing army would follow to take the city, and it was sparsely populated for fear the Woaden might one day put a torch to it. Those who tended the land near the city returned to the protection of the walls each day when the sun set. If the Woaden came raging across the hills, there was hardly more than forest for them to raze or pillage. If they got into the city, however, the matter was entirely different.

A door to Ran's right opened into the wind, then slammed closed.

'Marshal Gregon said I'd find you here,' said Brit without preamble. Their shared experience on the road from the front and weeks of working together on the defence of the city had bred familiarity between them that no longer required titles or etiquette. Ran needed Brit's honest advice, and appreciated it where a number of his father's advisors treated him like an uneducated idiot. Gregon and Lithor were the only other notable exceptions to the rule.

Ran lowered his looking glass and gave the watcher a smile. 'Aye, most days. The view is better here than at the wall.'

Across the fields, teams of workers laboured with shovels, cranking timber cranes, carts and horses, all struggling against the hard wind to finish Usmein's defences. From this height the workers resembled tiny game pieces, moving in random, chaotic patterns. For weeks, every hand the city could spare, including women and children, had been working from dawn to dusk. They all pinned their hopes for survival on the wild ideas of their young prince and Ran hoped their faith in him would not be misplaced.

Brit nodded and pocketed his hands. 'It's almost finished.'

'Now it just has to work,' muttered Ran. Each day he faced down his rising anxiety. His plan *had* to work. If it didn't, he'd have the blood of thousands on his hands; such a stain would never wash clean. He tried to smother the thought by changing the subject. 'What has Gregon got you doing?'

'Scouting for sentry posts, laying out archers' blinds.' Brit sounded bored, his voice low and dull, and without a hint of the cheek it had when they met at the front.

'That sounds exciting,' Ran quipped in an attempt to lighten the mood, but Brit's frown only deepened.

The watcher pointed at the western horizon. 'Not as exciting as that.'

Ran spun back to the view and peered through the looking glass. 'What *is* that?'

The stupid thing wouldn't focus.

The watcher slapped Ran on the shoulder. 'Time to test your defences. That's the duke's guard.'

Brit followed at Ranoth's heels, sliding down ladders from the dome until they hit the fourth-floor service corridor. They burst into the long southern gallery, the living quarters of the palace layered below their feet like a cake, all the way down to the servants' lodgings in the basement. Ran sprinted past a guard and staggered to a stop, thinking better of it.

'Go to the garrison and raise the alarm,' he ordered the man. 'The duke returns.'

He didn't wait for a reply and ran on. Marshal Gregon would be at the wall, overseeing the distribution of garrison soldiers across the defences. Some were finished and ready to occupy, others half done, but serviceable. There was cold comfort in the unfinished work at least providing a barrier to any Woaden thundering along behind Duke Ronart.

Ran led on down the stairs, not willing to wait for the lifts to crank all the way up to the fourth floor. When they reached the ground floor atrium Brit gave a high whistle to a group of guards and garrison soldiers at the east wing entrance. They all snapped to attention. 'Bring your blades, boys! To the wall!'

Outside they found Chancellor Lithor conferring with several palace officials by the forges. He spun towards the sound of hurrying boots on the palace entry stairs and his eyes widened at the sight of Ran running with garrison soldiers.

'Chancellor, have you a sword I can borrow?' Ran jogged over and Lithor, still in the unbreakable habit of wearing his blade every day, unbuckled his scabbard belt.

'What have you seen, sir?' The veteran kept his voice low and helped Ran fit the leather harness to his waist.

Short on breath, Ran waved towards the west. 'My father is in the hills. Now we discover if the Woaden follow behind him.'

'I'll lock the palace down.' Lithor waved sharply to his assistant, who darted off to enact the protocols for securing the palace compound.

'Aye, and my mother and the girls?' Ran said around a ball of fear threatening to choke him. He needed to keep his head on straight and his mind focused—people would look to him to set an example and though they might see a fifteen-year-old, a veteran of one failed command and greener than spring grass, they would not see the Palace Commander snivelling like a frightened child.

'They're prepared; I'll get them squared away.' The chancellor smacked him on the shoulder in a manly sort of good luck blessing and rushed off into the crowd. Bells began to toll in the city's long Guild Plaza, pealing a call to arms from atop the Silversmith's Hall.

There'd hardly been time to spend with his sisters since his return, but he'd not failed to plan for their protection. Ebonie and Nerola were to hide under the palace with the duchess and any of the court not involved in the defence of the city. If the walls fell, they could escape into the mountains. He didn't know how far they might make it if forced to flee. Marlow to the north was an ally, albeit a reluctant one, but the land between Usmein and Harbern was icy and sparse.

Ran shut a door on the thought. They wouldn't need to flee because he wasn't going to let his city fall.

He clambered aboard a troop wagon with the last of the soldiers and it passed through the palace gate which shut behind them with a dull boom. Dual steel portcullises, one either side of the two-foot-thick timber gates, fell at an eye-watering rate, clanking loudly as the chains ran unhindered through the winches. They slammed home into thin channels at the foot of the gate, locked in place underground by huge spring-loaded bolts. Now the only way into the palace complex was over the thirty-foot wall, or under a web of steel bars buried beneath the foundations.

The doors and shutters of houses and businesses banged closed, while workers poured through all four of Usmein's gates from the fields. Mothers rushed to gather their children and secure them in homes built of stone and timber, and Ran wondered how long their walls would hold if the Woaden breached the city. By the time the wagon reached the merchant quarter and trader's market by the city's main gate, the streets behind him stood empty.

Good, he thought. Perhaps they could avoid a massacre if people weren't running madly through the streets. Marshal Gregon waved from the gatehouse door, ushering Ran inside.

'Are they ready?' asked Ran, while Gregon led him to the stairs.

'As much as they can be, sir,' Gregon puffed, taking two stairs at a time up the spiralling stone flight. They exited into grey sunlight, hunched below the rampart and jogged across to one of the thickly barricaded archer blinds atop the wall. The gatehouse door locked behind them; the keepers sealing themselves in with the massive winches, plenty of torches, heavy stones and boiling oil ready for delivery through the murder holes.

Brit and a team of watchers were stationed in blinds along the wall with their keen eyes trained on the fields through peep holes. An eerie silence fell across Usmein unlike any Ran had ever heard and all grew still except for the flapping of the Palace Command banner. It stood proudly above the wall, the silver shield of his father's house on a black field, a black sash cutting across the shield to mark the absence of the duke. It only ever flew when the city came under attack, an ebony flag for Usmein's troops to gather behind in a time of dire peril. It had become Ran's banner—his standard.

The city was a veritable ghost town. Even at night it was never so quiet or empty. The thought sent a shudder through him, a reminder of the house of bones, the empty skulls and the girl. His hands began to burn again, tingling and aching down to the bones. His wrists throbbed with heat but this time no amount of squeezing or shaking eased the sensation.

He tightened his grip on the hilt of his borrowed sword and tried to ignore the sting biting into his flesh. He nudged Brit. 'Can you see them?'

'Aye, sir, our escort are leading them.' Brit let off two short whistles, followed by a longer blast and the signal repeated along the wall, relayed by other watchers. He looked away, blinked quickly and returned to squint through the eyehole. 'Not many left in the Duke's Guard.'

Ran's heart dropped into his boots and he peered around the blind to scan the fields. A plume of dust stretched south, carried on the hard north wind, a smudge of brown and black oscillating where the dust began.

Marshal Gregon dropped to his knees beside Ran, a looking glass resting on the edge of the rampart. 'Fuck, that's not many at all.'

'Marshal,' called Brit. 'There be flags at the south sentry post—they've seen the enemy in the hills.'

Away to the south, where the road wound down from the valley, two small red flags beat back and forth in a hurried signal. A signaller on the wall rushed to wave a reply with a set of flags, numerous colours signalling different messages in a variety of patterns.

'How far away are they?' Marshal Gregon asked with his looking glass on the approaching riders.

Another series of whistles echoed along the wall, down to the signallers and back before Brit answered, 'A few miles, maybe a little more.'

The marshal's looking glass snapped closed and he turned to Ran with a smile. 'We'll test your trap after all, your Grace!'

Ran tried to mimic the marshal's sentiment but his expression refused to cooperate. The muscles around his mouth were fixed in an anxious frown, anticipating the absolute worst, while his brain tried to decipher the circumstances leading to his father's army being whittled down to just a few hundred soldiers.

'Why are there so few men?' he whispered to the marshal.

Gregon shrugged. 'Better than none at all. You said our troops broke ranks and took off. No doubt a few hundred of them regrouped at other camps near the front.'

The watcher's whistle pierced the air and Brit leaned back from his eyehole. 'The duke's here, sir.'

Below, a mass of Orthian riders approached the gate at full gallop with an escort of garrison riders. The duke, thank the gods, rode at the centre atop his warhorse. The city gates groaned closed behind the remains of the Orthian soldiers and two portcullises, designed in tandem with the palace gate but twice the size, rattled into place. Ran fancied running to find his father among the men and horses, but checked himself. He needed to coordinate this last-ditch attempt to break the Woaden advance.

'Brit, send the signal to block the road and collapse the bridge,' ordered Ran, propping his looking glass on the rampart and taking a deep, steadying breath. He'd come this far on his own; his father's arrival changed nothing. He was the Palace Commander and responsible for Usmein's defence until he officially handed command back to Ronart.

Whistles echoed down the wall and flags snapped back and forth. On the far side of the fields, teams rushed forwards to dump cartloads of rubbish, furniture, boulders, and soil across the road, completely blocking where it came down from the hills. The carts and horses hurried away from the barricade, turning at specified markers and disappearing into the defences. Chains drawn by stout plough horses inside the city hauled a hastily constructed timber bridge platform away from under a layer of soil and debris before the gate. Beneath it ran a long, deep trench of foul, brackish water and clusters of sharp pikes. Ran's logic was simple, almost child-ish. He hoped the audacious simplicity alone would baffle the Woaden.

From the roadblock, earthwork embankments as tall as two men branched north and south to form two wide causeways. Four or five horses could ride abreast along these channels and quickly find themselves in a trench as deep as the bunds were high. There was no time to stop and avoid these channels when exiting the hills on the road; the blockade saw to that. A rider's only choice was to turn their horse left or right and charge down the trench or hit the roadblock head on. With a galloping horde of cavalry behind them, the riders were unlikely to attempt a stop and risk a crush in the bottleneck.

Ran watched the edge of the hills and the slice of road visible beyond the blockade, his pulse hammering in his throat, thudding in his ears. He waited and watched, certain in one moment that his plan would succeed then doubt-ing it completely in the next. He swallowed a lump from his throat.

Woaden riders thundered from the valley and poured out into the earth-works. A vanguard ten mounts wide, as many as could ride side by side along the road, stormed towards the blockade. Their horses immediately baulked and followed the channels by instinct, paying no attention to their masters.

'Yes!' Ran pumped his fist in the air, amazed and thrilled that the bunds worked.

Brit slapped him on the back. 'They're doing it. You *beauty*!'

A cheer echoed along the walls and men began to chant; *Black Prince, Black Prince…*

Hundreds of riders poured from the valley and vanished into the chan-nels, galloping down into the jewel of the defences; a vast network of trenches dug by the blistered hands of Usmein's residents. Soon the screams of dying soldiers and the whinnies of distressed horses reached the wall, dust clouds billowing up from unseen fighting.

Black Prince, Black Prince…

Too deep for a man to scale without tools, the network spread from the hills towards Usmein's walls, a twisting maze of trenches modelled on labyrinthine city streets. The soldiers of Usmein's garrison knew nothing of fighting on flat fields, but they were deadly in the winding canyons between buildings. The fields were now a dizzying maze riddled with drop pits, tar traps, and set about with ambush zones and dead ends to trap unsuspecting Woaden riders and unseat them from their mounts.

Black Prince, Black Prince…

'Why are they saying that?' Ran muttered to Gregon.

The Marshal answered with a nod at the black Palace Command banner shivering in the wind. He winked and smiled. 'They'll be calling you the Red Prince once this is over!'

'Maybe… If we win…' Ran's limbs tingled with elation and terror, still throbbing with uncomfortable heat.

Word of the defences quickly reached the riders coming through the valley and they slowed to avoid the barricade across the road. A good number, unable to stop in time, smashed into the wall of rubble and rubbish. Ran made sure the city's privies were emptied for the barrier—they might be the Empire's feared soldiers, but even the Woaden would shy away from climbing piles of shit. With the slowing of the charge, another challenge arose—the first of many heads appeared reluctantly over the roadblock and earthwork bunds, riders abandoning their horses and scrambling up to avoid the trenches.

'You see them?' asked Brit, his face pressed hard against the stone of his archer's blind, his eye on the peephole.

'Send the signal,' Ran replied and the whistles echoed again.

All over the field, beyond the borders of the trench network, arrows soared silently from camouflaged blinds to rain steely death on those stupid enough to peer above the embankments. The screams stung Ranoth's ears but he bit the inside of his lip and ignored the screeches of the dying—better them than the people inside the city.

A blast of blue light suddenly lit the field and a concussion wave hit the city wall with a shuddering boom.

Ran slammed into the rampart at his back and several men tumbled over the edge into the street, screaming all the way. If it hadn't been for the searing pain in his hands and forearms, Ran would have helped those knocked down by the explosion, but he couldn't lift his own weight from the stones.

'Mage! They've got a *mage!*' Brit's bellowing sounded like a whisper in a thunderstorm to Ran's ringing ears.

'What? What is it?' Ran cried, struggling to stand and falling gracelessly to his side.

The watcher turned and hauled the prince to his feet by the front of his tunic. 'A mage, mate—they've brought a wizard.'

CHAPTER TWELVE

Usmein, Orthia

Woaden mages were a rare but powerful weapon deployed in the Territory. Ran had seen firsthand what they could do, scything through lines of soldiers as though they were wheat in a field. The battle for Signal Hill had turned against him on the power of a magic-weaver, and only swung back again once they'd been eliminated by an elite squad of Orthian cutters. Such people were forbidden in Orthia, their powers a danger to the people and the state. Only the Woaden dared court such strangeness, bringing cursed children to train in the Academy and bolstering the ranks of the Congress of Mages.

'Fuck,' Ran breathed. He snatched up a looking glass in his trembling hand and peered through the lenses, the view at the other end shivering as though the earth itself trembled. 'I can't see…'

'The roadblock's gone!' Brit shouted and immediately Marshal Gregon began bellowing orders.

His knuckles turning white with effort, Ran focused the looking glass and cursed under his breath. The roadblock was indeed gone, vaporised as far as he could tell, leaving a few scraps of twisted steel and smouldering timber remaining. Through the dust and smoke, soldiers and horses charged forwards with weapons drawn. There was precious little space for people to run along the road and more than a few tumbled into unseen trenches. The horses went down hard, snapping their necks and throwing their riders from the saddle when a trench unexpectedly appeared before them. Archers fired and did well to hit their marks in the haze but too many Woaden made it through.

Ran's survey of the field settled on a figure standing motionless on the road, horses and men charging past like a river flows around a boulder. Ran focused the looking glass and felt his jaw drop.

A woman in silver robes stood calmly amongst the chaos, her elegant hands folded together as though she watched students practicing their letters in absolute silence. The serenity she affected while surrounded by madness and death was entirely unnerving. Her long black hair couldn't be straighter if it was ironed flat and her skin showed not a mark or crease. Her robes should have been covered shoulder to foot in dust and grime, but they flowed in the icy north wind, beating against her body in a steady rhythm, untouched by dirt or imperfection.

The battle vanished from Ran's consciousness and for a fleeting moment he imagined it was all over.

He liked that idea.

He wondered if it might be all right to just stay here and watch this woman for a while.

She was beautiful…

Grey eyes, the shade of an impending blizzard, met his gaze through the looking glass and Ranoth froze. She did not blink—not once.

I see you, Ranoth. I smell you. I know what you are. The woman's low, hoarse voice echoed in his mind.

He shuddered hard and dragged his eyes away from the woman standing amongst the chaos.

The fuck?! She can smell me? What is she—

Another glance through the looking glass told Ran it didn't matter—she was atop a horse and riding for the city with the other Woaden intent on scaling the walls.

'Prepare!' Marshal Gregon ordered, his voice akin to a thunderclap. From the blinds along the length of the wall, archers leaned out and nocked arrows dipped in alcohol hard enough to strip skin from bone. The smell alone made eyes water at close range and anyone dim enough to drink it didn't last long. Braziers warming the blinds lent flames to the noxious liquid and the arrows glowed hot in the grey day.

'Draw!' Gregon called and the steady creak of bows easing back filled Ran's ears. 'Loose!' The flames made a gentle slapping sound as arrows arced through the air and into the field. Two hundred feet from the wall's base, they plunged into the deep trench full of murky water and everyone on the rampart ducked for cover.

The explosion took Ran by surprise despite waiting for it in the archer's blind. In the trench, a mixture of tar and alcohol ignited with a deafening roar and a blinding orange fireball tore into the sky, skirted by a thick veil of oily, black smoke.

Another cheer went up, accompanied by a smattering of calls of *Black Prince*. Ran wasn't sure he liked the title, but he knew he didn't have a say in the matter. For what it was worth, he was now covered in soot and ash, the silver of his armour and tabard muted so that only the black showed.

The watchers whistled back and forth and Brit turned to Ranoth with a relieved smile. 'That worked well, your Grace.'

'Seemed to,' Ran nodded and perched his looking glass on the rampart again. The trench stretched the length of the city wall and crackled with angry fire. The charging Woaden had nowhere to go but back the way they came, along the road or into the trenches. Those atop horses weren't given much choice, the frantic animals bolting across the fields and slamming into the various earthworks. Orthian archers from the city garrison, positioned at the borders of the fields, resumed their volleys, picking off runners and anyone thinking of returning to the hills to regroup.

Clanking and shouting drew Ran's attention from the rout of the Imperial Army to the square inside the gate. Below, on the cobbles, among fountains and ancient granite buildings, Duke Ronart rallied the troops he'd led back to the city.

'Form ranks!' Ronart thumped a clenched fist into the chest plate of his dented and filthy armour, its shine and lustre scuffed out completely. 'If those Woaden bastards want this city, they can come over that wall and pry it from our cold, dead fingers! Dark will be the day Orthia bends a knee to that seething horde of motherfuckers!'

A heartened battle cry echoed up the wall and a surge of pride rushed through Ran's veins. Dark indeed would be the day his people surrendered to the Woaden. He glanced at the sky and smiled. It would not be today.

'Prince Ranoth...' Brit's low, uneasy drawl brought Ran back to reality atop the wall. He turned to the watcher and realised the reason for his disquiet. A thin section of roaring flame had extinguished immediately in front of their position, while the rest of the trench continued to burn, happily feasting on the toxic mix of tar and booze. Ran shielded his eyes and scanned the trench, his gaze falling on the woman in silver robes, her hands stretched towards the fire.

Her face contorted with concentrated rage, the flames reflected perfectly in her intense stare. The extinguished section of the trench expanded and Ran stiffened; she was bringing down his wall of fire.

'Marshal!' he called, keeping the woman in his sights. 'We need archers!'

A team of archers rushed forward, trained their arrows on the mage-woman and fired. The flames vaporised the shafts before they found their mark but the volley continued. If she expanded the gap any further, surely she risked the wrath of the arrows? To Ran's surprise, her grey gaze found him again as she twisted her fingers to extinguish more flames.

I know what you are, Ranoth Olseta...

As if conjured by her words, heat flashed down Ran's arms and throbbed in the ends of his fingers. His looking glass cracked under the pressure, the soft copper warping under the pads of his fingers. He threw the tube and stared. Tiny flashes of silver pinged across his skin, little sparks of energy snapping between his fingers like lightning. Despite the heat throbbing through his bones, there was no burning or smoke, no outward sign of what had happened other than the sparks and flashes.

Horrified, he glared at the woman who stood still, impervious to the rain of falling arrows. Beside her soldiers collapsed, riddled with feathered shafts and yet she remained untouched, as if protected by a transparent shell.

She smiled.

There was no hint of joy in the expression, shadows descended over her eyes and her pale lips twisted into a sneer. With a flick of her fingers, a wave of heavy soil erupted from the ground and crashed into the trench, flames and tar exploding towards Usmein.

The blast wave hit the wall below Ran's feet and shattered every window in the city for a mile. The mortar in the wall broke along its age-old seams and the section beside the gatehouse began to slowly collapse. Ran struggled to keep his feet, the stones shuddering and slipping against each other while soldiers and archers hurried to safety on the unbroken wall to the south. Brit turned to catch Ran's arm and missed by a hair's breadth.

A four-foot wide block between them disappeared, leaving a chasm and a deadly drop. Ran's footing faltered and he staggered backwards, the wall tipping away from the city into the field.

The mage-woman appeared in front of Ranoth on the rampart, materialising out of thin air. She shoved at him with open hands and a blast of blue light slammed into his chest. His feet left the stone of the falling rampart and he flew backwards across empty space, sailing through the shattered window of a nearby building, and sliding wildly across rugs and a flagstone floor.

Breathless and stunned, he groaned and tried to heave himself up from the floor. The room around him was furnished as a bedchamber, but was mercifully empty of occupants. His hands stung and throbbed, heat building and swirling then easing only to build again a moment later.

The woman appeared in a flare of light and walked calmly across the chamber, flexing her fingers. Outside, the crash of battle echoed up from the square. The remaining Woaden had crossed the crumbled section of wall to meet the defending Orthian army and Ran thanked the gods his father was down there.

She flexed her hands again and a spark ignited between the tips of her fingernails. Slowly, she drew her fingertips wider and revealed a web of sizzling lightning arcing between each outstretched finger. He staggered to his feet and glanced down, his own fingers sparking.

Oh shit...

'Oh shit, indeed, young prince.' She opened her palms towards him and displayed two glowing webs of energy pulsating across her hands. 'You are untrained, but I still sensed you all the way across the plain. The trail began at that ugly old house off the road and led me right to you. My condolences... The same magic flows through both our veins.'

The woman thrust the energy at Ran and he ducked and rolled. He crashed through a door and stumbled into the next room as the wall behind him exploded in a shower of splinters and flame.

He turned and brought his hands up to shield against the next attack, a brilliant flash of blue heat bursting from them to engulf what remained of the doorway and a day lounge. The energy scoured through him—blistering, shocking and violent—but he had no way of stopping it.

The mage staggered back and laughed between gulps of air. 'Good form, boy, good form! Let's see if you can do it again, shall we?'

She sent another cracking bolt across the room. Ran crouched and imagined a wall of blue light between them, a defence she couldn't penetrate. Her shot hit something beside his head and dissipated with a loud zap. Ran's ears filled with a high ringing and he glanced over his outstretched hands.

The mage-woman crawled to her feet and glared, her once perfect robe shredded down the left side, revealing a thigh puckered with the scars of an old burn. His mouth went cotton-dry and he edged away, aware that the woman knew this power better than he could possibly hope to. The darkness in her eyes deepened and she limped forwards, hands generating and weaving strands of crackling magic.

'It strikes me as amusing, young prince, that you've no clue what's happening in that tiny brain of yours. You might as well be sprouting tits for all the use this gift will be in your clumsy hands. You're a black-blood Orthian, not worth the cost of feeding. I will never understand why the gods insist on blessing errant scum like you with magic.' She shot another withering bolt of lightning at Ran and he dived for cover behind a nearby sofa. The sustained stream of energy carved through the wall and an already broken window, following him as he scrambled to escape.

'I heard them call you Black Prince. Is that because of your curse?' the mage-woman shouted over the furious sound of magic. 'It might be best if I do all Coraidin a favour, and eradicate you! It should save us all an *enormous* amount of—'

Ran launched at her from behind a solid timber desk, hands wide and full of wild magic. He closed them around her neck and slammed her back onto the stone floor, his full weight on her chest.

Her ribs snapped and she screamed, magic vanishing from her desperate hands which were clawing his face. Her nails bit into his cheeks, her teeth snapping at the inside of his wrists as she fought to break his hold. Ran dug his fingers hard into the creamy flesh of her neck and let go of the energy coursing through his bones.

Under the force of his clenched hands, the woman jerked and shivered, beating wildly at Ran while his magic tore through her skin and pierced the bones of her spine. There was a jolt and his magic shattered the walls of something within her. The tendrils of his energy burrowed into the source of her power and pulled, drawing away what remained of her magic.

'No!' she screamed, her voice harsh through the grip of Ran's large hands. He was covered in her blood up to his elbows, but she flailed against him without weakening at all. 'I—won't—let—you!'

The claw of a hand found purchase in his dark hair and yanked down hard. Ran ground his teeth and bit back a scream as her fingernails dug into his scalp, desperation shaking her clenched fist. She pulled harder and drew him towards the floor. If she brought him any lower his balance would tip and she could well throw him off.

Ran lifted the mage by the neck and slammed her head back to the cold floor with as much force as he could manage. He lifted and hammered her skull into the stone again, thumbs and fingers buried in her flesh. Blood splattered across his face as his magic seemed to swirl, entirely out of control, building with intensity like a fire-storm roaring through a tinder dry forest.

The excess magic pulsed up and down Ran's arms, his muscles bulging with added power, his chest heaving with strain. She continued to thrash like a fish out of water, and again he lifted her head then drove it down onto the floor. This time it cracked like an egg, split from the back of her skull to between her wild eyes.

The pulsing spark of her magic went out.

The thrashing stopped.

Her arms fell with a wet slap into the expanding pool of blood and her legs slid away from where she belted Ran's back with her knees. A final breath escaped her pale, blood-flecked lips and her chest caved under his weight with a sickening crunch. Ran pulled his shaking hands from the wounds in her neck and rolled away, blood leaking in a slow dribble from the holes left behind.

Vomit surged into his mouth and he hurled his lunch across the floor. He heaved and retched until nothing remained but acidic bile burning his tongue. Ran gasped and sniffed, his eyes watering with tears of exhaustion, and he sat against the legs of a crumpled chair, his hands drawn to his chest. Her blood dripped from his elbows, once hot, now as cold as ice in the wind and smoke swirling through the room. A white speck landed on his cheek and melted into a tear; the first of winter's snow blowing through the collapsed exterior wall, the heavy clouds finally relinquishing their cargo.

For a good while he sat and stared at the cooling body of the Woaden witch. She'd been sent to assist the Imperial Army in their invasion of Orthia and if not for her encounter with Ran, she might well have succeeded. Now she lay motionless on the floor of some unknown Orthian's home, bleeding into their fine woven rugs.

Despite the crack in her skull, her intense beauty remained in her unseeing gaze. Those grey eyes, the colour of a midwinter storm, pale as the stars, stared through the torn ceiling into an abyss Ran's vision couldn't penetrate. He should have felt relieved, victorious, even glad, but he trembled with guilt. It took all his strength not to collect the woman's lifeless body and cradle her against his chest while begging for forgiveness.

They were entirely alone in the upper level of the house. There were no witnesses to the battle or the outcome, nor to his lack of a stomach for killing. Yet as the snow fell, he became aware of another, crouched across the room, watching. In his right mind he would have been terrified, but he was too numb, too exhausted to feel anything but empty. After what he'd just witnessed, the appearance of a ghost in the corner of the room hardly felt unusual at all.

'You did the right thing, Ran.' Her voice slid across his frayed nerves like cool silk, and he shivered. The ghost girl sat in deep shadows, as broken as she'd been in the house of skulls and bones. Her white blonde hair fell past her shoulders in a sheet of rippling silver, her torn shift all she had to cover her nakedness, if only slightly. 'She would have killed you and massacred your people without a second thought. They don't let sane mages go to war, Ran. They send the rogues; the ones they know will lose control as they grow.'

'What?' Ran's voice, harsh from the exertion of the fight, did not squeak or break. It was a man's voice now, though he wasn't sure the price was worth paying. 'Did you say *grow?*'

'Yes,' the ghost watched him with a vapid blue gaze. 'She was fifteen.'

The mage-woman's—no—the mage-*girl's* slight build made sense now. How had he not seen it before? She lay there on the flagstones and the puzzle fell into place.

'She was an apprentice mage; too young to be fully trained.' The ghost continued, unmoved by his shock. 'The Woaden send children to the front, those who are already showing signs of rebellious powers and an inability to control them. They are called derramentis—without control of their minds. The Disputed Territory is a guaranteed death sentence. They are always cut down before they do much damage because they are so inexperienced.'

The witch's poisonous words, spat hatefully while she tried to kill him, suddenly became the desperate, angry cries of a child struggling to understand her powers and ready to fight for her life. Did she fear the magic bubbling up from the depths of his soul? Did she sense he might be her end?

He threw up again.

'Prince Ranoth, you mustn't mourn something that is not lost.' His ghost girl didn't move, but her clear eyes followed him carefully. 'She would have burned this city to ash and enslaved anyone she was too bored to murder. She had nothing to lose and the world has lost nothing in her death.'

'When someone dies, they ought to be mourned,' he snarled. He wiped a trail of vomit from his chin and sat back heavily. 'Did anyone mourn you, shade?'

The ghost shrugged and glanced at the dead girl and the damaged room around them. 'The gods are at fault, Ran, not you. You must understand that.'

He glared at her. 'Are they responsible for turning me into *this*? Or was it you?'

He lifted his shaking, bloodied hands and a spark of lightning arced between his fingers.

'I had nothing to do with it.' She shrugged again. 'You might have lived your whole life without your magic ever surfacing. For magic to appear, one must first be exposed to it.'

'I was *exposed*? Where?' snarled Ranoth. The ghost girl raised a brow, as if the answer were obvious. He searched his fractured, haunted memory to recall the first time he felt the aching heat in his hands, the first sign of his magic stirring. 'The house?'

'I told you to run,' the ghost girl murmured. 'I said they would find you if you didn't run.'

'I ran!' Ranoth shouted as she faded into the shadow.

'Not fast enough...'

CHAPTER THIRTEEN

Usmein, Orthia

The blood on Ranoth's hands cracked and peeled away in flakes as he scooped the limp body of the Woaden mage from the floor and cradled her across his arms. Her frame was parchment-light, but the dead weight still pulled on his shoulders and back. Unable to open the chamber's door, he kicked the handle until the timber splintered and swung away to reveal a dark, empty corridor and the landing of a flight of stairs.

By the god's mercy, the stairs were wide and he only once smacked the mage-girl's head into the balustrade, stumbling around another landing to descend the final flight to the ground floor. A small door under the stairs creaked open and two cautious faces emerged, their wide, bright eyes trained on Ran. They remained still and silent, watching him shuffle across the foyer to the front door. He put his back to the door, his boot resting on the timber.

'You've got a hole in the ceiling,' he said to the observers, and kicked backwards at the door. The lock gave easily and the door opened to the chaotic street outside. The girl's limp body folded enough at the waist to fit through the threshold and they emerged into a gathering of soldiers milling by the gate and the crumbled wall.

The fight was over, swords sheathed and bows silent, but the activity in the square was frenetic. Folk ran beside horse carts and worked quickly to clear the rubble of the wall. Loads of broken stone left through the open gate alongside carts heaped with the dead, all in various states of injury. The muscles in Ran's arms began to ache with the weight of the corpse, but in the din, he couldn't think where to put her.

Beyond the wall, through settling dust and falling snow, the trench continued to burn merrily, blanketing the city with thick smoke. It would take a week to burn out the fuel and extinguish itself, unless heavy snow choked it. Judging by the blue-grey clouds, the sky seemed fit to unleash a sizeable blizzard, so the city might be relieved of the miasma after a few days.

On the steps before the house, gazing wearily at the marketplace teeming with soldiers, Ran wondered if the home's owner knew their door could be so easily breached, with no more force than a stout kick. Usmein's citizens placed too much faith in the height of the outer wall and the defences in the Territory. Today proved a rude reminder that, given the right circumstances, such barriers were easily surmounted.

'Ran?' His father's throaty voice, savaged by screaming commands, reached through his fatigue to grasp his attention. Duke Ronart trotted his horse through the market square to the steps of the half-demolished house and stopped short, staring at the body in his son's arms. 'What in the name of the Rider happened, boy?'

Ran blinked and separated his cracked lips to taste blood on his tongue. 'They brought a mage…'

'I know, son. We're looking for him now. Need to make sure the cursed creature isn't lurking in the city or making a run for it back to the Territory.' Ronart dismounted and approached slowly. 'I meant, what happened here? Who is this girl?'

'This is her… This is the mage, Father.' Ran's knees gave out and he slumped to the cold stone of the top stair. The duke lurched forwards to steady his son but did not take the weight of the girl. He retreated as soon as Ran sat with the body in his lap, her blood dribbling down his trousers. 'She came with them and broke the wall, then came after me.'

'*She* is the mage?' breathed Ronart in disbelief. Ran nodded and his father bellowed over his shoulder for someone to find Marshal Gregon.

They waited, the noise of the recovering city shifting in and out of Ran's mind, at times so loud he thought his ears would burst, then fading until nothing remained but a piercing ringing fit to shatter glass. His eyes grew dry and itchy, no matter how often he blinked or rubbed them and his mouth had all the moisture of a sandy desert wasteland.

Gregon arrived, panting, with a bandage wrapped about his forearm. 'Sir?'

'Prince Ranoth tells me this girl was the Woaden mage brought in from the Territory.' The duke turned his back on his son.

Gregon nodded with his hands on his hips, still regaining his breath. 'Aye, sir, that's her. She tried to knock out the fire trench and used the flames to blast the hole in the wall.'

'She's a *child!*' exclaimed Ronart in a hard whisper, pointing at the girl's body as if Gregon hadn't noticed the thin frame and soft features. The marshal's hazel eyes met Ran's, bordered by a deep frown.

'I know, sir. I would doubt the tale myself had I not seen it with my own eyes. I commanded my archers to take her down but not one arrow touched her. She appeared on the wall and knocked the prince straight across the street into this house.' Gregon shook his head and glanced up at the ruined corner of the building's roof. 'It's a wonder he survived, your Grace...'

The duke's eyes darted between Gregon and Ran. 'Magic is not easily defeated... and she came after you specifically?'

'Yes, Father,' Ran nodded. 'She said she knew who I was, that she could "smell" me.'

Ronart crouched and scanned the girl's body, her torn robes and shattered skull, the ripped flesh around her neck. His hand hovered over the black bruises inflicted by Ran's fingers before pulling away.

'If she was truly a Woaden mage, then she was indeed a grave threat to Usmein, if not all Orthia. What she did here was powerful and deadly, not a party trick. If Gregon is right, neither my garrison soldiers nor a team of my best city archers could bring her down. Yet here she is, dead as a doornail, dripping all over the market master's front stairs.' The expression in the duke's eyes turned Ran's stomach. For the first time in his life, his father looked upon him with fear. 'Who killed her, if she was strong enough to survive my army and breach my city?'

Terror and uncertainty rolled through Ran. If he told them the truth, they would know what he'd become. The words tore themselves from his throat, unheeded by his anxiety.

'I did, Father.'

Duke Ronart ordered soldiers to take the mage-girl's body and quickly herded Ran into an escort of guards three men deep. Marshal Gregon's expression as they departed left Ran with a sense of heavy foreboding he could not shake. The look in the older man's eyes, his furrowed brow and shaking, bowed head signalled a kind of sad resignation. Gregon had guessed, as had his father, as soon as he'd told them the truth. He'd seen the realisation carve its way across their features. He'd seen the knowing glance they'd shared.

In the crowd of gathered soldiers, he heard whispers, 'The Black Prince?' 'That him…?'

The mage's words bit into him. Did the soldiers know about his magic too? Had news of what he'd done rippled through the ranks, telling all and sundry of the curse that had awoken in him? The fatigue in Ran's head and limbs consumed his thoughts, leaving room in his mind for little else on the long walk back to the palace.

The guards surrounding Ran ushered him through the palace doors behind the duke. When they did not remain outside, or return to the wall, he realised the guards were not to protect him, but to contain him. He staggered to a stop under the weight of his understanding and stared at his father, stalking ahead and yanking off his gloves. A guard shoved him in the back and he tripped forwards on shaking legs.

'Father?' he called, but the duke did not turn.

'Harkon! Have the stewards fetch the duchess and Tutor Master Perce. Bring them to my apartments.' Ronart's order to his chief steward silenced the crowded atrium and stopped everyone cold.

They stared at Ran, surrounded by the escort and covered in dried black blood, and their duke, equally filthy and trailing a dark cloud of fury behind him. The duke continued, unperturbed by their attention and turned right to march down the echoing gallery of the south wing.

Up four flights of wide, carpeted stairs, Ran struggled to keep the relentless pace of the soldiers and his father. His heart pounded, his mind scrambling to catch up. He had magic now. Magic was forbidden. Magic was evil and awful and derided in Orthia and now he had it, like a disease that gripped him in a burning fever that he could not shake.

He tripped more than once and was recovered by the hard hands of the escort, dumped on his feet and hurried along without a word. Obviously, they didn't fancy falling behind the duke as he raced up the stairs to the fourth floor and the private apartments he shared with his wife. Despite the system of platforms and pulleys, the duke enjoyed the challenge of the stairs. Ran didn't appreciate the sentiment today, his legs were almost numb from exertion.

They arrived to see Chief Steward Harkon waiting by the door to the main reception chamber overlooking the atrium and the arching marble dome. He'd come via the platform lifts and bowed as the duke approached.

'I have escorted her Grace and the Tutor Master to the chamber, as requested, sir.' Harkon opened the door and Ronart strode through, the guards peeling off to stand by the entry.

Ran stopped at the threshold and swallowed hard. He didn't want to go in, to face his mother and teacher, to see their eyes when they realised the muck on his arms was another person's blood, or their horror when he explained the mage-girl's death. He certainly didn't want to hear about what would happen next, or face the questions that would be thrown at him, because deep in his heart, he already knew the answers.

'Ranoth Olseta, get in here before I have those guards strap you in cuffs!' The duke roared and Ran grimaced. He glanced through the door to see his mother standing by the fire and his old tutor in black robes, his bald head reflecting the firelight.

'Ronart, there is no need—' Duchess Merideth began.

'There is every need! Ran, get in here and shut the bloody door!'

Ran slipped through the entry and stood no more than a few feet inside the chamber. High windows reached to the ceiling on the far wall, bathing the chamber and its fine furnishings in cool evening light. Candles and a large hearth offered plenty of warmth, illuminating the wide-eyed anxiety in his mother's face and the barely controlled rage of his father.

'What is this about, Ronart?' Merideth spoke quietly, her blue eyes trained steadily on her husband. 'You should be congratulating Ranoth for his exceptional defence of the city, not frog-marching him through the palace like a criminal!'

'That remains to be seen. The Woaden had a mage; one who rode in from the front and nearly tore the city apart. She toppled a section of the wall and we only just pushed them back through the gap before they realised more than half their number were dead and retreated. She was derramentis—one of the young exiled ones.' The duke pointed a finger at his son. 'He killed her.'

'He did *what?*' The duchess's gaze snapped to Ran, and the duke crossed his arms with a nod and stared at the fire. 'Oh, may the White Woman save us...'

'Indeed...' Ronart turned back to Ran.

'Mother, Father; I'm sorry...' Ranoth rubbed his aching head with the palm of a trembling, bloodied hand. He'd encountered the term derramentis before, but only briefly, in treatises on the Woaden and their penchant for encouraging magical abilities. What he could remember was fractured by his fatigue, his limbs heavy and his spirit spiralling down under the weight of his parent's regard. They stared at him in silence for a long moment, neither moving nor speaking, the duchess' eyes welling with tears. Ran's breath caught like a fishbone in his throat, strangled by the sight of his mother's sorrow. His heart hadn't slowed since the fight, hammering in his chest, skipping anxious intermittent beats and thumping back into time with a sickening lurch that made him gasp.

Ronart's frown deepened and he paced slowly towards Ran. 'You know of the mages, Ran—you know what they can do. You know they cannot be killed from any distance with a spear or arrow. That's why we have the cutters, to get in close and sever their spines. But you killed that mage with your bare hands.'

Tutor Perce cleared his throat. 'Your Grace, there is one other way to kill a mage, derramentis or otherwise: draw off their magic.'

The duke nodded and continued to study Ran sternly. 'How does one draw off a mage's magic, Tutor Master?'

'Only another magic-wielder can draw power from a mage, your Grace.'

The duke turned back to Ran. 'Now, Marshal Gregon said she came after you on the wall? Threw you off into the house?' Ronart continued without waiting for an answer. 'Then you appear holding her mangled corpse, claiming to have killed her. She's still got her head on her shoulders, albeit barely, her spine still attached to her skull. You're not trained to make the kill with a knife, and clearly haven't decapitated her; so I'm left with only one possible scenario to entertain.'

Silence filled the chamber, broken only when the duchess sniffed back quiet tears. The sound cut Ran through to his soul, burning as it did, searing him from within. The duke took to a chair by the fire, black and embellished with silver and grey. He didn't offer a seat to anyone else.

Perce remained beside the hearth's mantel, pale eyes carefully watching Ran under bushy white brows. It was impossible to read the old tutor's expression, an impassive mask fixed firmly in place, never revealing a hint of his thoughts before he meant to. With his hands clenched in fists to stop them shaking, Ran stood across from his father. The duke leaned forward, elbows on his knees, hands clasped together.

'How did you kill her, Ranoth?'

Ran's eyelids slid shut and he swallowed the fear welling in his throat. 'I… I deflected her magic and tackled her. She tried to fight me off but I was too heavy. I got my hands around her neck and…'

'You cracked her skull?' asked the duke softly.

'Yes,' Ran replied, eyes closed. The scene replayed in his mind, one gruesome moment at a time.

'What happened to her neck?' The duke probed.

'I don't know…' He shook his head, the repeating vision of the event blurring and shifting, unclear despite the memory being fresh in his mind.

'Your Grace, if I may?' Perce interceded. 'Prince Ranoth, how did you survive the mage's magic?'

'I put my hands up and imagined a wall between us. When I looked up, she was coming back to her feet, as if recovering from a fall. Her robes were all tattered.' Ran frowned as he recalled the fight. 'I don't know how, I just *did* it…'

'And her neck? What happened there?' Perce continued, his voice closer, approaching slowly across the fine hand-woven carpets before the fireplace.

'I held her down and my hands… My fingers went through her skin…' His eyes opened to see his mother, hands gripping her gown, with the tracks of tears down her face. Her distress was palpable and Ran's heart skipped a painful beat. Tutor Perce appeared and put an ink-stained hand on Ranoth's shoulder.

'Was there energy? Did anything pass between you when your hands touched her skin?' he asked. When Ran nodded, Perce turned to the duke and duchess and gave them one solemn nod, then returned to his place by the fire. 'Prince Ranoth used magic to defeat the mage, sir. The wounds you describe are consistent with a mage drawing power from another without consent.'

A sob escaped Duchess Merideth and her arms wrapped across her chest. The duke sat back and sighed, looking at his battle-scarred hands. Perce stared at the fire, and for a long while no one uttered a word. Ran glanced at them, searching for a friendly face in the gathering, but found none. He was alone here, cast adrift like a ship torn from its moorings by a vicious summer storm.

Ronart finally growled into the silence, 'Well, he didn't get it from my family—'

'How dare you level this at me!' Merideth snapped at her husband. Ran wished he could sink into the floor.

'The Olseta line was cleansed of magic and you know it, woman!' The duke stood and paced across the room.

'Ha!' The duchess turned, her eyes rimmed red and lips curled in a savage sneer. 'Cleansed? You're as bad as the Woaden, with their pathetic ideology of fine-bloods and black-bloods. You can't *cleanse* a family of magic, it's written in who you are, by the gods no less! It's not up to you or any of your ancestors to decide who is born with or without it!'

'I'm afraid her Grace is correct, sir,' Tutor Perce bravely interjected. 'Magic can return after generations without any direct links to another practicing mage. Ranoth may simply be unlucky.'

'Unlucky, my arse!' Ronart rounded on his son and approached with lightning speed. Ran didn't have time to back away. 'What happened to you, boy? When did this start? How long have you been hiding it?'

'I haven't hidden anything!' Ran cried, glancing desperately at his mother for assistance. She stared helplessly then averted her eyes as though the very sight of him pained her. 'I… When I came home from the Territory, the watcher and I sought shelter in a house not far to the north of the road.'

Everyone turned and stared at Ran. Their gazes bored into him like hot pokers, their scrutiny unwavering.

'What house?' the duke murmured, the colour draining from his face.

'A small farmhouse, a full day's ride from the front. The watcher insisted we keep moving, but I wanted to stop. I went to the house thinking the owner might lend us a bed for the night.' He looked at the three adults and frowned at their expressions of increasing horror. Had they heard of the house before? 'What we found was *unexpected*…'

'Prince Ranoth, did you go inside the house?' Perce asked in the serious, low tone he used for delivering grave tidings, typically of Ran's awful performance in grammar exams. Ran nodded to his tutor and Duke Ronart slumped into the nearest chair, the duchess covering her mouth to stifle another sob. 'And your magic began to stir after this?'

'Yes, Tutor.' When no one responded or elaborated, Ran decided there was hardly a better time than the present to bring up the name Brit Doon mentioned on the last day of their journey. 'The watcher told me to ask about Lackmah?'

'Fucking Lackmah, all right…' Duke Ronart spat the words and put his head in his hands. 'I should've burned it to the fucking ground.'

'Father, please, I don't understand!' Desperate for answers, Ran's resolve broke and his eyes filled with hot tears, stinging and blurring his vision.

The duke didn't answer. Instead he went to the door, muttered something to the soldiers outside and then stood back as all four of them entered.

'Ronart?' Merideth's eyes darted among the soldiers. 'What are you doing?'

'The law is clear, wife.' The duke lifted his chin and held Ran in a steely gaze. 'Escort Prince Ranoth to the dungeons.'

'NO!' The duchess screamed and a soldier leapt to catch her as she dived at Ran. The other soldiers rushed him and he threw a frantic glance at his mother as she vanished from sight.

'Mother!'

'Don't do this, Ronart!' Merideth's pleas echoed through the room as the first of the soldiers got Ran's arms in his grip. He spun in the circle of armoured bodies, ready to fight them off. His muscles fired and he felt a tiny flicker of magic spark, then die. The power that flared to life on the ramparts failed to ignite, and he was left with nothing but flailing hands and unsteady feet.

'Ranoth!' His mother cried from somewhere behind the wall of guards.

A fist crunched into his nose and the room plunged into darkness.

CHAPTER FOURTEEN

The palace dungeons, Usmein, Orthia

Ran's neck ached and the back of his skull smarted as though it had been hit with a forge hammer. Pain lanced forwards to a place between his eyes and spread its burning tendrils through his face. His nose throbbed cruelly each time he drew a breath through his cut and bloodied lips, and the swelling under his cheek bones pressed against the underside of his eyes.

He opened one eye and found there was little point to the exercise, so shut it again. There was hardly a sliver of light to be seen, just a murky glow off to the right. It was enough to see the dark smudges of prison bars and the slick sheen of the slimy stone floor, but it revealed no other features. Under his head he felt the reeds strewn across the ground to soak up moisture and excretions, but thanks to his blocked and swollen nose, he couldn't smell how long it had been since they were last changed.

He lay in a heap, his father's words floating through his head.

'The law is clear,' he'd said.

The law *was* clear, or more specifically, a single part of it—the part kept in the massive volumes that were under lock and key in the library. It was the part that detailed the Duke's Justice for anyone of age found to harbour any magical ability. An image of what awaited him flashed in his mind, and if he'd had anything left in his shrunken, painful stomach, he would have thrown up again. Terror shivered through him and he clenched his fists against it.

Lackmah…

The name echoed in his head, and his thoughts chased the trailing sound down a dark hole. Brit had known that name, and so had Perce and his parents. Was it the house of bones? Why hadn't he heard of it before now?

Footsteps echoed in the corridor outside his cell. Curiosity forced his eyes open again, and he immediately regretted it as a flaming torch rounded a corner and bathed the cell in bright light. It felt as though someone had thrown hot coals in his eyes and he slammed them shut against the scorching pain. Ran groaned and tried to turn his head from the offending light, but only succeeded in twisting his already painful neck and making his suffering worse.

'Oh,' Perce started and shuffled back several steps. Ran heard the old man mount the torch in a sconce and hurry back, his robes whispering over the floor. 'I am sorry, your Grace. I should have known your eyes would be terribly sore.'

A stool scraped across the corridor and the sound screeched through Ran's head like cat claws on glass. His tutor sat, and for a moment blessed silence filled the cell.

'I brought you some bread. It was all I could get past the guards...'

Ran's stomach growled and forced him to crawl towards where he last saw the cell bars, despite the agony in his face. A small loaf of bread pressed into his outstretched hand and he drew it to his chest, wishing for the first time since he woke that he had a sense of smell.

'How long...?' he croaked in Perce's general direction.

'A night and a day,' the tutor replied with a sigh. 'They are waiting for you to wake.' He sounded resigned, disappointed and weary, as though he hadn't slept an hour since Ran was locked under the palace.

'Mother?' Ran asked as he tore a small chunk of bread from the loaf and set it in his mouth to dissolve. His jaw didn't have the strength to chew yet.

'The duchess is... coping.' Perce didn't sound convinced of his own words, which gave Ran no comfort.

He hadn't seen his mother's face before the guard's fist crunched into his nose, but he would remember her cries until his dying day. He curled around his bread with a painful moan and tried not to think about the terror in her voice.

'Ranoth... Ranoth, listen to me, boy.' Perce's voice dropped to a whisper and Ran heard him shuffle closer to the bars. 'I don't have long, so you really must listen. The guards think I'm here on orders from your father, but...'

This piqued Ran's interest. He turned to the tutor's voice, years of slogging through lessons training him to heed the man's words.

'The duke doesn't know I'm here, but I told the guards you need to be tested. I told them I need to collect evidence for your trial.'

Ran managed to lift his head and squint towards Perce. The old man was a hunched shadow on a low stool, huddled close to the bars, his face pressed between them as he hissed his secrets into the half dark. 'When I call them, they'll come with the key, shackle you and hand you over to my custody. I've told them I'm taking you to your father for a few hours. It's all the time I could buy.'

'I don't...'

He wanted to tell Perce he didn't understand, but he did. Deep in the foggy recesses of his beaten brain, he knew what the tutor planned. He wanted to tell him not to bother, not to take the risk, but the old man was already on his feet and turning towards the torchlight. The dome of his bald head shone as he leaned around the corner and shouted, returning when heavy booted footsteps replied to his calls.

All Ran could manage was a groan before a pair of guards appeared with another blazing torch and blinded him. He didn't see them open the gate in the bars, but he felt their gloved hands heave him from the floor and hold him steady as an icy pair of manacles were clamped around his wrists.

At the exit of the cell, the guard handed Perce a guide chain, linked to Ran's manacles by a thick lock. 'You reckon you can manage him on your own, Master?'

'Oh really, dear boy,' Perce affected a tone of distinct distaste. 'Look at him—he can hardly stand upright. He's no more threat than a new-born kitten.'

The guards gave a chuckle and marched off down the corridor, leading Perce and Ran towards the massive steel doors at the dungeon entrance. Unlike the city prison, the palace dungeon was mostly empty, reserved for insubordinate soldiers of the garrison and the odd circumstance where a criminal might be caught within the palace walls. It was still a freezing, filthy place Ran would be glad to see the back of, but at least it wasn't filled to the brim with rotting convicts and lunatics.

'When will you have him back?' A guard shuffled in behind a desk with a wide ledger book spread across the table top and dipped a quill in ink. Ran squinted but couldn't read the scrawling script through his puffy eyes.

'In a few hours, but don't panic if I take longer,' Perce's hand tightened on Ran's arm as he swayed, the hallway spinning at a sickening rate with his blurred vision. 'These things can take a little more time if the subject is, shall we say, *unwilling*.'

'Be careful, Master Perce. You've heard what he did? Used his curse to draw the Woaden right up to the gates.'

'Oh, I heard,' Perce gave Ran a shove in the back. He stumbled out into a subterranean passage and slammed into the opposite wall. 'Black Prince indeed...'

Despite his advanced age, Tutor Master Perce Crofter moved with the swiftness of the north wind. His black robes billowed behind him as he hurried Ran through the maze of passages under the palace, all pretence of stealth abandoned. He stopped periodically to check around an approaching corner with his torch, then returned and urged Ran on. Ran's head began to clear as they moved, the stuffiness in his nose and face receding enough for his eyes to focus on the path ahead. His head still throbbed as though a hundred angry men were drumming on his skull, but he could at least see and keep up with the older man.

He assumed their travels took them away from the dungeon complex, but to where and in which direction, he couldn't tell. He'd never had the time nor the inclination to explore these tunnels, despite knowing they were here. It was this very maze he intended for his mother and sisters to shelter in if the Woaden breached the city, though he hadn't expected *he* would use them to flee just days after the attack.

They walked for what felt like forever, though it might have been under an hour, winding through hallways and past storage rooms, never encountering another soul. Their path led through inky darkness and Perce held his torch aloft as they continued into the gloom.

Had Ran heard those guards correctly? Had they said he used his magic to lead the Woaden to the gates? How could they think such a thing after the weeks he spent preparing to defend the city? Rumour was a poisonous thing. He staggered as the realisation hit him, the truth of what the world above these gloomy tunnels must think of him—and what he'd become—slamming into him. In the space of a day the battle at the city wall had morphed from a glorious victory on his part, into a catastrophic betrayal of the Orthian people by their prince and heir.

He was a monster now. A cursed thing, fit only for the executioner's block.

Yet when he had tried to defend himself in his father's audience chamber, his magic had failed. The soldiers had no problem defeating and incarcerating him.

'Perce!' Ran croaked and staggered to a halt. 'I'm cured! The magic—it's gone!'

He searched for the spark he felt on the wall and in the ruined house, but found nothing, and the ghost who had followed him from the house had not shown herself since the day of the battle. Hope and elation dared to lift his heavy heart!

'No, Ranoth, it hasn't.' The tutor clasped his arm and led on, down a set of stairs to a rusty gate set in the landing at the bottom. Beyond it a stream of sewage trickled past. 'I wish it *could* be cured, my boy, but it cannot.'

The walls here dripped, coated in a layer of green slime and their single torch threw eerie dancing shadows across the roughly hewn surface. From within his robe Perce retrieved a bunch of keys and rattled through them, muttering as his fingers flicked and turned them in the dim light.

'But I can't feel it anymore. It's gone…'

Perce found the key and jammed it into the lock, opening the creaking steel barricade and shoving Ran through the gap. He locked it again and found another key in his bundle to unlock the manacles around Ran's wrists. 'With a few days rest and good food, it will return. That's how it works. It takes training to keep some in reserve. I don't know how they do it, but according to the texts, it can be done. Once the magic is awoken, there is nothing in the known world that can halt it.'

The tutor continued the hurried lesson as they splashed into the water at the base of the tunnel and hurried along with the flow. 'The Olseta family *was* cleansed of the curse of magic many generations ago, though I fear your mother's more foreign blood may have reignited it. Tell me, do you know why Orthia is a duchy, not a kingdom?'

Ran shook his head. He didn't have the breath to spare on an answer.

'I wasn't permitted to teach this version of history, so an abbreviated lecture will have to do.' They rounded a corner and Perce caught Ran as he slipped on something sludgy that he hoped wasn't a turd. 'Orthia *was* once a kingdom, until the long line of kings was broken by the failure to produce an heir. The Woaden had not long since formed into a united force from the once warring tribes they had been before, but they were powerful and ambitious even then. They agreed to marry one of their minor royal sons to a distant niece of our dying king, thus bringing Orthia under Woaden protection.'

Ran's heart pounded harder by the moment and he suddenly felt very ill. He was a descendant of a Woaden prince…?

'Orthia became a Woaden duchy from that moment on,' Perce puffed between hurried sentences now, his robes dragging heavily in the muck around their ankles. 'Generations after the alliance, the two split in a dispute over the distribution of resources. Then came the cleansing—the cleansing of families and of our history.'

They stopped to catch their breath. How far had they come? Ran might have asked but Perce barrelled on with his story despite his heaving chest.

'Your ancestors feared those with magic might be sympathetic to the Congress of Mages in Wodurin. They ordered them executed. Beheaded… Children with the curse were sent away.'

Ran narrowed his aching eyes and held his side to alleviate a stitch in his chest. 'Even the children?'

'Even the children…' The tutor opened a pouch on his belt and held a scroll tube towards Ran. 'This contains the edicts issued by the duke at the time. It's the section of the law they will use against you.' Their eyes met and Ran saw fear in the tutor master's face unlike any he'd ever witnessed. 'Ranoth, you are fifteen summers old. You are no longer a child. They can use the full force of the Duke's Justice against you,' Perce shoved the tube into Ran's shaking hand and held it tightly. 'And trust me when I tell you, they *will* use it.'

The truth of it rocked Ran and his knees buckled. He knew the punishment for harbouring magic, but until now he had hoped, somehow, in some vain way, that his father wouldn't go through with it. But the pain in Perce's face told him otherwise. The duke would deploy the full force of the law against him, because he had no choice. He could not allow his son to live if he could not do the same for others.

'What has this got to do with Lackmah?' he asked suddenly, remembering his father's blunt response to the name.

'Forget Lackmah! Keep your mind in the present!' The old man snapped. Before Ran could counter his tutor, Perce hurried off down the tunnel and splashed to a stop at an inconspicuous ladder mounted on the wall. 'This is where we exit.'

He clambered up and put his shoulder to a disk of stone recessed into the roof. It shifted and a slice of moonlight cut into the darkness of the tunnel as Perce pushed up. The disc rose high enough for the tutor to slide it onto the surface above, then he carefully peered over the lip of the hole.

'Damn!' he hissed between his teeth, ducking back into the tunnel. 'Soldiers everywhere. Come up as quietly as you can.'

Ranoth followed Perce up the ladder and hauled himself through the hole on arms weakened by battle and beating. They emerged in a laneway cluttered with shadows and old furniture, just off a wide thoroughfare.

'Where are we?' Ran asked in a painful, nasal whisper.

'A street or two over from the South Gate,' Perce pointed past a pile of old chairs dusted with snow. 'We need to get through the soldiers on patrol. I have a horse waiting a few miles down the South Road, hidden though, off the road. You'll need to search for him. Look for an old shearer's hut and he'll be in the copse of trees behind it.'

'How?' It was all Ran could think of.

Perce shrugged. 'I called in a favour. You take the horse and you go south, understand?' He didn't wait for an answer, but as he made to hurry down the laneway, Ran grabbed the tutor and pulled him to a stop.

'Why? You signed me out of the dungeon. They'll know it was you. They might already be searching for us.'

'That is correct. And another reason why we shouldn't delay—'

'But *why?*' Ran pressed.

Perce threw a glance down the lane, then turned back. In an instant, Ran felt like a child again, under the watchful eye of a man who often came closer to filling the role of father than the duke ever did.

'Because, I don't believe you did what they say you did. I don't believe you're evil. I don't believe you're derramentis. But what I believe doesn't matter. The law is the law and your father is bound by it. You will be tried as a derramentis and executed. Your father will do it with his own hands if he has to!'

He gripped Ran's hands, squeezing his fingers around the scroll still held in his palm. 'This document is the law they will use against you. It links magic with Woaden blood and after what happened in the city, Usmein's citizens will scream for it to be spilled in penance. Too many people saw what happened on the wall, Ranoth. There is no altering the past. We can only circumvent the future. Do you hear what I am saying to you, boy?'

Ran nodded stiffly.

There were tears in the tutor's eyes; desperate pools of unshed grief. 'While I breathe, Ranoth, I will not let them kill you.'

Before he could reply, Perce hurried to the end of the lane and stole a glance down the street. With a wave, he signalled for Ran to follow and they darted across the thoroughfare into a darkened side street. Beyond another street and the rear of a saddlery yard, a wide space opened near the towering South Gate. If they were lucky, the guard might be thin with most of the soldiers attending the breach repairs to the west.

They crouched and weaved through the fences of the yard, through an open gateway and paused in the shadows of the workshop's front entry. The saddler and his family were probably asleep in the apartments above the shop and work sheds. No lights glowed in the front window, so neither Perce nor Ran cast a shadow into the street.

In the guard house on the opposite side of the road, a couple of soldiers played cards by the light of an oil lamp. It had to be close to midnight, a half-moon high above the city, hiding behind thin wisps of cloud. It gave them enough light to see the small door in the gate, held shut by a heavy iron latch. Getting through without being seen or heard would be close to impossible. Ran swallowed and made to grab Perce, but the tutor slipped out from his grasp and wandered casually up to the men in the guard house.

'Evening fellows!' He sketched a bow and leaned against the door frame. His body blocked most of the light spilling from the guard house, and importantly, obscured the view the guards had of the saddlery and the small door in the gate. 'I wondered if I could bother you for a minute of your time...'

Ran noticed Perce clasp his hands behind his back, and one of them waved hastily at the gate. The hammer of his pumping blood filled Ran's ears and he didn't hear the rest of the nonsense Perce delivered for the benefit of the guards. It was likely they would count him as a drunkard and send him on his way.

In a few quick steps, Ran was at the gate with his hand on the door latch, the thick iron giving way slowly to the pressure he forced down on it. When it finally released its grip, he let go of a breath that was screaming in his lungs and swung the timber door panel outwards.

'Oi!' A shout shot across the night and bounced off the cold walls of the buildings at either side of the road. 'Halt!'

Ranoth paused, his heart thumping wildly in his chest. He turned, one foot through the doorway, the other still inside the city. Perce began to talk louder, quicker, laughing, but it was farce to distract the gate guards. It did nothing to divert the soldier astride a horse in the centre of the street, moonlight glinting off his dented armour and greying hair.

Gregon was unmistakeable, even in a saddle, and Ran knew his jig was up. Recognition furrowed Marshal Gregon's brow and he leaned forward. 'Ranoth?'

'Damn it—' came a curse from his left, and Perce spun away from the guard house, abandoning his ruse. He shoved Ran in the chest and through the open doorway. 'Go! Get out of here!'

Ran tumbled into the night on the far side of the gate and scrambled to his feet. Shouts went up and the men at the gate launched into action. They tackled Perce into the timber barricade and the old man went down bellowing. Voices rose in anger, someone somewhere barked an order, something about a Black Prince, and Ran barrelled headlong into the woodland beyond the gate.

CHAPTER FIFTEEN

Hummel, Tolak Range, the South Lands

Moons waxed and waned over the Tolak range, and the dry season showed no sign of breaking to bring relief from the cold, parched air. The atmosphere vibrated with tension: Sellan watched Erlon; Lidan studied them both; and the clan silently eyed all three. Lidan stayed clear of her parents as best she could, keeping her thoughts to herself and her presence discreet. The less they noticed her, the less likely they were to use her as a pawn in their games.

Restricted by his injury, Erlon remained in the village and busied himself in the forge or the stables. Usually, at this time of year, the clan saw neither hide nor hair of the daari; his time spent hunting game and ranging the borders. Hummel always felt smaller with Erlon in it, as if he took up more space than the average man, and the place became almost claustrophobic the longer he lingered with his simmering anger. He paced like a caged animal, tense and careworn, his brow furrowed with deep lines and his temper quick to break. Lidan wished her father's malcontent was due solely to the conflict with his wife, but the trail of blood from the bush to Hummel's gate spoke of deadlier woes.

Since the first ill-fated hunt, four parties had returned beaten and scarred, while another failed to return at all. Grent worked to save the wounded, packing poultices into the deep gashes in their flesh and wrapping them in clean linen. For a lucky few, his ministrations dragged them back from the brink. For too many, he could do nothing but delay the inevitable slow descent into agony and death. None of them recalled who or what attacked them. They spoke of being ambushed by shadows, or refused to speak at all.

Lidan stood at her workbench in the bonesetter's treating rooms, a clean bandage hanging idle in her fingers and little bone needles waiting to be sharpened and cleaned on a nearby table.

'First Daughter?' Grent called without looking up. Lidan started and tore her eyes away from the wounded man sweating and grinding his teeth on the bonesetter's table. 'Have we any black-stump left?'

'Y—yes.' She let the unrolled bandage fall to the table and reached for a small, stoppered urn. It held no more than a cup full, but Grent only needed a few drops on the man's tongue to calm him. The mouthful Grent administered to the man would knock him out completely, his senses dulled and his mind closed. The shivering and sweating eased a few moments later but the broad shoulders of the bonesetter hunched in defeat, the back of his bloodied hand rubbing the bridge of his nose.

'I'll need you to go out and get more of that, Liddy... I can't leave...' The morning was still young and already Grent's voice was an exhausted croak.

'Yes, Master Grent...' She gave him the title after endless weeks assisting in the treatment rooms, her fingers deft at the finer tasks Grent struggled to complete, or simply hadn't the time for. Another group of rangers, equally injured and desperate for help, followed each one they healed; the search for food quickly turning into a fruitless pursuit of the mysterious attackers. The folk of the clan spared what they could to help, but Lidan devoted all her time to helping the wounded, glad for the distraction and an excuse to remain well clear of the hall.

A boy, one of Grent's helpers, stuck his head around a screen shielding their work from the others resting in the rooms.

'He's here, sir,' he murmured and disappeared, replaced by Daari Erlon's wide frame. Erlon gave Lidan a nod and folded his arms, stern eyes on Grent.

Grent sighed. 'He's calm but he won't last more than a few days.'

'You're sure?'

'We've done all we can.' Grent lifted a dressing of linens covering a wound in the man's chest and the daari swore.

While the top layers of cloth remained clean and white, the undersides were soaked with dark blood and a slick discharge that smelled of rotting fish. The wound was a haggard mess, packed with honey, healing leaves and ground bark, its edges puffy and the skin worrisome shades of red, purple and black. Swelling pulled the glossy flesh tight and the whole thing looked fit to burst at any moment. Early on, Lidan lost her lunch into the nearest bucket at the sight of badly infected wounds, but she'd seen so many they were now as common as piles of horse shit—still foul but frighteningly ordinary. The lines of anguish around her father's eyes struck a chord in her heart and she swallowed a lump of despair.

'Burns me to say it, but if you think it's best…' Erlon muttered.

With a nod Grent returned the dressing to the wound. 'Liddy, best you get back to those bandages, eh?'

She slipped back into the shadows at the rear of the room without glancing at her father. The request was simple enough, but she knew what it meant. This wasn't the first man Grent had seen go beyond the reach of his aid.

The first few he'd fought hard to save but they'd gone eventually, some of them screaming at demons hidden in the shadows, others sucking hard for breath as unseen hands squeezed their throats shut. Since then, she watched for the signs; the sweating and shivering, the same discoloured skin, and saw Grent's shoulders drop in defeat. She knew then her father would be called by one of the boys—Grent never sent her on the errand—and Erlon would come. She would retreat to her bench and pretend to roll bandages until…

Snap.

Her fingernails bit the tabletop and her teeth drew blood from the back of her lip. Her chin quivered, but she straightened. This was not the first time her father visited a final mercy on one of his suffering rangers and a wave of dread told her it wouldn't be the last.

Her meal at midday tasted of ash, her appetite stripped away by the sight and smell of death earlier that morning. Lidan felt hollow, in her heart and her head. Fatigue weighed her down and she wondered if it showed on her face. Her days were spent tending the wounded, but by night the daari's long and loud meetings with his rangers kept her wide awake. At first, she tried to sleep through the overhead conversations, until the muttered words drew her from her bed to listen through the screen of reeds, hidden like a mouse in the cracks of a wall. She scratched notes in a bound bundle of parchment, rudimentary symbols and drawings of the things and places they argued about.

Apart from the constant discussion of the attacks on the rangers, anyone with a few moments to spare whispered of the dana's comings and goings. Lidan caught snatches of rumour here and there, when the women helping Grent thought she was too far off to hear or when the dana again failed to appear in the hall for the evening meal. While she pretended not to notice, Lidan devoured every word, filtering fact from exaggeration and laying the pieces of the puzzle out so she might understand them.

At first, Dana Sellan vanished for a night, then two. Before long she was absent several days at a time, the whispers certain she'd taken ill and gone to stay with the Crone. When another hunt staggered back through the gate and she disappeared again, they said she was casting auguries and trying to discover the culprits, for that type of work took days and the clan eagerly sought any sign the ancestors might deign to send. Erlon made no mention of Sellan's absences, so deeply consumed by the more pressing problems of the clan that he failed to notice, or was too weary to care.

Lidan wasn't about to enquire after the dana, either. In battle, those who stuck their heads above the parapet for the sake of curiosity got shot, and this was not a matter worth an arrow between the eyes. Sellan always returned eventually, as she had today—silent and sullen—her bright eyes dull and sunken into shadowed caverns of weariness. Auguries and the work of reading them were taxing, Lidan knew well enough from observing the Crone for hours on end, but they didn't take *that* heavy a toll.

Weary beyond reckoning, Lidan ignored her mother and the rippling mutters of conversation in the hall. She didn't have a spark of energy to spare and she couldn't think where the rest of the clan found the time to gossip. Instead she stared at her plate and pushed the thick stew around with a crust of slowly disintegrating bread, leaving a trail of sodden crumbs in the gravy. She was at serious risk of falling asleep right there on the table.

There was every chance her father would announce another hunt, especially after losing *another* man to his wounds. The losses made the daari wild with anger and desperate enough to send more rangers out in the hope of finding whoever laid waste to the hunters. Lidan didn't fancy watching the faces of the clan folk fall at the news, or shadows of resignation creep into the eyes of the remaining rangers and hunters, wondering if their patrol was next.

She glanced at the nearest door to plan her escape when the clan's midwife crossed her line of sight, approaching the daari's table and bowing deeply. Her fatigue evaporated immediately and the noise of the hall vanished, leaving Moyra's words to echo alone amongst the beams.

'...news of your wife, Farah.'

'You have what?' Erlon leaned forward, straining to decipher the woman's statement.

'I bring news of your wife, sir.' Moyra repeated and folded her hands over her apron. Lidan stared at her mother across the hall, watching every inch of her for a reaction. 'I can confirm Mother Farah is with child.'

Sellan's knuckles turned ice white around her knife, the other hand strangling a cloth napkin beside her platter. Moyra continued to announce Farah's pregnancy to the clan, the unborn child conceived five moons ago, and Lidan gaped at her mother's shaking hands.

'We were unsure of the cause of her illness... Your fourth wife has not bled in some time, which is well for a strong womb and babe,' Moyra shouted over the wave of excited mutterings. 'The child will arrive near the time of the first rains, a good omen for a prosperous wet season.'

Erlon smiled and his men clapped; the clan needed good omens.

'I can say, Daari, Farah's illness is surely a sign from the ancestors that the child is a boy...'

The hall erupted with roaring cheers, drowning anything else Moyra had to say, fists hammering the tables and platters clattering together with the vibrations.

Lidan stood and hoped her legs would hold her as her mothers and sisters bestowed a blessing on the daari for his good fortune. To her dismay, an anxious knot balled up in her stomach.

It was real.

Her mother and the Crone were right. For all her efforts to distract herself from the truth, there *was* another child coming and there was nothing to be done to stop it. What if Moyra was right? What if the child was a boy?

She couldn't meet her father's eyes when she congratulated him with a swift embrace and a kiss on his stubbled cheek. He looked through her as though she were made of nothing but the wind, hardly recognising her through the joy shining in his eyes and the bright smile stretching across his face. Whatever pain he might have carried from the morning in the treatment rooms seemed to vanish as he hoisted a cup high and shouted for the tine-women to bring all the ale they could carry.

Lidan shuffled back and stood behind her half-mother's shoulders, her sisters crowding to the front of their family's cluster, giggling and smiling. The older girls whispered and grinned at each other, while Abbi held on to her mother's skirt, watching the sudden explosion of emotion and activity. The younger girls probably had no idea what was going on, only that the day was suddenly full of smiles after so much sadness and anger.

Tine-women appeared with urns in hand and the roaring commotion of the hall grew louder still. Lidan rubbed her temple and wondered if she could find something in Grent's treatment rooms to dispel a headache. She turned to find a doorway and walked straight into her mother's chest.

Her breath caught in her throat and she tried to back away before her mother noticed she was there, but the dana snagged her arm in a vice-grip and hurried her through the doorway to the kitchen, pushing tine-women aside.

Lidan swallowed the words that would dare to ask where they were going, her mother's rage obvious in the swing of her hips and the savagery of her steps. It seemed Sellan didn't want to stay for the drinking, the songs, or the blessings. Lidan's heart skipped when the trail to the Crone's decrepit hut came into view, fear saturating her limbs and her muscles beginning to bunch. Was she being dragged up there for another round of punishment, another beating or another night in the pit? Her hands began to twitch, her body preparing to make a break and run. She didn't care if she had nowhere to go, she wasn't going back to the dank horror of that hole.

A whimper escaped her throat and Sellan tsked, yanking hard on Lidan's arm to hurry her along. 'Oh, don't get all frightened on me now, girl. I'm not sending you to the pit. I've more important tasks for you.'

'But—' Lidan killed the questions on her lips as Sellan shoved open the Crone's door, strode in and slumped into a chair by the fire, leaving Lidan to stand amongst hanging bunches of herbs and badly tanned hides reeking of dead flesh and urine. She stayed by the door and the only fresh air to be had, and tried to slow the hammering of her heart. She felt like a cornered bouncer, sensing imminent danger and desperate to escape it. Her time in the Crone's hut had done nothing to endear the place to her, and she didn't think she would ever be comfortable in the structure's damp heat and the lingering stink of unwashed human.

The Crone poked at the fire casually and gave a wet, throaty sigh. 'The midwife confirmed it, then?'

Her eyes flicked to Lidan and saw straight into her soul without a single ounce of effort. Lidan was as vulnerable as a new born babe beneath that stare. Could the old woman reach into her mind and pluck out thoughts at a whim?

'Of course she did!' Sellan snarled. 'Now the whole place is in an uproar. The stupid man has a smile on his face wider than his arse crack.' The dana leaned towards the Crone with her palms up in supplication. 'Doesn't he realise the risk he's taking? He'll be dead before the boy is old enough to match or rule in his own right. And Farah isn't close to ready to rule as Mother-Dana. Gods save us! It'll be chaos...'

'What do you expect him to do with all those wives? Watch them sew?' The Crone folded her hands on the top of her walking stick and winked at Lidan, who paled and leaned into the wall. Had she just made a *joke?*

'If he was smart...'

'He's a man, Sellan. Intelligence and the males of our species are opposing forces and should the twain ever meet, the whole bloody cosmos would collapse under the weight of realised impossibility.'

'Pah!' Sellan stood to pace the room. 'If she has a boy and Erlon dies before he's old enough to stand as a daari on his own, his cousin's son might move to take the clan...'

'So sweet of you to be concerned with the clan's future...'

'I don't give a fuck about the clan, Thanie!' the dana snapped, baring straight, white teeth. 'I give a fuck about *me*. Things will change for us if he goes. How long do you think we'll last? I can control him for now, but if he passes the clan to any other bastard, mark my words, we'll be lucky to survive the first night! We'll be cast out, or worse. And what of *my* girls?'

Comforting, Lidan thought, staring at a dusty beam in the ceiling. Today was not the first time she'd been an after-thought to Sellan's concerns for her own wellbeing.

'What other option does he have?' The Crone seemed unmoved by the outburst and scowled at the dana. The old woman was the only person Lidan ever witnessed considering her mother with such an expression. 'Who will take the clan if not a son of his own, or a son of the western clans?'

'I've already told you.' Sellan stopped and looked intently at Lidan, her green eyes darkened by shadow.

CHAPTER SIXTEEN

The Caine, Tolak Range, the South Lands

The Crone followed the dana's gaze and snorted. 'She might be his heir now, but the clan won't like it. He's determined to sire a son for a reason, Sellan.'

'She is his *first born!* It shouldn't matter if he has a dozen sons. She came first!'

'But she is a woman! Or at least she will be. Who will follow her? Who will stand behind her in battle? What other clan would fear to tread in her territory? None, I'd wager. And as far as I understand the customs of this place, it would take a phenomenal amount of effort to change that fact.' A wad of the Crone's phlegm hit the fire and hissed angrily as if to signal the end of the discussion.

Lidan cleared a hard lump of fear from choking her throat and pressed harder against the wall. If she kept up the pressure, perhaps it might open up and swallow her so she could escape the conversation. Her mother approached the Crone with the smooth agility of a snake and pressed her hands onto the arms of the dusty chair the woman was perched on. Her face lowered to an inch from the Crone's nose and Lidan shuddered. How could she stomach the smell?

'She is a daughter of mine,' Sellan ground out and glanced at Lidan with narrowed eyes. 'If she heeds my word, the sky will fall at her command. Customs be damned. She will be his heir.'

'So, your plans are unchanged, then?' The Crone raised a brow.

'They remain as we discussed.' The dana withdrew to the fire.

The Crone nodded once and fixed her clear grey eyes back on Lidan. 'Good. After all that business when he got back from the hunt, I began to wonder...'

For some reason, no matter how often Lidan swallowed the ball of fear, it returned, her chest tightening with each breath. They were serious about fighting for her to remain as her father's heir, regardless of the child Farah now carried? Did they care what she thought? What she wanted? Evidently not, as they went on discussing her future as if she was no more than a piece of furniture in the room.

'He can't get enough of that Namjin whore, either.' In the blink of an eye Sellan changed the subject to her disdain for Farah and ran a hand through the dark red waves of her hair with a sigh. 'Boils my blood...'

'Do you want the potion?' The Crone's words turned Sellan, and the intent Lidan saw in her mother's gaze chilled Lidan's blood to ice.

The potion? What potion?

Sellan's eyes settled on Lidan.

Not that potion, surely?

'The one given to Bandi Napper?' asked Lidan. 'When her baby died and had to come out early?'

The room stood silent, the crackling fire the only sound between the three of them; Lidan stared in disbelief while Sellan chewed her lip in thought. The Crone gave a casual nod to the affirmative and Lidan's stomach did a sickening flip.

'You can't *do* that...' she whispered, barely loud enough to hear over the fire.

'The dana can do what she likes, girlie.' The Crone shrugged. 'Sometimes these things must be done. Isn't as if she hasn't done it before.'

Lidan met her mother's bright green gaze and couldn't believe what she saw. It was true, Sellan had done, and would do, whatever it took to secure her daughter's ascension, even if it meant destroying another woman's pregnancy. Disgusted, Lidan spun to the door. Her mother caught her arm with hard fingers and cupped her face, leaning close with wide, sad eyes.

'I don't like doing what must be done, Liddy.' Sellan caressed Lidan's cheek lovingly, her hand soft and warm. It felt like an age since her mother called her "Liddy". It was long ago, before all this trouble with Farah and the hunts.

'Why did you bring me here?' Lidan pulled away from the dana's grasp. She knew what those hands did when angered. If she enraged her mother, the penalty would be fiercer than a thousand summer suns. Would Sellan leave the Crone to punish her, or do it herself?

'I don't trust them, Liddy, my petal... You've seen what they are like! As soon as something more appealing comes along, they drop you like an old doll. We've been forgotten, you and I.' Sellan clicked her tongue and tucked Lidan's black hair behind her ears, just as her father once had. 'I brought you here to get you away from that stupid man and his celebrations. You don't deserve to have the loss of your inheritance rubbed in your face like that.'

'You can't kill her baby, Mam. It's cruel!'

Sellan nodded slowly and threw a glance at the Crone.

'Nor do I wish to. I only want what's best for our clan, nothing more. This requires more thought. It pains me to see them treat you like this, my petal. I hate it; every time he gets his seed to take, it's the same...' The dana slowly paced before the fire. 'I'd hoped to spare you the worst of it. You were young enough to forget what he did when the other girls were conceived, but if he insists on making more children, you will witness it again and again...'

'Mam, it's all right—' Lidan clasped her hands together, begging her mother to stop.

'All right?' Sellan's upper lip curled like a maddened dog shielding a bone. 'All right? You're going to throw it all away, hand it over to an unborn child who isn't likely to be of age before his father kicks off? You'd give up your status and sink into obscurity? You're content for me to disappear beneath Farah's new found glory as the mother of the heir? I think not! Perhaps I should just match you to the nearest horse-herder now, get it over with and let him fuck you senseless?'

'No!' Lidan cried.

'It's what you'll get if Farah drops a boy in the wet season!'

'No, Mam, please, I didn't mean—'

Sellan towered over her daughter and Lidan shrank instinctively. 'Then you understand what I'm faced with? The chance I'll lose you to some awful fate unless I act now and protect you?'

Lidan nodded. Her mother was right. *Stupid girl...*

'Liddy, I do this for you; only for you.' Her mother drew close, her soft voice soothing her shattered emotions. Lidan did understand, but the cost of securing her future tore at her heart. Perhaps it was best if she paid less attention to the path she must take and placed her focus on the destination. 'I won't let them take what is rightfully yours. I won't let them deprive you of the inheritance you deserve.'

'Please, just don't do anything to Farah or the baby. It isn't her fault...' Lidan didn't know if begging would change her mother's mind, but she had to try. She couldn't live with herself if she caused something awful to happen to her half-mothers or sisters, born or unborn. Sellan's face darkened and for a moment Lidan thought she would refuse. She reached and took the woman's perfectly manicured hand in hers, long pale fingers cupped in her small palm. 'Mam, promise on my life you won't hurt them. Farah and the baby?'

'Why?' The word came out cold and hard. Lidan let go of her mother's hand and the darkness deepened, their locked gaze unwavering. 'I see no other way to stop this before it gets out of hand.'

Frantic, Lidan searched her mind for the answer. She hunted the dark cavities of her heart for the one thing that might stay her mother's hand and came up with nothing but a scrap of an idea, a sliver of hope and a chance to forestall something awful.

'I'll do it,' she said.

Her mother started then frowned. 'You'll kill the baby?'

'No! I'll show Father that he doesn't need another heir. He has one already, doesn't he? Me. I'm the Tolak heir.' Lidan set her jaw and squared her shoulders. The Crone raised a brow at that, but Lidan chose to ignore the old woman's doubt. 'Let me show him.'

'And if you fail?' her mother put voice to the question banging on the inside of Lidan's skull.

What if I fail? What if he doesn't choose me?

For a moment she and her mother shared a look that spoke more than words ever could. Under the red-haired bluster and fiery temper, her mother was desperate. Sellan was terrified of losing her daughter's position in the clan and entirely prepared to do anything to secure it. Suddenly Lidan understood. Her mother would never agree to the plan without a safeguard.

'*If I fail, then you can do whatever you think is right...*'

The concession tore itself from Lidan's heart and the space left behind knotted into an ugly, blackened scar. If Sellan was surprised by her daughter, she hid it well. Lidan couldn't help searching her mother's face for a sign of her agreement, and found it in a minuscule nod of approval, before the dana vanished out the door and into the freezing afternoon.

Lidan remained frozen in place, her heart pounding.

Outside, a wind blustered in from the north, as hard and sharp as eagle talons, moaning through the gaps in the hut's roof. Her gaze found the Crone and for a moment, the smallest fragment of time, she caught the woman watching the empty doorway. She stared at the place Sellan had been with an expression Lidan could only describe as bone-deep sorrow. It was etched in every line and smudge, every twitch of muscle, every blink.

The sharp grey eyes met hers but Lidan didn't flinch away this time. She held her place. She wouldn't be afraid.

'She isn't serious, is she?' Lidan's question hung in the thick, hot air like vegetables in a soup.

'Oh, by the stars, she's as serious as she's ever been.'

'And if Mother Farah has a boy?'

The Crone raised her brows and shrugged. 'Best prepare yourself. You're on a high ridge between disappearing from here altogether or becoming the first woman to rule this place. It's up to you which way you fall. Not even the ancestors can tell what your mother might do.'

Lidan shook her head. 'She won't *do* anything until Father decides. She promised.'

'She's promised many things in her days, girlie. Not all of them good, and not all of them honoured and seen through either.' A gnarled finger stabbed towards Lidan and she recoiled. '*You* have to decide your path through this mess. Follow her, follow your father, or cut your own way? No one can tell you what's best.'

'I don't want anyone to get hurt...' Her voice was hardly more than a whisper, almost lost in the groans of the wind begging to be allowed in.

'It might be too late for that, girlie.' When Lidan gaped at the Crone, she whisked her aged hand and coughed. 'Get gone, before she comes back looking for you.'

Four steps outside the door Lidan broke into a run. What had she agreed to? How had she let those awful, evil words come from her mouth?

If I fail, then you can do whatever you think is right...

She had all but signed the child's death warrant! Even if she didn't commit the act herself and her mother's version of events came to pass, Lidan's hands would be dripping with blood—invisible, guilty stains that would never fade.

The echo of the words thumped in her ears as she hurried down to the village and slid breathless through the door of the stables. The place was abandoned, all the rangers and apprentices joining the daari in the hall to celebrate his next child and leaving the horses standing in their stalls. They looked at her, curious and wondering if she'd come to deliver more food to their feed-bags. Could they see the tears in her eyes?

By the ancestors, what was happening to her family? The pillars of her world were crumbling, dragging with them the fabric of her life. *She* was the reason her parents bickered and fought. *She* was a girl. If she were a boy, there would be no reason for them to fight; there would be no competition between her mothers, no impetus to produce a son and her father could live happily with his legacy secure. Instead, he had only girls—ten of them!

She shuddered and smudged tears across her cheeks as she unlocked Theus's stall door and swung it wide. Because of *her*, the clan's future stood in jeopardy and to secure their differing visions of how things should be, her parents seemed prepared to tear each other apart. Her mother was ready and willing to commit murder.

Theus greeted her with his head high, and stamped a hoof as if demanding to know why he remained trapped behind walls of timber. Lidan stood before him, blocking the doorway and tried to let her racing heartbeat slow down.

Mam says I can't ride you... Da says I can't ride you... What use is an heir who can't ride?

Before she could second-guess herself, or the horse could figure out what she was doing, Lidan slipped a halter over his head.

No one would notice she was gone. Why would they? She was invisible. The Crone said she would become nothing once a brother was born, but she was wrong. She was already nothing. No one cared what she did, or what happened to her. Her father wouldn't care once he had a son. Her mother wouldn't care once she wasn't the heir.

She was invisible—invisible and alone.

The horse jogged behind her to the stable door and out into the dusty common where Hummel's gate stood open for a group of rangers and their mounts. Not waiting to see if anyone noticed, not giving them a chance to disagree or halt her, Lidan ran.

Perhaps a voice called her name.

She shut out all sound except for the rasp of her breath and the thump of her blood. With her horse at her side she ran into the valley at the foot of the Caine, the grass browner than tanned hide, the sky an empty expanse of azure blue, stained only with the promise of sunset. At the creek they splashed through the shallow water to the other side, Theus pulling at the halter, eager to sprint along the open valley without restraint. She ran harder, pumping her legs faster, her boots slick with the remains of last night's frost.

At the far western end of the valley, where grassland gave way to bush and the creek emerged from the hills and tablelands, Lidan ran out of breath. Theus snorted and pawed the ground. He wanted to run, further, deeper into the high country, but Lidan shook her head.

'No,' she panted, 'I'm going to break you. And once I do, all on my own, Father will know I'm just like him, that I can be his heir. He doesn't need a son. And Mother won't have to fight him anymore. She won't have to worry about other children. I won't be invisible anymore. I'm going to break you and prove them all wrong.'

The length of a fallen tree offered a step to Theus's back, but the black horse wanted no part in her plan.

She pulled the reins and slapped him, tried to drag him closer to the tree and shouted every command she could think of, but they all echoed unanswered through the trees. Theus stamped backwards and threw his head, held it high, and danced and kicked. Lidan scrambled to avoid the jab of a sharp hoof and slid away from a prancing rear Theus aimed at her chest.

All the while she kept the leather reins in her hands. The rangers said to never let go when breaking a wild horse. They said the battle was lost once the beast took the reins. She found a thin stick and whipped him, and he snapped at her with huge flat teeth. He caught the stick like a hound might snag himself a bone and ripped it from her grasp, the rough bark slicing her palm wide open. In utter frustration she screamed until her throat burned and hammered his side with her fists.

Beaten and exhausted, her chest heaving and salty tears streaming down her face, Lidan let the leather straps fall from her fingers and threw her hands in the air.

'Go! Go back where you came from! They aren't ever going to let me ride you, so what's the point?'

The horse started and trotted away with an offended snort. Lidan sank to the ground, sobbing.

Stupid girl... Failed before I even started...

If only she could be the clever girl her mother wanted. A clever girl would appreciate her mother's efforts to secure a better future and eagerly take the opportunity in both hands. A clever girl would be interested in how she looked and how to tie her hair, so the sons of rangers and daaris noticed the long, fine lines of her neck, rather than scampering about in the mud with a forge apprentice and playing with babies in the garden. A good first daughter would be on her mother's side, ensuring no one ever undermined her position as heir.

It all seemed simple enough. It was a game, played by folk pretending never to move their pieces across the board. Could she play along and win? She knew she wasn't ready for the consequences of losing...

She stared at the creek as the eastern sky deepened from blue to black, night crawling closer, following at the heels of sunset. In the bush at her back, flocks of leafy tree dragons squawked, flapping between the trees in search of insects. The massive burnt orange monolith of the Caine stood majestic and imposing in the sky. Visible for miles in any direction, watching over the land, the silent sentinel stood strong against the forces of time in the harsh South Lands. How could she dominate such a place? She was a girl; a first daughter, but a girl nonetheless.

She was nothing without the power of her title and position as heir. She might be invisible now, but she risked vanishing altogether if she allowed others to encroach on her status. If she wanted to be anything more than a daari's first-wife, she had to employ the sparse tools and resources gifted by her birth. If she wanted to survive, she had to prove everyone wrong. She wasn't a weak little girl—she was the Tolak heir.

Her sobbing subsided and the black muzzle of the half-broken horse exhaled hot breath across her hand. Lidan looked up at Theus. 'You want something from me, horse?'

He snorted and shoved his nose under her hand. The animal understood the human tongue better than a beast should.

'If you want something from me, you can earn it. Nothing comes without a price; nothing is given without charge. You want carrots and bush apples, let me ride you.' She pushed his nose away and expected him to trot into the bush and never return. Instead, Theus wandered a while cropping grass, but glanced back as if unsure what to do about this human.

Her eyes followed his careful moves and she wished Behn could see the obvious intelligence in the animal. The apprentice reckoned he'd borne too many kicks and been stamped on too often to have any time for wild horses from the high country. He said the thin air made them stupid. Lidan disagreed. Theus was a careful, considered thinker who, once his mind was set, could not be deterred.

She could be like that.

He found his way to the fallen tree and stamped his hoof, obviously incensed that Lidan hadn't noticed his cleverness. From her seat on the damp ground, eyes stinging from so many childish tears, she gave him a smirk. 'Think you're smart, don't you?'

Theus tossed his majestic black head and she climbed to her feet, the naïve girl she'd been for so many years falling to the dirt, dead and discarded like old snakeskin. Before she committed to riding him back to the Caine or dying in the attempt, she held his head and stared him in the eye. Perhaps if she said the words aloud her ancestors might see to helping her succeed.

'No more fear, Theus. I won't be afraid anymore. I'll show them what I can do.' Lidan tousled the mane between his ears. The log gave just enough height to get her knee over his back, and with stony confidence, Lidan swung up and took the reins as she'd seen the rangers do. 'Walk on,' she commanded and Theus lowered his head to oblige.

When they strode calmly through the gate, two figures stood above the lintel on the wall. Siman and Jac stared at her in the fading light of the evening, not a word passing between them or Lidan as she continued beneath their feet. They knew the girl left with a half-broken horse, having never ridden one of her own. They knew she'd gone without the usual tools for the job; a light leather saddle, a long rope and a hair whip. They knew she didn't have the experience to master such a beast, and yet here she was, riding him bareback, with hardly enough time passing for her to teach him a simple command.

They showed no awareness of the old woman watching them from the ridge above the village. Lidan saw her, but made no move to acknowledge the Crone. She didn't need to. The old woman knew what had happened and what it meant.

Lidan wasn't invisible anymore.

CHAPTER SEVENTEEN

Hummel, Tolak Range, the South Lands

Theus didn't protest returning to his stall. He had a strange air of content-ment, framed by the sweat on his flanks and the jets of hot breath clouding from his nostrils. Fed and watered, he settled for the night alongside the other horses as if he'd been born among them.

Lidan shouldered her way through the door into the windy night. On a night like this the clan kept to the safety of sturdy walls. Hungry things found their way to villages on a bitter wind—namorras eager to feed and grow their tribe of the soulless. Tales of their long claws and sparse white hair whispered in her head as she hurried towards the light of warm fires and the protection of a thatch roof. The hall's thick walls only slightly muted the noise echoing into the valley, windows and doorways burning bright, drums and pipes playing a beat so loud it vibrated in Lidan's chest as she drew near.

Across the common, Sellan shouted curses at a tine-woman and Lidan slipped into the shadows beside the empty forge. The hall suddenly lost its appeal. Her mother sounded like she was well into a rage, and by the volume of the raucous laughter, a fair amount of ale had already found its way past men's lips and into their minds. The other children would already be in bed, saving them the sight of their drunken parents.

Despite being the eldest of Erlon's daughters, she was never allowed to partake in these sorts of festivities; her father sternly disapproved of his daughters witnessing feasts beyond the traditional formalities. Bed was the best option by a long shot, away from the world of a clan's leaders and their troubles, or injured rangers and their sickening wounds. Hugging her arms around her chest, Lidan picked her way through the kitchen garden to the back of the hall and made for the rear entry to the women's quarters.

Grunting and gasping stopped her dead, a mess of heaving bodies and tangled limbs revealed by the dim light of torches and stars. Lidan slapped a hand over her mouth to stifle a scream and started backwards. A man's bare backside and a woman's limp, bare legs jerked and pumped in an inconsistent rhythm, the rest of them hidden deep in shadow.

The grunts quickened, as did the thrusting visible in the half-light. Lidan's foot hit the leg of an old table stacked high with preserving urns and the whole pile crashed to the ground in a deafening smash. She fell and hit the cold dirt on her rear, utterly mortified and scrambling to escape the attention of the couple she'd stumbled across.

'Oi!' The man shouted, heavy steps staggering in her direction. 'Show y'self!'

Lidan froze.

No...

She prayed her ears betrayed her. She prayed she was wrong. His hand reached down and pulled away the fallen table, drunkenly stumbling sideways with its weight. Light spilling from the hall washed over his face and Lidan grimaced.

'Liddy-girl?' The voice became a soft, inebriated version of her father's. She shuffled further back and fought the smashed urns for freedom. 'S'all right, girl! Just me!'

Of course it was him—who else would it be? It wasn't enough to overhear him fighting with her mother and bickering about Farah, but now she found him mid-way through a tryst with only the ancestors knew who! She made it to her feet and ran for the light at the end of the wall, where the only remaining route to her bedroom lay through the kitchen. Her father's huge hand snagged her arm and she spun, shoulders held tight in his grasp.

'Let me go!' screamed Lidan and Erlon shook her.

'What's got into you? It's *me*, Liddy!'

She stopped struggling and glared. Over her father's shoulder, a young tine-woman slowly corrected her clothes, covered her legs and slipped into the darkness as though nothing was out of the ordinary. Erlon followed Lidan's gaze and rolled his eyes. 'Don't mind her—'

'I said, let me *go!*' Lidan pulled from his grasp and stumbled back.

Erlon checked his belt and ran his hands from forehead to chin, glancing again over his shoulder. Who was he looking for? A daari could lie with any of the clan's tine-women—they belonged to him—given as payment by other clans, or captured in raids. His encounter with the kitchen girl wasn't an issue. Why was he nervous, so eager for silence?

'Liddy,' he cooed.

Lidan spat at his feet. 'Don't call me that.'

All her plans for proving herself vanished. Burning in their place was a ferocious hurt that would not be silenced. How dare he, after abandoning her to the hands of her mother? He pretended to care, but he didn't. He didn't care when Sellan locked her in the pit, freezing to death and bleeding. He didn't care enough to send the Crone away even when he swore he would. All the anger and uncertainty, the pain and horror, boiled to the surface and rushed her thoughts with an avalanche of raw emotion. Her hands shook, clammy and sweaty, her skin prickling with bumps at the surge of adrenaline pumping through her veins.

The daari's face darkened to a scowl and he raised a finger in warning. 'You've had a fright, but that's no way to speak to your father!'

He was right. He was terrifying, but she'd gone past the point of no return. Her words couldn't be reclaimed. She had very little to lose, if anything at all. Between him and her mother, they'd already dismantled the world she thought she knew.

'Maybe I shouldn't speak at all, just shut up and disappear. Maybe I should, so you can pretend I don't exist!' shrieked Lidan, tears blurring her vision. Her mother's voice echoed in her ears and the words shot out before she knew what they were. 'You've got something better on the way now— your precious boy. That's what you really want. A boy. Only a *boy* can be the heir. I'm nothing because I'm not a boy. I'm an heir who can't be an heir. Well, you're wrong! You're all wrong. I can be, I'll show you—'

'What in the name of the ancestors is going on here?' Sellan rounded the corner behind Lidan and immediately pulled her into a protective embrace.

'You!' sneered Erlon and stepped forwards, drawing up to his full, imposing height. 'What poison have you poured in her ears? What lies have you told?'

'The truth is all I've ever spoken, Erlon. The truth about you and your priorities. I won't have her world crushed when she's usurped by that whore's by-blow! Lidan is your true heir.' Sellan filled the space between Erlon and Lidan, levying her height on him even though he stood a full head taller.

His drunken gaze cleared and rage flashed across his eyes, recognising his wife's challenge. Lidan backed into the shadows. She didn't want to see what happened next.

'Watch your mouth, woman,' Erlon growled at his first wife, fists clenched tight, his knuckles paling with tension. 'You've no idea what you're talking about.'

'I know perfectly well, and so do you,' accused Sellan.

Erlon turned to where Lidan hid in the shadows, rigid with anger and wondering if her world was about to come crashing down around her ears. In the silent darkness, trimmed at the edges by the rambling trill of pipes, her father watched her.

The lines of his face softened and his brows arched in fleeting plea. 'Liddy, please, come with me. I'll explain everything.' He hadn't given up on her yet.

'It's too late, Erlon. She knows too much. Your lies are a waste of breath and time. You're going to forget us all when that whore whelps a boy—'

The back of Erlon's massive hand struck the side of Sellan's fine-featured face with a crack and Lidan sprinted into the gloom of the common, desperate to escape their fiery bickering. Their shouts and screams shattered the night and the wheeling music of pipes and drums stopped hard.

Ahead, the forge stood empty, the glow of the hearth fire illuminating enough of the workshop for her to slip through without unseating Rick's tools and benches. In a corner behind the hearth, she collapsed on a pile of coal sacks and stayed there, her head buried in her hands and her legs curled against her chest.

Never in her life had she felt so entirely lost despite knowing exactly where she was. Never had she felt so alone while still at the centre of her ancestral lands. Never had she questioned so deeply her place in her family, her home, her people, than the night her father lifted his cup to thank the ancestors for his unborn child. Never had she thought she would grant her mother sanction to murder her brother. Never had she known so keenly that she would fail miserably and everything she held dear would be stripped away.

'Lidan?' Behn asked from beside the hearth.

She snapped up and scrambled backwards into the icy darkness, blinking tears from her eyes as her skin cried out for the warmth of the glowing coals.

'Oh, hey… It's only me…' The small taper in his hand cast a glow a little further than the hearth and Lidan paused at its edge. 'What are you doing in here?'

'Don't pretend you didn't hear…' she croaked, her voice worn by sobs.

'I did hear something. It didn't sound great…'

Lidan turned away and curled into a ball on the floor of the forge. 'Leave me alone, Behn.'

'Liddy… What's happened?'

'Why do you care?' said Lidan from beneath the shield of her arms.

Her friend failed to answer, and his footsteps receded into the night beyond the forge hearth. Lidan's heart sank, and if it were at all possible, broke a little more. He wouldn't come back. She wouldn't have, not if he spoke to her the way she had. He would be within his rights to never speak to her again, and she would deserve it.

Footsteps returned from the common, but Lidan didn't look up. A shovel began to shift the coals in the hearth and timber crunched down among the embers and ash. At this she lifted her head and opened one eye to glance over her arm.

Behn stood at the hearth side, stoking the fire with dry timber. At his feet lay a pile of blankets and furs, unfolded and crumpled in a heap. They weren't spare bed covers, but his very own, hastily gathered from his room at the back of the workshop. He nodded at the fire as if satisfied with his work and collected the blankets, fashioning a nest at the hearth-side with his back to the clay bricks that ran in a circle around it.

'You came back?' she said, as if he might be about to change his mind.

'You're my friend, Lidan.' Behn shrugged. 'I can't say I understood all that yelling, and I can't say I really want to know what was said, but if it's anything like the fight they had in the hall, I wouldn't want to go back over there either. So, if you can't go home, you have to stay here, and I won't let my friend sleep in the cold.'

Their eyes met and for the first time in days, Lidan felt a wave of peace wash over her heart.

The dreams came thick and fast, one after another, then all at once, then none at all. The time of empty limbo was the worst, no sky overhead and no earth underfoot. That was the time of true nightmares—the time the darkness and the shadows morphed into something altogether awful and slithered out from the crevices of Lidan's mind to taunt and torment. She'd had strange dreams before, some that made sense and others that were completely bizarre, but never as vivid as this.

In brief moments of respite, she saw old dreams, harsh and broken as though time had corroded the memory to a shuddering series of still images flashing one after another to give the impression of movement.

They weren't her memories—of this she was certain.

She had never seen a structure so massive, soaring above the height of the tallest tree, wrought entirely of stone and glimmering, capped with brilliant snow. Walls thicker than four men shoulder to shoulder kept some things in and others out, but it was impossible to tell which applied when.

She followed other children, some taller but most at her height, none with a face of their own. The memory let their features fade, holding only critical information in place rather than losing the whole thing to the ravages of time.

There were flashes and children lay twisted on the ground, mortal wounds torn in their small bodies. She felt sick and jolted. Her body refused to wake, and her mind became frantic. More flashes and flame. This time hot blood showered her face and her hands dripped with the stuff. The nausea redoubled and she shivered under the strain. Her body sought to purge the interloping memories but they played on.

Now a hand dragged her through dark passages, her chest burned and her legs pumped hard. The hand belonged to someone bigger, but not full grown. It was soft but strong, and it led her with purpose. The fear driving her down the corridor was unyielding and physical—it rippled up and down her limbs like wavelets on a lake, lacking any obvious beginning or end and increasing in pace.

When they broke free of the darkness, the leader turned and threw something powerful over their shoulder at a target Lidan couldn't see. The leader's clear eyes startled her to a stop.

She knew those eyes. She'd sat under their scrutiny too often to mistake them for another's, though the face was older now, wrinkled and weathered almost beyond recognition. But the eyes were the same—clear and grey, the colour of cloud before rain.

Realisation hit her in the chest with the force of a charging boar and threw her screaming from the dream. Behn's hand held tight to hers as it had when they closed their eyes, and he slept on as if nothing had happened. He grunted where he lay on the furs and rolled away, taking his cover with him and leaving her with the thickest among them. Behn was that sort of friend—he gave up the best of what he had.

Reluctantly, Lidan returned to the fur and put her back against his. Despite the warmth of their bodies trapped under the covers and the fire still feeding greedily on the timber among the coals, she lay shivering with her eyes wide and her teeth chattering. If she shut them, would the dreams return? Her head wanted to see more, to delve deeper, but her heart paled at the idea. She couldn't bear to see the Crone's eyes again…

Chapter Eighteen

Hummel, Tolak Range, the South Lands

Dawn broke and sliced through the restless sleep Lidan managed to glean from the remains of the night. At least the forge had been quiet, which could not be said for her room in the rear of the hall. She rose and found Behn had abandoned his post sometime in the early morning, probably to see to chores for Master Rick. His absence made her morning easier to swallow. She didn't fancy facing any questions he might have thought up in the night.

She folded Behn's blankets away, and found a warm place to sit beside the forge bellows and watch the village wake as the sun cleared the darkness from the sky. Her eyes were heavy from the lack of rest and Rick nodded at her as he went about his business, unperturbed by her quiet presence, common enough before she made her way to Grent's treatment rooms to begin her tasks.

By the way the clan folk groaned and dragged their feet across the common's dusty paths, last night's ale had hit them hard. Their eyes narrowed as though the sun shone a hundred times brighter and to a man, they spoke with hoarse, overused voices. A pair of boots attached to motionless legs poked through the pig pen's open gate, the pigs happily snuffling around, enjoying rare freedom in the common, trotting about unhindered. If it weren't for the low fences around the clan's small garden plots, the precious few things still growing in the harsh light of the dry season would have been swilling through the swine's bellies by day break.

A deep growl rolled through Lidan's stomach, which she ignored with animosity. Her insides enjoyed playing out her weaknesses—this time of the flesh rather than of the mind. She didn't need a reminder that she was hungry. The events of the previous evening left her without a meal and gave nothing in return except a terrible night's sleep. She knew breakfast was on the table in the hall, but she'd be damned if she was about to wander in and sit down as though the world were right again. Even by the light of a new day, she wasn't ready to face her parents. It was too high a price to pay for porridge and toasted bread.

To her left, Rick cleared his throat and handed her an earthenware mug of tea, steam coiling up in the cool morning air. He said nothing and wandered away to inspect his tools and stoke the fire to a crackling blaze. Her fingers closed around the belly of the mug and settled into the ridges baked across its surface, the bellow's huge leather lungs drawing deep before exhaling in a long wheezing breath.

Had Rick heard the screams and name-calling after the moon rose? Surely half the South Lands heard the argument echoing off the face of the Caine, the awful cacophony of her parents tearing their matching apart. The only people oblivious to the noise were either dead or deaf, yet Rick made no mention of it.

He *was* a quiet man, never keen to commit to one side of an argument too soon, if at all. He wasn't known to pass comment on rumours and gossip, though he might utter a word of advice from his homeland in the north. Rick swung a hammer for a living, a tradesman in a world where hunters and rangers reigned, yet Lidan's father trusted his counsel. Lidan suspected there was much more to Rick Anvail than anyone knew.

She thought Rick to be more mystery than man, and a source of quiet wisdom in a clan of hotheads who attacked their problems with spears rather than reason. Rick was the judicious, cautious type, unlikely to stand before unstoppable forces, and while she wished it otherwise, her parents' conflict had become relentless. This man from north of the Malapa would not be fool enough to throw his weight behind either side.

The sun crested Hummel's timber battlement, a bright white orb glaring down on a village full of weary revellers, and painted the common with the colours of day. She shaded her eyes and felt the ache of her pupils contracting to block out the harsh light. Men skulked into the shade around houses, sheds and the buildings set at the foot of the wall, muttering thin excuses for continuing their work where the sun's rays did not yet reach.

Gateman Jac wandered from the hut at the top of the wall and lifted his face to the sun, soaking it in with the peaceful expression of a hound lying lazily in a warm corner; eyes almost closed, nostrils flaring to draw cool air deep into his chest. He was among a small group of gatemen and rangers who stood watch last night and had no reason to curse the sun and the daari's ale this morning. With a glance at the boots of the sorry soul snoring in the pig pen, Lidan wondered if Jac begrudged spending the night sober.

The gateman turned, leaned folded arms on the rampart and lifted two fingers to Lidan in a silent greeting. He'd been with Siman when she returned riding Theus. How many rangers and tradesmen had he told? Had word already reached her father before night fell, before their argument in the dark, behind the hall?

She nodded back and crossed the common with her eyes cast to the ground and her mug hugged to her chest. She prayed no one would notice her. If they couldn't catch her eye, they might not realise she slipped by. If she kept to herself, they might not recognise her, despite inheriting her father's unmistakable height and charcoal black hair. If someone called her name, *everyone* would stop and stare, whisper and mutter. She was the reason her parents fought and howled in the darkness. *She* was the reason the daari's wife rebelled against him. They knew. They all knew…

Lidan smacked her forehead against the gatehouse door.

'Damn it!' she cursed and kicked until the door shook against the hinges. Staring at the ground was effective for avoiding eye contact, but a guaranteed way to slam into inanimate objects. Her hot tea dribbled over her fingers and she bit her lip to distract from the scald. A few people nearby looked up at the disturbance, then quickly averted their eyes when they saw the furious scowl etched on her face. On any other day, they'd offer a witty joke or a greeting. Not today. Not in the state they were in, and not after last night.

Lidan heaved the door open and gave it a swift flick as she came through the threshold. It picked up speed and slammed into the frame. The impact shook years of accumulated dust from the ceiling and walls, light brown trails and puffs of fine dirt raining down. She wished she could see the pained grimaces of those nearby, the sound echoing through their fatigued, ale-shrivelled brains. The thought was enough to dampen most of the heat in her anger.

The heavier weight of disappointment quickly replaced her anger, increasing with each step up the creaking stairs. By the landing at the parapet it pulled so insistently at her shoulders that she paused, closed her eyes and sighed, willing the feeling to disperse. It stubbornly refused, and introduced its stable-mate, utter desperation, to her heart. Together, the disappointment and desperation put a shoulder to the little hope and happiness she had left and thrust them off a cliff into a miserable abyss.

Oh, how she wanted to leave this place; despite the homely scent of baking, the familiar clang of the forge and snorting of horses in the yards. Not for the first time, she glanced at the sky and wondered if the ancestors might show her a way out.

'Why is it, when the older folk drink all night, the young ones wake before the sky is full blue?' Jac asked, cracking her reverie with unwelcome precision. He sat with his back to the rampart wall, feet up on a chair, his arms crossed and sharp eyes scanning the valley. More at ease with the sun than those nursing sore heads, he made the most of the warming rays rather than keeping to the chilly shadows.

'Revenge, mostly,' she replied and Jac raised a brow. She put her mug on a table, leaned a shoulder against the wall of the landing and tried to rub the gooseflesh from her cold arms. Hidden from sight under an awning on the rampart, Lidan watched the eastern side of the common and the wide expanse of land at the far end of the valley awash with the rising sun's light. Only Jac could see her here.

'They do say a little revenge is good for the soul,' he turned back to the valley.

'And for the mind...'

He didn't answer but Lidan didn't worry. She didn't keep company with Jac and the gatemen because they were good at conversation. She came here because they were exactly the opposite. They kept quiet, only muttering amongst themselves and doing their jobs with the fierce concentration it required. Up here, the clamour of the common dulled, stripped away by the breeze blowing across the wall. The smell of horse manure diminished to something a little earthier and a whole lot more pleasant, and the chances were close to nil of being disturbed by her family. When she wasn't assisting Grent or tending to Theus, this was her favourite place in the world.

Thinking of Theus, she opened her mouth to ask Jac who knew about her breaking in the horse.

His voice cut her off before the words formed on her tongue.

'Liddy, throw me the looking glass?' Jac extended his hand and sat forward, brow furrowed and jaw set.

From a shelf inside the awning, Lidan snatched a metal tube full of fine glass disks aligned with magical accuracy—the product of another northern horse trade. There was only one looking glass on the Tolak range and Jac guarded it jealously. He snapped it open and held it to his eye. 'Fuck your mother backwards, not *again!*'

The big man rushed under the awning, shoving the looking glass at Lidan and pushing her aside. Mystified, she spun out to the rampart and mimicked Jac's action with the tube, the smaller end of the cylinder pressed against her eye.

Nothing but brown grass blurred across the end of the tube, then a smudge appeared that might be a line of trees. She slowed her hand and looked again. The tree line on the far side of the valley, close to the foot of the steep tablelands and hills, became clear and Lidan slowed further, concentrating, watching.

The smudge moved, a black shape jerking from the trees, struggling to break free from the tangled undergrowth. The tube turned in Lidan's hand, incrementally, and the image sharpened, clear as day. A man staggered and stumbled, arms waving in a weak attempt to attract attention. He tripped and pitched forward, his face thumping into the dry earth with such force his head bounced. Then nothing.

Any warmth Lidan felt from the morning sun vanished in a fresh wave of gooseflesh prickling across her skin. If it wasn't for the wind shifting through the tinder dry grass, she could have sworn time itself stopped.

A long box strung end to end with a leather strap hit her in the stomach and she gasped, clutching it and fumbling the looking glass between her hands.

'You're coming with me.' Jac snatched the tube and hurried down the stairs.

The box in her hands was familiar—Grent handed her one when rangers needed attention as they staggered through the gates, his own box bigger and with two thick straps. Boxes like it littered the village, stored away for emergencies then appearing as if from nowhere in moments of need, like when her father returned from his ill-fated hunt.

'Lidan! Come *on!*' Jac bellowed up the stairs.

She scrambled down and exited the stairwell as Jac hit a bank of tight ropes on the wall with the business end of an axe. The cords severed and the ends snapped up through holes in the roof. A violent, deafening whir filled the gate's housing and an almighty creak shuddered through the walls.

Lidan sprinted after Jac. Nearby, horses saddled and ready for any emergency, pawed the ground, sensing Jac's tension and Lidan's utter confusion. 'You need Grent, not me!'

'No time. You'll have to do.' Jac hoisted her by the waist into the nearest saddle. In the yards beside the stables, Theus let out an indignant whinny and trotted along the fence with his nostrils flared. There was no time to saddle him or even explain why she was atop some other horse.

A boom shook the length of the wall. The gates, free of their ropes and the burden of a counterweight, swung open and pounded into the walls to either side. The smack Jac gave her horse would've woken the creature from death, let alone encouraged it to move, and the steed launched into a full tilt gallop. Before she had her hands correctly on the reins, they were out the gate and flying across the valley.

CHAPTER NINETEEN

Tolak Range, the South Lands

The dark smudge of the trees at the base of the foothills stood a mile or so from the wall, along with the stumbling man Lidan saw through the looking glass. Their horses vaulted a stream flowing towards the creek and charged across the open space beyond, Lidan following as close to Jac as she could safely manage. She didn't want to lose him if he pushed on into the bush.

An awful, acrid stench hit the inside of Lidan's nose and burned the skin with caustic ferocity, worsening the closer they came to the trees. Her stomach rolled and the back of her throat recoiled, gagging at the smell. Try as it might, her body couldn't expel the odour once it settled in her nostrils. It was utterly foul, like the stink of a thousand rotting carcasses. The wretched miasma of an untended midden came a close second; even the Crone's armpits emitted a more pleasant aroma.

Jac's tall bay horse baulked and wheeled away, offended and spooked by the reek. It pulled at the bit, eager to take off in the opposite direction. Lidan's horse reared and angrily tossed its head, whipping the coarse hair of its mane across her face.

The gateman gagged and coughed, and soothed his horse before swinging down. He collected his weapons and Lidan eyed them in silence, unsure what he planned to do with the flint hand-axe and long bronze dagger. He let the bay trot off to a distance it preferred and hurried towards the bush and the source of the odour, waving at Lidan to follow.

With the strap of the attendee box slung across her chest, she ran through the grass, stumbling over clumps and unseen piles of loose stones. Blades of grass clung to her under-trousers and skirt, forcing her to wade as if she were in fast flowing water, seeds sticking desperately to the fabric and hoping to hitch a ride to unfertilised ground.

'Over here!' Jac shouted and ran on.

Lidan scanned the grass but failed to recognise what he'd seen. She didn't have a gateman's sharp eye. When Jac fell to his knees in the shadow of the hills a few feet from the trees, she knew he'd found the motionless man. She hurried to him, slipping the box strap over her head and holding it out for him to take.

The gateman didn't turn; his attention fixed on the filthy figure slumped in the grass. He grasped the man's shoulders and flipped him to his back, exposing a face pale as ice and splattered with old, dark blood.

'By the ancestors, it's Loge! Hand me the wake tonic,' Jac ordered without looking up. He began examining the man's arms, revealing deep gashes to the underside of each, black blood crusted on the sleeves of his coat. His tunic and lightweight chest armour were equally slashed and bloodied, wounds hidden beneath a thick layer of accumulated dirt and tattered clothing. Bloody spray seemed to paint him from head to toe, but it was hard to tell if it belonged to him or some other poor soul. 'Lidan!'

'Oh.' she started and stared at Jac. He waved an extended hand, palm up, waiting for the wake tonic from the box. 'Yes, wake tonic... wake, wake...'

The lid eased back and her fingers rifled through a compartment lined with soft wool and packed with clay urns, each stoppered with a little tanned animal skin and a carved cork of wood. Painted symbols on the bottles revealed what each contained; pictures of the ingredients so one could distinguish wake from halestrom. The required bottle appeared and she tossed it at Jac, who shook it and yanked the stopper free. He held the skin from the stopper, soaked with liquid, under the fallen man's nose and waited.

Nothing.

Wake tonic was powerful, especially in this concentration. It should have stirred the younger man from his stupor faster than a horn rouses rangers to battle. Jac swore again and handed the urn, stopper and all, back to Lidan and leaned to press his ear against the man's chest.

'Come on, Loge...' he murmured. 'Come on, mate... Where are you?' His hand squeezed and patted the length of Loge's pallid neck then stopped. 'You're still there, mate. I can feel it. Chuck me the burner tonic and a dressing.'

Lidan obliged in silence, terrified and enthralled. Was the man dead? She hadn't recognised him under all that grime and gore but Loge Baker was the eldest son of Wiull, the man who ground the clan's grain into flour. At about seventeen years of age, Loge was almost a fully-fledged ranger—quite an achievement for the son of a tradesman. If he passed his training and lived to tell of it, he'd rank among the highest men in the clan. Exactly what happened since he left with his ranging masters looking for the hunt attackers was a mystery. They'd gone and failed to return for weeks.

The burner tonic rubbed on Loge's neck suddenly took effect, the pain was enough to rattle him awake, and he lurched up from the grass, gasping and wheezing. Jac hurried to pour a bladder of water across the young man's skin and dilute the tonic's sting.

'All right, Loge—you're back now. It's all right—'

Loge seized the lapels of Jac's coat with bloodied hands and fixed wild eyes on the gateman. Jac froze, as did Lidan, staring at the young man shivering on the ground. His cracked lips parted and he drew a ragged, laboured breath.

'Fucking *run!*'

'Wait on—' Jac tried to prise Loge's grip from his coat, but the ranger held tight.

'No, no, no. No waiting. Run. Just fucking *run!*'

A deep throaty snarl rolled from the shadows amongst the trees and Lidan gaped at Loge, her mouth dry and chest heaving with quick breaths. The ranger's wide eyes, half hidden behind a ragged mess of dark, wavy hair, held her entranced and horrified all in one moment. Light brown, almost gold, they flashed with panic. She tightened her grip on a flint knife in the depths of the attendee box, but Loge shook his head slowly as she drew it out. She dropped it back amongst the dressings and bandages and cold terror crawled up the back of her neck.

'There's no weapon to defend against what's in there...' He didn't blink. Not once.

Lidan let the box strap fall from her fingers, the urns clinking in protest where it landed.

The snarl came again.

'What is it, ranger?' Jac kept his eyes on the trees and stood carefully, drawing Loge to his feet and angling the wounded man so he stood behind him. One of Jac's thick arms held Loge upright, the other hand weighing the small axe.

'There's no name for what stalks in there...'

'Make one up then!' The gateman demanded through clenched teeth. 'I'd like to know what's gonna fucking eat me before it gets a chance!'

Loge's eyes never left the trees. 'Remember those stories... about the boys who wandered too far from their clan and ne'er came back?'

'I remember,' whispered Jac.

'This is worse. Worse than the pankars, worse than the namorras who suck your soul from your neck bones. It's hunting, stalking, wandering from one kill to another.'

The hidden creature howled and the bush trembled as it darted left then right through the shadows, crashing through the undergrowth. The stink was as thick as steam and just as difficult to breathe through. It clogged every available orifice. Jac motioned for Lidan to stand and she slowly came to her feet, fingers shaking no matter how tight she balled them into fists, her heart thumping faster with each chilling growl.

It snarled again and crashed closer, almost to the very edge of the trees. The trunks shook, dry leaves raining down in a curtain of pale green and gold. Lidan's empty hands ached for a weapon—a knife, a stick, a rock, anything! Without her bow she stood as defenceless as the day she was born, naked and vulnerable in the sight of the creature lurking behind the trees.

'Liddy, get your horse,' murmured Jac, gesturing with his axe.

She took a step back and stopped dead. A pair of glowering eyes in a hollow among the ghost-bark trees told her there was no point. There was not a horse alive that could outrun it.

A guttural growl rumbled from beneath eyes glimmering with reflected morning light. The creature's top lip curled back to reveal a row of broken, decaying teeth with only the ancestors-knew-what wedged between them, rotting there since its last meal. Lidan glanced at Loge, tracing the gashes across his torso and the shredded clothes sagging from his frame like torn flags.

She'd seen those wounds before, etched in the flesh of Tolak rangers. They weren't the stuff of arrows or stone axes. Even a blade wrought in bronze couldn't cut so clean or so deep. They were the marks left by an iron edge.

'What is it, Loge?' Lidan squeaked through her tightening throat. 'What does it want?'

'Us...'

'The horse, Lidan; *now*, damn it!'

She stepped back, one foot at a time, through the clinging grass and felt around blindly in the vain hope of catching the reins without taking her eyes off the monster in the shadows. The soft breath of a horse blew against her palm, the mount too well trained to abandon its rider, and for a moment she dared to hope they might escape alive. The leather of the reins rubbed a sense of reassurance into her skin, but it couldn't dispel her terror.

The creature roared and the bush shook for a hundred feet in all directions, birds and small wildlife scrambling to escape in a whir of frantic activity.

Jac seized his chance in the distraction and spun away, dragging Loge towards the horse as Lidan led it forwards to meet them half way. The gateman heaved the injured ranger into the saddle and turned back for Lidan as the creature lurched from the darkness into the sunlight. The horse shied and pranced away with Jac jogging after it, clutching at the reins.

The creature, now exposed to the day, was something that might once have been a man, but had since lost the essence that distinguishes humanity from beasts. There was recognition in its glare, but only that of a predator sizing up its prey. The man who might have lived behind those eyes and dreamed within that head was long dead. By the look of the body, it wasn't long for this world either. Great sheets of puckered skin peeled back to reveal bone and black, festering bands of muscle, with no sign of fresh red blood. The creature was hunched and malformed in the back, the disfigurement affecting the way it moved. It prowled, more than walked, low to the ground, with its large arms hanging and fingers welded around the hilts of two long knives—filthy, but sharp. It eased its weight from side to side, couched over thickly muscled legs and bare feet. If a man, a wolf and a bear ever birthed some unnatural offspring, this thing was it.

It sniffed the air and drooled frothing saliva from pale lips. It lifted its chin and shuddered with primeval pleasure, as if the scent of their fear sent its blood rushing and made it hard for the hunt. Men boasted of how the hunt made them feel, how it thickened their loins as they charged down their quarry and Lidan hadn't understood what they truly meant until now. She hadn't thought anyone could get such a rush from something so banal, so everyday, but now the salivating beast stood across the waving grass, staring with hungry, hollow eyes, she knew. There was a need there, a raw desperation that had to be slaked. It was going to take them down and enjoy every bloody moment.

'Liddy…'

'Jac…' she murmured; chin quivering.

'Come towards us.'

'I can't.'

'You can, girl. 'Course you can. One step, then another.' The gateman's reassurance was almost enough to convince her that she could, in fact, outrun the beast across open ground. But those eyes… 'Come on, girl.'

'Hey, fuck-face!' Loge jeered and threw something at the creature to break its concentration.

That seemed to be enough and Lidan ran, while heavy, bounding steps thundered up behind her.

Fast—too fast.

A roar, a flash of shadow, and the horrid stink, and all she could do was scream.

Chapter Twenty

Tolak Range, the South Lands

She tripped and hit the dirt and grass, sliding to a stop, ripping the soft skin of her shoulder and arm on the hard ground. A wet hiss leaked from the creature, so close its spit hit the back of her neck. Lidan squeezed her eyes shut and sent a desperate prayer to anyone who might be listening.

She didn't want to die. Not yet. Not like this.

Her fingers dug into the dirt, determined to hold on to the earth for all she was worth, and her hand curled around the unseen length of a branch. She allowed her eyes to open a crack and glanced down. It was less than a foot long, dry and brittle, but sharp at both ends. Red splinters jutted from beneath mottled grey bark, knots and the buds of broken twigs biting her palm with more reassurance than Jac could ever offer. Jac was too far away to offer any help, and she could use this.

The thing snarled and grunted as it leapt forwards for the kill.

Barely hearing Jac's howl, Lidan rolled and held the branch in front of her face with both hands. The creature hit with its full weight thrust forward, knives scraping past her shoulders, jaws wide.

It struggled and gagged, its bulk pressing down on her slight frame.

Lidan pushed against the branch, the muscles in her arms shivering with effort. She thrust the branch forwards, a grisly, wet crunch echoing in her ears as she drove her only weapon into the creature's mouth and down its throat.

It coughed and heaved and tried to pull back.

The skin on her palms tore and her voice rose to a guttural scream. With the last of her fading strength, she rammed the branch through the back of the creature's neck, and its body shuddered violently.

Lidan expected blood, but there was nothing but a strange, oozy blue-black pus. With its jaw wedged open, the beast's saliva dripped from its teeth across her face. She gagged and shivered, her body descending into panic, her mind swirling and her lungs screaming for air. It wheezed and shuddered again, then slumped dead across her body like a sack of grain.

'Get off her, ya slug!' Jac hauled the body of the beast away mere moments before Lidan ran out of breath under the solid weight.

'She all right, Jac?'

'You right, Liddy? Got all your parts in the right place?' Jac dragged her to her feet and held her at arms' length.

She nodded but words didn't pass her lips.

Her legs failed and she stumbled into Jac, relying on his large, weathered hands to carry her to the waiting horse. Her hands shook and her chin refused to stop quivering even when she bit her lip so hard it bled. The pus and drool smeared thick across her shirt stank something awful, but it was only half the reason tears slipped from her eyes.

'What're you doing, mate?' Loge called to Jac, but Lidan didn't look up to see where he'd gone. She sat atop the horse and kept her eyes on the middle ground, the empty space between earth and sky, trying to scour the image of the creature from her mind. In her head, it still hunched in the grass, its yawning maw inches from her face.

'Taking it back with us.'

She turned sharply at that. 'You're *what?*'

Jac straightened and wiped sweat and blue slime from his brow. 'You want to explain this without evidence?'

He was right, damn it. Who in their right mind would believe a word of what happened unless they saw the beast for themselves?

Nearly thirty rangers blocked the gateway to Hummel, their spears and arrowheads trained on the horses walking slowly up from the creek. A hastily erected barricade spanned the opening in the wall, the gates standing where Jac left them. The creature's body bumped gently behind on a towrope, feet bound and the head wrapped in a length of bandage.

The branch Lidan wedged in its mouth remained in place, the oozy pus still leaking from the corpse but losing its stink. Either she'd grown used to it, or in death the thing ceased emitting the foul odour she'd smelled on it before. In either case, she was thankful it wasn't nearly as nasty as it had been.

'What's happened, Jac?' Siman frowned over the barricade, questioning Jac but not shifting his gaze from Loge.

'Saw young Loge stagger out of the bush, then this thing attacked us.' He nodded his head to indicate the creature lying motionless behind the horses.

'Is it dead?' Siman tightened his grip on his spear.

'It's dead. I'll swear on it,' said Loge. 'The daari needs to see this, sir.'

'And where are the others from your party, apprentice?' asked Siman. 'I've a mind to keep you out here with that thing. How am I to know what'll happen if we let you in?'

'Ranger!' Daari Erlon shouted from inside the gate and the guards moved aside until he appeared behind the barricade. 'Is that my *daughter?* By the ancestors, what is she doing out there?'

'Helped me save Loge, sir!' Jac called and drew Erlon's attention from Siman. The daari's sharp eyes found Lidan and if she could have shrunk further into the saddle, she'd gladly have done so. 'She killed this beastie…'

They all stared at her then. Some visibly gaped, others sneered or frowned. Erlon didn't move a muscle in his broad body, his eyes locked on Lidan with stern intensity. There was a question in them that she couldn't read. It was hidden under all of his confusion, shock, horror, anger and concern. He looked fit to fly into a rage and send her crying to her room for behaving so recklessly, but instead he hesitated and bit his tongue. She saw the muscles jump in his neck and knew it took all his strength not to snarl.

'Let them in,' he ordered, still carefully watching Lidan.

'But sir—' Siman started, and swallowed his protest when Erlon turned his cool gaze around and stepped towards him.

'You'll let them pass.' He didn't raise his voice or lift a hand. He didn't need to. The rangers and gatemen made a path for Jac to urge his horse along, the corpse jolting across the ground and Loge's mount wandering calmly behind. 'I'll inspect it in the stables. Clear them and keep everyone away until I say otherwise. Send for Grent and Rick.'

Her father might have said more to Siman and those he trusted most with the clan's security, but Lidan moved out of earshot. The usual chatter and noise of the clan died as they dragged the beast's corpse across the common. Lidan turned away and stared at Jac's hands on the reins near her waist, focussed on the wall of his chest at her back and the steady rhythm of the horse's gait. For all her talk, right now she wanted nothing more than to become invisible.

'Loge?' called a woman across the common. 'Loge, is that you?'

'Yes, Mam,' he replied and the woman burst into tears. It was likely she had resigned to never seeing her son again, as so many other mothers never would.

'Thank the ancestors... Wiull, he's back! Loge's back! Oh, thank goodness...' She ran towards them followed by a man in a leather apron with dusty white hands. Loge's reunion with his parents vanished behind Jac and even if he hadn't blocked her view with his wide shoulders, she didn't risk looking back. Her father was there, and the creature's bouncing carcass—neither of them sights she fancied.

***

The stable doors shut with a muffled thud and strands of hay and dust billowed in the wake of the tall timber panels. Jac helped Lidan from the saddle and held her steady as her shaking knees threatened to give way beneath her weight.

'You all right?' he murmured, just for her to hear. Lidan nodded and blew out a trembling breath, and he squeezed her hand. 'Get a perch on that crate and stay there. Let me sort this out.'

She obeyed his command and he turned to untie the dead creature from his horse's saddle, releasing the mount into an empty stall. Her hands shook and her stomach rolled, her throat contracting each time she glanced at the creature's corpse. She wanted to vomit.

What was that thing? She'd never seen or heard of anything like it.

But she had...

In the incoherent death ramblings of rangers. In the garbled screams in the night when she sat watch in the treatment rooms. None of what she'd heard had made sense at the time, but now, with this monster's glaring eyes and hot, stinking breath still fresh on her skin, she knew what those rangers had seen.

The stable doors whispered as they opened; Grent, Rick, and Siman slipping through the gap before they shut again and smothered the noise of the common. The weariness left over from the previous night seemed all but forgotten in the commotion of their return.

The two tradesmen clasped hands with Daari Erlon before turning to the creature. They bent their heads together, voices rumbling in a low murmur, arms folded into muscled knots of worry only broken by a few sharp gestures towards the dead thing in the middle of the stable floor. Her heart hammering, Lidan shut her eyes and drew in a deep breath.

A flash of teeth and a hot, foul snarl snapped at her face.

She started and her eyes flew open.

The thing remained as it was, dead on the floor, twisted and oozing, but in her mind, it lived, stretching its jaws wide to fit her between its teeth. She shuddered and bit hard into the raw flesh on the back of her lip to keep her chin from quivering.

No tears in front of Da—no tears and no fear.

Erlon glanced at her as if he'd sensed her thought, his eyes unsure as they went from the creature to her and back again. The other men ceased muttering between themselves and followed the daari's gaze, equally uncertain, brows creased and lips pressed into thin lines of concern.

'Gateman Jac?' Erlon began, his attention lingering on Lidan before turning to the gateman. 'You saw this thing from the wall?'

'No, sir. I saw Loge come from the bush. Didn't see this 'til we got out there to help him.' Jac clasped his hands behind his back and nodded at Lidan. 'Loge was injured and I needed a healer's help. The First Daughter was the only one 'round to lend a hand. Good thing too—it was her that killed it.'

'How?' her father frowned and stepped closer to inspect the corpse without leaning too near.

'Shoved a stick down its throat, I believe...' Jac glanced her way and winked. She tried to return his kindness with a smile, but she felt numb and there was no way to tell if the features on her face obeyed her instructions. They more than likely remained locked in an expression of startled horror.

'Grent,' Erlon waved at his bonesetter and stood back. 'What do you make of it?'

'Looks like a man, or perhaps it was a man once...' He crouched over the creature and prodded its arm with a length of wood.

'Too big and brutal to be a pankar,' said Siman as Grent moved around the corpse. 'Look at the size of it, and the claws...'

'They aren't claws, my friend.' Rick knelt beside the corpse and yanked a mean blade from its grip. The creature's finger bones snapped and gave way, peeling back and reluctantly giving up their prize. 'This is a blade, not grown, but made. Northern metal, wrought in a forge like ours but from a different ore.' Rick held the knife up to a beam of sunlight, his fingers tracing the edge and hilt. 'Steel, worn and badly cared for, but steel.' He threw it at a nearby timber pillar and Lidan jumped at the sound of the blade driving deep into the wood and shivering in place. 'Sharp for all the wear. Bone or ivory handle, folded iron blade... good quality or else they wouldn't have lasted in this condition.'

The pair of knives were long, about the length of Lidan's forearm from tip to hilt, and the handles were half that length again. 'Can you tell where they came from, just by looking?' Lidan asked quietly.

'If you know what to look for.' The forge master glanced at the daari. 'Imperial, most likely.' Her father raised his brows at that and Lidan frowned. Imperial? What under all the sun and stars did *imperial* mean?

Catching her confusion, Rick added, 'From way up north; across more mountains than the clans have ever seen.'

'Not bronze?' Erlon asked.

Rick shook his head and spat. 'No, and not from the clans, unless they've got themselves a northern forge master. We'd have heard about it before now if they did. No way they wouldn't brag about it.'

'Like we did when you decided to stay and fire our ore?'

'Aye, sir, just like you did.' Rick nodded at the door. 'Every clan this side of Fracture Pass knows I work metals for you and they're jealous as the sun.'

'Blood-oath they're jealous!' Erlon remarked proudly. 'But they didn't do *this*. This is wandering death, with weapons we hardly know how to fight.'

'Ngaru.' Lidan said the name the clans gave to unknown creatures like this, her voice rising into the silence left by her father. 'Night wanderers...'

Her father glanced at his countrymen and they nodded.

'Ngaru,' he repeated and a heavy, considered silence settled in the air. Lidan remained sitting on a creaking timber crate of horse leathers and wished she was anywhere but here…

'Liddy?' Erlon asked, their eyes meeting across the stable, his brow creasing into a frown. 'It got you with those knives, didn't it?'

'I…' She glanced down, realising at the top of both arms, an inch or so below the shoulder, two gashes in her shirt shone bright red. 'I suppose it did…'

Grent hurried to her side and pulled her shirt up over her head to expose the skin beneath the torn white sleeves. Her undershirt saved her some dignity but the pain seeping from the wounds banished any embarrassment. Grent treated her like the rangers they tended in the treatment rooms, unbothered by her gender or the presence of the others. His fingers probed the gashes and she winced, sucking air between clenched teeth and arching away.

'These need cleaning,' he announced and threw his jacket over her bare shoulders before leading her towards the door.

Siman cleared his throat to get her father's attention. 'What'll we do, sir?'

'We do nothing,' the daari replied.

Lidan baulked and turned in Grent's gentle hands, her pain forgotten. 'What?'

'You heard me, Lidan Tolak—we do nothing.'

'But Da, those things…'

He held up a hand and her protest evaporated.

'We know what they are now. I won't waste more men on searching them out, or risk drawing more of them towards Hummel. Until the rains come, we bar the gates, and we stay here.' His dark brows furrowed over stern eyes. 'They won't get past our gates.'

The glint of sunlight on the knives caught Lidan's eye.

Follow her, follow your father or cut your own way? The Crone's words echoed in her mind and drew an idea from the depths of her thoughts.

'What are you going to do with the knives?' she asked. The thought of them ending up on the midden unsettled her stomach but she couldn't put her finger on why. Perhaps she hesitated at the idea of throwing away something as rare as iron from the north, or perhaps... 'Can I keep them?'

The words were out before she knew she'd said them.

They all looked at Erlon and she wished she could decipher the expression on her father's face and read his thoughts, even for a moment.

Erlon shot a questioning glance at the forge master, and Rick inclined his head. 'I *could* fix them. What's in your mind?'

She squared her shoulders though her skin stung white-hot around the wounds the knives left in her flesh. 'They put scars on me that I'll wear 'til I die. They owe me a debt.'

'They're weapons, First Daughter. Not toys,' Rick remarked. 'You'll need training.'

It was a request that went against all of her mother's wishes. The woman wanted her daughter to be the heir, but without risk-taking or danger, without training or ranging. Lidan knew such a thing was impossible, and perhaps if her mother had relented sooner, she might have been well on her way to showing her father that she was as worthy an heir as any son. Instead, Lidan was bound to a sickening promise, and these knives offered a chance to fulfil it.

As she watched Erlon, she saw recognition pass over his face. He understood what she was asking and why—she was challenging him to defy the dana. She was challenging him to treat her as his heir, to allow her to show him what she was capable of, despite the promise of a son, and despite the wishes of his first wife.

He watched her, his eyes taking in the way she lifted her chin in defiance and held herself proudly. She'd done the impossible and broken in Theus, and now she'd killed the creature lurking in the bush and slaughtering rangers. He *had* to let her prove she could be his heir.

Erlon put his hands on his hips and sighed, as if feeling the weight of the decision and the burden of the consequences. In that moment she knew he would refuse, and her heart sank. He looked back at his daughter and her hands clenched into tight fists, her teeth biting into the back of her lip to keep it from shaking.

'To the victor go the spoils,' her father said with a nod. 'You killed the ngaru, so the knives are yours. You will train.'

CHAPTER TWENTY-ONE

The Southern Reaches, Orthia

Voices pursued Ranoth into the darkness. They followed him as he fought his way through the trees and thick undergrowth. Their torches threw dancing shadows and revealing shafts of light into the woods which threatened to expose him at every turn.

He hurried through the night, reaching out with whatever senses hadn't abandoned him in the cold of the dungeons, hoping to find a way through the darkness towards some sort of safety. He kept the road to his left and obscured his trail, waited for the soldiers to pass before he circled down behind them and sprinted across to the northern side of the road. If luck hadn't abandoned him then the darkness would cover his tracks until morning, but if the soldiers found Perce's promised horse before he did, his efforts were for naught.

A deep drain beside the road hid him from sight and he crouched, hurrying through the wet slop at the base of the ditch. For what seemed like hours he kept to that drain until a line of stones in a pile indicated the remains of an old paddock fence. Across the field in the faint moonlight, he saw the leaning structure of a low shed, the surviving timbers of a ramp at either end, and a livestock yard barely standing after many years of neglect. The building stood on stone pillars as high as Ran's waist, though some at the northern end had crumbled.

He swallowed the memory of the last abandoned building he encountered and covered the exposed ground without taking a breath. Were it not for Perce's guarantee of a horse, Ran would have avoided the place like the pox. In the shadow cast by the ramp at the northern end, he huddled and waited.

The sound of his pursuers had fallen away, the light of their torches fading until he felt he was quite alone, but the chances they had given up on him were close to nil. They were in the woods, hiding and hunting.

The sound of his breath and the hammer of his heart grated against his nerves, the ice cold of the night biting into his hands and fingers. Nothing moved in the woods where he'd been, no sign of men or beasts following his trail, so he slipped from the shadows and hurried down the back side of the building to its southern corner. Across the field stood the copse of trees Perce mentioned, and if his luck held, the horse and supplies. Without them, he was as good as dead.

He stepped from the shelter of the building and straight into the chest of a soldier.

Ran's forehead smacked into the man's nose and sent him staggering back. For a moment, Ran thought he'd run into a post. His recovery was quicker than the soldier's, who reeled backwards then bent double, pinching his bleeding nose and cursing.

Before the other man had a chance to look up, Ran grabbed him by the shoulders and spun with him back into the shadows behind the shed. The soldier's head hit a stone footing with a crack and Ran dropped him.

The soldier moaned as Ran stood over him, his face a mess of black blood in the pale moonlight. Ran glanced around. How many more men were in the trees? How many were waiting for him to break cover and head for the horse? If this soldier got up and went back to the city, he would reveal the direction of his escape.

Thoughts piled up in his brain faster than he could sort through them while the soldier held his head in his hands and rolled onto to his knees. He would be on his feet in a few moments, then Ran would have to deal with an armed opponent and nothing at hand to defend himself with.

A glint of light on water drew his eye and he grabbed the man by the back of his tunic. The soldier tried to stand, tried to throw his weight backwards, but Ran kept moving, dragging him the few feet across the dirt and snow to a trough.

He didn't think about it. He didn't reason or make excuses. He lifted the man by his clothes and shoved him face first into the icy water and held tight.

Shock hit the soldier first, a jerk through his whole body as he recoiled from the freezing water. Ran's muscles screamed as he threw his weight down on the man's back.

The soldier began to thrash, his legs kicking and torso bucking like a wild horse. His arms flailed and grappled for Ran, desperate for a purchase on his skin, his clothing, or his hair. Ran pressed down harder and jammed his elbows into the man's spine, pinning him against the edge of the trough with everything he had.

The frantic lurching and heaving soon subsided to a feeble quiver, then ended entirely. The body gave a few unconscious twitches, then lay still, floating in the shimmering water as wavelets slopped over the side onto Ran's boots.

For a while Ran didn't move. He couldn't.

The silence of the night filled his ears like the water filling the soldier's lungs, and he waited. He waited for the man to move, to start fighting again. He waited for the soldier to launch up from the water and gut him, but his body lay motionless with its legs stretched out across the dirt.

When Ran stood, his chest sucking in great gulps of air, the body stayed as he left it. His hands shook and his legs threatened to give way but he remained upright, staring at the body in the water and the ripples slowly fading from the surface. The man was dead, of that there was little doubt.

What the fuck have I done?

'Saved yourself,' a voice spoke from nowhere and everywhere. It filled his head and he clamped his eyes shut. It stung his ears and set off a sharp ringing he couldn't dislodge, but the voice was right. The soldier would have alerted others and they in turn would have found his trail. He couldn't let the man live, not after finding him at the shearer's shed. He would lead the duke's soldiers back here, find the horse's tracks and follow them. The man couldn't live…

Ran glanced around and hoped the soldier had been alone. He didn't have the guts or the strength to kill any more of them.

He rubbed his face with quivering hands to shake off the horror, the guilt, and the memory of what had happened and crouched beside the body. He choked as he flipped the corpse onto the ground and tried not to look at the man's face, now washed clean of blood. He rifled through pockets and pilfered coins and basic supplies; a dagger, a purse, a spare pair of boots and some gloves, a thick coat and a good leather belt with a sword and scabbard were his rewards for murder. The threat of vomit deterred him from stripping off the man's clothes entirely.

If someone found the body it would be immediately obvious that the man was of the city guard or an Orthian soldier, but he didn't have the time or tools to dig a grave. For want of a better option, he rolled the body under the floor of the shed between two of the stone footings. A nearby fence lent him a length of timber and he wedged it under the base of the trough. With every ounce of his remaining strength, he leaned on the timber until the trough began to lift. It eased up from its base and began to tip towards the shed until the volume of the water overcame the weight of the stone. The whole thing flipped and thumped down over the corpse, trapping it in a solid stone tomb. Unless the smell escaped the seal of the stone against the soil, there was no way a passer-by would notice the trough or suspect a body lay rotting underneath.

It was a lonely burial, but safe from curious eyes and the teeth of wolves. At least the soldier would keep his secrets under the weight of stone.

He found the horse waiting in the darkness, tied to a tree, with sad-dlebags stuffed with provisions. The animal seemed well muscled, enough to withstand a hard ride; but as much as he wanted to tear off into the night, he checked his fear.

If he rode the thing until it died, his pursuers would surely catch him in a few days, if not sooner. If he took it slow and kept off the road, he and the horse might yet survive. Too much had been sacrificed to buy him this freedom, and he would not—*could* not—let that be in vain. Soon after abandoning the field and the shearer's shed, he found a riverbed and fol-lowed it south for as long as he could stay in the saddle.

He had no clue what fate Perce had suffered; no idea if the guards at the gate had let him live or beaten him to death. If the tutor survived his arrest, then the Duke's Justice awaited him for aiding a criminal in his escape. Both Ran and the old man knew what that meant. Ran's stomach rolled at the thought and he turned his face from the pale dawn, as if the light made the wound in his heart harder to bear.

Perce would be furious if Ran let his emotions get the better of him. He would scowl and snort and tell the prince to be a man about it. He didn't have the patience for sentiment, though a little shone through the moment he gave Ran the scroll tube and admitted it was all he could do to save his life. For that, Ran hadn't had the chance to thank him, and probably never would. He wept when he lay on his saddle to snatch a fitful rest as another night fell, despite what the old man would think of him.

It took two blizzards covering his tracks before he felt he might have finally lost his father's soldiers. Snow smothered the trail of his horse, and he stayed in the highlands where the terrain was more difficult for soldiers and trackers to cross. He had no doubt that as soon as he descended from the hills, scores of the duke's troops would be waiting to drag him back to Usmein.

Ran made the provisions last as long as he could, but close to a month had passed and things were tight. All of his fresh food was gone and the preserved meat and hard tack were running dangerously low. He ate only on the days when he travelled, and tried to ignore his hunger on days when he and the horse rested. To fill the gaps, Ran resorted to stealing from small farms and cottages by the cover of night, pinching from smoke houses and pantry stores in barns. If the locals noticed the tracks through their yards, they never raised the alarm, and no one ever followed him back into the high ridges and gullies.

The weather closed in at the turn of the moon and he found refuge in a cave at the apex of a valley choked with snow. As he stripped the saddle and blanket from the horse and led the beast inside, Ran wondered if his father's men still searched for him or if they'd given up and gone home. Surely it was madness to hunt a boy into the mountains and forests only to bring him back for execution?

Even as he wondered, he knew the answer.

Ran knew his father and the lengths the man would go to in order to protect Orthia, his house, and his rule. He could have ended the war in the Disputed Territory decades ago, just by bending a knee to the Empire, but he would not. Ronart would defend Orthia until his dying breath, even if it meant sacrificing every one of his subjects. Even if it meant ripping his only son's inheritance from his cold, dead fingers. No price was too high for freedom. He couldn't just let his cursed son vanish into the wilds and escape justice. What message would that send to the people? How could he control the threat of magic among ordinary Orthians if he couldn't follow the law in regard to his own son? It cut deep to admit it, but his father wouldn't allow the search to end until they found him, dead or alive.

Ran glanced at his gloved hands in the orange light of his campfire and sighed. Was it his mother's blood that carried the curse, as his father so loudly accused? Her horror and sadness, the disappointment in her eyes, haunted Ran in the small hours of the night, when he lay awake turning the past over in his head as if he might find a place to wind it all back. Back to when he was home, before his stupid insistence on going to the Territory, back before he lost everything.

His eyes filled with tears.

The thought drove him to his feet and the campfire flared with the rage that fuelled his magic. He paced the cave and drew shaking breaths to calm his angry heart. Furious at his failures, furious at his stupidity, he spun and punched the cave wall. Burying his fear and sorrow deep into the rock, his fist cracked the granite. If there was pain, he couldn't feel it, his hands burning with magic.

The cave groaned in protest, dust and stone chips raining down like the snow outside.

Oh shit... He pressed his palms against the wall and cooed as if his soothing voice might convince the mountain not to fall in on him.

'You've gone and done it now...' her voice slipped from the darkness at the back of the cave, husky and mocking.

Ran didn't bother to look in her direction anymore, sick of searching and not seeing. His ghost girl came and went as she pleased, and she'd not shown herself to him in almost a week.

'You always pick the *finest* moments to visit,' he spat and sat his shivering body beside the fire, though it was not the cold that made his skin crawl and his muscles quiver. He shook like a terrified puppy every time his magic roared to life uninvited and burst out to inflict itself on whatever stood nearby. Today it was a cave wall, last week it was a persistent, noisy bird keeping him from sleep; tomorrow it might be a tree.

Whenever his magic flared, he understood the law. He was dangerous. Too dangerous to be around innocent people, too dangerous to trust with the care or leadership of others. As much as he missed his home, he was glad to be far from Usmein and anyone who might catch the edge of his wild and unpredictable powers. Ran glanced up and was surprised to see the ghost, watching him, her pale blue gaze wandering from his shaking hands to his face.

'Have you opened it?' She asked the same question whenever she came.

She knew the answer but asked anyway, waiting patiently for him to reply before saying another word. Once or twice since leaving Usmein, he hadn't answered at all, and the silence that followed was something close to the worst thing he'd ever heard. Her eyes fell on the saddlebags beside his thin bedroll but he didn't move to touch them.

'No, not yet,' he replied and poked at the embers of the fire instead.

'Why?' She cocked her head to one side like a curious bird. She'd never asked him why, only *when*, as if fishing for an invitation to an unveiling party. The wicked old wound in her neck gaped a little as she moved, and Ran suppressed a shudder. Mostly, he could ignore it, hidden as it was in the shadows beneath her chin, but when she strained her neck like that, it yawned open to remind him that she was, in fact, quite dead.

'I...' he began, then stared at the saddlebag.

Tightly wrapped in layers of woollen clothes and oiled leathers, buried under provisions, a map and a water bladder, was the scroll tube Perce pressed into his hand during his escape. It felt as if the shiny tube hummed under all that camouflage, singing to him as he rode or walked up windswept ridges. He slipped past villages and hamlets, and all the while he felt the tube in the saddlebag, weighing him down like a stone.

Their eyes met across the fire again and Ran shrugged away her question. 'I know what it says.'

She rolled her eyes. 'Of course you do. You've got a whole story in your head that tells you exactly what it says and why you've got no reason to open it.' She paused and lifted her chin, her scrutiny cutting through his warm winter clothes until he felt entirely naked and completely helpless. 'We both know that story is a lie.'

He swallowed a retort and a few too many curses, and clenched his jaw. Provoking the ghost was unwise if he hoped to get more than an hour's sleep in the next few nights. She tormented and haunted him when he spoke rudely or cursed at her, or threw his magic her way, but hadn't yet turned her powers of persuasion to forcing him to act.

She was a little odd like that.

With a sigh, he opened his hands towards her. 'A lie it might be, but it's my lie, *my* make-believe tale. I don't need to see the words to know the truth at the heart of it.'

'Perhaps,' she said, 'not yet.'

Her hand reached through the flames to hover over his, her flickering form unmolested by the heat. For a moment she considered him with a worried frown and pity in her eyes, an expression her usually stony features had not made in Ran's presence.

'But one day you'll want to know, you'll *need* to know, and you'll beg to see the ink your fear and pride blinded you to. By then, it might be too late.'

'What? Why?' His brow creased into a frown. What could she possibly know about the scroll that he didn't?

'No...' she said with a sad smile. Her translucent hand touched the faint stubble on his cheek, a frozen whisper across his flesh. 'That's not for me to tell. You have to do this yourself.'

He glanced at the saddlebag where the scroll lay hidden, his heart thumping. What did she know? He could find out if he just opened it, but he was bone tired and not entirely sure he was ready. Reading what Perce had hidden in there would make it all real; his father's anger, his mother's sorrow, his future evaporating into the air. He swallowed and looked back at the ghost.

She vanished with the next howl of wind and his horse snorted and stamped his hoof, as he did whenever she left them alone. Ran despised her when she lingered and sorely missed her when she left, an awful see-saw of emotion tipping wildly back and forth as the loneliness of his existence settled in. Her words echoed in his mind and he shook his head to dispel the sound.

'Maybe it's time we found some human company, hey fella? Find a farm to get you some more feed?' he asked the horse, and grimaced as the wind at the cave mouth whipped up to an icy roar. 'Though maybe not today.'

The horse didn't respond, as always, and returned his attention to the small chaff bag on the ground. He probably understood that if Ran's only company remained a mute horse and a ghost girl, then he'd be well and truly mad before the thaw of spring.

For another two nights and a day the storm continued to dump snow in front of Ran's cave, each passing hour blurring into the next, only distinguished by increasing boredom and solitude. When the second morning broke with a clear sky and a singing bird, the sunlight on his eyes felt like hot needles and a noise other than the howling wind was something of a foreign language.

He used a flat stone to dig a channel out of the cave and into the morning. The forest on the mountainside was blanketed in sparkling white. The horse eyed him suspiciously when he approached with the saddle, but Ran smiled.

'Don't worry; I'm not going to make you carry me. Just the tack.'

Without knowing the depth of the drifts, he risked breaking more than the horse's ankles if he rode. With a long lead they could pick their way across the terrain and find their footing, avoiding a fall, breaking something on the horse, or himself, and dying in the cold.

'If we're lucky,' he murmured to the horse, 'we'll find somewhere nice and stay the night.'

The horse snorted, which Ran took as agreement, and they slipped and skidded beside each other down the slope to an unused road shrouded in gnarled trees and low shrubs.

They needed more supplies if they were to survive the winter, so an excursion to a village was inevitable. He hadn't planned much further than the thaw, when the snow would dribble away to the streams and the heavy clouds would lift. He knew he had to survive, but to what end he was yet to decide.

When he did break cover and enter a town, Ran made a point to never stay more than a few hours. He posed as a messenger and spoke only to the few merchants he traded with. Perce's saddlebags offered up enough coin to get him what he needed, quickly and without too many questions, but he always left town feeling the eyes of the residents on his back. If soldiers or scouts came through, would they tell the tale of the messenger when asked if they'd seen anything strange? Would they recall his face, his features, or the direction he left in?

Often, he circled the settlements and came at them from the south, as if travelling towards the capital and he always made sure to leave to the north. He let his sparse facial hair grow and kept himself fairly filthy to obscure anything that might be a trait worth remembering. He even added a drawl to his words, dropping his voice to a low tone and peppering his speech with enough curses to hide his noble education.

If his luck held, the locals would think him nothing more than a rider or vagrant and he'd slip from their memories altogether. All he had was hope. He needed a rest in a real bed and a hot meal in his belly after so many nights on cold, unforgiving rock. Otherwise, the winter might do his father a favour and put an end to his troubles.

They rested at midday. Despite the cold in the wind and the damp in his boots, the faint warmth of the sun at its zenith was glorious against his frozen skin as he closed his eyes and leaned back against the wide trunk of a tree. The road arced down from the mountainside ever so slightly and he guessed it wound towards a town, or a wider, more heavily trafficked highway. It galled him to need the respite a town offered, but he was unwilling to get any closer to desperate than he already was. He'd read enough in his lessons about what starvation did to men's minds and he wasn't at all keen on experiencing it first-hand.

A twig snapped in the woods to his left and his eyes flicked open. The peace of a few moments' rest vanished in an instant, replaced by hollow fear. His horse stood unmoved and unconcerned by the sound, his head down but ears swivelling back and forth. The sound had not startled the beast, who had proven as good a guard as any hound he'd ever met.

The storm of the previous night had carpeted the snowfall with leaves and branches, sticks and tree nuts. The leaf litter rustled again and he paused, scanning the trees at the edge of the snowy clearing. Stealth had been hard to come by in such conditions, and he'd given up on it some hours ago after cursing every hoof fall that loudly crunched through the debris. Whatever moved through the shadows was making an extra effort to remain unseen, but it had been heard. With silent steps he collected his bow, slipped the quiver belt around his hips and stretched the string into place.

Careful to place his booted feet between the fallen matter and on the soft, powdered snow, he followed the direction of the sound and let his magic roll away like a transparent fog. Trees slipped by, their shadows shifting across his vision, drawing his eyes to seek villains in the lee of trunks, boles and boughs.

Leaves crunched and he spun to confront the attacker, bow up, fletched arrow at the corner of his mouth, ready to bury itself in the chest of his hunter.

What the merry fuck…?

A puff of white rabbit stood still as stone, stupid enough to back itself up against a dark tree trunk. Its sparkling red eyes watched him, its small nose twitching as it caught a touch of his scent on the air. Before he could think to stop it, his magic rose and bore down on the rabbit, twisting its hand of influence until the creature did not move at all. Even the quiver of its fine whiskers slowed to a stop.

His attacker, nothing more than a potential meal, stood paralysed in the face of his magic and his arrowhead. Ran blinked rapidly and steadied his hands, drawing a breath then letting half of it go. Time slowed until the motion of the trees dancing in the wind eased and ceased, the hammer of his heart the only sound to fill his ears.

Without command, his fingers loosed the shaft and in that moment, time and all her realities resumed. The arrow nailed the rabbit in the skull and burrowed into the tree, the kill so quick the animal hardly had a moment to realise its fate and squeal for mercy. Other than the gentle hum of the arrow shivering in the tree trunk, the forest was silent.

Blood trickled from the wound and the shock of glaring crimson against the blistering white sheen of the snow shook Ran from his trance. The magic dissipated and his hands and fingers shook as he unstrung his bow and moved to collect his quarry. A quick tug brought the shaft and head from the tree's bark, the rabbit yielding to his touch as he scooped it up and turned.

The ghost barred his way.

Ran choked on a curse and his teeth jammed down on the inside of his lips.

She stood atop the snow, her weightless feet not sinking into the drifts, the blue orbs of her eyes trained wide and unblinking on the rabbit. Her stare pinned him to the spot, her intense focus on the dead animal in his hands. On her face, the tracks of three bloodied fingers drew lines from her forehead to chin, across her perfect pale lips. Smeared in blood, they parted as if they ached to speak some painful truth but could not form the words.

She met his gaze and Ran swallowed hard. Where had the blood come from? There hadn't been blood on her before, at least not since...

His hands lifted the rabbit between them and he glanced down. Instead of one small wound in the animal's head, a wide, ragged gash glared up at him from the creature's throat, its head twisted away at a sick angle.

It was the same wound he had seen on the ghost in the house. The same awful mess that gaped at him whenever she moved her head. His heart leapt and he startled, flicking his hand to throw the dead rabbit away. His arm flailed but his fingers held tight, failing to heed his commands.

What the fuck is going on?!

His mind screamed at him to run but he couldn't move. He shot a glance at his ghost.

Her throat gaped wide. The old wound, once dried and empty, blackened and bruised, surged with a gush of blood that washed down her chest and onto the white carpet of snow. Her eyes rolled back and she vanished in a burst of power.

Ran dropped the rabbit in the snow and fled.

Chapter Twenty-two

Graupen, Southern Orthia

Ran rode the horse as fast and as long as he dared. He knew deep in the recesses of his mind that what he saw in the forest could not be outrun and could not be left behind. His magic had opened a door to something and it was a portal he could not close. It was a part of him and would go wherever he travelled, but he would be damned if he was going to spend another night in the frozen mountains at the mercy of his magic and his dreams.

By sundown, the outskirts of Graupen blinked into view through a hammering fall of ice and snow. Thin slivers of light glowed from behind shutters closed tight against the wind, not enough to banish the night, but enough to lead Ran through the howling storm towards the little mining village.

He guided the horse along the road, their heads bowed low against the sting of ice, their steps heavy and laboured. The mount shied at a drift and yanked the reins in Ran's hand, the jolt tipping his balance and sending him diving to the ground. He bit back the curses and screams at the ache in his knees and the hunger in his belly and staggered to his feet, soothing the horse and regaining the reins.

Graupen had no wall or gate, no outer defences or guardhouse. The road ran straight through town and out the other side, and by the look of the lights winking in the distance, it ended almost as soon as it began. They stumbled up the street, Ran squinting up at the timber-clad buildings as they passed, searching for any sign of an inn. One building somewhere near what he thought might be the centre of town seemed to glow stronger than the others, emitting a smell that could be roasting meat, or a burning corpse.

They passed a well, the steel pump beside it frozen solid, a bucket hanging above the black abyss swinging with a quiet creak in the wind. If it weren't for the light escaping the buildings, Ran would have sworn the place was entirely deserted. He stopped several feet from the door of the large building and swallowed his thumping heart. Graupen was a speck on any Orthian map, if it was mentioned at all. The chances of encountering the duke's men here, in such weather, were slim to none. He would have to keep telling himself that as he stepped through the door, or else he'd draw the eye of every cart-driver and pick-swinger by dint of looking nothing short of terrified.

The horse gladly slipped into an empty stall in the inn's stables and set to scoffing a pile of hay in the far corner. Ran looked for a stablehand to take the tack but the attendant's small room stood empty. He shrugged his coat closer to his shoulders and supposed travellers arriving in such a foul squall were uncommon. Why sit out in the cold waiting on no one? For a moment he considered unsaddling the horse himself, then thought better of it. If he needed to leave on short notice, he'd not have time to faff about saddling the beast and convincing him to take his bit. He took the saddlebags, and left everything else in place.

The entrance to the inn beckoned and he pressed one gloved hand against the door. He tried to ease it inward, but the wind snatched the panel from his grip and whipped it into the opposite wall with a loud crack that echoed through the smoky taproom.

The noise was enough to shake the filmy glasses lined up behind the bar, and Ran's mind flew into a panic, but hardly anyone in the dim room looked up to wonder at him. He swallowed his heart again and heaved the door closed at his back, willing his face to relax and his eyes to not appear quite as startled as he knew they seemed. He couldn't afford to stand out—he was a messenger, nothing more or less. Less would be much better in this case, but the messenger story had held up so far against the drunken enquiries of tavern types. By now he was close to comfortable with the mummer-act he put on when slipping into the unsavoury watering holes of Orthia's towns and villages.

The keeper glanced up and placed a tankard on the bar.

Obviously, the glass is kept for the respectable folk...

'Ale?' asked the keeper, his jug already hovering over the tankard.

Ran nodded in a nonchalant way, the kind of shrug he'd seen a thousand times in other taverns, followed by a grunt of neither agreement nor refusal. 'And whatever food you've got going.'

The keeper turned to bellow the order through a doorway and Ran took his tankard of dark beer to a seat in the corner. Corner seats were the rarest and most sought after in a tavern. They ideally gave you somewhere shadowy to hide and watch the rest of the drinkers with both eyes without the worry of a knife finding its way between your ribs.

A man in a greasy apron lumbered towards him with a plate of ham, a heel of bread, and a small bowl of soup balanced beside them. They were deposited on the table and Ran glanced up to mutter the obligatory thank you. He expected to see the man's retreating back, not his dark eyes staring down as he wiped his hands on the soiled cloth at his waist.

He had a similar look about him to the barkeep—a wide, crooked nose and heavy brows. His forearms were thickly muscled and better suited to swinging a pick and shovel than the finer arts of preparing food fit for human consumption. When the man's hands came to rest on his hips, Ran noticed at least half of one was missing, along with the thumb and first two fingers. Now he understood why the giant toiled in the inn's kitchen rather than a mine.

'You a messenger?' the man asked, folding his arms over his chest so the injured hand vanished into the shadows behind his elbow.

Ran blinked. 'Pardon?'

The cook leaned forward. 'I said, you a *messenger?*'

He rolled the words from his tongue slowly, as if to help Ran understand them better.

Fear slipped a hand around Ran's neck and began to squeeze. Had they heard of a messenger coming this way? Had they been told to watch for one?

'What makes you say that?' His voice was hardly more than a squeak and only a speck louder than a mewling kitten.

'Int no one else daft enough to travel in this weather.' The man might have been making a little joke, but there wasn't even a glimmer of humour in his eyes.

'O'course...' Ran mumbled. He drew heavily on his tankard and tried to spark his tired and terrified mind into action.

'Got any news?' The cook persisted and Ran ground his teeth against the rim of the cup. He had news, but nothing he wanted to share with these folks. All he wanted was a quiet meal and to sleep for a few hours out of the wind.

He wiped his mouth with his sleeve and shrugged, hedging his bets and hoping his acting skills were better than his disguise. 'Not much. Not been near many settlements lately. Chartered messages only this time of year.'

'Oh,' said the cook, turning to nod at the barkeep, who must surely be his brother. 'Chartered, eh?'

He wandered off at that and took a seat on a stool at the bar, the gentle murmur of conversation resuming as the keep poured the cook an ale. Ran's fingers reached for his tankard but the low rumble of conversation was again cut by a voice, this time from the opposite side of the room.

'You know how the duke's boy escaped? Tha' Black Prince? The one with the curse?' Silence killed the conversation and every eye turned to a man of middle years with greying hair poking through holes in his well-worn winter cap. He hesitated at the sudden attention and the muscles in his neck twitched as he swallowed his nerves. 'I heard tha' duke's offerin' a bounty.'

Ran bit the inside of his cheek to stop himself from choking on his bread. He took another long, casual draw on his drink and settled into his chair. A bounty? The duke was still hunting him and had a *bounty* on his head? Ronart must be desperate to bring him in if he was willing to offer cold coin for the transaction. For an odd little moment Ran wondered how much was on offer.

'You been in the strong stuff again, Thom?' The barkeep looked down his nose at the man.

'Ain't no drink talkin'. It's true!' Thom insisted and waved his tankard in a wide arc. 'I got word from my niece in Lisor. Duke's men are all over the place.'

Lisor was a few weeks to the north of Graupen, maybe longer if the storms kept the roads thick with snow. But if the weather slowed his father's men, then it was bound to slow him. That decided it then. No more towns or villages. He'd have to hole up somewhere and steal enough supplies to get him through. He'd go into the hills, find a cave—

'S'that what you heard, messenger?' The cook's rumbling voice stripped away Ran's thoughts and left him staring across his plate at a room full of filthy miners all waiting on his word.

'Dunno,' he replied automatically. He'd given the answer to his mother enough that it came as a natural response when he had no idea what to say. 'Like I said, haven't been that way.'

The cook gave him a dismissive wave and returned to his ale, muttering to his brother as the rest of the taproom's occupants decided he wasn't all that interesting and turned away.

The taproom cleared as the night ground on and the wind continued to moan along the street outside. Ran extracted himself from his seat and eased his aching legs and back between the tables to the bar. He slid three copper coins towards the man and nodded at the stairs. 'This enough for the drink, food, and a bed?'

'Aye.' He scooped the coins into his calloused hand quicker than a dealer collects his cards. 'End of the hall.'

The stairs creaked a little more than Ran thought safe as he climbed to the landing and limped past closed doors to the end of the hallway as instructed. He was a good rider, and a fit one, but he'd never ridden or walked in weather like this. The warmth of even the coarsest blankets called as he closed the door and dropped his saddlebags to the floor. What passed for a bed in these parts wasn't much, but the lumpy mattress across the room was better than a thin mat on a cave floor.

He used the flint from his bag to strike a flame amongst the logs laid in the hearth, and flopped down on the bed. His eyelids fell heavily across his vision, blurring the darkness and the faint light of the flames. He hadn't expected to see the ghost there, sitting in the corner with her knees to her chest, but she appeared and stared at the fire.

'The fuck happened to you?' he muttered, lying face down on the bed, his feet still in his boots and hanging over the end of the frame. 'Back in the forest?'

'The magic...' she replied, her eyes trained on the fire. She rocked, ever so slightly, back and forth where she sat. He'd never seen her this agitated before and Ranoth's blood ran cold.

'What?' Frowning, he pulled an elbow under him and sat up a little.

'What you did in the forest, with the rabbit... the magic... you held it in place...'

'To shoot it for food.' What could be so wrong about that?

She shook her head.

'That's what they did to me… Used the magic to hold me in place while they...' Her eyes met his, cold and angry, tears sparkling like diamonds falling through water. 'There is untold agony in staring at your death without the power to run for your life.'

'It was only a rabbit!'

The ghost sprang to her feet and rushed over the floorboards. He flipped onto his back and scrambled across the bed until he toppled off the other side, the ghost scything through the wooden frame with her translucent form as if it wasn't there at all.

She leaned over him and sneered, a red spark of rage flashing in the pupils of her eyes and a dark shadow further hollowing her already gaunt features. 'Aren't we all rabbits, powerless to stop the strong from doing us harm? Aren't we all hunted, like frightened rodents through the forest? It was only a rabbit, but it was no different from me, no different from *you!'*

She vanished. Her departure sucked the warmth from the small dusty room and left him frozen to his very core, his face stinging as though she'd slapped him. The fire guttered but held in the embers, glowing and returning slowly to life as breath filled his lungs and slowed his heart. Despite the icy air and his exhaled breath clouding like smoke, sweat dribbled down his neck and forehead, his fingernails biting the boards of the floor. His hands shook—a slight tremor that vibrated through his entire body until it built into a sob and escaped his lips with a falling tear.

The ghost was right. She was always right.

He was no different to the rabbit, no different to any game animal pursued through the woods, whether for sustenance or pleasure. He was as hunted as that rabbit, and he'd turned his power on it, despite his already superior strength. What might he do if his pursuer cornered him the way he'd cornered the rabbit? Was it only a matter of time before the walls closed in and the escape routes vanished, only a matter of time before his father's men tracked him to a dark corner and he too stared at his death without the power to run?

He curled his knees to his chest, lying on his side on the floor, and knew not even the softest blankets or feather down covers could ease the chill shivering in his bones or quiet the sobs choking in his throat. Ran wrapped his arms around his chest and held tight to his coat, burying his tears in the worn, oiled leather and ignoring the smell.

He was as alone as he'd ever been in his short life.

He'd lost everything, and he was nothing.

A hard kernel of loneliness and hate solidified deep in the well of his soul, near where the magic dwelled. It swirled and he slammed a door on it. He had no time or patience for it now—it was, after all, the reason he was running for his life.

Just like a rabbit...

CHAPTER TWENTY-THREE

Graupen, Southern Orthia

It wasn't the creak of the door that woke him.

Something else, something he couldn't quite trace, whispered along the fibres of the boards to his ear, pressed hard against the floor. Only his eyes responded to the call, easing open while the rest of him, from crown to sole, remained silent and as still as stone.

The door knob turned until the latch gave way, the aged metal protesting as a strong hand pressed it into service. The panel swung inward without admitting more light than the struggling fire already gave, no illumination to flood the bed or reveal his whereabouts. Whoever stood at the threshold valued stealth over sight.

Ran swallowed and licked his lips, flexing his fingers against the leather of his coat. His hand ached for a knife, but it lay sheathed in his saddlebag on the opposite side of the bed, between him and the intruder. A real messenger would have slept with a weapon in his hand, especially in an unknown village surrounded by drunk strangers. In lieu of a material weapon, his magic swirled to life and tingled up his cold fingers. It coiled and pooled, collecting itself and preparing.

A foot stepped through the doorway, a soft whisper of movement on the boards without a hint of a creak in the timber. Another pair followed, less carefully, clipping the leg of the room's solitary chair with its heel. A voice cursed and hissed, scolding the noise the chair made as it scraped over the floor. Another voice swore a whispered apology.

There was a thump as a fist hit a chest, and a whispered, 'Shhh!'

Silence.

The feet edged closer, shuffling across the room as carefully as two giants could manage until Ran saw them through the space under the thin bed frame, halting together in two pairs of enormous leather boots. Ran guessed the owners to be the barkeep and his greasy cook of a brother, the latter a little too drunk for the covert operation his sibling enlisted him in. His ankles swivelled and his feet stumbled, while the other pair stood solid and sure in a wide stance.

'You sure 'bout this?' The drunken cook asked.

'You heard him—chartered messages only. He'll have more than coppers on him for sure. 'Less you want to be an inn cook the rest of your life?'

'No, but—'

'Then quit your whining!' The cook must have agreed with his brother at that, because he didn't offer another word in protest. 'Ready,' the barkeep said. 'Now!'

The business end of a sword scored through the mattress and slammed to a halt beside Ran's nose. His arms arced up, hot magic catching the bed frame like wind in a sail and flipping it into the wall above the fire. The cook and the barkeep fell back howling, the splinters of the frame catching their faces and exposed arms. The drunker of the two landed on his backside and shattered the chair on the way down, his weapon clanking across the floor, out of reach.

Ran snatched his saddlebag and looped it over his shoulder as he bolted through the doorway into the hall. A roar echoed in his wake, the barkeep recovering and realising his quarry was escaping through the inn. He ordered his brother to his feet and the heavy running steps of the giants pounded after him, thundering in the cold silence and stirring other guests from their slumber.

'Get him!' The barkeep bellowed as a door swung open and a bleary-eyed miner from the taproom appeared, gawping at the commotion. The daze cleared from his eyes quickly as Ran sprinted towards him and a gnarled hand shot out to grasp at his coat. Ran shoved a hand at the man's chest, meaning to shunt him back into the room, but the magic flared and a blue burst of light hit the old fellow square in the sternum. He soared back, crashed straight through the opposite wall and wheeled down into the street below. Ran didn't stop to hear if his scream ended abruptly in the snow.

His ears rang with a pitched whistle that drove him on, the voices of his pursuers growing louder as he scrambled down the stairs into the empty taproom. He pushed forwards, tables and chairs skidding untouched from his path like water parting before a prow, collecting in a tangle at the far edges of the room. He spun at a crash at his back and saw the drunken cook lying face down at the foot of the stairs, and the keep glaring from the top.

Ran retreated until his back was against the door. He glanced again at the barkeep, skidding down the stairs and stepping over the groaning man at the bottom with a snarl of murderous intent. Ran raised his hands and urged the magic forward, imagining a wave rising under the toppled tables and carrying them into the path of his attacker. They hit the man with enough force to lay him out beside his brother.

Ran didn't linger. He shouldered the door and burst into the waiting blizzard. A crater and debris in the snow drew his eyes to the figure of the man he sent sailing down from upstairs, now a twisted, motionless form dusted in white.

Someone tackled Ran from behind and drove him into a drift on the road, sludge and mud only inches below the fresh powder. He kicked and swung his fists, fighting to turn around so he could face his attacker, but the man's weight pressed heavy against the minor strength of a fifteen-year-old boy. Desperate and scrambling, Ran latched on to the first thought to cross his mind and acted.

His magic pulsed again, this time directed at the road under his prone body. The force of the blast lifted him, with his attacker still clawing his back, into the air and across the street into the outer wall of the inn. The timber creaked and the stone cracked, both brittle and frozen and not built to withstand the weight slammed against them. The man on his back grunted and fell away, his arms limp and hands no longer grappling at Ran's neck and face.

Ran staggered and fell into the street, collecting his lost saddlebag before spinning to catch a glimpse of the man. The drunken cook lay at the edge of the snow crater, still, but breathing while his brother stood in the doorway with his slightly bent sword held ready. Ran began to back away and lifted his hands in warning.

'It's *you*, in'it? The cursed one—the Black Prince? You might run, boy,' the barkeep sneered and stepped into the howling blizzard, recognising Ran for who he was. 'You might run, but there 'int a place in the world you can hide.'

Running in snow was hard. Running in mud was harder. Running in snowy, icy, filthy mud was nearly impossible. Somehow Ran's legs kept lifting and pressing over and over in an action his brain thought was running, but he wasn't convinced he was going anywhere at all. The ground was somewhere beneath the drifts that at times extended upward to encase his ankles and shins. He pushed on, blinking sleet from his eyes.

Voices at his back, bellowing in the night and jeering for his blood, were all the motivation he needed to keep moving in the storm. What lay ahead was unseen and unknown, but it was a whole lot better than what he knew lay behind. Their torches grew close, the light enough to see by, and he baulked and ran harder. Memories of escaping Usmein leapt to his mind and he staggered forwards, scrambling for some sort of safety in the night. The better the light, the closer they were, and the closer they got, the nearer their swords came to his back.

Thom the miner made no mention of the duke's bounty being conditional. For all these men knew, a dead derramentis mage was as valuable as a live one, and a damn sight less dangerous to his captors when the body was relieved of its head. His chances of returning to Usmein alive were dwindling by the second. In fact, his chances of being alive to do anything were drastically shrinking at a rate he wasn't altogether happy with.

A shout echoed among the trees and he dove to the left, stumbling down a hill and seeking darkness. The ground beneath his feet vanished and he pitched forwards. Before he had time to scream his face hit a jagged slope and he tumbled in a shower of stones and ice into a black abyss. The hard ground punched through the layers of clothing to mark him with bruises and the toe of his boot caught a tree root, jerking his ankle in a painful twist.

A stand of bracken arrested his fall as the hill plateaued to flatter ground, the tangle of thick vines holding him still and pinning his coat among its thorns like pegs on a washing line. By the grace of the gods he hit the savage shrub with his back, sparing his face the onslaught of the barbs and branches, and affording him a view up the hill he'd just skidded down. High up through the branches of tall, snow-laden trees, the glow of torches moved, marking the search for him in the storm. The wind whipped the falling ice into his face, stinging his skin and eyes, burning his lips, but he saw enough.

The glow, a dancing light among the trees on the ridge above, receded until darkness reclaimed her dominion over the woods and left Ran dangling with his feet above the ground like a limp scarecrow. They might have diverted their search, thinking he'd run in the other direction, but their torches would tell them his tracks led over the ridge and down the hill. Their torches would lead them back to the road and their local knowledge would bring them to the base of the hill by another, more comfortable path than he took.

He couldn't afford to be here when they arrived, swords shining and teeth bared in glaring, greedy smiles. Ran yanked on his arm, heaving against the strength of the bracken until either the thorns or his coat gave in. One limb at a time, he pulled and ripped, glad with every rent stitch that it wasn't his skin against the bush's blades. He could get another coat in time, or repair this one if his saddlebag survived the escape, but wounds could spell death if they fouled.

A serious cluster of thorns were well entrenched in the area between his shoulder blades and despite all the pulling and wriggling he could manage, they weren't willing to release their catch.

'Fuck it,' he muttered.

He slipped his arm out of the coat's sleeve and left it hanging in the vines like a corpse. His other arm followed and he dropped to the ground, weary legs staggering under his weight. For a moment he waited and let the exhaustion ebb and flow across his skin and seep through his muscles, one hand grasping the hem of his coat for stability. If the magic hadn't left him weak and shaking, the race through the woods had done the job for certain. Again, his legs quivered and threatened to cave. Then they cracked like brittle timber hollowed by rot and ants.

Ranoth glanced down.

Knees shouldn't crack like timber.

The ground opened with an echoing crunch and Ran fell, his coat following him down like a torn flag.

CHAPTER TWENTY-FOUR

The Southern Reaches, Orthia

A few small stones peppered Ran's brow, enough to let him know he was alive.

He wasn't yet sure he liked the idea all that much.

Being alive hurt—a lot.

It hurt in his head and his shoulders, in his back and his hips. It hurt his legs and it probably hurt his feet, but he couldn't be sure if they were still attached. One hand hurt so badly it burned with all the fire of a summer sun, but the other was as absent as his feet; neither gone nor present, neither comfortable nor in the same agony as the rest of him.

More stones and dirt landed on his face, but he could not open his eyes to see the source. Perhaps the pursuers had found him and now set about burying him as they thought him dead.

No. They hunted him for a bounty, why bury him in the woods? Unless he was already in Usmein, dragged back in unconsciousness and tried in absence…

In the distance he thought he heard a throaty growl, like a bear, or a dog, or both mixed together. He couldn't be sure. He wanted to go back to sleep.

'The heck are you doing down there?' a voice murmured from above, a whisper meant for its owner and no one else.

A bigger, heavier stone thumped into his chest.

'You alive?' the voice called, louder this time.

His arms and legs refused to respond to the question, sprawled in a limp, defiant mess on a cold, very hard floor. He tried to move them, but they would not obey. The voice above didn't sound malicious or threatening. It sounded curious and perhaps a little worried. It made him think of trusting and obliging, and of things other than putrid, unwashed miners in a taproom. All his effort moved to his eyes. If they opened, the voice would know he lived.

The growl rumbled in the earth again. It sniffed, except the earth doesn't sniff.

With all the force he could muster, Ran peeled his eyes open a fraction, enough to let the blinding light of morning flood in and burn at the insides of his brain. He grimaced and slammed them shut.

'Are you...?' the voice asked again, an anxious waver in the words, uncertainty in the way the sentence hung in the air.

Ran prised his eyelids open again, thin slits to keep the light at bay but moving enough to answer the question whispered from above. Against the light and the black walls of the hole he languished in, she peered over the edge, flame-red hair glowing in the white of the morning. If only he had the strength to groan.

Laying in the darkness of that hole, Ran had believed his hand and both of his feet were truly lost. He imagined himself dismembered, with body parts strewn about his bleeding figure. Now a sense of warmth curled around his arms and legs, soaking into his bones and swarming along his veins, and he knew his limbs had survived intact. The burning in his fingers and toes, the sting in his skin, was beyond the burn of magic or the release of its power. It was harder than ice and as bone deep as the coldest chill, and held nothing of the comfort warmth should. It burned like a brand and there was nothing Ran could do to escape it.

His limbs shivered and his back ached but he didn't dare try to move. Only the gods knew what he'd done to himself in that fall. Enough soldiers fell from the city wall for him to know what such a height could do to a person's spine. If he survived with nothing more than a few broken bones, he'd be extremely fortunate.

A door nearby opened but did not close. The visitor did not plan to linger.

A figure sat beside him and pressed a cup to his lips, thick liquid lapping at his mouth. He tried to refuse it, but all he managed was a throaty gasp.

'Drink it or you'll be howling in an hour.' The same voice as before issued the order without a hint of room for compromise. Her accent spoke of the Orthian highlands, rolling her R's and extending her vowels. 'Won't have you keeping everyone awake 'til sparrows.'

Ran obliged and let the liquid pass, his tongue doing its best to ignore the bitter flavour barely masked by berries and mint. The effect of the tonic swirled into him instantly, taking with it the agony in his face and neck and dragging it down his throat. It collected pain as it travelled, scooping it from one place and the next, balling it into one throbbing ache at the small of his back, before soothing it to a dull pulse. It settled there, warm and numb, present but calm, and content to rest until the tonic wore off and it could return to the places where he bore his injuries.

He hoped she'd made the mixture good and strong.

He did not wish to feel the pain again.

He woke, shivering and weeping, the pillow at either side of his head sodden and cold in contrast to the heat of his fevered skin. His rescuer sat on the bed again, dabbing a cool cloth to his brow. She whispered quiet incantations and words of comfort, urging him to find peace in the pain when there surely was none.

Ran choked on a sob and opened his eyes a fraction.

She removed the cloth and buried it in a bowl of snow balanced in her lap. Her fingers were red raw from the ice, but she persisted and returned the cloth to pat his cheeks and neck. Her eyes met his and she smiled. 'Hoped to keep you sleeping.'

The cloth felt lukewarm as it settled on his brow and moisture dribbled through his hair to mix with sweat and tears.

'Sorry...' he croaked, his voice hoarse with lack of use.

'Aye, fever will do that. Close your eyes.'

It cost him. Pain lanced through his skull at the movement of his eyes, but it was well worth it for a glimpse of the flame-red curls pulled back from her face, wrapped in a cloth to keep them contained. She pulled the compress down from his forehead to cover his vision, leaving him no choice but to heed her command.

His fever broke in the night and Ran finally fell into a restful sleep.

The ghost girl appeared then, sitting in the corner, watching in silence. He said nothing to her, nor did she speak to him, her hard gaze wandering across him with an expression of flat disappointment. She vanished before he shut his eyes but he didn't have the energy to wonder why she'd gone.

Morning peeked through the curtains across the room, and his strained, injured muscles relaxed for the first time since he'd escaped Graupen. Ran felt safe in this room, as though the terrors of the outside world could not penetrate its walls. His head knew that to be a lie, but his heart held fast to the idea, unwilling to concede what his mind knew to be true. It would not be long before he had to move on. There were few places in Orthia he could call safe or secure, where his father's scouts might not happen upon him or where his face might not be recognised.

But where was he going? What was he doing except running headlong into the wilderness without a plan?

Dreams of the western coast and the Syod Archipelago had flashed through his fever, leaving him in little doubt that his future lay beyond the edges of Coraidin. The continent was vast, and he knew from his lessons that it was not the only land to be seen. There were strings of islands stretching away to continents far larger, and with many more places to hide.

All he needed to do was survive long enough to get there.

Such places were a haven for people fleeing old lives, looking to make a fresh start where no one asked questions or cared where you were from. Many would be willing to accept a young man with magic in his blood and the skills to read and write and fight.

Yet, as appealing as disappearing into obscurity beyond the borders of Coraidin seemed, setting such a course meant leaving his entire life behind. What of his place in his father's house—his rightful place, as the duke's son and heir? Did that not warrant some response on his part? Anguish twisted in his belly, and he knew a clean break for the coast wouldn't suffice. He wasn't ready to throw it all away just yet.

Surely there was a cure for this curse. Surely there was a way to reverse the magic, or suppress it. He knew his father and the Orthian people would never accept a magic-weaver as their future ruler, and this reality left him with a single choice—banish his magic, or accept a life on the fringes of the world. Perhaps the answer lay in Isord, in his grandfather's court. Surely his mother's family would help—

The door opened to his right and a young woman entered with a tray. A bowl of soup steamed beside a pile of fresh bandages, the smell alone setting his mouth to watering.

'Well, you look better today.' She smiled briefly and set the tray on a nearby table. Ran checked himself as she approached, realising she was at least his age, if not a few years his senior. Her hazel eyes scrutinised him in his sickbed with the same cool professionalism he saw in the palace infirmary and from his childhood nurse. Her hands were not shy of work, fine scars and short nails attesting to hardship.

She went to the end of the bed and drew back the covers. A cool puff of air curled up Ran's legs and he realised with a start that he was arse-naked under the sheets and blankets. He recoiled as much as his weakened body would allow, but his nurse raised a brow and smirked.

'Today isn't the first time, sir. Seen one, you've seen them all.'

Ran looked away as she removed a bedpan and returned to examine his feet and ankles, calves and knees. She probed a place in his upper thigh and he jerked away from the sharp pain that lanced through his muscle like a startled cat.

'That's healing nicely,' she observed, then returned the covers to their rightful place and sat beside him. She took his hands, one at a time, turning them in the light and manipulating his fingers and wrists. 'You're lucky I found you when I did, and that you had decent gear. This one was frozen stiff and I thought it might have to go.'

She lifted his right hand so he could see the peeling skin on his fingers and the back of his hand.

'Snow-burn. It will heal but you need to keep it warm and cream it often. At first, I thought you managed to avoid breaking anything...' Her eyes appraised him again, this time as if she expected him to admit a secret. 'I thought it strange until I saw your ankle.'

The woman went to the end of the bed again and pulled the cover back from his foot, gently lifting it to her shoulder. She rested his heel under her collarbone and held the weight there, pointing to the bulging bone on the inner side of the joint.

'This, was over here,' her finger moved to point at the front of his shin and Ran felt his eyes widen in surprise. 'These toes were here,' she pointed to the empty air past her shoulder. 'And the whole thing was set rock hard.'

Ranoth swallowed and shrugged.

She raised another sceptical brow and laid his leg back on the bed, then crossed her arms and cocked her hip.

'No way you ran through the woods on a foot that badly deformed, so it wasn't an old injury. I saw your tracks and you had two normal feet before you fell down that shaft. You near snapped that foot off when you fell, and in the time it took for me to find you and drag you here, it set itself, albeit badly.' She shrugged and sat down, folding her hands in her lap. Ran tried to look at something else, but her eyes were all he could see. 'I thought maybe it was frozen, so I corrected it. Found out the hard way that it weren't frozen. I had to break your ankle to get it back in place.'

His mouth ran dry and his heart thumped hard. What was she saying? His ankle had broken then mysteriously healed itself?

'I thought it would take weeks to heal again. It took *days*.' Her gaze bore down on him. 'You've been here a fortnight. I've treated men in the mine, crushed under loads or wheels, so I know how long it's meant to take. No one heals a broken bone in less than two months, let alone a couple of days.'

Ah, shit...

The magic. It was the only explanation, the only force strong enough to change him so rapidly and without his control or command.

When he offered no answers, she stood and brought the soup. She fed it to him in silence, his hands too weak and aching to hold the bowl or spoon. The broth was simple and probably the blandest thing he'd eaten in his life, but in that moment, it was divine and warm and all the things he needed. When the last drops were finished, she set about changing the bandages on his arms and legs, a dressing above his left eye, and situating a clean bedpan, all without a word.

By the time she piled the soiled bandages on the tray and stood at the end of the bed preparing to leave, Ran thought he might have the strength to utter a word or two of his own. He opened his mouth, but she beat him to it.

'Look, I don't know who you are, or what you were doing down that old vent shaft, but I know injuries and I know wounds. What I saw when I looked down that hole was a man nearer to death than any I've seen.' She eyed him carefully. 'You should be dead, yet here you are. I could claim it as my handiwork, but that'd be a lie. I helped break the fever, but something else healed you.'

Ran froze.

Beyond the closed door and the walls of the room, footsteps and the murmur of voices lingered then moved on. The young woman did not turn to acknowledge the sounds, instead kept her gaze firmly on her patient and his reaction. It was as though she saw right past his skin and bone to his soul and its secrets.

'They won't come in unless asked by me. They have other chores to see to and hardly have time to nurse an injured vagrant back to health.' She took a step closer, a fire burning in her hazel eyes and lines of worry in her brow. 'I know *what* you are, sir. Believe me when I say you are safe in this room, in my care, but know your secrets have shown themselves and you're lucky it was only I who saw them.'

She went to the door and a croak escaped Ran's throat. She turned, her hand on the latch.

'Name?' he asked, squeezing the word out, his hand flexing with the effort.

'Sasha.' She inclined her head and left, Ran's ears ringing with the pounding of his heart and the sound of that one word.

Chapter Twenty-five

The Southern Reaches, Orthia

Sasha wandered in and out of Ran's room as days passed, requiring him to move around and forcing him to work his weary legs more than he liked. He slept hard, the exercise taxing but rewarding. Every day he saw improvements in his injuries, which gave him hope. He'd feared he might never be able to gain full use of some of his limbs. His foot and ankle gradually took more weight, his badly lacerated thigh hardly smarting at all as he walked with Sasha's help from his bed to the window and back. By the fifth day of exercising, he was able to make several circles around the room, and refused to lie in the bed unless to sleep after dark.

If Sasha thought he progressed well, she kept it to herself. Ran did see her smile as he circled the room while she stacked clean clothes and linens in a chest by the wall. He saw the gleam of pride in her eyes and the smallest crease in her cheeks when she thought he wasn't looking, but try as he might to break through her icy exterior, she kept herself aloof. The coolness of her manner threw him, seemingly at odds with her otherwise caring nature.

She came to soothe him back to sleep when nightmares stalked his dreams. He dreamed often of his father, the soldiers and the men from the tavern hunting him through the trackless woods in his mind. She sat by his side, smoothed the creases from his brow, and sang songs like those his mother had when he was unwell. The duchess never let another care for her children when they fell ill; her hands were always ready to treat a cold or fever.

All of this, knowing how his mother was when her children were poorly and watching Sasha in the moments when he needed her most, confirmed to Ranoth that the flame-haired young woman was no icy matron. She was hiding herself from him, holding back, unwilling to let him know her. He asked questions but her answers, if they came at all, were blunt and singular. She left very little room for him to investigate or enquire.

'You know,' he ventured, stretching his thigh tentatively and rubbing the muscle to warm it before walking the room again. 'I've been here nearly three weeks and I still know nothing about you.'

Sasha's hands didn't stop folding the clean clothes, nor did her eyes turn in his direction. 'Best for everyone it stays that way.'

'Everyone?' He continued to massage the muscle but his exercise was forgotten. 'Who else is here? I've only ever seen you and heard footsteps and muffled voices.'

'Best you don't know of them and they don't know of you.' She placed a shirt on the pile and reached for another. Ran moved as fast as his limp would carry him and caught her wrist.

Sasha froze and met his eyes with a glare. He expected to see fear, but her anger shocked him and he dropped her hand as quickly as he'd taken it.

'I don't understand, Sasha.'

'I told you when you woke up; I know what you are.' She jerked her head towards the door. 'How long before they find out?'

Her honesty stunned him and the truth of her words stung like salt in a wound. His broken ankle, healed too quickly, and the unnaturally fast recovery of his less severe injuries, had marked him out and revealed his curse.

Sasha dropped the shirt she was folding and put her hand on her hip with a sigh. 'I don't think you're dangerous, but it's better if you don't know anything more about me or the others in this house than you need to. And the same goes for us. Why do you think I haven't asked your name?'

She was right, of course. If someone came looking for him, it would be her name as well as his on the executioner's list after a short trial for treason and assisting a fugitive. Did she know about the bounty the duke had put on his head?

'I'll leave as soon as I'm able, I swear.' He pressed his fist to his chest and gave her a small bow.

'But not a minute before,' she countered. 'I've not spent three weeks dragging you back from death to watch you run off into the woods and get yourself killed.'

Ran inclined his head again and began his ritual of pacing the room in silence while Sasha returned to her folding and stacking. The tension between them slipped from the atmosphere as though their conversation had cleared the worries clouding both their heads. Ran was as happy not to tell Sasha his name as he was not to know anything more about the other occupants of the house. He didn't want to know where they were or what the nearest settlement was, though he suspected Graupen was the closest. He'd not run far enough to escape its rural borders.

Outside the room, a door slammed and Ran started. His hand fell by instinct to the door latch on his left, and he stopped and listened. Sasha appeared at his side in seconds, her ear pressed against the timber panel and her finger held up to order him to silence.

'Where is she?' A deep voice boomed, loud enough this time to make the words clear. Sasha stiffened at the sound and, for a moment, he thought he saw a glimmer of fear in her eyes.

Another voice answered the man's demand, too soft to discern.

'I don't care what she said, she's not hiding anymore!' the man bellowed. Heavy steps thundered closer. Sasha shoved Ran aside and he staggered into the adjacent wall. She snapped the latch and opened the door, darting into a hallway. The footsteps stopped abruptly, the door creaking to a stop, slightly ajar.

Ran could see neither the man nor Sasha, the wall between them blocking his view, but he knew he stood a mere foot from the person angrily making demands. Again, his weapons were well out of reach, locked in a cupboard across the room to which Sasha held the key. If things went sour, he had only his hands and a pair of unsteady legs to defend himself with.

'Afternoon, Father.'

'Time you let me see your guest, Sash.' The man's voice softened. It sounded almost pleading, as if he'd tried for an age to get past his daughter's guard to see who she was keeping in the room.

'I'm sorry, I can't. He's too ill.' Her flat response drew a growl from her father's throat.

'I've been to town. I spoke to the inn-keeper...' He let the words hang, as if they should be enough to convince her that something was amiss.

'And?' Sasha prompted, obviously unimpressed.

'There's a bounty on the prince's head, for using magic. He was in town and near ripped the inn apart, Sasha. They said he ran and vanished in the woods.' The man paused and cleared his throat. 'I won't have a criminal under my roof.'

'You've no evidence to say he's the prince.' Sasha dismissed her father's claims out of hand and Ran grimaced. She must have some power in this house if she'd kept him hidden from her parents for three weeks.

'It's no coincidence,' the older man growled.

'He is protected in my care, Father. You know the healer's law—'

'You might work for me down that bloody mine as a healer, but while you're under my roof, Sasha Hale, you're still my daughter!' he shouted now, his fist hitting the wall where Ran leaned close to listen.

'You have *no* right to accuse an injured man of crimes you have no evidence he committed!' Sasha countered. 'Besides, he is not nearly well enough to face any sort of interrogation, or to travel.'

'No? Tomorrow he's coming to town with me and we'll see what they have to say. If he has the same face as the man who destroyed the inn, then he'll be dealt with. Let him plead his case to the judge.' Sasha's father stormed away, leaving the hallway silent and Ran sweating with panic against the wall.

They know! Shit. They know. They'll have sent word to Usmein, or the nearest garrison and soldiers will be on their way...

Sasha appeared in the doorway, frowning and chewing her bottom lip. Her hand went to the latch but paused, her gaze settling on Ran standing in the corner, shivering.

'In bed,' she said quietly and shut the door without further explanation.

Suddenly very cold and very afraid, Ran obeyed, but he would not sleep. He needed to get out of here. Had Sasha's irate father mentioned his daughter's patient to the folk in the village? Had the coincidence dawned on him in the solitude of his mind, or had the innkeeper helped him piece the story together? If Sasha's father knew who he was, likely everyone in town knew. If he stayed, he was as good as dead.

'Wake up!' Sasha hissed in Ran's ear.

He jolted up and glanced around, stunned. He'd fallen asleep after all, his body ignoring his mind's pleas to stay alert and concoct a plan of escape. Instead, he'd slumbered and let precious hours slip by.

'Shit!' He sat up, her hands still pulling insistently at his shoulders. 'What time is it?'

'Late enough without being too early,' she replied and scooped his legs out of the bed to settle his feet on the floor. 'Put this on.'

She shoved a thick coat at his chest and began forcing his feet into a pair of boots that were only just big enough. His own were long gone, sliced off by Sasha when she tended to his broken ankle and frozen toes.

'Up, up, up, let's go!' She heaved him to his feet and went to the window.

'It's locked. I tried it,' Ran muttered, fighting to get his hands into the gloves Sasha threw at him.

She raised a brow at him and waggled a key between her fingers. 'Locks have keys.' True to her word, the lock gave in to the press of the key and the window eased open to the cold of the snowy night. 'The snowfall should be heavy enough to cover our tracks—'

'*Our* tracks?' Ran caught her elbow as she moved to step onto the chest below the window, snow swirling through the open space and collecting on the furniture. 'You're not coming.'

'Are you the duke's son, the prince of Orthia? The one they call the Black Prince?' Sasha's eyes flashed in the light of the fire that was trying its best to warm the room. 'I know you have magic and frankly, you don't have the make of a boy raised behind a plough and draught horse, or down in the tunnels. You aren't from these parts. Are you the man my father thinks you are?'

Hot fear balled in Ran's throat. It could be a trap. She could drag a confession from his lips before crawling out the window to hand him over to his father's soldiers, or worse, the locals. Her arm twisted in his grasp until her hand curled around his.

'You go out there alone, you'll die; you stay here, you'll die. I told you, I didn't spend three weeks saving you from the hands of the Dark Rider just to send you off to die somewhere else.' She handed him his worn saddlebag and pulled a rucksack of her own onto her shoulders. 'You go, I go.'

Sasha climbed through the window and dropped silently into the drift below the ledge. She turned and offered her hands to help him through, but Ran hesitated. His fear was real and paralysing. The last time he stole into a blustery, snowy night, he'd come as close to dying as he thought a live man could and still survive.

'You stay, you die…' she repeated, in case he hadn't heard or understood the first time.

'What if we get caught?' He gave his fear a voice and it cut through the night. Sasha simply shook her head. 'We don't get caught, Prince Ranoth.'

The snow stung and the cold bored into his joints. He felt as though he hurried into the night with a hundred millstones hanging from his shoulders, the weight dragging him down into the banks of white. His ankle burned and the muscles of his legs screamed for rest. He was breathless within minutes and staggered along behind Sasha, doing his best to keep up while his body did everything it could to stop him.

Sasha tied a rope between them and walked at his side or in front, seeking the easiest track or the most sheltered pathway along the hills and valleys. Somewhere before dawn, in the darkest part of the night, Ran thought it would be better to cut the rope with the knife in his bag and just give in to the snow's embrace. If it wanted him that badly, it could have him.

Sasha wouldn't have any of that, though. She dragged him on at a pace fast enough to make progress, but not so quickly that he was exhausted entirely. She walked away from her parents' home like she'd dreamed of nothing but the day she could finally put her back to it. Confidence and strength pulsed from her like heat from a fire, unaltered by the driving snow and biting wind, determined to get her patient away from the house, her father, and the threat of the locals.

Had he not drawn strength from his little pool of magic in the darkest hours, Ran knew he'd have died among the trees and drifts of powdered snow, and not even Sasha's skilled hands could have saved him. But even that power source was finite. Eventually, when he reached down for extra fuel to warm his worn muscles and frozen feet, he found nothing but a scoured, empty pit. The reality of his situation hit him like a boulder to the chest and he stumbled, fatigue collapsing his resolve and gutting the single spark of resilience he'd carried from the farmhouse.

He hit the snow and his companion instantly hauled him back to his feet, taking his full weight on her shoulders. How she managed it he couldn't imagine; her frame was so slight under the layers of fur and wool he thought she'd snap under the pressure if he put an ounce more weight on her. But she pressed on, staggering through drifts and pushing him up rocky inclines, never complaining.

'Not much further,' she grunted, crawling up an embankment and reaching to pull him up through the falling white. Though it came down softly, it still left his face wet and stinging as though whipped.

As dawn light broke in the eastern sky at their backs, they stumbled into a cave in the high face of a mountain, not unlike those where he'd taken refuge after his escape. Ran's eyes searched the dark corners and crevices, expecting to see his ghost there, but she remained hidden in the shadows of his mind. Sasha dropped him on the floor and immediately stripped off her bag and brushed the snow from both their coats. She produced two tightly rolled blankets and tossed one at Ran before wrapping the other about her shoulders and sitting heavily on the ground beside him.

The wind couldn't reach its claws to where they sat in the cave, curled against each other and the rough wall. It wasn't warm, but it was better than the alternative. The sheer relief of not fighting the weather for every step was glorious, if strange. Ran felt weightless without the force of the wind and snow jarring against his every move. His body practically floated in the calm of the cave, the silence only broken by the whispered sound of gentle breath.

'Why are you helping me?' he asked, unsure if Sasha was awake but too sore and weary to turn his head to check.

'Innocent people don't deserve to die.'

'You don't know I'm innocent.'

She looked up at him, fatigue drawing her eyes into deep shadows, her lips burnt and raw, bright as blood against pale skin. 'No, perhaps not... You've got the look of someone who's seen death. But what they're accusing you of—the magic—it's not a burden you chose. Magic doesn't give you a say when it comes, it doesn't ask your permission.'

'You seem to know a lot about it,' he mused.

Most Orthians, if asked, would spit in the dirt and call it a curse, and a filthy Woaden curse at that. Had he found the only person east of the Morgen Ranges who didn't think so?

When she failed to reply, he glanced down. Her eyes were closed and her cheek pressed against his shoulder, her chest rising and falling with slumbering breath, a steady rhythm that drew him into a trance. His eyelids drooped and closed, and not even a glimpse of the ghost in the corner of the cave could keep him awake a moment longer.

Usmein, Orthia

Every year since her marriage, Duchess Merideth found comfort in the winter season, knowing her family was whole and safe from the threat of the Woaden. It was a time when soldiers returned from the front to become husbands, sons and daughters once more. Homes were full and the towns and cities of the duchy calmed. This year, the sense of peace did not arrive with the first fall of snow.

This year, there was nothing but pain.

Her home, as vast and opulent as it was, felt empty and cold—a corpse where once a living, breathing thing existed. There was no laughter in the halls, nor any colour or light. To her eyes, the world, and everything in it, was dead.

Her son, her only living son, was gone.

He'd been gone for weeks, or perhaps a month or more; she ceased counting when the days became too numerous for her heart to hold. She knew the longer Ranoth remained away, the less likely it was she would ever see him again. She knew as days became weeks, the weather would only get worse—colder and harder—until it finally froze the duchy solid and locked the roads and passes in ice. She also knew if her son lingered in the wilds of the world, the cold would take his life before her husband's soldiers found his trail.

She closed her eyes to hold in her tears, surprised there were any left to shed. No one saw her cry; she made sure of that. She kept her pain locked inside until darkness filled her room and sleep blocked the ears of her attendants. Only then did she allow herself time to sob and mourn; although there was no body to weep over, her boy was all but dead.

If they found him, they would kill him. If he escaped, he was as likely to die of exposure or in the gnashing teeth of something foul. And if he lived, by the grace of the White Woman, he couldn't ever return.

'Meri?'

'Ronart,' she replied and opened her eyes to the view from her window. Snow tumbled from the sky and whipped against the glass. She hadn't heard him enter her chambers, nor cross the floor of the receiving room. He stood a few feet behind her shoulder, wise enough not to approach within striking distance.

'No news today,' Duke Ronart murmured. 'I am sorry.'

Merideth sighed. 'Husband, you are many things. *Sorry* is not one of them.'

'What would you have me do?' he asked, frustration tightening his throat around the words. She turned to see his hands open in pleading supplication, but there was a shadow of anger in his eyes. He still didn't understand.

'Call off your dogs. Bring my son home. Love him, despite his faults.' She thought her demands simple enough. They had not changed since the day they dragged Ranoth into the dungeons, and had continued after they found he had escaped. 'These are things a father should do.'

Ronart's hands lowered to his sides and his shoulders sagged. If he thought her answer would change, that her mind and heart's desires would alter, he did not know her at all.

'I can't,' he finally replied.

Merideth shook her head. 'You can, you just won't.'

He left *when* he realised she had no more words to share. The ensuing silence was only broken by a knock at the door an hour later.

'The watcher has arrived, ma'am,' her butler announced from the threshold.

'Send him in.' She waited for the man to enter and clear his throat, and turned with her shaking hands folded as the butler closed the door. 'Brit Doon, is it?'

'Aye, ma'am,' he replied with a bow, a woollen hat clasped in his hands.

'I won't dally with formalities. There are things you must know. You are relieved of your commission to my husband's army and you have been transferred legally and entirely into my personal employment. Do you understand? You are no longer in the command of the duke or any of his marshals. You answer to me alone.'

His face drained of all colour and his eyes went wide. 'Yes, ma'am.'

'Do you have a family?'

'Aye.'

'They will be cared for.'

A muscle in his neck jumped but he nodded. 'Aye.'

Merideth stepped forwards but not so close as to startle the man. He was already wringing his hat to death between his hands. 'You returned my son from the Territory, is that correct?'

He only managed a nod.

'And you were there, at the house, when it happened?' She watched his head twitch and took it as an affirmative reply. 'I don't need to know what happened. Frankly, I don't care to. But I do need to know that you can be trusted. I need to know that you can take orders. So far, I see a watcher who did his best in a bad situation and followed his master's command, and you did not turn on my son when he was most in need. You helped him and returned him to me. Are you still that man?'

'Aye, ma'am.' He tried to clear the squeak of fear from his throat but failed.

'I need you to find my son.'

For a long while, Brit said nothing. He only stared and she wondered if he was searching for a way to refuse. 'The duke has soldiers—'

'Yes, the duke has men crawling all over Orthia looking for Ran, but my son is more resourceful than he is given credit for. My husband has sent infantry—common soldiers from the ranks. You, on the other hand, know my son. And you are a watcher. Watchers have good eyes, yes? You will track him and you will find him.' Merideth poured herself a cup of sweet tea from a nearby service and glanced at Brit, his eyes trained on the window. 'I would go myself, but I would not risk my daughters by leaving them alone in this city, not while folk bay for their brother's blood. You are the only option I have.'

He nodded. 'And if I find him?'

'When you find him...' At this she paused and sighed, hardly believing the words were to pass her lips. 'Take him as far from here as any map allows.'

Their eyes met and she saw recognition in the watcher's face. He knew exactly what she was ordering him to do and what it meant if either of them were caught.

'Do you understand, Watcher Doon?'

'Aye, ma'am.'

Chapter Twenty-six

While there was sense in her father's order to remain within Hummel's walls, Lidan doubted he quite comprehended the sheer boredom of endless days and nights of confinement. Used to running through the valley at the foot of the Caine no matter the season, she quickly grew restless as her infected wounds healed and her strength returned. There were only so many things a girl could do about the hall and with all but a select few confined on the daari's order, tasks were done faster than usual. At least she had her training to fill the hours.

Erlon made no apologies for restricting the clan as the dry season drained the colour from the range; refusing to allow them to gather or hunt food and insisting they subsist on the yields of their small plots and the livestock kept within the walls. The rangers and gatemen scanned the trees and valley from the top of the wall, weapons ready, wary of the shadows and what might linger in them. They all heard Loge's recollections and saw the body of the creature they called the ngaru, dragged back through the common and burned beyond the gates. They all knew what it had done and that there could be more lurking in the bush across the valley.

The clan's people watched the pyre of tinder-dry logs, marvelling at the blue flames reaching into the sky as the corpse slowly reduced to bone and ash. They muttered and wondered about what might happen next. Would more come, or was this a lone beast, hunting on the range? Everyone whispered, except the dana. She kept her distance and stared at the creature with wide, wary eyes. Lidan watched her mother from the shadows and corners, stayed out of sight and out of the way, but she watched all the same. She saw her mother biting her perfect nails and nervously picking at the skin on her hands.

The dana slipped away after the pyre burned to the ground and the tine-women came to sluice buckets of water over the ashes and dampen the few remaining embers. Her mother hurried to the Crone's hut and vanished behind the walls where Lidan did not dare follow and remained there for days.

When she did return, Lidan realised her mother had changed. There was an air about her, an anxious aura that caused her to startle at the smallest sounds, and she spent long spans of time staring into the middle ground where nothing existed but her thoughts. Shockingly, at the sight of the ngaru's corpse, her mother had transformed into something Lidan had never seen before. Her mother was terrified.

For the most part, Lidan kept clear of her parents in an effort to avoid crossing paths with their fighting. She couldn't stand the tension and anger that oozed from them both, whether or not the other was near. She knew her mother was furious at the daari for allowing her to train to fight, apoplectic that he willingly put his daughter in what she saw as utterly unnecessary danger. But her mother was at war with herself. In one moment, Sellan was content that Lidan seemed on a path to securing the succession, regardless of the sex of Farah's unborn child; but in the next, she was consumed with anxiety and riddled with concern that Lidan's training would get her killed.

The daari seemed equally riled that his wife had tried to turn his eldest daughter against him. Lidan felt her father's eyes on her back as she trained or took riding lessons from Siman in the common. He smiled to cover his cool scrutiny, but she felt it like the heat of the sun burning against her skin. He was watching and waiting, though she had no idea what for.

More than once her mother scowled at her as she wandered in, slicked with sweat and streaked with dirt. Sellan clicked her tongue at the bruises on Lidan's forearms and hands, and made barbed, underhanded comments about the grazes on her knuckles. She hissed a hundred questions at Lidan when she limped in one afternoon after slipping from her stirrups and twisting her ankle. Otherwise, her mother kept to herself, and the silence was almost as bad as the screaming Lidan was accustomed to. In some sick way, she wished her mother would go back to being her old, unpredictable self. Instead, she was pale, jittery, sullen and paranoid, always glancing over her shoulder and never entirely settled.

The training also kept Lidan away from the ever-present sound of Farah vomiting her meals into a pail by her bed. Despite herself, the sight of her half-mother's growing belly made Lidan's heart thump and her mouth run dry. In a few more months, as the dry season waned and the days grew longer, that belly would birth a baby and from that day on, Lidan's whole world could change. It might collapse like a house made of sand, her position and value in the family diminished as one tiny human took its first breath, unaware of the damage he did with that one small act. Or the child could be a girl, another in a long line of daughters and no threat to Lidan or her sisters. It turned her stomach that she saw danger growing in her half-mother's womb.

The impending arrival and the abundance of spare time gave Lidan plenty to mull over, her mind flicking through possibilities and decisions. She tried to play them out to their ends, attempting to see the future of each path before she was forced to take one above another. None of them struck her as better than the rest, all of them with pitfalls and dangers, unpleasant and fraught to the last with choices she wished she didn't have to make. Among them lingered her mother's awful suggestion, and the shadow it cast followed her day and night.

The day was overcast and cold beyond the eaves of the hall, the north wind howling down from the tablelands with sharp teeth of ice to gnaw at any exposed skin it might find. Days like this found the common empty and the entries to homes barred tightly against the weather. The dry season was coming to an end with all the fury it could muster and Lidan ached to hear the far-off roar of an approaching summer storm and smell the promise of rain. The time between the depth of the dry season and the height of the sweltering, humid summer was the most glorious and no one in the village prayed harder than Lidan for the cold to crawl back to the mountains.

The training yard between the stables and the ranger's barracks echoed with the satisfying crack and clack of staves meeting with force, the whisper of leather boots on hard packed soil and the laboured breath of fighters. Healed of his wounds and elevated to the status of ranger, it had been several weeks since Loge volunteered to oversee Lidan's training when all the other rangers and gatemen stared open mouthed at Siman's request.

None of them had the slightest idea how to train a girl of twelve, almost thirteen, in the way of the blades. Some of them were skilled close quarter fighters, but preferred axes or the clubs they hung from their saddles. Rangers and gatemen were more accustomed to hunting and shooting arrows at their prey, be it man or beast, not slicing it into submission. Knives were used to cut meat or rope, not to battle an enemy.

Lidan suspected her mother of sowing seeds of doubt among the rangers by way of their wives, muttering in their ears about the danger of training a girl who stood so far above their station. What if they hurt her? She was the heir after all...

Loge either hadn't heard the dana's whispered threats or didn't care for them. He knew well how to wield the shorter knives some rangers carried and offered to train Lidan once he had recovered. She quietly suspected he did it to distract himself and fill his days with anything but cleaning tack or tending horses.

His encounter with the ngaru haunted his eyes in the moments they rested between bouts, though it had left the miller's son with an unparalleled knowledge of how the creature manipulated its weapons. Of the other rangers who survived the ill-fated hunts, Lidan's father included, none of them recalled the form of the creature that attacked them or the weapons it used. They had vague, blurred memories of a shadow in the bush and its screams, the heat of their wounds and the terror they'd felt, but none of them had evaded or fought one for as long as Loge. This was something he and Lidan shared, a place of darkness they'd both experienced and didn't ever wish to return to.

Loge's stave slapped the still-raw skin below her scar. Lidan cried out and scurried to the side as pain radiated up her arm to her shoulder.

He pointed to his eyes. 'You weren't looking.'

She reset her stance and pushed the pain down to the soles of her feet, willing her energy to give her strength and speed. Her eyes focused on Loge and his staves, while hers rose to a ready position. He lunged and struck high and low, forcing Lidan to deflect the blows and spin away from his weight. Taller and broader than his student, Loge's first lesson was in balance.

'Good!' he said and moved to a nearby awning. His light brown skin shone with sweat and he ran a hand over his brow and through the waves of his thick black hair. Lidan snatched at the chance for a drink and gulped water from a bladder. 'Your opponent will be bigger and stronger than you until—well, forever. Your size gives you the advantage of speed. You're light and you need to move where they can't. Stay inside their circle.' He took the bladder Lidan offered and drained it. 'Big guys can't move like that.'

'Shouldn't I stay out of their reach?' Lidan asked. She sat on a bench under the awning, her body shivering with pounding blood and adrenaline.

'Look.' He crouched in front of her and held his arm straight towards her shoulder. He took her arm and straightened it beside his, her fingers pointed at his shoulder. His fingertips touched just at her collarbone, while her outstretched arm only reached just past his elbow. 'Their circle will be this wide, or bigger again. Yours is much smaller, even if you grow to be as tall as your da. Now, add the length of a club or an axe to my arm and my range is even longer. If you try and stay out of my reach I'll smack you in the head before you get a hit in. If you get in close with those knives, you'll have me butchered like a pig for the spit in no time. I can't get any sort of force in my hits this close.'

He demonstrated by pulling her to her feet and flailing his arms around her head until she burst out laughing and pushed him away. Loge dropped down on the bench and rubbed at an ache in his knee. 'Why do you want to fight, anyway? Word is your mam isn't too impressed.'

Lidan shrugged and leaned against the awning post, letting the wind wick away her sweat and cool her head and body. 'I wanted to keep the ngaru's knives, so Rick and Da decided I needed to learn how to use them. I don't want to be stuck behind these walls when summer comes. I want to ride and see the range like the other girls.'

'There aren't many girls who become rangers.' It was his turn to shrug. 'Plenty apprentice but leave when they're matched. Nothing to say you can't, but you're the First Daughter...'

Lidan knew what that meant all too well. Tolak girls trained to be rangers, they knew how to ride and shoot, forage and hunt; but it was a courtesy. It was something to keep them occupied and make them more appealing to husbands when they were old enough to match.

Lidan shook her head. 'I'm not allowed to match until I'm eighteen. I'll be damned if I'm going to spend the next six years sewing and waiting for a husband.'

She kept the rest of her plans tucked securely away behind her lips. Loge didn't need to know that she planned to have her father declare her his heir, even if Farah had a boy. She didn't want to let that secret loose on the world just yet. For now, the knives were reason enough to train, and that's all Loge needed to know.

'Fair enough.' Loge nodded and threw her coat from the back of the bench seat. 'Put that on and do your stretches. Don't want sore limbs for tomorrow.'

She shoved one arm through a sleeve and a whistle from the wall cut the air. Loge's eyes met hers and they paused, listening and waiting for the following warning. What had the gatemen seen?

'Rider!' a man bellowed and the village sprang to life beyond the confines of the training yard.

CHAPTER TWENTY-SEVEN

Hummel, Tolak Range, the South Lands

Lidan frowned. 'A rider?'

'No riders have gone out in a week or more...' Loge started running as rangers emerged from their barracks and hurried through the yard's gate to see what the call was about. Lidan ran through the gathering crowd as the gates groaned open and a horse staggered through. The rider straightened, blinking his eyes.

'Catch him!' someone cried as he slipped from the saddle and pitched towards the ground. Spinning around, Lidan shoved her way to the back of the crowd and took the steps to the hall two at a time. She reached the door as her father burst through from the other side, the scrape of benches across the floor echoing at his back as his advisors stood at the interruption.

'Da!' Lidan panted. 'A rider!'

'What in the—?' He scooped Lidan from his path with a heavily muscled arm and put her behind the wall of his back. 'Who is he?' he called down to the men helping the rider approach the steps.

'By his symbol, he's Namjin.' Jac scaled the steps and held out a roll of tightly bound leather. 'He's carry'n a message.'

The daari took the roll and flipped it over to find the markings of the clan who sent it. From her vantage at his elbow, Lidan saw the faint impression of two mountains and the sun, enclosed in a circle—the mark of the Namjin clan who commanded the range to the northwest. They thought themselves descended from Jin; a giant they said made the world. Erlon said the story made them arrogant and overly assured of their own superiority. They were in a constant state of conflict with the Tolak and a message from them was a rare and important thing indeed.

'Get him inside and set a patrol in the valley.'

Jac nodded and stepped away as the messenger limped up the stairs behind him. A pair of men helped the rider through the hall door and Lidan followed behind them, half the clan and their children filing in after them to see the newcomer. She pushed her way to the front, using the space left in her father's wake, and stopped at the edge of the crowd beside the fire pit. Warm soup and a blanket appeared before the messenger, and a stool for him to sit on and rest his legs. Grent slipped from the gathering and crouched beside the man while the daari collected himself and glanced around to make certain everyone of importance was in attendance.

Seeing an opportunity to be at the centre of things, Lidan squeezed between the shifting bodies and squatted beside Grent. His eyes smiled at her despite the blood on his hands and he nodded at his attendee box, the lid already off and the contents a jumbled mess. Lidan shook her head and handed him a dressing. She'd organised all his kits before she started training with Loge, and in a fortnight all her work had been undone.

'You've come from Namjin?' Erlon asked the rider and the hall fell silent.

'Yes.' The man winced as Grent dabbed a wound in his back. 'Fast as I could...'

Erlon's eyes scanned the man from head to foot, taking in the filth and blood. 'You were brave to travel alone.'

Lidan could only stare at the rider's back. Something had torn through the man's coat, his leathers and his shirt to score deep lacerations in his skin. They gaped, wide and angry, and were almost rancid with infection. She knew those wounds...

'I was one of ten riders who left to deliver this message.'

A murmur of confusion rippled through the hall.

'Pardon me?' The daari leaned forwards in his audience chair.

Lidan continued to stare at the man's back and sat on her heels, her heart pounding so hard she could hardly hear over the frantic beat.

'A party of ten left for each clan in the South Lands, all with the same message. Of my party, all but me were killed on the way. Argh!'

He flinched away as Grent poured alcohol over a wound and cut away fabric glued to his skin with dried blood. The wounds became clearer under the dirt and muck, and Lidan shivered.

'Killed by what?' The gravity in Erlon's voice told Lidan he already knew the answer. *She* already knew the answer.

'Ngaru,' she replied without thinking. The eyes of the room fell on where she sat crouched at the man's shoulder and the messenger turned to the small voice at his side. She looked at him and saw the same shadows lingering in his eyes as they did in Loge's. 'Black creatures in the forms of men, with weapons of iron?'

'The like I've never seen before...' the rider replied, his voice wavering. He swallowed hard, and Lidan noticed the tremor in his hands. 'Monsters...'

'How many?' Erlon broke the moment between his daughter and the messenger. 'Did you see them?'

'Can't say for sure, sir. We rode hard to get away from it, until the horses died. Could have been one or more, or maybe different ones as we went. They don't come out in the open. They stick to the shadows...' He reached to point at his injured back. 'I got this when my last companion was snatched from his horse—' His voice broke and he coughed, a shaking breath rattling his chest and only barely suppressing tears. His chin shook as badly as his hands, so Lidan gently took the soup before it spilled. 'Still don't know how it missed me, and got him...'

The daari turned to consult Siman and the messenger kept talking, staring at the fire as if he saw something there other than embers and flame.

'They attack our villages at night, when the guards are tired and the people are unawares. They don't make a sound when they come over the walls, no screeches or howls, just silence, like they don't need to speak to know what to do.' The silence in the hall pressed down; even the children stared. Lidan's stomach flipped and a dressing fell from her limp fingers, forgotten in the despair of the messenger's story. 'But in the bush, they scream...'

'They attack *villages*?' Siman's voice rose with shock, a sound alien to Lidan's ears, the stoic bravery of the ranger waning in the face of the news.

The ngaru had only ever attacked Tolak ranging parties. Never had they made an attempt to enter Hummel. How many more of them were out there, waiting in the trees and in the lee of the tablelands? Lidan's chest tightened, her mind spinning at the thought of a plague of the creatures seething out of the ravines and canyons.

213

'Once a week, then almost nightly at the new moon, then less as it rises again. All over the south we've heard stories. Some Namjin villages have been cleared out completely. That's why they sent us.' The messenger looked up at the daari and their eyes locked. 'They've called a Corron.'

Chatter burst into the silence and Lidan flinched away, the sound ripping at her ears. Her head started to throb as her father held his hands up to plead for calm.

'A Corron? There hasn't been a Corron in two generations!' The daari glanced at the shadows to the right and found Sellan, her arms crossed and lips pressed into a hard line. She kept her eyes on the messenger, studying him as if trying to read a deeper meaning in his words, but she made no move to speak.

The messenger shrugged. 'Our daari feels this matter requires a united approach.'

'Clear the hall!' Erlon bellowed and people started, then hurried to comply. 'First Wife, see the messenger has all he needs.'

Sellan stared at her husband. 'But, I—'

Erlon's fist slammed into the armrest of the chair, a boom echoing through the emptying hall and cutting his wife's words from the air. 'I will call for you when I have need of you!'

The dana's stare turned to the messenger and with a flick of her head she had him limping after her to the kitchen. It was only then Erlon saw Lidan crouched beside the stool at the fire pit.

'You too, Liddy. I'll send for you all soon.'

Us all? She didn't have a chance to ask what he meant before Grent ushered her from the hall. Beyond, she found Loge sitting on the steps with Behn and a cluster of rangers and tradesmen milling at their feet.

'Make yourself comfortable.' Loge patted the step beside him. 'We'll be here a while.'

It was well after dark before the door opened again and Siman's face appeared. He looked at his rangers, then at Lidan, then at the brazier they had burning at the base of the stairs to fight off the encroaching cold. 'Rangers and daari's kin only.'

He slipped back inside and Lidan threw an apologetic glance at Behn. She darted inside, ignoring the ache in her knees and the sting of the hall's heat on her face after hours sitting outside in the cold. Her father sat where she'd left him, and her mothers and sisters gathered before him, silent and waiting. His eyes seemed to have sunk into pools of fatigue as the hours passed and this struck a chord of worry in Lidan's heart. The message must have brought grave tidings indeed.

'They're all here, sir,' Siman murmured.

The daari nodded and leaned forwards in his chair, elbows resting on his knees, his hands clasped tightly together. 'The Namjin have called a Corron to discuss the ngaru and what can be done to stop them. As the messenger said, they've hit the northern clans the hardest and refugees are fleeing south. It seems we've been lucky, by comparison, and have only encountered a few on our borders.

'This Corron will be held in Namjin, at Daari Yorrell's hall in Jinloh.' He licked his lips and paused, seeming to think carefully on his next words. 'And the Law requires each daari to travel to the meeting… with their family.'

'What?' The dana put her hands on Marrit's slight shoulders, hugging her youngest daughter against her skirt. Abbi shuffled in beside Lidan and the little girl's soft hand slipped into hers. Lidan gave her hand a gentle squeeze and Abbi leaned into her leg. Kelill and Raeh looked at each other with wide eyes, an unspoken question passing between them. Sellan scoffed, 'Your whole family? That is the most ridiculous thing I've ever heard!'

'Of course it is, but that doesn't change the fact of the matter.' Erlon looked at them all in turn, his wives, his rangers and his daughters. 'We must all go.'

'What in the world for? What possible use are women and children on such a journey?' Instead of her usual scornful scowl, Sellan's frown deepened to one of genuine concern. 'Have they no regard for the dangers?'

Lidan felt sick. Craving a little freedom beyond the walls of the village was one thing. Travelling for weeks through bushland infested with ngaru was something else entirely. She glanced at Loge and saw the same fear mirrored in his eyes, dancing with the glimmer of the fire and torchlight.

Erlon shook his head. 'The risks are shared across the clans. Everyone has to bring their family and their rangers. We have no choice. The Corron is called and we must attend.'

'And what of Farah?' Raeh asked, balancing a weary Cerise on her hip. 'The poor woman is surely too ill to travel.'

Silence fell across the gathering and the daari sighed heavily. 'All my children must attend, even the unborn.'

Lidan's mother spat on the floor. 'I will not let you take my daughters beyond that gate to be fed to whatever monsters wait in the shadows!'

Abbi burst into tears beside Lidan and she scooped the child up, settling her on her hip. She bounced Abbi a few times and kissed her forehead, and the little one pressed her face into her sister's neck. She might not be old enough to understand what her parents were saying, but the emotion in the room was enough to set her on edge. Her slight body shivered despite the warmth of the fire pit. Marrit's wide green eyes found Lidan and she saw the girl biting her lip to stop it quivering. She gave her younger sister a wink and a small smile. It was the only reassurance she could manage across the space between them.

'We'll have every able-bodied ranger with us, Sellan. This is not a negotiation.'

'What in the name of the ancestors do the Council want the children for?' The dana snapped.

Erlon's gaze shifted to Lidan and held there; bearing down with a sudden weight of expectation she hadn't anticipated. 'They are my heirs.'

Chapter Twenty-eight

Hummel, Tolak Range, the South Lands

Dawn broke to the snorting and stamping of horses, the muttering of rangers and the grumbling of tired children woken too early from their beds. Two wagons, brought out from storage in the stables, had been dusted off and were now packed high with provisions and weapons. Under the flat beds, boxes held stores of arrows and spears, spare bowstrings and axes. Along the sides, spears hung in leather ties, ready at a moment's notice to be snatched from their bonds and turned against an enemy attack. Lidan wondered at them from across the common, thinking to herself there might be more weaponry than food in either carriage.

Theus shied and she soothed him with a pat on the nose. A crowd emerged from the hall, clustered around Farah as she came awkwardly down the stairs with a hand clutched to her belly. It was big but not as large as it should be for her term. Beside Lidan, Moyra clicked her tongue and sighed.

'Poor girl,' the midwife muttered. 'She's only a cycle or two shy of having that baby, if she lasts that long.'

'I thought it wasn't due 'til the rains?' Lidan countered with a frown. The group moved across the common and helped Farah into the wagon; her gaunt face and shaking legs disappearing under the arching hide cover. The weather was markedly warmer with each passing day, but the air remained so dry it seemed impossible that it might turn and bring rain.

'The rains *are* due in a month or two, First Daughter. It's this dry that won't let up! We've had cold rain before, but it's not the usual.' Moyra and Lidan looked at the clear, empty sky. Only a handful of high, white puffs of cloud lingered above the tablelands. 'No chance of those bringing rain.'

Lidan looked across at the older woman, a large woven basket in her hands, covered in fabric and tied with a rope. 'What's that for?'

'Midwife's travel kit.' Moyra nodded at the basket.

'Midwives have travelling kits?' Lidan frowned again and tried to recall if she'd seen such a thing in Grent's healing rooms.

'They do now,' the midwife sighed and walked towards the carriages, climbing the same step as Farah and disappearing behind the hide door flap.

Lidan's sisters piled into the carriages, followed by their mothers, all glancing around the village common as if they'd left something behind. Finally, the dana appeared at the top of the hall steps, her dark green eyes scanning the common. While the messenger had urged the daari to depart for the Corron immediately, the dana had refused, insisting on at least three days to prepare the convoy.

For the most part, Lidan didn't mind the delay. She spent her time training with Loge and working to make sure Theus was ready to ride, staying out from under everyone's hurrying feet. Even the forge was too busy for her liking, ringing day and night as Rick and Behn raced to prepare weapons. The delay chafed at her father though, as much as he tried to hide it behind his smile and booming laugh.

He talked to the girls about adventure and exciting new things to see. He promised to show them the river to the west and let them swim if the weather grew warm. It was only when he looked away from his daughters, excitedly milling at their father's feet, that Lidan saw the truth in his face. His smile never reached his eyes, never set them to sparkle as they used to. She knew then how dangerous the journey was, how much of a risk he took taking them to the Corron.

Erlon lifted Marrit into a wagon and went to Titon, already saddled and waiting at the head of the convoy. Loge appeared beside Lidan and she started, so fixed on watching the others she didn't notice his approach.

'Time to get up,' he murmured, lacing his hands together palms up and offering her a step to use. Her leg swung over the saddle and her hands squeezed the reins. Suddenly she felt at home.

'What do you think you are doing?' Sellan's voice echoed against the walls.

Lidan looked up to see her mother striding towards her with a fire in her eyes. Had she not been in the saddle she would have run. Theus sensed her anxiety and bounced on his front hooves, snorting and shaking his head at her mother. With a cry Sellan staggered to a stop and held up her arm as if to defend herself against a snarling beast, drawing the attention of everyone assembled in the common.

'Lidan Tolak! You will get down from that beast this instant, or mark my words—'

Titon's hoof falls cut the tirade as her father rode over.

'What is going on?' he hissed, pulling the horse up and leaning down to his wife, who stepped stiffly away from the giant black stallion.

'What is she doing up there?' Sellan snapped, pointing at Lidan as though she was an errant toddler climbing too far up a tree.

'I'd say she's preparing to ride out, like the rest of us.' Erlon lowered his voice to a growl. 'I suggest you get in a carriage unless you want to ride in a saddle yourself.'

'I would rather walk over hot coals than ride one of those hideous things.'

'Then get aboard.'

'Lidan, get down. You're coming with me.' The dana waved her hand as if the words were all she needed to say, and stepped towards the wagons.

Erlon cleared his throat. 'There's not enough room. Lidan is apprenticed now. She rides with the rangers.'

'She's—' Sellan began.

'She's quite capable in the saddle, wife.'

'She is your *heir!* What if something happens? What if she falls or, ancestors forbid, that wretched thing throws her to her death?' Her mother glared at the horse as if it had the face of a monster and the temperament to boot, but Erlon leaned down further to face her.

'Lidan broke that horse with her own hands. You know the Law. It's hers, and it will keep her safe.'

She waited for a retort to burst from her mother's lips, but somehow Sellan kept it imprisoned behind her clenched jaw. With a final glare at Theus and not so much as a glance at Lidan, she turned on her heel and stormed to the waiting carriages.

A breath Lidan didn't realise she held burned in her chest and she exhaled, her stomach twisting like writhing snakes. They hadn't even left Hummel and her parents were already at each other's throats. How much worse would it be after a week or so of hard travel?

Erlon paused for a moment, then turned Titon to face his daughter.

'As much as she is wrong, she is right.' His stare left her in no doubt he was deathly serious. 'Stay with Loge or Siman or I'll put that horse on a lead and make you sit in a wagon. Don't make me regret my decision.'

'Yes, Da.' She nodded and glanced over at Loge, still checking his horse's tack.

The young ranger came around to pat her on the elbow and check Theus's bridle for the last time. 'You'll be right. I won't let anything happen.'

A sharp whistle rose from the commotion and Siman's long arm waved. Jac waved back and the huge timber gates groaned open against the dry soil, dust whirling up in their wake. Horses and men pushed forwards, carriages creaked and their wheels began to turn. Lidan gave Theus a little slack in his reins and pressed her boots into his side, urging him forwards alongside Loge and the other rangers.

They passed under the lintel of the gateway and into the valley, the land she'd been separated from for weeks finally opening up before her, blades of grass swaying in greeting with the wind. The breeze hit her face like a wave and she breathed deep, pulling all the scents and freedoms of the range into her chest and willing them to never leave.

'Oi, Liddy!' Rick shouted from somewhere in the common behind the convoy. She pulled up and searched the crowd, his sandy brown hair weaving between the horses and riders to her side.

'Here...' he said breathlessly, holding up a belt with two fine leather holsters and garters stitched on the ends. 'Yours... you'll need them. And happy birthday.'

Gleaming bone handles flashed in the morning light, a hint of the fine new blades hidden in the holsters. She took the belt with careful hands and strapped it across her hips, the garters at the ends of the sheaths wrapping around her thighs. They were a little awkward to fit while sitting in the saddle, but once she had them clasped, the leather and the knives sat perfectly against her legs.

The ngaru knives. Her knives.

Rick pointed at Loge. 'Keep training her. No more staves.'

Loge nodded as the forge master backed away from the press of riders moving through the gate and Lidan couldn't help smiling broadly, pride swelling in her chest.

She had her knives.

With a click of his tongue, Loge moved his horse, Striker, into the convoy, drawing Theus and Lidan with him down into the valley.

At the western apex of the valley, where the track led up into the bush and the foothills of the tablelands, Lidan glanced over her shoulder before the trees could envelop the view of her home. Far off now, standing against the blue of the sky and the pale green and brown of the land, the Caine watched them leave.

She shivered. How many of them would live to see it again? She locked the image of the monolith in her mind and dread settled in her heart.

Chapter Twenty-nine

The Southern Reaches, Orthia

Spear fishing through shattered river ice required a talent Ran didn't possess. After standing at the river's edge for over an hour, stabbing at shadows and the slightest movement of waterweed, he gave up and left the task to Sasha's deft hands. She already had two good-sized fish on the bank, gutted and skewered, while he remained empty handed and hungry.

Her packed provisions only lasted them a week, rationed and eaten sparingly when they stopped to rest or avoid the weather. Their diet of dried meat and thick, hard bread, dry leaves brewed into a tea and some sort of oat biscuit, was only rarely interrupted by the addition of a rabbit or a small fox. He left the hunting to Sasha as well, happy that she could track and shoot the game faster than he. Outwardly he blamed an ache in his hands for his lack of hunting success, but the memory of the ghost and the rabbit still chilled his bones, and he dared not draw an arrow against a target for fear of inducing a similar reaction.

Sasha didn't seem to mind his avoidance of hunting. She gave him a wry smile and he wondered if she thought him incapable and soft—a weak little prince from the city with no woodland skills to hold to his name. While he wasn't weak or little, compared to her, it was a wonder he'd survived on his own.

The young woman's spear shot down and flicked back up with another fish flapping wildly at the end. With cool efficiency, she yanked it free and cracked its head on a nearby tree root. Ran turned away and began collecting wood for the fire instead. He could build one of those well enough and use a little magic to light it without a flint.

He practiced caution with his trick after it backfired at least once. He'd been distracted and the fire he was building burst into an explosive inferno, engulfing a tree and almost destroying their travelling packs. Sasha kept her distance when he lit the fire from then on, her eyes wide as she watched him each evening, as if she still couldn't quite believe what she was seeing.

Ran found a hollow up the bank from the river and set about making his fire and clearing a sheltered place for them to sleep. He tied a canvas sheet to a tree and pegged the corners to the ground, fashioning an awning to keep the snow at bay should it decide to fall in the night. By now, nearly three moons had passed since he escaped Usmein, and with Sasha's help, they stayed well clear of roads and villages.

Soon, the fire crackled happily in a ring of stones, warming the hollow, and Sasha returned from the river. Ran's weary eyes stared vacantly into the flames until she crouched beside him and set the fish over the heat to roast.

'I still don't understand why you want to go to Isord,' she murmured into the silence. They'd discussed his plans weeks ago and agreed to make for the Ruken mountains, then follow them west to Isord and the capital, Kotja.

'My mother is from there. I can seek out her family and get some help.'

'Help for what?' she frowned.

He spread his hands before him. 'This.'

A little spark shot between his fingers and Sasha raised a brow.

'Ran, they can't help you with that.'

'Well, maybe they can help me negotiate with my father.' Ran poked the fire with a stick and the smell of the roasting fish set his stomach to growling, a sound so loud he worried it might shake the snow from the mountain at his back. His mouth watered as Sasha passed him a skewer.

Their fingers touched in the exchange. His skin prickled with goosebumps, but Sasha flinched away as if stung and Ran's heart raced with panic. Had he hurt her with his magic?

She shuffled back and dropped her gaze, busying herself with skinning her fish and fussing over the embers. He might have whispered an apology but his throat tightened and the words evaporated. She reacted the same way whenever their bare skin touched, as rare and fleeting as the moments were. When covered head to toe with coats, gloves, and boots, she had no problem taking his hand to help him climb a ridge or curling up beside him to conserve warmth when they slept. It was as if the feeling of his skin revolted her, despite weeks spent tending his wounds and cleaning his body.

Did she fear the magic, or him?

Perhaps, even though she vowed to help him, he repulsed her, as with every other Orthian. The magic made him disgusting and untouchable and more besides—it made him dangerous. No wonder she recoiled.

'Best get some rest...' He tossed the used skewer into the flames and crawled under the awning to his thin mat and blanket. Sasha remained silent beside the fire. By the time Ran's eyes closed and sleep claimed him, she hadn't moved a muscle.

A cold hand on his chest woke Ran with a start, his heart pounding, his limbs paralysed. The ghost leaned over him, the awning flapping in the wind above her head.

'What the—' His protest ended when her finger pressed to her lips, commanding silence.

You're still asleep... she spoke to his mind, her mouth unmoved. Her eyes searched his face and her hands spread across his chest like fans. He felt his muscles relax under the pressure of her touch and she sat back on her heels, drawing her icy fingers into her lap.

What's going on? What's wrong?

Nothing. She stared at him for a while, her expression unreadable in the faint light from the fire. Have you opened the scroll?

For fuck's sake—no, I haven't opened it! In case you didn't notice, I'm busy running for my life!

Her lips pressed into a line and she let out a frustrated huff. *Don't say I didn't try to warn you...*

Warn me about what? Ran tried to sit up but the ghost vanished before he could call his limbs to action. He closed his eyes and pushed her face from his mind, her words lingering like an echo in a long empty chamber. Whatever obsession the ghost girl had with the scroll, he was not about to indulge her. Perhaps she was going mad, or perhaps *he* was the one losing his mind, driven from sanity by the endless white and ice. In any case, he would have plenty of time to read the stupid scroll when he was safely in a tavern in Kotja.

A blizzard howled down from the north two nights later. Their little awning collapsed and he and Sasha huddled together under a tree, hoping the worst would pass by morning. If they were lucky, it would be the final snowstorm of the season, but it was impossible to tell in the wilds of the mountains. When the sky finally did lighten in the east, it hardly looked like much of a dawn. Thick cloud roiled in the sky, blocking most of the day's light and all its warmth, boding ill for the coming day.

'We need to get out of this or we'll freeze to death.' Ran's teeth chattered around his words, his body shivering uncontrollably despite Sasha's warmth and the blanket and canvas covering their heads.

'I know,' she replied, her hands curled in tight, shaking fists, her breath fogging like smoke. 'I saw a road to the west... should be a farm house...'

'Not ideal,' he muttered.

'They have a shed we can hide in.'

That sounded safer. He didn't fancy knocking on a farmer's door in a foul blizzard and facing their awkward looks and barely hidden suspicion. No one travelled at this time of year unless it was extremely urgent—a matter of life or death.

'Hope so. Don't feel like explaining myself to anyone.' He heaved the canvas cover off, dislodging the built-up snow, and dragged Sasha to her feet. 'Hasn't worked out so well in the past.'

Sasha nodded, or she shivered so hard her head moved involuntarily. 'Aye,' she whispered.

They shouldered their bags and tied the rope between their belts. In a howler like this, they risked losing each other as easily as if it were moonless and midnight. For what seemed like hours their path took them along the face of a steep incline, the ground falling away to their left as they picked their way between trees and through thick drifts of snow.

Sasha slipped and the rope snapped taught, pulling Ran savagely off his feet. They slid down the icy hillside, picking up speed until a tree flashed between them and snagged the rope. The force of the jolt was like a punch to the guts as the rope yanked hard on Ran's belt and it tightened around his belly. On the other side of the tree, Sasha groaned and swore.

'You all right?' Ran shouted into the wind.

'I think—' she sucked a breath through clenched teeth and he saw her hand reach for her leg. 'Twisted my knee a bit.'

Ran climbed to his feet and staggered across the snow, releasing the rope from the tree and then kneeling by Sasha as she struggled to stand.

'Here,' he croaked and hooked his arm around her waist. 'Let's get onto some flatter ground, hey?'

She nodded and accepted his help. Together they found their feet, and Sasha looped an arm over Ran's shoulder before they began to shuffle down the hillside to the valley below. The going was hard and slow, with Sasha grinding her teeth beside Ran's ear for most of the journey into the valley and along a frozen river.

'We can rest here,' he shouted through the wind and snow.

Sasha shook her head and rubbed at the top of her knee. 'We stay here, we die. It's not far.'

'How can you know?'

'I came this way when I was training to be a healer. We stopped at the farm. We can rest there.'

'Only if you're sure? We can find a cave or something...' He glanced around at the forest, but Sasha shook her head. 'Right then. You tell me the way.'

A barn loomed from the falling snow, at first an ominous shadow, then growing clearer as they staggered closer and finally fell against the door. Ran couldn't see the lights of a farmhouse, nor hear any dogs or animals. Perhaps the farmers Sasha remembered had moved on, or were caught in town by the storm. Either would suit him. He needed somewhere safe and warm, but most of all hidden so they could recover their strength without risking discovery.

He put his shoulder against the door and heaved it open. They shuffled inside, shaking snow from their clothes and stamping their boots. Ran glanced up, expecting to find the place brimming with livestock and the warm, earthy scent of manure, but every stall stood empty.

He balked at that. Shouldn't the farmer's animals be locked up safe and warm in weather like this? He threw a glance out the door, scanning the

foul weather outside to see if anyone or anything stood beyond the protection of the barn, but nothing moved.

Still as a graveyard... The ghost's voice slipped through his mind and he
shuddered, shoving his shoulder into the timber of the door and ramming it
shut against the snow. At the far end of the barn, a hayloft stood above more
stalls, all of them as empty as those to his left and right. He tried to ignore the
strangeness of the place and helped Sasha towards a stall under the loft.

She lowered herself onto a milking stool and a frown creased her brow
as she glanced around. 'Where are the cattle?'

Ran swallowed his apprehension. 'Maybe the farmer moved on? Crops
failed, or something?'

He dumped their bags on the ground and went to rifle through the stalls.
He found a few horse rugs and another canvas sheet—not exactly luxuries
but enough to keep them warm and spare them the icy coffin that was
waiting outside.

'No, I don't think so...' Sasha murmured as Ran dragged a few bales of
hay into their stall and spread a decent thickness of straw over the ground.
He helped Sasha lay back on the loosely piled hay and she gladly accepted
the rugs Ran folded around her, grimacing when he lifted her injured leg
up onto a bale. He turned to search the other stalls, but Sasha caught his
sleeve. 'In my bag... there are some leaves.'

He nodded and searched her belongings, coming out with a handful of
small cloth bags. Sasha picked one from the selection, took a dark green
leaf from the bag and put it in her mouth. She handed the bag to Ran and
pointed. 'For pain and swelling in the joints. You should take one too, or
your ankle will be useless in the morning.'

With a raised brow, he sniffed the bag and gagged. The scent was something between acid and rotting potatoes. Sasha gave him a stern look and
a pointed finger, so he shrugged, took one, and began to chew.

'Ugh, do I have to swallow?' he choked around the leaf and tried not to
lose his stomach.

Sasha shook her head and lay back on the hay, her eyes closing with a
peaceful sigh. 'Just chew and suck.'

Then the wave hit him, joyous numbness flowing from his chest through
his hips to his feet. It circled there, warming and pulsing, spreading along

his aching limbs, settling in the bones and easing the muscles. Ran sat on the hay beside Sasha as the juice of the leaf sought out his injuries.

He had planned to sit up and keep watch, to light a fire and mull over his plans. He had thought the fall on the hillside had left him unharmed, but as he twisted to lie down, his waist and hips ached and burned. There were bruises under the layers of clothing protecting him from the cold. He couldn't see them, but they were scored through his flesh; a painful reminder of how dangerous his journey was and how often he walked the fine line between life and death.

CHAPTER THIRTY

The Southern Reaches, Orthia

The sound of shuffling in the hay woke him and he sat up fast. The wind had eased and he realised he must have slept. It was impossible to tell the time of day, or night, by the light seeping into the barn, the roof as well as the fields outside were layered with several feet of fresh snow. Ran glanced around and saw Sasha sitting up, rummaging through her bag.

He groaned and flopped back down, relieved it was only her and not some armed invader.

'How are you feeling?' he asked, rubbing his hands over his face to dispel the numbness. The leaves were gone from his mouth, so perhaps he'd swallowed them after all. His ankle and waist didn't ache as badly as they had the night before, and he circled his foot to test its range.

'Better. Just a little bruised,' Sasha croaked, handing him a water bladder. 'Drink this. We can melt snow to refill it. You don't want to get a headache.'

He took the bladder and drank deeply, the cold water flooding him and drawing his body back to consciousness as the chill spread through his belly. 'What was that stuff?'

'Caya leaf.' She handed him a biscuit and took the bladder. 'It's not easy to find so we use it sparingly. If cattle find it they'll eat the whole bush until they're laid out in the field, moaning and completely mad. They love it.'

'Bloody heck.' Ran wondered at the idea—a few dozen cows lolling around in a field as drunk as ten men at midsummer.

'And speaking of cows...' Sasha turned to the empty barn. 'We need to find out where they've gone.'

'Farmers probably left—'

'There's no way the Parrys would leave.' She shook her head. 'They've worked this farm for five generations, maybe more.'

'How far is the farmhouse?' Ran came to his feet and brushed hay from his coat as he opened the stall door.

'Just across the field,' Sasha replied with a raised brow. 'Where are you going?'

He was two steps from the barn door. 'The house will tell us for sure if they've gone and for how long. We need to figure out how long it's safe to stay. We need food as well.'

'And if someone sees us?' she asked. She clambered to her feet and limped after him, helping to pull on the barn door and open a space wide enough for them to squeeze through, the threshold barred by drifts of snow.

'You said you came here when you were training?'

Sasha nodded as Ran scanned the snowy fields outside.

'If they recognise you, we can make up a story about you travelling to see another healer.'

'How do I explain you?' She folded her arms, challenging a plan she rightly thought he was making up as he went along.

'I brought you the message and I'm taking you back to the sender.'

She rolled her eyes. 'Fine. Come on, it's this way.'

Ran helped Sasha through the snow, around to the left and along the length of the barn. At the end, under the hayloft, they paused and watched the grey day and flurries of snow for any signs of life. There was no smell of burning firewood or the wafting scents of breakfast, no animals or human noises. For a few hundred feet in all directions, all they could see were snowy paddocks and fences. Directly ahead, a dark shadow stood at the edge of visibility.

'Over there, in the yard with tall pines at the back of the garden.' Sasha moved cautiously into the snow, her feet sinking past her ankles and dragging long lines in the drifts. They waded on, fighting the white just to move a few feet closer to the shadow. 'What I'd give for snow shoes...' she growled under her breath, stumbling and staggering in a battle to remain upright.

At the trees, Sasha paused, peering through them to the rear of the house. In the yard, a flimsy washing line stood empty between two leaning posts, while everything else lay hidden under mounds of snow. There might have been a bench or a wood block, but they were nothing more than lumps under a pure, white carpet.

The windows of the house were shuttered—not unusual in foul weather—but he couldn't see even the slightest flicker of movement between the timber slats. Ran pointed at the roof and Sasha followed his hand. The two chimneys poking up from the collected snow were clear of any smoke.

'If someone is home, they're very cold.' He edged forwards, his hand folding over the hilt of his knife. The farm's still silence sent a creeping sense of terror up his spine and around his neck, a chill born of more than just the snow shivering through his limbs. The last time he'd approached an abandoned farmhouse, he'd seen a ghost and been exposed to enough magic it drew his own to the surface, like fire drawing a blister out of burnt skin.

He swallowed his fear and touched the rear door, rapping a knuckle on the wood. Sasha leaned forwards at his shoulder, watching and waiting. The door creaked and Ran realised it was open, swinging in at his touch and allowing snow to fall on the flagstone floor inside. He laid a hand on the panel and pushed, forcing the reluctant hinges to give way so the door could open fully.

'Hello?' he called, not for a minute expecting a reply.

A strange odour coiled in his nose as they moved through the room at the rear of the house. The acidic scent of spoiled onions and potatoes wafted from the pantry to his left, and from a leg of ham hanging nearby. All were well beyond usefulness, despite the cold. The smell they gave off told him no one had been at the Parry farm for weeks.

'I'd say no one's here,' he said, coughing and covering his nose with his sleeve. The rotten pantry wasn't the only foul smell in the place. They moved from the pantry and buttery and into the house, following a corridor and passing room after room, all with their doors closed to the world. Ran reached for the handle of the nearest one, but Sasha laid her hand on his arm. She shook her head and slipped past, leading him up the corridor to the front of the house.

The smell worsened until they emerged into a sitting room. The fireplace stood cold, the chairs empty and dusty. It was a tidy room with minimal, comfortable furniture and enough seats for a large family, decorated hereabouts with the ornaments and trinkets of a well-loved home.

And a lot of blood.

It was old blood, sprayed from floor to ceiling in great gouts and spurts, splattered across rugs and chairs, blankets and wall hangings. Even the cold couldn't keep it from stinking. A gagging sound next to him signalled Sasha's reaction. She held her hands to her mouth, her eyes filled to the brim with sparkling tears. Even as a healer, accustomed to blood and gore, she wasn't immune to the room's aura of soul-hollowing fear, or its stench.

Ran had been very wrong to think he'd seen true horror in the cottage near Usmein, or at the front in the Disputed Territory. This place reeked of it, as if the terror of those who had died here had burned itself into the very timbers of the structure. He drew his knife from its sheath, ignoring the tremor in his hand and wondering what use the blade would be if he encountered the monster that did this. It had to be a beast of some kind—a bear or a wolf.

The backs of the chairs bore the scars of claws, tears in the upholstery exposing padding and the ribs of the frames. Another near the doorway had been crushed completely, reduced to splinters and dust. Had the family tried to barricade the door, desperate to keep the thing out?

When he reached the threshold, Ran expected to find the door hanging on its hinges. Instead, he found the hinges ripped from the wall along with the door, gaping holes left in the timber cladding over the clay wall filling.

'What in the Underworld did this?' he whispered and turned to Sasha. He expected her to blame it on the local wildlife, but she stared past him and didn't breathe a word in reply. She was ashen, the usual bright spots of colour in her pale cheeks extinguished. Her eyes were wide and her mouth gaped, her chest rising and falling as if she fought to catch her breath. Ran tore his eyes away and followed her gaze, turning to look through the yawning doorway into the snowy garden beyond the porch.

Dark smudges under the freshly fallen powder drew him from the house and out into the yard; seven of them, scattered across the space in grey mounds of various sizes.

'Seven,' Sasha whispered. 'There were seven Parrys who lived here; the parents and five children… the youngest was a baby I helped deliver…'

She choked on the final word and a sob escaped her throat. She bent double and crumpled onto the porch with her head in her hands. Ran hardly heard her anguish over the rushing sound of blood in his ears and the thud of his heart. His panic and terror set a fire under his magic, enough to send it shooting along his arms to pool in his fingers without so much as a word of permission.

The dark shapes drew him into the garden. The largest was near the gate and the others were spread out haphazardly across the space between the garden wall and the porch. To his right, the smallest of them glared up at him, daring him to scoop back the snow to see what lay underneath. He didn't give in to the taunt, knowing he didn't have the stomach for whatever he would find.

'What could have done this?' he called and glanced back at the house.

Sasha shook her head. 'I have no idea. Animals, maybe. They don't normally attack houses, though...'

She was right. Ran had heard of lone farmers in fields, or travellers in the road falling victim to predators in the woods. He'd heard of bodies found in trees, stashed for later by a frugal beast preserving its next meal. When camps were attacked, the creatures took the bodies for food. They didn't leave them scattered and exposed in the snow and wind. They never went into homes, through barred doors and slaughtered the occupants to the last.

In the distance, against the shadow of a stand of trees, hidden behind the trunks, his ghost girl watched. If she knew the answers, she kept them to herself. She slipped into the darkness and vanished, leaving Ran none the wiser, and all the more frustrated.

He went back to Sasha and helped her stand, her legs and hands shaking.

'They're all dead...' she whispered, her eyes searching the garden.

'I'm sorry.' It was all he could say for a family he'd never met, nor cared for. As the duke's son, all Orthians were his people and he loved them as such. But that was nothing compared to midwifing a birth only to find the entire family massacred in their home a few short years later.

He held Sasha to his chest and let her cry.

By midday he managed to convince Sasha to leave the site of the slaughter and return to the barn to rest. Improved though she was, the longer she spent out in the cold, the worse her knee would become. She settled in the hay of the stall and eased her leg up onto the bale, the fear in her eyes making her bright red hair seem all the wilder.

'What if the beast comes back?' she asked, her voice hoarse and raw.

'I doubt it will. It killed everyone here, so why come back?' Ran pulled a horse blanket up to her chin. 'I'm going to see if there's anything worth salvaging from the house. I won't be long,' he promised and slipped back out the door and into the snow.

Some stores had survived abandonment—dried meat and a few small barrels of oats. Jars of preserves and some hardier cured meat hidden against the cold stone of the pantry wall, but everything fresh had turned. They could salvage some flour and make some coal bread, and porridge with the oats, and pack the rest for their journey. At least the bread and porridge would give them both the energy they needed to keep moving.

With the last bundle of food and an armful of dry wood from the stack inside the house, Ran stepped into the deepening evening, content with his day's work. It felt good to do something practical, and useful, while Sasha recovered. It seemed such a small thing, compared to all she had done to help him. The aches in his limbs were the reward of hard work, rather than the result of injury, and he could sense his body healing, despite the exhaustion of—

A high-pitched howl echoed in the hills above the farm and froze him in his tracks. He stood halfway between the house and the barn, knee deep in snow with darkness rising from the east to bring the night. It wasn't the call of any owl he'd ever heard, nor an eagle or mountain cat. It wasn't a wolf or a bear. It was different, more guttural, and far more desperate.

He swallowed his fear and hurried to close the space ahead, slamming the barn door shut and dumping his cargo on the floor. Sasha jerked up and stared wide-eyed from the stall, watching as he searched through a tool cabinet near the door.

'What's wrong?' she asked, arriving at his side and scooping up the food. Her gaze followed him as he moved back to the door and started to nail a piece of timber above the lock. The lock wasn't in the best condition and this was the only thing he could think of to barricade the door.

'Nothing. I just thought we could use the extra security.' He didn't want to tell her about the scream in the woods. He took a length of thick wire and wound it through the door handles and then twisted the ends together, spiralling tighter and tighter until the wood and iron groaned with tension.

Stepping back beside Sasha, Ran hoped his lock would not be tested. It looked pathetic and flimsy in the face of the destruction in the house, and if whatever ripped the door from the farmhouse came to the barn there was little chance his defences would hold.

'Ran,' she said slowly. 'What did you see?'

'Nothing,' he repeated without looking at her, certain she would see straight through the lie if he did. He picked up the firewood and led her back to the stall, pretending not to see the questioning frown on her face.

CHAPTER THIRTY-ONE

The Parry Farm, Southern Orthia

Their meal started and finished in silence, with neither of them offering to light a fire against the dark and cold. A couple of candles stolen from the farmhouse lit a small circle within the confines of the stall, a softly glowing orb with Ran and Sasha sitting at its edges. Ran's magic shifted under his skin, hot and itchy, fuelled by anxiety, ready at a moment's notice to burst forth and defend him.

As useful as it was in an emergency, he hated the idea of his power moving as it pleased, without his control. What if he woke in the night and lashed out with it, only to find he'd attacked Sasha as she slept? What if he had a nightmare and it discharged without him realising it? He could burn the barn to the ground in a matter of minutes, incinerating them both in the process. Shuddering at the thought, he forced his power back into the recess it crawled from, working hard to hold it there.

Across the circle of light, Sasha fidgeted with strands of hay, twisting and weaving them into bands of plaits. She might have been making a basket or a bag, or just passing the time as the silence stretched between them; Ran's untrained eyes couldn't tell.

'Who is she?' Sasha asked quietly, her voice cutting the stillness and making Ran jump.

'Who?' He stared at her with wide eyes. Sasha was the only woman he'd seen in months.

'The girl you talk to in your dreams.'

Their eyes met and there was nothing Ran could do to escape her scrutiny and nowhere to hide. She watched him for a lie, waiting for him to try and deceive her.

'Ah...' Ran cleared his throat and shifted awkwardly. There really was no way to explain it without sounding like a crazy person. Sasha probably thought he was mad already—a little more wasn't going to make much difference. 'She's a ghost.'

'Why does she haunt you?' she asked, reaching for another strand of hay and continuing her weaving, her eyes on his face.

'I didn't kill her, if that's what you're implying,' he countered sourly. He ran his hand through his hair and prepared the story, searching for words to describe a night he'd tried so hard to forget. 'On my way back to Usmein from the Disputed Territory, I stumbled on a place full of magic, and she was there. The magic triggered my powers and she's been following me ever since.'

'And that's why you fled Usmein?'

'Because of the magic, yes.' A sad laugh escaped him and he shook his head. 'I didn't get a chance to tell anyone about the ghost. Doubt it would have mattered.'

Her hands paused for a moment while she watched him and not for the first time Ran wished he could tell what she was thinking.

'Our people have a hard time with magic...' Sasha's eyes fell to her weaving as she spoke. 'We don't like it because we don't understand it. Not so long ago, healers were treated with the same suspicion, our hands able to work wonders that normal folk can't manage. Healing and magic are the same in a way—they both work with forces the eyes often can't see. We treat coughs with leaves and broken bones with creams and in the minds of folk, it shouldn't work like that.'

Frustration roiled in Ran's stomach. 'Why mistreat someone trying to help you? That's just stupid.'

'People fear what they don't understand and hate what they can't control.'

'So why help me?' he asked, letting the question hang in the air like smoke. 'Why risk yourself aiding a magic-user who escaped the Duke's Justice?'

Sasha put her weaving in her lap and let her hands fall still.

'I'm not an only child. I had two younger brothers who I haven't seen since they were toddlers. My father sent them away without a word of warning or a moment to say farewell. He said he caught them playing in the wood shed, flicking sparks of power between them like normal children might pass a ball...' She bit her lip, her eyes wandering to the small candle flames. 'That was ten years ago, maybe even longer. I've no idea where they went or if they survived the journey. My mother never forgave him for it; never speaks more than a few words to him. She'd probably like to see him dead if she thought she could get away with it.'

The weeping face of Duchess Merideth flashed in Ran's mind, her red, watery eyes heavy with disappointment and sorrow. How many mothers in the duchy had their children taken from them, never to be seen or heard from again? How many husbands and wives shared their beds with this sadness; blame wedged between them like an unwelcome visitor? Ran couldn't imagine his mother publicly railing against his father—she knew her place and her role as his wife. But in private, when they spoke the truths in their hearts, he wondered if she, like Sasha's mother, could ever forgive her husband.

'I'm sorry for your brothers, Sasha.'

She shrugged and returned to her weaving. 'No point crying over things that can't be helped. When I was young, I thought if I learned to heal, I could find a cure for magic and bring them home. I dreamed I could go into the wilds and find them, fix what must be broken in them and bring them back to my mother.'

Ran waited for her to continue, but a small tear streaking down her cheek told him she didn't have the words to go on. 'There isn't a cure, is there?'

She shook her head and yanked hard on the weaving, pouring her anger into the strands, tying it into the braid with all the force her fingers could manage. He decided she wasn't making anything useful, like a bag or basket; she was binding her pain and sorrow into a prison of straw and grass.

'And that's why you helped me?'

'I told you when we left Graupen—magic doesn't give you a choice. You have it, or you don't. I wasn't about to let my father do to you what he did to my brothers.'

'Well, thank you,' he murmured, bowing as deeply as he could while sitting on the stall floor. 'I'm sorry I've kept you awake with my mutterings.'

With a wave of her hand, Sasha dismissed his worry. 'She sounds like she keeps you busy. In any case, it's not wise to ignore the shades who haunt us. They get annoyed.'

That caught Ran's attention with two hands. 'What do you know about ghosts?'

At that, she gave him a sad smile. 'We all have ghosts who walk in our shadows, Ran. Just happens some are louder than others.'

When Ran heard the shuffle of feet on snow outside the barn, his first thought turned to Sasha. Was it dawn, or she had gone to relieve herself in the night? Reality slapped the thought from his mind, recalling that he'd locked the barn so tightly that it was unlikely she could get out without his help. His eyes opened but the rest of him remained still as stone under the horse blankets and canvas.

The candles were out, tucked away in their bags for another night, and the darkness of the barn was complete. Sasha slumbered beside him, rolled in her blankets and breathing the calm rhythm of sleep. She hadn't heard the footsteps. He listened hard, straining against the sound of his beating heart to discern the source.

To say he heard normal footfalls was inaccurate. It was more like a scraping noise than actual steps, like feet dragged through the snow, hardly lifted above it. Or perhaps more like crawling, as if the source crouched low and shifted itself with effort.

It continued for a moment, moving around the perimeter of the barn. It travelled down the long wall towards the door at the far end, hovering there and moving back and forth. The doors did not move.

The sound began to shift again, easing itself along the other wall, this time towards the end where Ran lay beside Sasha in their stall. His right ear rang with the noise, all other sound fading to nothing as he focused his energy on the thing outside. It seemed to pass within inches of his head, and the thickness of the barn wall did nothing to soothe the fear creeping into his chest, tightening a hand around his hammering heart.

To his left, in the snow beside the wall, the sound of movement stopped. It wasn't an uneasy pause, when one might shuffle their feet and wonder which way to go next. It was a dead stop, as if it had found exactly what it was looking for.

The thing outside drew a deep breath through its nose, sucking in the scent of everything around it. It came closer to the wall, sniffing and breathing heavily, following a trail no eye could see. Then Ran remembered the sound from a hazy place in his memory. He'd heard it before: at the bottom of the mine shaft where he'd fallen not so long ago.

Sweat beaded on Ran's forehead; his palms were clammy, and his fingers itched for his knife. He didn't dare move to grab it, his heart and lungs already working hard as he tried to minimise his breath in case the creature heard.

Sniffing and shuffling steps moved from near his feet towards his head, quicker and more insistent as it approached then stopped again. It drew another long, deep breath and exhaled with a satisfied sigh that sent a cold shiver through every bone in Ran's body. A wet splattering sound pattered against the wall of the barn, and the snow hissed as hot liquid hit the ground.

It can't seriously be taking a piss?

He screwed up his nose at the acrid stink wafting up through the panels of the wall, stinging his nostrils and turning his stomach. The creature finished relieving itself and shuffled away quickly, retreating across the snow until Ran's ears lost the sound of its awkward steps to the night, a howling scream echoing along the valley to signal its departure. Not for the first time, he thanked the gods that Sasha remained asleep.

It took a moment for the creature's behaviour to make sense despite his fear. With the foul stench of the urine still burning his nose, Ran's heart skipped before thumping back into a frantic beat.

Whatever the creature was, it had marked its territory like a dog, claiming the place and sending a clear message to any others who might pass this way.

This barn, and whatever lay inside, belonged to *it*. Its territory. Its property. Its food.

CHAPTER THIRTY-TWO

Namjin Range, the South Lands

The ngaru found the convoy a few days out from Hummel and tracked it across the Tolak Range, keeping pace through the trees and shadows. At times the creatures retreated out of earshot, sometimes for a few days, sometimes only for several hours. When the creatures did retreat, the relief among the travellers was palpable, but their respite always ended with an echoing howl as the ngaru returned. Lidan knew their sound as well as her own voice, the howls shaking the hide covers of the wagons and the resolve of the rangers. One hand went to her knife by instinct, squeezing the handle, while the other held tight to the reins, waiting for the moment the monsters leapt from the trees to snatch her from the saddle.

She waited, but they never came.

At night the rangers set fires at the edge of the camp after the Namjin messenger suggested the creatures disliked the flames. From Lidan's experience, ngaru paid no mind to light or warmth. She'd seen them attack in the day when the sun was high in the southern sky, so she doubted the effectiveness of the fire pits and torches carried by the perimeter patrols.

In her gut she knew it was something else that kept the ngaru at bay—some sort of wariness or uncertainty that she didn't understand. She heard them off in the bush, scuffling around in the under-growth and yowling to one another. She closed her eyes and tried to shut them out, her hands shivering at the effort, but nothing kept the sound from her ears. With Loge nearby, always within reach and never out of sight, she felt safe enough, but it was a false sense of security. If those creatures wanted to take the camp, no fire or ranger could stop them.

The question remained: why didn't they?

Each evening when the convoy set camp, Lidan and Loge found a place to train with their knives. The sound of metal ringing and clashing, a quickly uttered encouragement or correction, punctuated with the shuffling of boots and grunts of exertion, filled the air in the camp and forced back the noise of the ngaru among the trees. The exercise pushed Lidan's muscles until they burned beneath her skin and her blood thumped in her head, and at night when she curled into a bedroll beside her sisters, exhaustion swept through her, dragging her down into a heavy sleep that not even the ngaru's calls could disturb.

As night fell, Loge stepped back from sparring and bowed, breathless and sweating. 'That's enough for tonight. Well done.'

Lidan grinned. 'Have I worn you out?'

The young ranger laughed and shook his head as they walked back to the fires near the wagons. 'No, but you are getting faster and stronger.'

They stowed their weapons and took a drink from a bladder of water.

'Nights are getting warmer,' Loge said quietly. He was a good sight taller than Lidan, and his hazel brown eyes seemed to shine when he laughed.

'Days are longer too,' she agreed and glanced at the sky between the trees, the stars blinking through the long leaves.

They'd spent close to a month on the move, pushing through the foot-hills of the tablelands in a northwesterly direction, the sunrise at their back and the mountains to their right. The days were increasingly warmer, signalling an end to the winter and the coming wet season.

'Still no rain,' she observed and squeezed a stopper into the mouth of the water bladder.

By the coming full moon, they would be at the base of the hills where the Namjin clan made their home and in the relative safety of the Corron. Her father said the ngaru wouldn't dare attack such a gathering, reassuring his family and rangers that succour was near. Lidan had no faith in the idea of safety in numbers, but she hoped for her father's sake his word would hold true.

The ngaru in the distance howled again, screeching and screaming and sending a shudder of disgust through Lidan's core.

'What are they doing out there?' she demanded through clenched teeth, the noise of their hunters grating against her nerves like splintered wood on soft, exposed skin.

'Who knows?' Loge flicked a piece of bark at the fire and it flared bright before dying to ash. 'The one who attacked me tracked us for days. It's like they have to make sure they can kill you before they attack. They don't want to risk losing the fight.' His eyes scanned the trees. 'I thought they would have tried by now.'

'Maybe they decided we're too dangerous?' she suggested without a hint of hope, her words twisted by the sourness of sarcasm.

'Ha!' Loge laughed, a harsh sound in the tense clearing. A few rangers glanced their way before turning back to their meals and hushed conversations. 'Maybe, but I doubt it,' muttered Loge, as bitter and frustrated as Lidan.

The hide curtain at the rear of a wagon opened, and Lidan watched her mother climb down on shaking legs. Sellan carried a pail to the edge of the camp and tipped the contents into the bushes, the light of the fires showing her apron soiled with dirt and streaks of vomit for the first time in recent memory. With only a few tine-women travelling in the convoy, the bulk of Farah's care fell to her sister-wives, including Sellan. Her mother's face was as pale and drawn as Lidan had ever seen it and a jolt of shock ran along her spine.

Her mothers rarely ventured outside the wagons, fear and fatigue keeping them behind the hide walls with the children. More cries echoed between the trees and an unseen child began to wail. Someone tried to soothe her tears with whispers and a song, but they died away as the little girl's cries rang louder. The ngaru responded with their own howling song, as if calling to each other and asking what the noise meant. But it wasn't long before they were back to crashing through the bush, and by the sound of it, chasing some small animal and making it scream in vain for its life before cutting it short and snarling loudly over the scraps.

Lidan watched the dana in the shadow of the wagon, hidden from the camp. She dropped the pail and leaned against the side rail of the carriage, her auburn hair falling from its tail and into her face. She'd never seen her mother so unkempt and ragged. Even when Lidan's baby sisters kept the hall awake crying for milk and their mother's arms, the dana turned herself out in pristine fashion; not a hair out of place or a smudge of fatigue on her face.

The woman straightened, her hands on her hips, and drew a deep breath through her nose while her eyes remained tightly closed. Her lips moved without uttering a sound, whispering silent words into the night.

What is she doing? Lidan frowned. Her mother's fingers paled around her knuckles. Her arms shook and her face creased with effort, as if concentrating her will on blocking the sounds of the ngaru from her mind.

The racket finally eased and the dana opened her eyes to stare at the side of the wagon, her shoulders sagging as if a weight had been lifted. Then the dana turned and their gazes met. Had her mother sensed her presence?

It wasn't her unwavering stare that sent a shiver down Lidan's spine, or even the fact that her mother's mutterings seemed to have quelled the ngaru's snarling that turned her blood to ice. In the dark green of Sellan's eyes, she saw fear, and for the first time in thirteen years, she knew her mother was truly afraid.

The vision of her mother's pale face and wide eyes haunted every mile until the convoy broke the cover of the trees and a grassy plain stretched out before them. The sounds of the ngaru fell behind the riders as the wagons crossed into open ground, making their way to the dark, snaking line of a river and the track running along its bank. The sound of the world without the constant howl of their pursuers was nothing short of blissful.

For the first time in a month Lidan heard birds and insects and lily drakes chirping in the reeds and grass along the riverbank, the water rushing away to the south, lured by the sea. It whispered over stones and fallen branches, lapping in little coves and bubbling past, drawing the horses into the riverbed to drink. Starved by the dry season, it seemed too small for the width of the banks and awkward, like a child wearing her father's boots. Even so, it ran wider than the creek in the valley of the Caine and Lidan marvelled at the clear water and shimmering eddies, a smile spreading across her face.

She dismounted and jogged with Theus across the sandy riverbed, the rangers following slowly, their eyes on the line of sparse trees shading the gully. Lidan glanced back at her father, atop Titon on the bank, standing guard at the wagons as the women and children climbed out with expressions of relief. He nodded and waved his hand and the travelling party broke into an excited frenzy.

They stripped off their boots and waded into the cold pools, splashing their faces and laughing at each other for the first time in weeks. The horses hardly raised their heads from drinking while their riders rubbed them down. At least half the rangers kept watch, then swapped with their fellows for a turn in the water and a chance to rest their horses' backs.

Lidan closed her eyes and lay back on the warm, coarse sand, allowing her mind to rest and the joyful sounds of her family to wash her clean of the anxiety that had accumulated under the threat of the ngaru and the unsettling memory of her mother's unease. Perhaps the Namjin messenger was right and the ngaru *were* fearful of light and warmth, keeping their distance, never sure if it was safe to pounce. For now, by the rushing river in the peace of the gully, she didn't care. She was thankful she'd had no cause to use her knives for more than practice and relieved to have made it to the Namjin range alive.

A high whistle broke her tranquillity and she sat bolt upright, spinning to look at her father as rangers hurried to respond to the signal. She stood quickly and followed their gaze, catching sight of riders approaching from the north. Many carried spears, which was hardly considered polite for a simple welcoming party.

Until a month ago, the Tolak and the Namjin had been teetering on all out war along the border. Now her family had been invited to cross it under the pretence of a Corron, and Lidan began to wonder if perhaps it had all been an elaborate ruse to draw her father out into the open. Her heart rate rose, her pulse thudding hard as her throat tightened.

The Tolak group collected itself in a rush as the riders neared; her mothers and Moyra herding startled children up the bank and into the wagons with whispers of comfort. Her sisters stared wide-eyed at the commotion, never uttering a word of complaint. After a month living in fear of the ngaru, they didn't need any encouragement when ordered to hide.

Lidan scrambled to her boots and shoved them on, ignoring wet socks and sand, and snatched Theus's reins. Either she'd grown on the journey or become more flexible, as she was now able to reach her foot to the stirrup and swing onto the horse's back without Loge's help. As if summoned by the thought, the ranger appeared at her side and moved Striker in front of Theus, putting himself between Lidan and any danger the riders might present.

The man at the head of the group raised his hand and his companions slowed to a halt. Keen to hear their exchange with her father, Lidan pulled at the reins and turned Theus up the bank, but they both jerked to a stop. Loge's hand held the horse's bridle firmly and his stern hazel eyes told her without words that she would not be moving.

'Greetings, Daari!' The lead rider called, lifting his hand high then bringing it to his chest. 'Daari Yorrell Namjin bids you welcome.'

Lidan narrowed her eyes. By his clipped tone and clear words, the man sounded unlike any ranger she had ever heard. Though his clothes were scruffy and worn, covered in dust and more than a little mud, his horse was by far the most magnificent of the group. The glint of fine stones in a bone ring around his wrist caught Lidan's eye, and she wondered what game the man was playing at. He was no ranger, or advisor to a daari, nor a tradesman or master. Only a clan leader displayed his status with such finery.

'Greetings to you,' Erlon replied, mimicking the hand gesture and adding a slight bow of his head. 'We have travelled from Tolak to attend the Corron.'

The lead rider nodded and swept his hand to the side. 'Allow us to escort you.'

No one moved; Tolak rangers waiting on their daari's signal and the Namjin riders pausing for a response.

'You think you can fool me with that poor disguise?' Erlon asked the rider.

The other man turned his hands up and shrugged. 'It was worth a bloody try, wasn't it?'

Erlon smirked. 'It may have been a few years, Yorrell, but you haven't changed that much. You are going grey, though. Too many wives will do that to a man.'

Loge slowly released Theus's bridle and Lidan gave the horse some rein, guiding him up the bank and around the wagons with Loge close behind.

'I wish my nagging wives and your bloody rangers harrying my border were the extent of my problems.' Yorrell smiled, but it did not reach his eyes.

There was a shadow there that would not budge, a twin to the darkness haunting her father. Erlon sighed and nodded, a glance of understanding passing between them.

'Who is this strapping young lad?' Yorrell asked, changing the subject.

Lidan baulked and looked down at herself. Her breasts weren't exactly what she would have called prominent, especially under layers of riding leathers and her coat, but her long hair and finer facial features were surely enough to hint that she was in fact a girl. Then she looked to her right and her face flushed hot with embarrassment. Daari Yorrell was referring to Loge. The ranger stared at the Namjin leader with unveiled shock, unsure what to do or say.

'That joke was old the last time I saw you,' Erlon countered. 'You know I don't have any sons.'

A lump formed in Lidan's throat as Yorrell laughed at his jest.

'Still makes me laugh!' He turned to her with a smile and bowed his head. 'Lidan; you *have* grown since I last saw you. I almost didn't recognise the woman you're becoming.'

There was a sting in the way he said *woman*, the word rolling slyly from his tongue. She bowed her head instinctively, knowing her mother surely watched from the wagon and would slap her black and blue if she offended the Namjin daari.

'Thank you, sir,' Lidan murmured, hoping to appease him so he might take his attention elsewhere. Her strategy failed.

Yorrell urged his horse forwards and took her chin gently between his fingers, lifting her face to the sun. In the corner of her vision, Lidan saw Loge stiffen, his hands tightening around his reins and his lips pressing into a line. Striker sensed the tension and shied with a snort. There was nothing Lidan could do except meet the daari's eyes.

They were deep brown like his hair, framed with dark brows in a broad face with strong prominent cheekbones and skin only a touch darker than her father's. His jaw was square and his neck was a thick trunk of a thing that hardly tapered at all from the shoulders to the head. He seemed square, without any soft edges to speak of; like a brick of stone atop a horse.

His lips, however, were strange: too full for a man of his build, and the way he ran his tongue across them made Lidan want to slap his large hand away. Yorrell eyed her, his gaze wandering from her face, down her chest, to her legs, and back again before the grip on her chin tightened ever so slightly.

'She has her mother's colour, but the look of her father is there for certain,' he said, his riders watching with blank expressions while her father's rangers shifted uncomfortably in their saddles.

'That's because she *is* mine,' Erlon replied between clenched teeth and Yorrell's hand fell away. Yorrell shrugged and turned his horse back to his men.

'We will arrange for her to meet my son during the Corron. She and Cole will have much in common.' Daari Yorrell waved and continued past his companions along the riverbank. 'Come, you've had a hard ride. There is time to rest before the Corron begins in the morning.'

Lidan's hands shook where they gripped the reins between her fingers. Her entire body was rigid, her muscles bunched so tightly they began to ache. In all the times her mother had beaten and screamed at her, Lidan had never felt fouler or more used than she did right now, sitting on her horse among the very people meant to protect her. Her skin crawled where Yorrell had held her, burning as if his fingers had been made of fire and had somehow branded her. The thought of his wide lips, and his tongue running across them made her shudder, and the idea of meeting his son turned her stomach.

A hand gripped her shoulder as the Tolak rangers moved to follow the Namjin, and she flinched, her arm swinging up to turn the grasp away like Loge had taught her.

'Liddy,' a voice cooed over the rattle and rumble of the passing wagons and she turned to see it belonged to her father. He leaned back in his saddle and their eyes met. 'Don't think too much on it, all right? That's just how he is.'

Just how he is? Lidan repeated to herself, watching her father's back as he rode ahead to lead his family to the Corron. She bit her lip to stop it shaking and doubted her father knew Daari Yorrell as well as he thought he did.

CHAPTER THIRTY-THREE

The Corron, Namjin Range, the South Lands

The hills known as Jin's Brothers rose from the grasslands. They were dark, almost black, even where the light of the sun touched the stone. There was no vegetation along the ridges or crevices and a dusty skirt of grey soil surrounded them in a narrow space at the foot where grass did not grow. Much like the solitary Caine, the rounded monoliths stood guard over the clan below; their massive shadows stretching into the east, growing ever longer as the Tolak group approached and the sun sunk towards its rest.

For most of her life, Lidan had only ever seen people from her own clan. Every so often, when the weather allowed, traders from Isord or Arinnia braved Fracture Pass to come and barter for the horses her people broke and trained. They had the same faces as her mother; fair skin and bright hair, and their clothes, their finery and their speech all hinted at a world much larger than the one she knew.

Traders from the south and east also came across the desert, their skin as black as jet and their faces wrapped against the northern winds they swore bit at them with teeth of ice. They too came for the horses and haggled fiercely for a good price. She saw the cloth they carried and grew dizzy at the scent of their spice wagons, wondering at the places they came from, dotted along the Rinay Coast and the islands on the sea.

In those days of trading, when she was not much older than Abbi, she had marvelled at how so many people could live in one place. While the traders had only swelled Hummel's population by a quarter, at the time she felt certain if another person walked through the gates, the walls would burst apart in a shower of timber and dried clay.

Yet, as the track veered left and they turned their horses into the valley between the two hills, Lidan's breath caught in her throat, and she realised how sheltered her life truly had been.

The central Namjin village, Jinloh, hugged the base of the southern hill, walled like her home, with a long hall and clusters of homes and buildings among garden plots and animal pens. Jinloh was not surprising in itself—it was the sprawling camp between the hills that stole the breath from her chest, dwarfing the village and sending a murmur of awe through the Tolak riders.

From the base of one hill, across a wide, shallow valley to the base of the other, tents of all shapes and sizes shifted in the evening breeze. Colours and smells assaulted her senses, banners and flags adorned with clan symbols snapping back and forth to announce their owners' location. The noise grew as they neared, the clamour of people and animals, adults and children, warriors and tradesmen all crammed into one place rising above anything she'd ever heard before.

'By my grandfather's balls, Yorrell!' Erlon's voice carried on the wind. 'How many people did you invite?'

'Just the five clans, but they brought a few tag-alongs…'

The chaos of sound and movement swallowed their conversation. Lidan's ears rang with the voices of bakers hawking flat bread and butchers arguing with their customers over trade. Theus put his head down and followed the other horses obediently, and it was just as well. As the crowds closed around her family and their wagons, she lost all sense of direction and purpose, instead gaping at the sheer volume of the clans gathered at the feet of the Brothers.

The sun broke the horizon in the east and poured its light down the Namjin valley to the crowing of a rooster and the barking reply of an offended dog. Lidan's body felt like stone, her head aching as if it had been filled with mud overnight and beaten with a club. Her father snored in the back of their tent, likely nursing a dark mood and a roiling stomach after too many cups of Namjin berry wine with a few of his rangers and Yorrell.

Lidan had quickly made herself absent from their evening celebrations in case Yorrell had any ideas of introducing her to his son.

She slipped from the bedroll of pelts and collected her coat, wondering how long she might need it today as the sun rose and warmed the valley. She left her mother and sister sleeping in the same cot, Sellan's arms wrapped around Marrit for warmth and protection. Holding her youngest daughter close was the most intimate gesture Lidan had seen from her mother in a long time. She couldn't remember the last time her mother had held her in an embrace like that, or if she ever had. She bit down on a pang of jealousy. Perhaps a little fear was good for the dana.

Outside the large hide tent, the day seemed filled with the rising smoke of cooking fires lazily drifting in the still air, the smell of meat and porridge wandering through the tents to draw the clan's people from their sleep. The rangers took to cooking what food they'd carried in the wagons, awake before the rest of the family.

Loge handed her a bowl of sticky porridge and a spoon, then nodded at the village to the south of their camp. 'You're going to need all the energy you can get today.'

He moved away before she could ask him why.

Her gaze followed his gesture to the walled village and the hall at the centre, a single storey built into the soft earth at the base of the monolith, crawling with activity. The sun was barely above the tablelands and already the place hummed with the movement and voices of hundreds of people. Loge's meaning slid down her spine like cold water and she shivered.

Today the Corron began.

A deep cough, something close to retch, echoed behind her and she spun with surprise. Her father leaned against the side rail of a wagon and shook his head. 'I'm too old for this shit...'

Siman tossed him a water skin with a smirk. 'We're all young men when the stars are out and the wine's flow'n. Then we wake to find we're as old as ever and feel'n every year of it.'

'It's that bloody Yorrell. I never could let him get a drink ahead of me, and he knows it.' Erlon took a draw on the water skin, rinsed his mouth and spat beside the cart's wheel. 'Feel like a horse shat in my mouth. And he'll be up in that hall, fresh as a flower while I'm hack'n my guts up.' Erlon noticed Lidan and winked before taking a long drink.

A ranger offered Erlon a bowl but he waved it away.

'Got any wine?'

The ranger smiled and an urn appeared with a cup and the daari drained three cupfuls without a word, then looked at Lidan. She sat frowning, unsure what to make of this unveiled glimpse into the world her father inhabited.

'It's going to be a long week, Liddy. You might need a drink by the end of it just to dull the pain.'

After seeing what the Namjin wine did to her father, she doubted his assertion. Porridge would suffice for now.

'Have they sent word?' asked Erlon.

Siman glanced up from fitting the belt for his new bronze axe. 'Just after dawn. The Corron begins at midday in the hall. You can bring a second, but everyone else has to stay in camp.'

The daari nodded and glanced at his daughter. 'Hope you don't have anything planned, Liddy. You're coming with me, too.'

Lidan fumbled and almost dropped her breakfast in the dirt between her feet. When her father said the family must travel to Namjin lands, she thought it merely a formality and a show of pride. After all, how often did the daaris of all five great southern clans have the chance to parade their offspring before their rivals and allies? She didn't realise he meant for her to attend the Corron *with* him. What possible use would she be?

She scrambled to stand as he moved away, the wine urn under his arm. 'Father, I… why?'

He turned back casually—or perhaps drunkenly—and shrugged. 'You're my heir.'

He vanished between the tents and left Lidan by the cooking fire with her bowl hanging precariously from her hand. Elation warred with trepidation in the depths of her belly and she bit the inside of her lip.

There was sad resignation in his voice as the words echoed in her ears. She heard the scorn and ridicule in Yorrell's words the day before, mocking her father for his lack of sons and her cheeks flushed with heat. Erlon must be the laughing stock of the clan daaris, forced to bring a girl to the Corron when his peers undoubtedly had at least one son to their names.

Would it ever matter how well she rode or fought? Would it ever matter that she could read and write symbols and argue the Law? Would it ever matter that she could do all the things an heir needed to, as long as she was a girl and all her father wanted was a boy?

But he'd said it. He'd actually *said* the words. She was his heir, the one he was taking to the Corron, the one who would sit at his side through the meetings and face the daaris of the other clans, just as she'd promised her mother she would. She lifted her chin and squared her shoulders, ignoring the nervous thud of her heart and the weight of expectation settling on her shoulders, and prepared herself to leap into the unknown.

CHAPTER THIRTY-FOUR

The Corron, Namjin Range, the South Lands

Jinloh's gates stood open, the empty space between yawning like the maw of a great beast preparing to swallow Lidan whole. The walls loomed above the nearby tents, diminishing the sprawl of humanity at their feet as though they were no bigger than ants. They stood at least twice as high as the walls around Hummel and at the top wore a crown of timber spikes, which by the look of the wood, had been cut and placed recently. Were they to ward off ngaru or a human enemy?

Theus followed Titon, her father's broad back filling the gateway as they rode with Siman through throngs of villagers pushing past in the opposite direction. She noticed their curious glances, their whispers and their pointing fingers, and she lifted her chin, staring straight ahead in an effort to disguise her apprehension. Bundles of goods and children in hand, the clan folk hurried on around the horses and into the camp in the valley, leaving the village near empty and strangely quiet. Groaning timber caused Lidan to turn, the gates easing closed at their backs and booming as the thick locking beam fell into place.

The commotion of the camp faded, muted by the high walls and Lidan's blood ran cold. Loge was locked on the other side of those imposing ramparts, the spikes atop the wall standing between them, and she felt oddly uneasy at his absence. Sitting atop her fierce horse, beside her father and his chief ranger, Lidan should have felt untouchable. She should have felt safe. Instead, she felt like a mouse waiting for a snare to snap shut around her neck.

Yorrell emerged from the hall, waving as they dismounted and smiling with his fleshy lips. His brown eyes sparkled, not with joy, but an anticipation Lidan didn't care for. His gaze fell on her too readily, finding her too easily behind Erlon and Siman and lingering for longer than she liked. If her father noticed, he didn't show it. He approached the daari and clasped his arm with a smile on his face, albeit a weary one.

'You've arrived!' Yorrell remarked, taking his eyes from Lidan long enough to glance at Erlon. 'You Tolaks don't like to rush, do you?'

'Blame your wine,' replied Erlon, and Yorrell nodded knowingly.

'You're out of practice, old man.' He turned and gestured to the doors, open and waiting. 'Come, we have much to discuss.'

Smoke haze stung Lidan's eyes, unused to the choking way it collected beneath the thatch after so long away from home. Even at midday, the hall's central fire pit popped and danced while lanterns on the walls glowed to illuminate the great round table that encircled it.

Three men sat around the table, each with a younger boy beside them and another man behind their shoulder, while a tall boy and a man stood beside an empty chair directly across the fire pit from the door. As they entered the hall and the doors shut behind them, Lidan felt the eyes of the men move to track her and her father to the empty chairs on the left. Her hand itched to hold the handle of her knife, hidden under the length of her coat.

Her mother's insistence on an overskirt of dark green and a fine shirt and tunic seemed apt now that she saw the gathered men in their finery. Gemstones and beads flashed in their hair and beards; thick leather vambraces and bracelets of bone and fine polished wood adorned their arms. A polished stone axe lay on the table before each of them. The blades faced the owner, the handles pointed towards the fire, almost out of reach. It was a spectacle of intimidation and respect, on one hand showing strength while on the other, disarming each leader in the presence of his peers.

Lidan thanked the ancestors she had Raeh braid her hair before she left the camp. At least she looked regal amongst this not-too-subtle display of manliness. Her father wore his finest tunic and his hair tied back, fine braids from his temples flashing in the firelight with rings of bronze and copper. The eyes of the gathered men shifted as he drew closer, their brows creasing and lips curling.

It took a moment for Lidan to understand as she sank down in her seat, scanning the gathering and realising not one man in the room had a metal trinket on his person. Except for the three members of the Tolak clan, the adornments of the other leaders and their companions were strictly stone, timber and bone, and while they were beautiful, they paled in comparison to the lustre of her father's metal.

Erlon sat down, followed by Siman and waited for Yorrell to stand in his place at what could be called the "head" of the circular table. The Namjin leader drew his axe from his belt and laid it on the table, turning its shaft to the fire in silence, then gestured to Erlon to do the same. With a distinct nonchalance, her father hefted his axe from his belt and it thumped down on the tabletop, the bronze blade shining in the orange firelight. The sharpened edge seemed to sing as he gently spun the handle towards the fire, dragging with it the gaze of the daaris and their companions.

'And so,' Yorrell began, 'the Corron is in session. It is customary to spend at least the first day commenting on the progress of our clans and leave the talk of more important things to the coming days. However, we have no time for such formalities.

'As detailed in the messages sent last moon, our people have come under attack this season from an unknown and foreign foe. It has torn apart villages and harried ranging parties from the Wolban range in the north to the Daylin marshes in the southwest. It comes by night and takes the lives of our innocents as readily as those of our warriors.' He placed his hands on the table and looked at each daari in turn. 'This Corron will not speak of the progress of our clans, but the preparation and defence of them. We will decide what must be done to stem the advance of this scourge and how we can ally ourselves against it.'

Lidan heard her father shift in his chair but did not dare move to look at his face. She stared at the flames and committed every word to memory, etched in the stone of her mind. She would not forget the words spoken here. Today marked a tipping point, a place in time when the people of the South Lands put aside their differences and turned to face the snarling terror of the ngaru.

On the afternoon of the fourth day, Yorrell waved and a tine-woman approached with a wine urn. She filled the cups around the table, and just as her father predicted, Lidan held hers out to be filled with the rest of the men and boys. Her hand ached from days of scratching symbols on sheets of parchment, her fingers stained with ink. Her mother bit back on her disdain and only once muttered an underhanded comment about potential husbands disliking girls with ugly, inky fingers. Lidan suspected she did so only because her daughter was now at the centre of everything, finally acting as an heir, despite the impending birth of Farah's child.

Sellan became more restless as the days of the Corron progressed, fussing over Lidan's hair and clothes, scolding the girls if they left the tent with so much as a mark on their faces. She even worried after the younger girls, insisting they wear the finest things they owned and hurrying to barter more fabric from stalls in the camp's market when the supply of worthy clothing ran out. She had her sister-wives and the tine-women sewing through the day to produce garments for Lidan and the others, all in an effort to show the clan's wealth.

None of it made sense to Lidan until, on the fourth day, Yorrell leaned back in his chair, wine in hand and said, 'Now we come to the matter of alliances.'

Lidan's hand stopped squeezing the aches from her bones and she swallowed her mouthful of wine, slowly returning the cup to the table. She looked up and saw the daaris nodding, their hands never far from the berry wine while a few of their sons glanced at each other and smirked. A chill wrapped its hands around Lidan's throat, her gaze shifting to Yorrell and his wide lips. His eyes were on her again, flicking away only when her father leaned forwards and cleared his throat.

'Are we five not already allied against this threat?' asked Erlon. His wine stood untouched, as it had since the first day. His was the only cup the tine-woman never needed to refill.

'Of course,' Yorrell hastened to agree, then spread his hand to indicate the gathering. 'But even the strongest halls can benefit from repairs. We all know the best way to strengthen an alliance is by matching.'

Lidan's ears filled with the thumping sound of her blood, powered by her racing heart. In her naivety she thought Yorrell had forgotten the promised introduction to his son, consumed as they were with talk of the ngaru. Now the roving eyes of father and son found her and her skin crawled.

'What children have we between the five of us?' Yorrell asked, opening the question to the daaris. 'I have my eldest, Cole, four younger sons and three daughters.'

'My eldest is Trenor,' Daari Allin of the Wolban announced. 'I have six more sons and two daughters.'

'Brandt is my eldest,' offered Merk of the Marsaw, clapping his son on the shoulder. 'He has...' the older man leaned towards his son, who whispered in his father's ear, '... *five* sisters!'

Horice, daari of the Daylin clan, drained his wine and held the cup out for the tine-woman to refill. 'Harran is the heir to my range, unless one of his brothers is stupid enough to challenge him.' The young man beside Horice beamed, his blond hair shining in the torchlight, announcing the northern blood in his veins.

Then their attention turned to Lidan's father and silence fell across the room. Her cheeks flushed with heat, embarrassed on her father's behalf and utterly powerless to save him the shame of admitting his heir was a girl. To his credit, Erlon turned to her and placed a solid hand on her shoulder, a genuine smile lighting his eyes.

'My heir is Lidan. She has nine sisters, all as beautiful as their mothers and as fierce as their father.'

The swell of pride filling Lidan's chest deflated when Daari Yorrell snorted a laugh. 'My cousin has yet to give you a son?'

On her shoulder, her father's hand tightened, his fingers digging into the fabric of her tunic as if to funnel his rage away from his face.

He shrugged. 'Not for lack of trying.'

The other leaders laughed and Erlon grinned, nodding and winking at his fellows while Yorrell merely raised his brows and turned his cup idly on the table.

'Still,' Yorrell continued as the laughter died, 'such a failure on Farah's part should be rectified. It reflects badly on my clan.'

The men and boys turned to Yorrell, leaning forwards in silence, unwilling to miss a single word. Breathing deeply, Lidan tried to calm her hammering heart.

Please don't...

'If my cousin won't give you a son, I shall give you one of mine.' Yorrell smiled and bile rose in Lidan's throat. 'In exchange for Lidan, of course.'

CHAPTER THIRTY-FIVE

The Parry Farm, Southern Orthia

'Sasha, wake up!' Ran shook her by the shoulders. 'Come on, you have to wake up!'

'Wassit?' muttered Sasha, starting from her sleep and shielding her eyes against the light of the dawning day.

'Time to get up.' Ran pulled her to sit and shoved a handful of dried meat at her.

She blinked at him in weary confusion. 'Is the sun even up?'

'Barely, but we have to go.'

'Go where?' she asked, her voice growing stronger as the daze of sleep disappeared.

'Anywhere,' he said, hurrying to collect their things and stuff them into the packs. 'We can't stay here.'

'What's happened?' Sasha caught his arm as he passed and locked her gaze on his face. 'Has this got to do with you barring the door? What happened yesterday? Did you see something out there?'

The angle of her brows and the way her fingers held his coat told him she wasn't going to let him brush away her questions this time.

Ran sighed. 'It came back last night. Whatever killed the Parrys came back. It knows we're here, and it's marked us.'

'Marked us?' she repeated. She let him go and he returned to packing the few possessions they had.

'It pissed on the barn like a dog marking a tree.' He nodded when Sasha screwed up her face. 'Surprised the smell didn't wake you.'

'Well, now you mention it, there was something…' she muttered and collected her blanket, folding it into a pack.

'If I'm right, we have today to get a head start. If it thinks we're staying put then it will come back. We can—'

'You think we can outrun it?'

Her question halted his hurried packing. Ran looked at Sasha as she came to her feet, her injured knee wrapped with a strip of cloth beneath her trousers, her hair a mess of red curls and straw. Could they, with her knee and his ankle, against the snow and the wind and the mountains?

'I don't know. I don't even know what it is.' Ran glanced at the barn wall as if he could see through it to the day outside, the hills and snowy mountains. 'I do know it's coming back, and I don't want to be here when it arrives.'

Sasha nodded and hefted her bag onto her back with a wince of discomfort twisting at her features. She waved Ran away as he moved forwards to help. 'I'm all right, Ran, really—I'll be fine.'

'I'm sorry,' he said, shouldering his bag. 'I wish we could stay longer but it's not safe here anymore.'

'If we stick near the roads we'll make better time,' she suggested, pulling her knitted hat down over her hair.

Ran nodded and went to the door of the barn, ignoring the shiver of fear threading along his spine. He despised the exposure of the road but agreed with Sasha's assessment. It was unlikely that any ordinary folk would be out and about after the recent storms, but he couldn't say the same for his father's soldiers.

Had they persisted in following him after he escaped Graupen? Had Sasha's father told the townsfolk about his daughter's mysterious patient and sent word back to the city? For every foot of snow that fell in the path of the soldiers, another fell in his, hindering his progress as much as theirs. For all he knew, they were only a few miles behind them, with more provisions and better equipment.

Still, he didn't fear them as much as the creature that tore the farmhouse apart and marked the barn in the night. If all else failed and he was captured, he had some chance of mercy in a trial. He might escape execution if he could argue he was cursed by the magic and therefore, not at fault. He could *not* hope to reason with a beast such as the one that massacred the Parry family.

Sasha helped pry the nails from the door with a hammer, while he unwound the wire and released the door handles. From the tool store beside the door, Ran retrieved a pair of knives he assumed were once used to butcher animals, and handed one to Sasha. She looked at the blade with a raised brow and eyed the rust and nicks along the cutting edge.

'Better than nothing, I guess,' she muttered as she tucked it into her belt and Ran smiled.

He shoved his shoulder into the barn door and pushed out into the day. Their stolen knives were in terrible condition, but they were also large and sharp enough to do a lot of damage to anything they were thrust into. If that proved enough to give them time to escape a pursuer, or even kill them, he would gladly take his chances with a rusty butcher's knife.

The sunlight seemed to linger a little longer than it had in the preceding days, affording Ran and Sasha a few more precious hours of travel before their escape was uncovered. They hurried along the road, heading southwest as fast as their stolen snowshoes could carry them. Thankfully, the fair weather held, and only as the sun dipped behind the peaks did the wind begin to moan through the trees and catch its icy claws in the seams of their coats.

Sasha kept pace with Ran as they tramped across the snow, her limp growing more pronounced as the day dragged on. His lungs and legs screamed for rest, but his head warned him that every moment stopped by the roadside was a gift to the creature behind them. Even as night crept up the valley at their backs, his mind demanded they carry on and follow the road into the darkness, despite the dangers lurking in the shadows.

When the sun finally dropped from sight, they fell at the base of a broad tree trunk, sheltering beneath its wide canopy of thick branches and worked to catch their breaths. Ran's shoulders burned from the effort of carrying his bag, the straps digging into his skin through the layers of fur and fabric as if they weren't there at all. He'd be surprised if he could lift his arms by morning, let alone move his legs. It was possible they'd covered more ground in their haste than any day previous—and it was a good thing, too. The further they got from the farm, the greater distance the creature had to cover to find them. With the weather and wind on their side, the slope not too steep and the help of the weight-distributing snowshoes, they'd had a successful day of running away.

Sasha shivered beside him, her hands balled into tight fists, and suddenly Ran's elation at the gains of the day faded. Once more they were in the wilds of the world, surrounded by snow and ice and pursued by an unseen foe. It felt like he'd failed her.

'We can't light a fire, can we?' she asked through chattering teeth.

Ran shook his head as the darkness deepened. 'Not tonight.'

'Ah, shit,' she muttered. She pulled her blanket from her bag and shuffled closer. 'You'll just have to hold me, then.'

He laughed a little and lifted his arm to let her curl in under it, wrapping it around her shoulders. 'Reckon I can manage that.'

Fatigue took Sasha quickly to sleep, but nothing could tempt Ran's eyes from scanning the darkness as she rested in his arms. The moon peered through the clouds and trees, full and shining its silver light on the world below. It wasn't bright enough to travel, but it was enough to see the road and the woods clearly for several feet in either direction. The patches of moonlight and shadow danced, spinning and weaving against each other like lovers, bound in a waltz played by the wind.

He found himself staring at the play of light and shadow, wondering how long they had until their peace was broken. It seemed inevitable that someone, or something, would find them. It was merely a matter of who and when. Was he ready for the fight? For the consequences of being discovered?

Sasha murmured against his chest and he pulled her a little closer, ever more aware that if his father's soldiers captured them, she would face the executioner just for helping him. He could claim her as a hostage, an unwilling guide forced to take him through the mountain passes to Isord. He could try and get her to stay behind or return home, but something in the way she recalled her father's treatment of her brothers made him think that was impossible. She wasn't ever going back to that house.

Could he leave her in the next town, safe among Orthian people, rather than dragging her further into dangers that only the gods knew? Perhaps if he left her at an inn while she slept and stole away into the night he could put enough distance between them that she couldn't track him down. She'd never forgive him if he did that, but if he were hundreds of miles away and across the border, he would never see her again to face her wrath.

CHAPTER THIRTY-SIX

The Southern Reaches, Orthia

Shuffling footsteps woke Ran as they had the night before, scraping across the snow in quick spurts, then stopping, before moving slowly and stopping again. His eyes flew open and he registered the pale light of dawn in the east.

Fuck.

Sasha's hand pressed against his chest once, twice, then a third time—a signal that she was awake. Unfortunately, the relief wasn't enough to slow his heart. The creature was near; so near he heard it breathing and dragging itself across the icy crust on the snow, pausing every so often to sniff the air.

It was the same sound he heard from outside the barn and down in the mine, the same long, drawn-out inhalation that spoke of a creature tracking prey. Had his fall woken the creature from the darkness of the tunnels? Had it been following them since then?

He closed his eyes and tried to calm down, feigning sleep as Sasha's hand moved slowly under the blankets to pass him a knife. She pressed it into his hand and closed his fingers around the hilt, rolling her head as she did to draw attention away from the movement. To anyone watching, she remained asleep, resettling against his chest and growing still once more.

Under the blanket, Ran gripped the knife so hard his arm shook. Tension and fear shivered along his muscles, down to the tight fist clenched around the worn wooden handle. The rusty blade might not stand a chance against the thing stalking them, but it was all they had—two butchering knives and some magic. The power stirred under his skin, warmed by the fear in his blood.

It rose from a dark place in his soul, spiralling up to his shoulders and down his arms, pooling in his fingers and tingling like insects crawling across his flesh. Sasha drew a sharp breath and stiffened. At such close quarters, it wasn't surprising that she sensed the gathering power.

The creature moved closer, approaching with slow, purposeful steps. It sniffed and exhaled, snuffling hurriedly as though it caught the trail of its prey and didn't dare lose it.

Sweat rolled down Ran's brow, past his ear and under his collar, leaving a trail of ice in its wake. Panic and the heat of his magic burned across his skin, feverish in the snow and ice of the roadside. The creature had tracked them all night, following their scent to this place beside a tree as broad as a horse was long, and now it stood but a few feet from Ran's right shoulder.

He knew it had found them when the sniffing stopped with a satisfied gasp. To his left, still curled under his arm, Sasha slowly raised her head. Her body tensed, preparing to fight for her life.

'Ready?' Sasha whispered.

He squeezed her hand under the blanket in reply and heard her swallow her fear.

'Now!' she screamed and threw back the blanket.

She rolled away from the tree and Ran hurled himself forwards, kicking off the trunk into a roll. He came to his feet and spun, knife raised, to meet the attacker.

Across the snow, the beast skittered back, surprised by their movement, then opened its jaw to snarl and hiss. Its mouth yawned twice as wide as a man's could comfortably open, revealing broken jagged teeth, blackened by rot and dripping with slick saliva. Its lips were covered in pustules; one bursting as the flesh stretched around it, leaking blue slime down the creature's chin.

It roared and the branches above them shook, dislodging clumps of snow that thumped to the ground. The creature, a thing with the form of a human but the movement of a diseased, enraged hound, took advantage of the shower and sprang forward, clawed hands extended and its mouth snapping. It hit Ran in the chest and twisted, throwing him at the tree.

He slammed into the trunk with a loud crack as something broke, echoing under branches and more ice fell around him. He heard a scream and a barking howl and scrambled to his hands and knees, sucking a breath through his teeth and clutching his side.

Several feet away, Sasha lay sprawled across the ground, her knife knocked out of reach. The creature stalked across the snow, its lips drawn back from its teeth, circling Sasha as she dragged herself to her feet and balanced on her good leg.

'Ran?' she called and the beast paused, tilting its head to the side.

Black orbs regarded Ran from a sunken, hollowed face. Deformed and scarred, the creature's skin peeled away from bone and muscle as if decomposing where it stood, and what remained of its long, lank hair hung matted from its scalp like filthy curtains. It looked back at Sasha and snarled, crouching low on its thick hind legs and digging its clawed hands into the snow.

Ran's vision shifted, stuttering and blurring. He hesitated, and for a single heartbeat, he saw a person crouching before Sasha. Was it a woman he saw, naked and lithe, deadly and—

It pounced at Sasha and his vision flicked back into place, the image of the living woman vanishing beneath the rotting corpse. Sasha went down under the creature's weight and Ran screamed. His magic flared, a blast of blue power exploding in the snow beside Sasha and the creature, sending a plume of ice into the air. The monster skittered away and Ran staggered after it, launching himself at the creature through the cloud of falling ice.

He tackled it in the side and they rolled together onto the flat width of the roadway. The creature found its feet before he got a hand under his body and it turned back to Sasha, howling and shivering with exhilaration.

A cold shudder of terror caught Ran and he realised with painful clarity that the creature was enjoying their suffering. It saw Sasha look towards Ran for help and spun to swat him across the face with the back of its hand. Instead of flesh and bone, cold steel ripped through the skin along Ran's jawline, and he flew backwards, landing hard and skidding across the icy road.

'No!' Sasha cried, her voice filling his ears while his head rang like a bell struck with a hammer. Blood streamed from the wound in his face, burning as the heat of his body met the cold of the air.

Clutching his side, Ran hauled himself to his knees in time to see the creature begin to run. Its bounding leaps closed the distance and Sasha desperately scrambled to her feet.

She never had a chance.

The beast leapt and caught its claws in the back of her coat, sinking its teeth into the top of her shoulder. Sasha's scream cut the air. She hit the snow, thrashing under the weight of the creature, before she managed to turn and face it, hitting it with savage fists. She kicked and screamed, bucking under its hind legs, trying to squirm out from under it.

Finally, the thing had enough of her efforts and laid one hard punch straight to Sasha's face. The resulting crack made Ran's stomach lurch as he found his feet and staggered to a stop.

Across the road, the beast eased back from Sasha's motionless body as a bright red stain spread through the snow behind her head, glaring in the morning light. The creature backed away and put Sasha's prone body between it and Ran, standing behind it like a wolf displaying a kill to the pack.

Then it lifted a foot and placed it on Sasha's chest, right at the base of her ribcage. It put all of its weight on the foot and pressed down, her bones bending under the pressure, then opened its mouth to snarl.

Ran replied with a scream ripped from the depths of his chest and charged.

The beast threw itself forwards using Sasha as a springboard, launching into the air with its steel claws extended. They came together and Ran focused all his remaining magic on the tiny place between their grappling bodies. He might only have one chance to kill the thing before he spent his power and he wasn't about to waste it on missing his mark.

His magic exploded and the beast vanished in the burst of blue light that roared from Ran's hands. The energy from the blast hurled Ran backwards, slamming him onto the hard snow and cracking collected pools of ice. His body screamed and pain lanced from his chest down to his left ankle, burning a path through his bones like lightning.

Somehow, he found the strength to pull himself to his feet, staggering and stumbling back to the clearing around the tree. Several feet away, at the edge of the woods, the creature lay struggling, howling with frustration as its legs and one arm refused to respond. Ran limped past Sasha, still as stone on the ground and refused to look at her face.

He would not be distracted.

The beast spat at him as he neared and it received his boot in its face for its efforts. It snarled, helpless in the snow but unbowed, unwilling or unable to back down even when its defeat seemed inevitable.

'What *are* you?' Ran managed to growl between heaving breaths.

The creature slashed at him with its hand, the steel claws ripping into his trousers and slicing his skin. He cried out and staggered away, cursing and clutching his injured leg, pausing only to watch his blood run to the snow and stain it crimson.

'Fuck, that's it.'

Powered by rage, pain and magic, Ranoth leapt forwards and kicked the creature in the cavity under its chin. Its head snapped back and the neck split in half, the head and some of the attached spine skidding away across the ground in a spray of pus and mucus. The stuff oozed from the wound like gravy, fluorescent blue against the pristine white carpet of snow.

He stood and roared at the corpse, howling his victory to make sure it knew to stay dead. He half expected it to move again, somehow finding its head and reattaching it, but the beast remained still. After a good minute, Ran decided it was in fact dead, and turned away.

Only then did he look at Sasha's face.

She lay there draped in blood, her hair a darker red for all the crimson around her head. By some blessing of the gods her eyes were closed, spared the sight of his tears as he fell to the ground beside her. His hands hovered over the wound at her temple, a ragged gaping thing with a gash splitting across her forehead. Gentle fingers touched her face and turned her head to reveal the impact site of the creature's jaws on her shoulder. There was a crater in her flesh the width of a fist and shaped like a star burst; tears in her skin running away from it at all angles.

The bleeding had slowed now, the blood still warm despite the cold…

Still warm?

His hands slid to her neck and pressed under her chin, searching for the one sign he needed to keep his hope alive. He leaned closer to her face, and listened, scanning her body for movement.

A single breath whispered against his cheek.

Under the pads of his fingers, two beats thumped. Faint and slow, they were followed eventually by more.

'You're alive?' he murmured.

He searched her face. Her lips hung loose; her jaw was slack. There was no sign at all that she heard him. Only the slow, faint beat of her pulse under his fingers told him that somehow life lingered within her shattered body.

Across the snow, something drew his eyes and he snapped around to confront it. Instead of the creature he expected, he saw his ghost standing in a translucent shift, her bare feet unaffected by the ice and blood sprayed around the clearing. His heart nearly stopped when their eyes met, a shiver of recognition turning his stomach to a basket of angry snakes.

Her icy gaze held him still, while his heart thumped wildly against his cracked ribs. He felt every frantic beat and every quick, shallow breath.

'Now,' she said flatly.

'Now, what?' His voice cracked with emotion and the fatigue of too many weeks running, too many nights spent sleeping with one eye open and too many days hoping the next might be the morning he found sanctuary.

'Now will you open the scroll?'

Chapter Thirty-seven

'She's *dying* and you want me to open the scroll?'

'If you want her to live, I suggest you do.' She disappeared in a flurry of snow and left Ran cradling Sasha. Already his ribs hurt less, his breathing returning to a normal, painless rhythm, and the torn skin on his leg had stopped bleeding. Magic throbbed through his body, healing him from the inside despite the beating handed to him by the creature.

With as much care as his clumsy hands could muster, he collected Sasha's limp body and carried her back to the blankets and bags under the tree. If she were to die, it wouldn't be from his lack of trying. The bags yielded another blanket and among her healing supplies he found clean strips of cloth and some sort of rubbing alcohol. He applied those to her wounds, wrapping dressings tightly to stem the bleeding and encourage the skin to knit. The best he could do was keep them clean—he didn't dare use any of the poultices or creams she had hidden in the bottom of the bag. Without knowing what they were, he was likely to make her worse rather than better.

Rummaging for something to clean the gash on his jaw, his fingers brushed against metal and he paused. It was warm when it should have been ice cold, and it responded to his touch with a gentle vibration. His senses, heightened by magic and adrenaline, caught the faint hum of the scroll tube calling him from the depths of his bag, unseen but not forgotten.

He drew it out and held it to the light. The brass was as perfect and unmarked as the night Tutor Perce shoved it in his hand and urged him along the escape tunnels. Months of hard living and running for his life had left him broken and weary, but the scroll remained untouched, a stark reminder of the life he'd left behind.

With Sasha wrapped in all their blankets and continuing her slow, laboured breathing, Ran sat back on his heels, his fingers trembling as he unscrewed the cap on the tube. It turned easily for such an old thing, the filigree design on the metal distorting as the end of the tube spun and fell away. He tipped it up and let a vellum scroll slip into his hand, hard after many years but still supple enough to unroll. As his shaking fingers unwound the sheet, the message inked on the hide became clear.

A map, drawn with a fine hand in black and red ink, opened up before him. Several long paragraphs in a script he could barely decipher preceded and followed the map, centering it on the sheet that stretched from his fingertips to his chest. It was a long, detailed document, but one feature stood out.

In the mountains to the far south of Usmein, where the Ruken met the Morgen Ranges, was a keep, drawn in red. Given how far they had travelled, it was likely to be somewhere near where he and Sasha were now. His heart hammered harder.

Above the tiny image of the keep, a label read: *The Exiled.*

'Exiled?' he murmured.

He scanned the rest of the scroll, searching for the term in the text. He found it in a paragraph dedicated to the problem of those young children found to be cursed with magic, not old enough to be derramentis but deemed a threat nonetheless. He read the words once, then again to be sure.

It couldn't say what he thought it did… Surely there had to be a double meaning?

Letting the scroll fall into his lap, he looked up and blinked to clear his vision of rising anger and saw the ghost sitting beside Sasha's head.

'They send the children to a keep in the mountains?' he demanded.

She nodded. 'Any under the age of fifteen.'

'And the older ones?' He knew the answer, but he wanted her to say it. He wanted to hear the words.

'They are executed.'

'I told you; I already knew what this fucking thing said! I told you reading it was a waste of time!' Ran threw the scroll at the ghost and it sailed right through her translucent form. 'How is this going to help her?'

The ghost's eyes met his. There was no sympathy there, no understanding or patience. They were cold and they stared at him with unwavering precision.

'Your wounds have all but healed, Ranoth Olseta. Why?'

'Magic,' he spat and stood up, touching the wound along his jaw to find a scab where there should have been a gash and exposed bone.

'If you can heal yourself with magic, do you suppose magic can heal others?'

Her question hit him like a kick to the stomach through the fog of his anger. He turned and stared at her, now standing beside Sasha as pale and beautiful as the night he first saw her in the abandoned cottage of bones.

'I can't use my magic to heal her,' he growled. 'I can barely light a fire without burning down half the forest!'

She rolled her eyes. 'I didn't mean you.'

Now Ran frowned and stepped towards her, the pieces of her puzzle falling in to place. 'Then who? Where could I possibly hope to find a magic-weaver who can—'

She opened her hand towards the discarded scroll and the map.

'The keep?' Ran asked, a shiver of realisation washing over him.

'The keep,' she repeated. 'A nation's magic-weavers, all exiled as children to a place far from the eyes or ears of anyone who might care. They remain there, imprisoned, but not alone. They have teachers dedicated to training them to control their power. They also have healers.'

'They might send word to my father...'

The ghost shook her head. 'They are bound to secrecy. Even your father doesn't know of their location. That's why your tutor made you take the scroll. Can you imagine what your father would do if he discovered an entire keep of cursed children?'

Ran's blood turned to ice in his veins and visions of a massacre flashed in his mind. If Duke Ronart was willing to execute his own son, what punishment would he deliver to those not of his blood? 'What if she doesn't make it?'

The ghost glanced at Sasha. 'If you'd opened the scroll sooner, you might have gone to the keep instead of the farm...'

Her gaze met his again and the weight of his failure fell hard on his shoulders. She was right—had he listened to her, he would have known about the keep and the exiled children. He would have realised there was a safe place for him to hide. Driven by a sudden need to move, he stooped to collect the things scattered around the base of the tree and stowed them in their bags.

'You don't have time for that…'

He stopped and looked to where she stood, in the daylight beside the corpse of the dead creature. She looked at it, then at her hand, then at him.

'You need to get there before sunset.'

'Why?'

'The smell will draw them here and they will track you. You don't have time to carry her and the bags.' The wind began to blow and her form faltered, fading as a breeze gusted through the clearing.

'Them? Shit, *who?*' he demanded, desperate now. He needed his ghost more than ever; he needed her knowledge and her counsel. He needed her voice… 'My father? His soldiers?'

Her head shook slightly and her blue eyes stayed on him as she faded. 'Not them. Make haste, Ranoth.'

He sprinted forwards as if to catch her by the shoulders, not realising the futility of the idea until his hands passed through her like they would mist. 'If not him, then *who?*'

'The others…'

CHAPTER THIRTY-EIGHT

The Corron, Namjin Range, the South Lands

Lidan sat outside her father's tent and watched the shadows lengthen as night approached. She pulled her coat tighter, shivering despite the braziers to her left and right, and tried to ignore the chill in her bones. Siman sat nearby, fletching arrow shafts in an effort to look busy. She watched him and found she missed the feeling of her bow in her hand. It remained at Hummel, left behind in the rush to leave and replaced too readily by her knives, new and shiny and a sight more impressive. She hadn't realised the true value of the blades until she stepped into the Corron to see the four most powerful men in the South Lands wielding stone and flint.

By rights, her father's metal axe should make him a kaardi, higher in status and power than any of the daaris, and the rightful leader of all the southern clans. Yet, he didn't lord his wealth over the others. He treated them with respect—expecting the same in return, she was sure—but did they feel the same?

Daari Yorrell's proposal left her with the sense that he was the man with the real power. He hosted the Corron and chaired the meetings but more than that, the other leaders followed his example in almost everything. They ate and drank when and as he did, they dressed to match his fashion and at least two of the assembled sons had begun to wear their hair in a similar style. They looked to him for leadership and the idea made Lidan ill. If the most powerful and formidable men in the South Lands bent to the will of Daari Yorrell, what hope did she have of avoiding his proposal? What chance did she have of returning to Hummel with her family, instead of remaining here under the lingering gaze of those wandering eyes?

For almost two hours her parents had remained in the tent at her back, whispering and hissing at each other. They were discussing Yorrell's offer as discreetly as they could manage, which was a welcome change to the open-air quarrels they'd taken a liking to of late. Among their own people, they were free to spit and snarl, but surrounded on all sides by the other four clans, their words were carefully guarded and not to be overheard.

Lidan waited and bit her nails, her foot bouncing up and down to the beat of her anxiety. She hoped her father might ask her opinion though he did not legally need to. She hoped he might give her a chance to speak and lay her concerns before him. That he might give her a chance to change his mind…

There was little that begging and sobbing could do if he'd already decided. A man with ten daughters became quickly immune to the wailing of girls when they didn't get their way, deaf to the pitch of their voices and blind to their tears. There were four women in his life who might have a chance at talking him around, and the most powerful of them seemed to be struggling to plead her case.

Scanning the paths to the right, Lidan bit her lip and clenched her jaw. She waited.

Where are they?

'Sellan, it's a good match—' Her father's voice broke from the confines of the tent and her heart skipped.

Lidan sprang to her feet and slipped through the doorway before Siman could stop her. Her appearance startled her parents, arresting their conversation and turning their eyes to stare at her in shock.

She held up a hand to her father. 'Please, Da; you can't mean that?'

Erlon sighed and put his large hands on his hips, taking a moment to stare at his boots and collect his thoughts.

'Yes, I do,' he said finally.

'You hardly know the boy!' Sellan countered, pouring herself a berry wine and draining it quickly. She pointed the cup at her husband. 'You've got no idea what you're agreeing to.'

'I know Yorrell well enough, and I'm matched to his cousin. Cole has a good bloodline.' His hand opened towards Lidan. 'The match will strengthen our alliance.'

'Because your matching to Farah isn't enough?' Sellan spat the words, refilling her cup before Erlon snatched the wine urn away.

'It's an insult on his family that she hasn't borne me a son.' The urn slammed onto the table and Lidan jumped. 'One of his younger boys will come home with us.'

Sellan grew still and placed her cup carefully on the table before crossing her arms. 'Why?'

'I… because…' Erlon faltered, frustration reddening his cheeks. 'To be an heir for me, that's why!'

'You'd hand your people over to the Namjin, just like that?'

Lidan had never heard her mother's voice so quiet, yet so full of rage. She stood fixed to the spot, regretting her intrusion into the argument and wishing she could slip away again without them noticing.

'You don't give a shit about my people!'

'I give a shit about my daughters, and yours, and what happens to them once you're dead!' Sellan hissed and strode up to his face. 'If you name a Namjin boy as your heir, your body won't be cold before Yorrell rides through the valley and claims the range for himself. What do you think will happen to the girls then? Think he will find them good matches before his own kin? More likely they'll become tine-women and spend their days shovelling shit and scrubbing linens.'

Erlon glared at his first wife but didn't respond, his eyes wide with anger and his chest heaving. Then the dana looked at Lidan and nodded.

'You defied me with that horse and those knives. She doesn't need to do any of that to be a successful heir. If anything, it's an excellent way to get her killed. You won't defy me with her matching. I say no.'

'I thought you wanted me to match?' The words escaped Lidan's mouth before she could slam her teeth shut to stop them.

'Oh, I do, petal. When you're old enough and the right man is found, you'll be matched. You're the Tolak heir after all—your hand is worth a thousand horses and more besides.' She glared up at her husband as if to reinforce her point. 'But I will not leave my thirteen-year-old daughter with a clan I do not know, on the promise that she will be safe and whole on the day she turns eighteen. Not a chance.'

Lidan barely began to breathe a sigh of relief when her father shook his head.

'Times have changed, Sellan. I need to solidify the alliance with Yorrell. I need to match one of the girls to one of his sons. Why not his heir to mine?'

'Why not strip her naked yourself and send her up to him now?' A faint, hoarse voice spoke from beside the door.

In the arguing, no one had noticed Kelill enter with Farah, the pregnant woman's arm draped over her sister-wife's shoulders for support. Lidan's heart sparked with hope—her message had gotten through and her half-mother had come.

Erlon turned and staggered back, shocked to see his frail wife standing in the doorway, her distended belly illuminated by braziers and candles.

'Pardon?' he whispered.

'I said, why don't you just strip her naked and send her up there now?'

'I don't understand.' His eyes flicked from face to face, his first and fourth wife seeming to form an unfamiliar alliance in defence of his daughter.

'You think she'll be safe here; safe with Cole? Cole may only be fifteen but he is his father's son. The same blood runs through both their veins and the same darkness shadows both of their hearts.' No one moved as Farah spoke. It felt like an age since she'd been seen, let alone heard, and the force of her will bore down on her husband. 'Do you trust me so little, that you think I won't give you a son of your own? You're so desperate that you would trade your daughter off for a substitute heir?'

'You don't know it's a boy, Farah.' Erlon stated quietly and anger flared in Farah's eyes.

'If I had an inkling that it wasn't, do you think I would have carried it for all these months, enduring the sickness it brought on me?' She stabbed a finger at her stomach. 'By the blood of our daughter, I would have cut this child from me if I weren't certain it is the boy you so desperately want!' Tears spilled from her eyes and she stepped away from Kelill's supportive arm. 'Do you know why my father matched me to you?'

Erlon stared at Farah, stunned. 'It was a good match?'

'He sent me to you, to get me away from Yorrell. He was willing to match me away from my clan to keep me safe.'

'Safe from *what*?' Erlon's hands flew out from his sides in exasperation. Did he really not see? How could he not see?

'From Yorrell!' Farah was right in front of him now; the only thing separating them was her huge pregnancy and a tiny sliver of light. 'When Yorrell sees something he likes, he'll do anything to claim it, no matter the price. He was furious when I was sent away, enraged that his uncle had taken his favourite play thing and sent it off to match with a daari. I should have been a *first* wife, not a fourth, but it was worth it to escape him. If you leave Lidan here, you will never see her again. The girl she is, and the woman she will become, will die. She will never be the same.'

'But she's matching to Cole...' His defence faded under the sheer force of Farah's gaze.

'If you believe that, then you're a fool and I don't know you at all.' She shook her head and put her hand gently on his chest. The dana stiffened but did not move to interrupt. 'You think you know Yorrell, but there are shadows in him hiding things you have never seen. Don't leave Lidan, or any of your daughters here to discover them.'

Erlon's eyes met those of his gathered wives, then Lidan's, lingering there as he registered the fear and revulsion written on her face. Finally, he saw. 'What am I going to tell him? I can't just say no.'

'Da?' Lidan stepped forwards, taking the focus from Farah and allowing her to slip back to a chair provided by Kelill. The daari looked down at his daughter. 'I'm thirteen. I'm not allowed to match until I'm eighteen—the Law protects first daughters. You tell Yorrell I'm not old enough. You don't say *no*, you say, not *yet*.'

It was the most diplomatic response she could think of. It cut away the stark refusal her mothers wanted and found somewhere in the middle, protected by the Law all clans adhered to. First daughters could not match before their eighteenth birthday, and a plague of ngaru wasn't going to change that. Erlon waited a moment and glanced at the dana. Her green eyes levelled on her daughter but there was no way to tell if she was proud or happy or furious under the perfect mask of her pale face. With a slight nod, she agreed.

'Very well,' the daari submitted with a sigh. 'I will see what I can do.' He left them standing in the tent, the door flapping closed in the cool evening breeze.

Farah let go a long sigh and shook her head. 'I hope it works, for your sake.' Their eyes met. Lidan saw fear and doubt, and her blood ran cold. 'He won't get out of it without paying a heavy price.'

Kelill murmured something about checking on the children before slipping out into the gathering night with Farah. They left Lidan with her mother, alone for the first time in months, standing in complete silence. Lidan felt as though a gale, until now hammering against her and forcing her backwards, had suddenly fallen away. Her body felt light, her muscles relaxed and she allowed her shoulders to drop, relief taking the place of panic. For now, she was safe from Yorrell and whatever plans he had simmering in his head.

Her mother refilled her wine cup and held it out to Lidan. She stared at it, uncertain and surprised.

'Don't tell me you don't need something to settle your nerves.' Sellan pressed the cup into Lidan's hand and went to sit in the empty chair Farah left behind. 'Quite the master stroke telling Farah of Yorrell's plan.'

Lidan didn't answer. Instead she drained the wine and clutched the empty cup for comfort. She struggled to find somewhere to comfortably rest her gaze, so she focused on the floor. If there was a lesson to be learned from her mother's harsh hand and forked tongue, it was not to speak until asked a direct question, and then keep it brief. She felt the scrutiny of her mother's eyes and lifted her face.

'It was a move *I* should have thought of.' The dana remained perfectly still. 'How did you know about Farah's past?'

'I didn't,' Lidan replied.

'Then how did you know to send her a message?'

'I heard Yorrell ask Da if his cousin had given him a son yet.' She shrugged, wondering at how simple the idea had seemed at the time when she'd hurried to Raeh and asked her to pass on a message. 'Farah must have known Yorrell before she matched with Da, and if she agreed it was a good match, then perhaps I was worried over nothing.'

'And she didn't—a gamble you played and won. No doubt you knew how much stock your father places in her word.' The dana stood and took her daughter's shoulders in her hands. Lidan looked up and tried not to squirm. 'I'm impressed.'

Lidan couldn't help frowning. This wasn't what she imagined her mother's reaction would be. 'I thought you wanted me to make a good match?'

'Ah, but I do, Liddy.' Sellan's hand stroked her cheek, cold fingers against hot, flushed skin, then stepped away. 'I intend you to match with a great man, should one present himself, but you won't become the dana of another clan. You'll be the dana of the Tolak clan. You are the heir and it is your right. But, if Farah has a boy...'

A chill blew through the open door of the tent and dimmed the light of the fires as Lidan swallowed a hard kernel of fear. She might be her father's heir now, but that could change in a matter of weeks, perhaps days.

'So tell me, child. Do you want to remain your father's heir, or become some worthless minor daughter, usurped by a squalling babe?'

'I...' Lidan's heart pounded and she picked at the seam in her skirt as she searched for the words. 'I do. I want this more than anything.'

'Is that so?' Sellan folded her arms and eyed her daughter carefully. Lidan gave a quick nod, then glanced away, heat rising in her cheeks to declare her shame. She didn't like where this was headed. It felt wrong, like partaking in a plot that she had tried to hold herself apart from.

Sellan stepped in close, less than an inch from Lidan's nose, and her presence blocked out the world. 'So what are you willing to do, to claim what is rightfully yours?'

Chapter Thirty-nine

The Corron, Namjin Range, the South Lands

Her sleep was restless, haunted by the imagined snarls and screams of the ngaru and the ache in her heart left by her admission to her mother. As she lay staring at the glowing coals in a nearby brazier and listening to her father snore, Lidan wondered if all her efforts to protect Farah's child from her mother's schemes and to convince her father of her worth had been for nothing. If that child was a boy, what would she have to do to keep her place among the clan?

Lidan had no desire to leave her home, or match to a man she didn't know. Perhaps when she was older the prospect might not seem so terrifying, but for now it was an awful proposition. She knew her reasons for wanting to remain with her people—she felt, in her bones, that it was where she was meant to be. She was meant to be her clan's leader, meant to take her father's place when he was gone. On this one thing alone, she and her mother agreed.

It was hot; hotter than any night previous, and her skin beaded with sweat. She kicked off her blankets and, for the first time in months, cursed the warming coals beside her bed. Certain she would look no better than a ngaru when the sun rose, she lay on her back and prayed to the ancestors for some rest. Sleep claimed her well past midnight, the wide glowing moon vanishing behind clouds and finally plunging the range into darkness.

Daari Erlon waited for his daughter beside the cooking fires and nodded as she approached, rubbing the sand of sleep from her eyes. Above, the sky rolled with clouds, dark and low, driven from the south by a warm wind. It felt strange after so many months wrapped against the cold for the day to be so warm before the sun had barely risen, but it was a joy to leave her coat behind and feel the air on her skin.

Raeh handed her a bowl of vegetable stew and hurried off after one of the girls, yelling at them to stop hitting their sister and eat their breakfast. Lidan ignored the noise and watched her father, reading the signs in his shifting feet that he had something to say.

'Today may not be pleasant,' he started with a knowing look in his eye, watching as she blew on a spoonful of stew and listened. 'I might not be given a choice.'

Biting the inside of her lip, Lidan placed the bowl on a table and sighed. 'I understand...'

'I spoke more to Farah last night, and I want you to know, this is not a match I support. Under any terms.'

She felt a smile spread along her lips and Erlon raised his hand to stop it. 'That doesn't mean I can refuse it outright. Every daari is looking for a way to match his children to those of the others. I have four other proposals from the clans I need to consider for your sisters, yours being the fifth and most important. I'm going to need a good reason to refuse it.'

Lidan nodded and her gaze drifted to the ground. He was right—today *was* going to be unpleasant.

'Liddy,' he crouched in front of her and touched the leather of her knife sheaths. No longer disguised by the length of her coat, the handles of both knives stood proudly exposed, the straps of the holsters wrapping around her thighs under the fabric of her split skirt. 'You know how to use these?'

She nodded and grew still. She had trained with Loge every day since they left the Caine behind. There was a warning in her father's voice and worry in his eyes. It was as if he knew he was leading her into danger.

'When we get up there, you put them on the table, beside my axe. Let them be seen in the light.'

'Shouldn't I keep them close?'

'A good fighter can get to their weapon from the other side of the room. The table shouldn't stop you.' He tapped the sheath. 'Putting them on the table shows your strength and your status. Show them you aren't a toy or some pretty thing to be looked at and fought over.'

Lidan set her jaw and nodded again, her heart thumping with an injection of pride. She would stand beside her father and show the other daaris who she was. She was not a brood mare, to be traded over wine and laughter. She was the heir.

The daaris filed up the incline and through the gate of the Namjin village, their seconds and heirs following and dismounting in the common as the village folk left. Yorrell emerged from the hall and waved them inside, his eyes finding Lidan in the crowd almost immediately. This time she threw a glance at her father, standing at her side with one hand on the small of her back, and saw his eyes narrow in response. Her words the night before and the warning from Farah had hit home—now he saw what she'd seen all along.

Her heart swelled. The previous day, he'd been ready to throw her to these dogs like a scrap of meat, but now he saw the truth he'd been blind to. She lifted her chin and walked through the door, paying no mind to Yorrell or his son loitering in the shadows. Yesterday she looked down to avoid his gaze; today she passed by as if he wasn't there at all.

Inside, men worked to raise hatches in the roof, standing on ladders and opening portals to permit light and fresh air into the hall. Each portal stood open about a foot, wedged in place by thick lengths of timber braced against the frame of the roof. The gaps in the thatch were enough to let a breeze flow in, without the risk of rain pouring through in the wet season. It was a welcome change to the dim, smoky interior Lidan had been subjected to for almost a week.

Tine-women poured cups of wine and laid out platters of food: roast meat and root vegetables, flatbreads and preserves, as well as rare fruit hardly seen in the dry season. When the rains came, the bush would burst with the stuff, but for the moment it was a delicacy. Yorrell had saved his most spectacular hospitality for the final day of the Corron, yet it left no impression on Lidan other than sickness. What others might have seen as a potent display of status, she saw as audacious and crude—excess at a time when the people of the South Lands could least afford it.

The daaris and heirs gathered at the table, their seconds standing behind them. All reached for their axes and placed them on the table. They turned the handles inward to the cold fire pit and waited. Lidan felt a nudge and realised with a start that her father had elbowed her. Her mind flicked into action and she remembered his instruction.

She took the hilts of her knives and drew the blades from their sheaths, the metal singing as it left the leather and shone in the watery light of the hall. Eyes from across the room fell on her hands as she laid the knives on the table, turning them so the apex of each blade pointed towards her. As she straightened, she glanced at the gathered men and watched their faces twist with shock and jealousy at the display she laid before them. Suddenly, Yorrell's offering of fruit and abundant meat paled in comparison to her steel.

To her left around the table, Yorrell glared in barely veiled anger. Lidan tried desperately to suppress a smile as his gaze flicked between her father and the knives, for once never settling on her. She could sense the question in the Namjin leader's angry glare: who was this man, to flaunt such wealth in his host's house? Who was this man, who chose to gift his daughter knives of steel while he himself only wielded an axe of bronze?

Lidan bit down on a smirk. What would Yorrell do if he saw the massive sword hanging above her father's audience chair? If knives like these made him puff up with envy, she could only imagine the red in his face and the words that would die on his lips at the sight of a blade that grand. For the first time since arriving on the Namjin range, Lidan felt strong, and she swore she saw the corner of her father's lips turn up in a smile as they took their seats.

Yorrell cleared his throat and broke the trance set among the men by her knives. 'I trust you all had a pleasant evening and found great joy in delivering the proposals of matching to your families.'

The men nodded and some of the boys couldn't help grinning.

'Bloody hot last night,' Daari Allin muttered, prompting nods of agreement from those at the table. His clan hailed from the tablelands and foothills of the Malapa north of Namjin—the coldest of all the clan territories. If Lidan felt the heat of the night, then the Wolban people felt it more so.

'You'll be heading back to your frozen mountains soon enough, Allin.'
Yorrell waved his hand. 'We have one order of business to conclude today,
then the feasting will begin. My hall will be open to all, in celebration of
the matching contracts and our alliance against these ngaru.

'I shall begin. All those in favour of the alliance between our clans will
raise their axes. Should the call to aid come from our brothers, we will
furnish them with whatever rangers and supplies we can spare. We will
defend the lives of our fellow clansmen as readily as we would our own
kin. Who of you say aye?'

All five daaris leaned forwards and slipped a hand under the blades of
their axes, lifting them an inch or so from the table. The small gesture was
all Yorrell needed to cement the agreement and he nodded at his tine-
woman. She scurried to fill any cups begging for wine and the men drank.
All but Erlon slammed their cups on the table and wiped their mouths
with their sleeves. He placed his down carefully, and Lidan wondered if
he'd drunk any at all. She left hers untouched.

For the following hours, the men bartered and argued over the details of
their children's matching contracts. They debated the value of a bride's dowry
and what her family got in return. A husband's family were gifted fabrics
and household items when a girl matched into their family, supplies to provide
for the extra mouths they would feed when she gave birth to sons and daughters. The bride's family were given horses, livestock, or tine-women. The
helping hands the girl's family lost when she left to live with her husband
had to be replaced in some way, and a tine suited the transaction well.

Each daari at the table signed contracts for as many of their children as
they could manage, while some agreed that their ties were already strong
enough to not need a new match. In a few cases, the contracts were signed
in lieu of upcoming births, or transferred to the children of their brothers
or sisters. The whole proceeding reminded Lidan of horse-trading and by
the afternoon, her ears rang and her head throbbed. When a tine-woman
appeared with a platter of small cakes, she wolfed down a handful and
collected a few more for later.

Exhausted by the noise and the sheer effort of keeping track of the
contracts, she hardly noticed when the hall grew silent and the gazes of the
men fell on her side of the table. Yorrell leaned back in his chair and smiled.

'Now we come to the final—and undoubtedly most important—contract of the day.' His hand opened towards his son sitting at his side. 'The matching of my Cole, to your Lidan. It has been a long time since two heirs have matched, has it not, Horice?'

The oldest of the daaris nodded. 'It is rare for a daari to have only females from which to name his heir. Rarer still that the heir is matched before a brother is born. An occasion to be celebrated, I'm sure.'

Lidan tried not to wear her embarrassment on her face but her cheeks flushed and she looked down, training her eyes on the table. It wasn't her fault she was a girl, and certainly not her fault there had been no brothers after her. It was hardly something any living man had control over. Such things were the will of the ancestors.

'An occasion to be celebrated,' Yorrell repeated, drawing the last word out with a nod and a smile. 'I've consulted and decided to offer three tine-women, ten mares, two stallions and a hog as my son's matching gift to your family.'

A murmur of astonishment rippled around the table, eyebrows arched and heads nodded, all impressed with the daari's offer. Air left Lidan's lungs in a rush, as if she'd been kicked, and her eyes widened at the staggering value of the gift. The stallions alone were worth their weight in precious stones and would fetch a price much higher than her hand if traded to the convoys from beyond the South Lands. The addition of the tine-women gave her father increased status and would almost certainly mean her half-mothers might never lift a hand in work again.

Had Yorrell just handed her father an offer he couldn't refuse?

CHAPTER FORTY

The Corron, Namjin Range, the South Lands

Erlon took a breath and placed a hand on the table. 'I'm sorry, but I must decline your gift and the offer to match your son to my daughter.'

The silence was only broken by the creaking of chairs as men leaned away and crossed their arms. From their frowns, Lidan suspected this was not the response any of them anticipated. Lidan's mouth ran dry as she scanned the gathering. There was no way this ended well, no way the previous conflicts between the Namjin and the Tolak wouldn't surge to the surface and threaten to swamp them all. As relieved as she was to hear her father's refusal, the darkness descending over Yorrell's face chilled her to her core.

'I'm not sure I understand,' said Yorrell quietly, his head leaning to one side. 'This is an offer well within the value of Lidan's status.'

'That may be so,' Erlon conceded, nodding slowly. 'But it is not the value I take issue with. Lidan is only thirteen. She is too young for matching, even if she were a minor daughter. As First Daughter, she is to be matched only after the age of eighteen. The Law is very clear on this.'

Yorrell's chest began to heave a little more with each breath. 'Of course, she and Cole will not be matched officially until she has turned eighteen—'

'Then there is no reason for my daughter to remain here.' Erlon's fingers flicked as though they itched to take the axe handle, even just for the comfort of the shaft in his hand. Lidan felt the same tingle in her fingers, her hands begging for the knives she had laid on the table. 'When she is old enough, by the Law, we can revisit—'

'Hang the fucking Law!' Yorrell leapt to his feet and swiped an arm in Lidan's direction. His Second, a man with long ratty hair, sprang into action and came striding towards Lidan.

He covered the distance in a blink with nothing between them but open floor.

Lidan snatched her knives and tucked the blades against her forearms, launching away from the table and clearing her chair with a kick. The Second reached with his long arms and Lidan turned into his circle, putting her back to his chest and driving both knives under her arms. They found the soft tissue under his ribs and he roared beside her ear. She turned under his arm and twisted, ripping the knives out as she went. A rooster-tail of blood splattered across the table and the Second staggered, flailing an arm backwards to grab her collar.

Cole hefted his own axe and seemed ready to come to the Second's aid, but his father took him by the shoulders and held him back. Lidan ignored them and went slack in the fabric of her shirt. The shirt slipped over her head and she dropped to her knees, crouching in a chest-wrap of white fabric and her trouser-skirt. She spun and kicked the Second in the back of the knees, stealing his balance as his blood poured onto the floor.

She stood up behind the Second as he slipped in the slick of blood, flapping his arms vainly to regain balance he'd long since lost. As he turned towards her, Lidan's left knife plunged into his chest, driving him to the floor, where the other slashed through his throat. He twitched a few times while she crouched over his head, knives held ready, unwilling to move until she was sure he wasn't getting up again.

She sucked breath into her lungs as the last wheeze escaped the Second and his body grew still as stone.

To her right, Yorrell stood with his son, holding him with straining knuckles, both of them stiff as boards and staring with shock. To her left, her father straightened from a ready stance and placed his axe back on the table, careful to turn the handle back to the fire pit. It was a signal to Yorrell that the fight was over if he let it be, and Siman followed suit, stowing his knife and axe.

Lidan stood and let the Second's blood drip from her face and hands. Her hands shook and her muscles sang under her skin, blood pumping through her veins and throbbing through her ears. Had Loge not taught her the way of the knives, she would have been dragged screaming into the back rooms of Yorrell's hall before her father could do anything to stop them. The ensuing fight would have been a bloodbath. At least for now only one man lay dead while the rest stood stunned. Trenor, Daari Allin's heir, nodded approvingly with a small smile but it vanished under his father's glare. Clearly the clans had wagered on Yorrell as the dominant force, not expecting Lidan or her father to react the way they had.

'As I was saying,' Erlon continued, as if the fight hadn't happened. 'When Lidan is old enough by Law, we will revisit the matter of matching. Until then, I will not discuss this, or any other proposal for my daughters' hands.'

'*Any* of them?' Daari Allin shouted across the table. 'We've all agreed to match our children to make this alliance! You can't withdraw your family just because—'

'None of my girls are old enough, Allin; and neither are most of yours. We all know the Law and why it exists. If we can't find a way to make the alliance work without bartering our children like horses, then we have greater problems than the ngaru!' Erlon's voice rang under the hall's roof and silenced everyone within earshot.

Yorrell shook with rage where he stood, letting go of Cole and taking a step towards Erlon. Lidan stiffened, her arms tensing as he approached, but her father raised a finger—a signal that he had things in hand.

'You have brought shame on my hall and my clan, Daari.' Yorrell's voice wavered, his hands clenching and unfurling as if they yearned to strangle her father. He'd be lucky to get close enough to try—even then, his hands wouldn't make it around the muscle. Yorrell was a big man, but not superior to her father's strength. Equal, perhaps, but not superior. Yorrell spat at Erlon. 'You bring insult on *all* our clans.'

Allin nodded fervently, but Merk and Horice merely watched. Both daari's lands neighboured the Tolak range and they knew her father well. Horice's clan, being the furthest to the south, hardly had anything to do with the Namjin in everyday dealings, and held his alliance with Tolak close. It was the first thing her father taught her when reading maps—know where your allies are and the holes where your enemies hide.

'No, Yorrell. You insult *me* by offering me your minor son as my stand-by heir. You insult my *wife*, so pregnant she can hardly move, by accusing her of failing to provide me heirs.' Her father jabbed a finger into the surface of the table. 'And you insult our ancestors and our Laws by demanding we match our children before they are old enough.'

'What, then, can we do to rescue this alliance?' Horice held his hands up and nodded at the warring daaris.

'I want them.' Yorrell's hand came up to point at Lidan and the eyes of the men turned to regard her. 'I want those knives.'

Lidan tightened her grip on the bone handles. She'd be dead before they prised them from her fingers, before she willingly gave them to anyone. Yorrell most of all. There was no way she was handing them over.

'And as compensation for the shame you bring here and the death of my Second, I want the plans for the metal-forge.'

'What?' Erlon barked a laugh. 'You can't be serious! You're lucky we don't try you before a Hearing for conspiring to break the Law!'

'I am owed compensation for what you have done here! If you will not ally yourself against the ngaru through matching, then you will allow us to arm ourselves with weapons such as yours.' Yorrell's eyes were wild now, glistening and wide. 'You will pay for what you have done here.'

Daari Erlon straightened and took his axe from the table. With a nod and a pointed finger, he indicated to Lidan to grab her bloodied shirt and stand beside Siman. She hurried to comply as the rest of the daaris leaned back, watching and waiting for Erlon's next move.

Erlon pointed at Horice, Merk and Allin. 'My alliance with you stands regardless of the proposed matchings. Should you ever call on me, I will come to your aid with whatever I can spare. The Tolak clan will not abandon its fellows to the darkness of the ngaru. Should you choose to do the same for us, we will be forever grateful.' His gaze fell on Yorrell and the tone in his voice dropped.

'As for the Namjin… while I would not leave you to suffer, I will not arm you with weapons you do not understand, or know how to wield. I would sooner trust my axe in the hands of a child. My own rangers do not ride with weapons of metal, and this—' He hefted the bronze axe '—I save for special occasions, like showing off in front of fools like you. I suggest you don't give me a reason to use it.'

Her father nodded his head at the door and Lidan moved with Siman, slipping the bloodied shirt over her chest wrap and jogging to keep pace with him. Erlon turned more slowly and followed, taunting Yorrell with the sight of his back.

'Is that a threat, Tolak?' Yorrell spat in their wake.

Erlon spun in the doorway and pointed the head of the axe at Yorrell. 'You bet your arse it's a threat! You come after me and mine and you'll feel more than the bite of this axe in your neck. There'll be flames, and nothing you recognise as yours will be left standing.'

There was a rush from inside the hall and Siman practically threw Lidan into Theus's saddle before swinging into his own beside Erlon and Titon. Yorrell appeared from the darkness to stand in the doorway, steaming with impotent rage. There was very little he could do—the Law protected Lidan and her father, and Yorrell knew it. Unless the three other daaris sided with him, there was nothing to be done to change matters.

She watched as Merk and Horice shouldered past Yorrell and whistled for stable hands to bring their horses, but Yorrell hardly seemed to notice. He only had eyes for Erlon. He pointed a thick-fingered hand at Lidan's father and his lip curled as they turned their horses for the gate.

'You get off my land! If I see you or any of your cunt brats at dawn, I'll see they are shown how a stone axe can split a skull,' he bellowed at their backs. 'The Marsaw and Daylin too—all of you! Get the fuck off my land!'

CHAPTER FORTY-ONE

The Southern Reaches, Orthia

It frustrated Ran how often he had to admit that the ghost girl was right. She'd been right about the scroll, and she'd been right about the difficulty of carrying Sasha across the snowy hills and fields and into a narrow valley. According to his map and the cryptic hints the ghost gave him every few miles, the keep lay at the head of the valley, nestled against the mountains with a stream at the foot of the wall.

When daylight began to fade and still the keep hadn't appeared in the distance, Ran began to panic. The ghost said he had until nightfall, and then the others would come. She said he had to get to the keep before they found them because this time, there wasn't one creature, but many. He hoped she was wrong. He hoped she was exaggerating and making a fuss, but to date he had no reason to doubt her.

Just as she had told him, he *did* regret not opening the scroll sooner. Heck, he regretted not opening it the first night away from Usmein. It was his own stupid pride that had stopped him, and perhaps a deep and unshakable fear of what it revealed about how Orthia treated those born with magic in their souls.

The knowledge of the keep and the succour it provided for magic-weaving children might have saved him a whole heap of trouble and pain. He might have bypassed Graupen altogether and never have met Sasha, saving her the gruesome injuries she now suffered

As things stood, they'd be lucky to make it to the keep alive. Ran carried Sasha across his shoulders, his arm looped through her legs and behind her knee, her right arm cradled against his chest. He'd seen soldiers carry their unconscious comrades from the Territory in such a manner, but never thought he would ever have reason to use the method himself. Her head bobbed against his shoulder with every heavy step and he cringed whenever he slipped on the uneven ground. It was a faint track, and seemed undisturbed, so it was unlikely anyone had been this way in some time. Over his shoulder, sunlight faded from the valley. There had been no fresh snowfall overnight and the snow beneath his feet was slushy; and Ran left a set of distinct footprints that a blind man could follow.

Ahead, the ghost girl waited on a rock beside the road. The boulder was as high as his shoulder and she crouched atop it like a mountain cat, watching his approach with a blank blue stare. Ran rolled his eyes and wondered what she wanted this time, thankful only for an excuse to pause and rest his legs.

'Almost nightfall,' she murmured when he grunted to a stop and eased Sasha to the ground. He covered her with a blanket he'd kept from their packs and leaned back to stretch his legs. The ghost tilted her head at Sasha. 'She's fading with the light.'

'Shut up,' Ran snapped.

'Pardon?' The ghost glared at him, incredulous.

'I said shut up! I know she's fading and I can see that the sun is setting. I don't need your constant commentary.'

'Without my "constant commentary", you'd be dead!' she snarled back at him.

'I'd have a moment's peace beforehand,' Ran countered. He turned to look down the valley. 'Feels like I've walked a thousand miles.'

'If only.' The ghost slipped silently from the rock and moved around it.

Annoyed but curious, Ran followed her. The track circled the rock, and on the other side, the valley lengthened between two soaring mountains. Down to his right, a river bubbled over stone and whispered in eddies, thawed snow running away from the mountains as the surest sign spring had arrived. The track paralleled the river, following it up the valley and disappearing around a bend.

'Up there,' the ghost said, lifting her chin. 'Follow the river.'

'How much further?'

'The distance doesn't matter, Ranoth,' she replied, and began walking up the track, leaving him in her wake. 'It only matters that you cross it.'

He collected Sasha and somehow managed to settle her on his shoulders without dropping her on her head. As much as he hated the cryptic riddles of his ghost and her habit of never telling him what he needed to know before it was too late, he agreed with her. It didn't matter how far ahead the keep was. He needed to travel the distance if he hoped to survive, or the whole effort would be for naught.

The first howl echoed up the valley at Ran's back as the sun's last rays faded to indigo and black. He and the ghost spun around, scanning the trees and low shrubs for movement. A chill raced up his spine.

'I thought they didn't travel by day? How can they be so close?' He whirled to confront the ghost and her form began to wane.

'An easy mistake to make,' she said. Her eyes stared past him as if she saw right through the trees and hillsides to the creatures themselves.

'You said they didn't travel by day!'

'You *assumed* they didn't! I told you to reach the keep by nightfall. I told you they were coming. I said nothing about how or when they hunted!'

'But the other one—' He lost his protest in the sound of a barking call, two distinct replies following in the silence left behind.

'Ranoth!' The ghost was in front of him in an instant, as opaque and human as she had ever been. 'Curse you for a fool! Fucking *run!*'

He ran.

Sasha bounced on his shoulders, her dead weight dragging him down with every step, but he ran. He put one foot in front of the other and ignored the screams of the creatures. He silenced the voice of dissent in his head and reasoned against its warnings.

He would make it to the keep before the creatures found him. He would make it or die trying.

A glimmer of hope lit the falling twilight as he staggered around a bend in the track. Ahead, torches flickered in a line that could only mark the top of a wall. Through the sweat and tears of exertion, he couldn't see much of the structure, but the light was enough to set a fire in his heart.

The keep was there, just a few more steps, just a little further. It was as real as the skin on his hands and it was right there, waiting for him with light from torches to guide his way. The creatures howled and barked, three distinct voices echoing in his wake. He couldn't tell how far they were, or how fast they moved.

It didn't matter.

He was going to make it to the keep.

Black walls loomed from the trees, rising several stories up the face of the mountain. Within the grounds, three thick towers stood in defiance of the elements, their roofs capped by snowfall, tiny slivers of light escaping into the night from behind curtains and shutters. Only along the wall and its shorter intermittent towers did torches burn bright.

The track widened, then spread into a clearing. The keep wall stood on the opposite side and his heart leapt at the sight. The clearing was several hundred feet across, and empty. Not a building or a shack stood in the space, no wagons or awnings; it was clear of snow and grass, and the trees at the edges leaned back as though they'd long ago decided it was a fool's errand to put down roots in that soil.

Ran stumbled from the forest's eaves into the emptiness and the glow of the torches on the wall, his heart in his throat threatening to block the air from his lungs. His legs began to fail and he reached down for his magic, depleted and weak after the fight with the first creature and healing his wounds. He touched it and drew on what little remained, powering his legs and willing them to carry him a little further and a little faster.

Thwack, thwack, thwack.

Ran staggered to a stop and stared at his boots. Three arrows quivered in the soil no more than a foot in front of him. He looked up and narrowed his eyes at the shadows above the walls. There were no faces, no signs of life except for the warning shots at his feet.

The creatures screamed again, raising the hair on the back of his neck. They were close; they could smell him and they were close. The keep was right there, waiting. Safety, succour for him, for Sasha—right there, yards away. So close he could reach out and touch it.

But death waited no matter which way he turned. Arrows raining down from the keep would end him as quickly as the creatures behind him, and once more he was stuck between a rock and a hard place with nowhere to go and no one to help him.

Fuck it, he thought. He hadn't come this far, and sacrificed this much just to lay down and die.

He stepped forwards and a fourth arrow slammed into the dirt. It shivered beside his boot, and he again stared up at the wall.

'Please! I need help!' he pleaded with the darkness in the vain hope it might hear him. Someone was shooting arrows at him, so someone had seen him. They *had* to help him. They couldn't leave him out here. 'Please! We need—'

A deep, guttural growl rolled from the woods at Ran's back. For a moment, he squeezed his eyes shut and waited. Perhaps he'd heard wrong. Perhaps the thing was still far away...

Another came from his left, a heavy snorting breath heaving with the effort of the chase. Then the third, skirting to his right and sucking a breath before exhaling with a satisfied sigh through its mouth.

Ran turned and put himself between them and Sasha. Had the watchers on the wall seen her hanging from his shoulders? They would now, as the foul creatures slipped from the trees to surround their prey. The light from the torches didn't bother them, unperturbed by the flames or the warmth. He'd been a fool to think they would be affected by it, or that they were all the same.

They slunk forwards, hands reaching down to the dirt. They crouched, the thick muscles across their shoulders bunched and ready to launch at Ran. A flash of light drew his eye.

In the hand of one beast, he saw a blade. Its hilt vanished under the skin and hair of its arm as if it had been inserted and attached as an extension—a deadly steel appendage. Another had two blades sewn into its right forearm, one on either side of its long, mangled fingers, and they scraped the ground as it crawled forwards. The third had two swords protruding from its collarbones and a shorter knife jutting from its forehead. It looked as though all it needed to do was charge and impale its victim to win the day.

All of them were torn, rotting and deformed, and under their foul exteriors, all had human forms. They were not wolves or bears. They were not serpents or mountain cats. They moved like wild things, their hands and feet half-built in the shape of an animal's, but true animals they were not.

Ran backed towards the wall, scarcely noticing that no more arrows fell in warning. He heard voices, but their shouting seemed a hundred miles away. A high-pitched ringing in his ears drowned out even the snapping snarl of the creatures as they closed in.

He lowered Sasha as carefully as he could, laying her at his heels and straightening again without taking his eyes from the beasts. They stalked forwards and smacked the saliva on their lips, baring rotting broken teeth and black stumps of severed tongues.

Free of Sasha's weight, he raised his hands and willed what remained of his magic to surface. He let his fear and revulsion fuel it, stoking the fire of anger at his own impotence. Sasha had protected him from her father; she had healed him, helped him escape, and when she'd needed him, he'd failed. He'd let one creature nearly crack her skull and a pack of others hunt them through the woods to their deaths.

He'd ignored his father and insisted on going to the Territory, costing dozens upon dozens of lives in pursuit of his own achievements, he'd ignored Brit Doon and insisted on approaching the cottage in the night. He'd ignored the ghost for no reason other than his own pride, and his stupidity was about to cost him not just his own life, but that of a young woman who'd deserved better. He'd done nothing but lead himself, and now Sasha, into deeper danger, ignoring every sign and signal otherwise.

He let the rage at his incompetence build, the heat scoring the core of his bones and arcing along the outside of his skin. The magic surfaced near his elbows, blue light scorching the sleeves of his coat and shirt until they fell away as ash. It swirled along his outstretched arms to his hands, held up in defence, now presented in defiance.

The faces of the creatures narrowed against the light, but they were undeterred; they were not afraid.

For a moment Ran pitied them.

Fear might have saved them.

He pointed his hands at the ground beneath the creatures' feet and let go.

The magic boomed, blue power exploding the earth under the creatures and enveloping them in lightning and flame. Their screams disappeared into the echoing thunder of the blast and Ran staggered back.

His heels snagged on Sasha and he fell, the blue and the darkness blurring in front of his eyes. He heard voices, shouting and orders. He heard a gate groan open and saw figures rush into the clearing. He saw more flashes of light and heard the death throes of the creatures as they were slaughtered where they lay injured and wailing. He felt hands grasp his arms, then he saw nothing.

CHAPTER FORTY-TWO

Namjin Range, the South Lands

Lidan should have guessed by the heat in the previous night. She should have seen the signs in the gathering clouds and the rolling wind blowing from the south. She knew what a turn felt like, yet with all her energy focussed on escaping Yorrell, she hadn't noticed.

Their convoy of two wagons and mounted riders followed the track along the river, the same way they'd entered the Namjin range only this time without an escort. At her back, the other clans packed their things, their rangers and their horses and made a hasty retreat into the late afternoon. On Yorrell's orders, the Tolak, Daylin and Marsaw clans had to leave and Lidan did not doubt for a moment he would make good on his threats if anyone of them remained at dawn. The Wolban, it seemed, were not included in the eviction.

Her mothers wasted no time lamenting the need to leave before dark, all of them happy to put the Namjin far behind them as quickly as they could. Together with the rangers, they threw everything in the wagons and urged the horses on, thankful they hadn't dragged the rest of the clan with them on the journey.

Lidan didn't think of the ngaru until the noise and commotion of the Corron disappeared behind the bulk of the southern hill. Only in the silence did she remember their calls and cries, promising to wait for her return and hunt her back to Hummel. She shivered despite the sticky warmth in the air, heavy with moisture and drawing sweat from her brow. They were in the trees and they were waiting.

Overhead, the first roll of thunder announced the storm she'd felt coming all afternoon. It came from the south, dark clouds laden with rain inching closer on the wind. She knew the smell of the trees and grass as they readied themselves for the coming rain, yet she didn't recognise it for what it was until it stood right over her head.

The wet season had returned.

They managed to cross under the trees as the first splatters of rain hit the ground. The smell of it filled her nose with its heady aroma, enough to make her dizzy. The rangers turned in their saddles, untying bags and drawing out long, oiled leather coats with wide hoods. Loge pulled Striker to a stop and threw a coat at Lidan, dragging another from a second saddlebag.

'Put it on and draw it in tight,' he shouted over the thunder as another crack of lightning flashed in the grey sky to their right. She obeyed his instruction and shouldered the coat before more than a few drops of rain could soak through her clean shirt.

The leather was light and water beaded off the surface, running in tiny streams from her shoulders past her ankles. The hem of the coat fell past her boots, long enough to protect her from the heaviest downpour. She snapped the hood over her head and the noise of the convoy drowned in the thrumming of rain on leather. Suddenly every ranger looked exactly the same—all covered head to foot in dark, oiled skins, faces hidden in the shadows of their hoods. The water turned the horses' hair from bay to brown, and chestnut to black. The few white horses soon became grey and wore socks of mud above their knees.

A loud whistle pierced the trees and someone waved their hand. At the signal the convoy moved faster, the wagons bouncing and jostling over the rocky path in protest of the increased speed. Theus put his head down and powered forwards, following Striker into the storm. It wasn't for another hour that Lidan realised Loge had tethered her bridle to the back of his saddle and had been leading her horse all along. She ground her teeth and tried to push her anger away. He was only doing as her father had ordered and making sure she didn't get lost in the weather.

The rain hammered on well after dark and the convoy of rangers and horses continued without any sign of stopping. The riders lit torches doused in animal fat, the flames defying the weather but lending only a little smoky light to the path ahead. Eventually a message was relayed from the front of the column for Loge and he unhitched the lead on Theus's bridle.

'Stay beside the wagons 'til I get back!' he shouted.

She didn't think he saw her nod and didn't suppose it mattered. She wasn't about to take off into the bush on her own. She knew what was out there and just because she couldn't hear them over the thunder and the rain, she knew the ngaru waited at the edge of the light. She felt their eyes on her skin, as though she didn't have a stitch of fabric on her body. She felt them leering and could almost see them salivating, wondering at how they might separate her from the group. She was smaller than the rest, thinner and weaker; perhaps not as satisfying, but worth the wait.

Lidan shuddered and pushed the thought from her mind. She wasn't going to let them eat away at her resolve. They'd already cost her father an alliance with his neighbour and slaughtered dozens of his rangers. She would not allow them to take anything more from her or her people.

'Lidan?' Raeh's face appeared through the flap at the back of the wagon. Lidan urged Theus through the rain and squinted up at her half-mother. 'Get up the front and tell your father we have to stop.'

'Why? What's wrong?'

'Farah's babe is coming.'

The woman slipped back into the wagon. Over the sound of horses and the rattle of the wagon across the rocky track, Lidan heard a gasp and a pained moan. Her heart skipped a beat. She spurred Theus, giving him the length of the reins, and hurried forwards to the head of the group.

Rain streamed down, spilling from the oiled leather coats and across the flanks of the horses. She glanced under each hood as she passed, the rangers' heads all bowed against the onslaught of water. Ahead she recognised Titon and drew up beside him, tugging her father's sleeve to get his attention.

'Liddy, what are you doing out in this weather?' He glanced around as if someone should have been watching her more carefully. 'You should be in a wagon.'

'Raeh sent me with a message. We need to stop.'

He slowed Titon and rangers filed past them, under orders to keep moving. 'Why?'

'It's Farah…'

'Halt!' he bellowed and the caravan of horses and wagons came to a stop, voices echoing in the trees as riders soothed uneasy mounts. 'Now? Right now?'

'That's what she said,' Lidan shrugged. Thunder crashed overhead and lightning arced along the belly of the clouds, illuminating the trail and bush in eerie black and white.

The daari swore and stood in his stirrups to whistle at his rangers. 'Spread out and clear a perimeter! Set shelters and light more torches with the oil. Keep your eyes on the bush.'

His rangers moved as ordered and strung small hide covers between trees, lighting torches against the darkness. Without the creaking and rattling of the wagons or the stamping of horses' hooves, the bush was filled only with the sound of the storm. Farah cried out and people glanced around, then nodded their understanding and fell into hushed conversation to distract from the noise of labour.

Erlon turned to Lidan. 'You head back and see what can be done. Bring me word when you can.'

She hurried to oblige, tethering Theus to the wagon and helping the driver light the ring of oil torches around the rails. When they burned and hissed in the rain, she climbed the ladder and poked her head through the door flap.

Inside was a steamy cluster of sweating women, each working silently at their tasks while Farah crouched on her hands and knees, rocking back and forth. How long had she been like this before they called for a halt? By the exhaustion on their faces, it must have been hours.

Moyra sat behind Farah, her hand massaging a circle in the small of Farah's back, while Kelill wiped the woman's brow with a damp cloth and moved her hair from her sweat-slicked face. Raeh worked to mix a pain-relieving tea and Sellan crouched over the instruments from Moyra's kit. Her lips moved, whispering hurried words, the same silent phrases she repeated on their last journey through the bush. The women started at Lidan's intrusion, and the dana's lips grew still.

Before Lidan could speak, a ngaru's howl rent the air outside the wagon. The dread sound was followed by the pitched wail of a dying man, then the bush erupted with the roar of men and beasts in battle.

Sellan dove towards Lidan and wrapped a pale hand as hard as stone around her arm. Her eyes were wide with fear and she grimaced at the sound of the rangers and ngaru warring in the storm. 'Lidan Tolak, you make sure your sisters are in that wagon and not one of you is to come out until I give the word. Understand?'

'But—'

'Go!' Her mother shoved her out into the rain and Lidan scrambled to shelter under the second wagon's tray. She crawled through the mud and tried to ignore the stones cutting her hands and tearing the fabric of her skirt and trousers. To her left a ranger screamed and vanished into the bush, snatched from between his fellows as quick as lightning flashed overhead. The rangers roared and charged after the ngaru with their axes and spears, disappearing beyond the wagon's light.

She climbed out at the rear of the wagon and three rangers nodded at her, their weapons ready as others further off tried to keep the attacking creatures at bay. These rangers were the last line of defence between the horror of the ngaru and her sisters, and Lidan planned to add another. The beasts would pry her knives from her cold, dead fingers before she let them pass into the wagon.

In the doorway of the wagon, she saw Elva and Bridie; so close in age they could be twins had their mothers not been different women. Bridie gripped the rear rail and stared into the stormy night while Elva held her by the apron with clenched fists and pale knuckles. Both girls' eyes searched the gloom, and they winced as thunder crashed across the sky.

'Girls, get inside!' Lidan shouted, reaching to climb the ladder and shove them back inside.

Both of them started as if only just realising she was there, staring and shivering. She tipped back her hood so they could see her face in the next flash of lightning but neither of them relaxed. A cold shudder rolled through Lidan. In all their lives she'd not seen her eldest sisters so terrified.

'What's wrong?'

'It's Abbi…' Elva glanced at Bridie who continued to stare through the fighting into the bush with darting eyes.

'Elva, what's happened?' Lidan demanded. She grabbed her sister's rain-slicked arm as the dana so often did to her.

'I don't know!' Elva shook her head and glanced again at Bridie.

'Bridie?' Lidan snatched at the girl's shirt and pulled her down to meet her gaze. 'Where is Abbi?'

'She's gone.' Bridie's bottom lip quivered.

It took all Lidan's restraint not to slap the girl. 'Where? Gone *where?*'

Bridie lifted a shaking hand to point at the darkness of the bush. 'She must have followed Mam out after she checked on us.'

Panic drew Lidan's heart into her throat and horror rippled over her skin. 'She went out there? She went into the *bush?*'

Both girls nodded and Lidan's heart nearly stopped dead.

CHAPTER FORTY-THREE

Namjin Range, the South Lands

'Get back inside and tie the door down,' Lidan ordered, spinning into the rain.

Her sisters vanished and the hide cover of the wagon snapped taut as they secured the ties on the inside. There was no time to alert her father and no one spare to form a search party. Abbi might only be a short distance beyond the reach of the torches, probably searching for her mother, and with every minute of delay she wandered further into danger.

Lidan yanked her hood over her head and stole a torch from the rail of the wagon. She was in the bush and away from the trail in moments, rain hammering down and dripping across her vision. Lightning flashed and illuminated the trees, black shadows and brilliant white then nothing. It all vanished to pitch darkness except for the small circle of orange light from her torch.

The drumming rain drowned out everything but the echo of her breath beneath her hood. She pushed it back and opened her ears to the scrubland, ignoring the screams and howls behind her. She willed her heart to slow and reached out beyond the splat of huge raindrops on dry leaves and the roll of thunder.

A rustle in the undergrowth drew her attention, but it was too small to be Abbi. Lidan listened harder, focussing on those sounds that were not natural to the bush, sounds not made by rangers or horses or labouring women. She closed her eyes and waited.

Someone screamed and a crash echoed between the trees. Eyes open and trained on the direction of the sound, Lidan darted after it, led by the torch and the lightning and her churning gut. The crashing continued, followed by another scream, louder, closer this time. She charged on, vaulting a fallen tree and scrambling to a stop on the other side.

A child screamed again, terrified and alone.

'Abbi!' Lidan cried in reply, hoping somehow her sister would hear her through the chaos and fear. There was no answer, no sign the little girl heard her at all. 'Abbi! Where are you?'

A growl shook the bush ahead, followed by the rumble and crack of thunder and a furious gust of wind. The rain stung Lidan's face, forcing her eyes to narrow and her hand came up to shield against the onslaught. The wind clawed at her coat but she pushed on, the torch guttering before coaxing itself back to life.

Just beyond the edge of her light, Lidan heard the hurried breaths of a child. She lifted the torch in a vain attempt to throw the light in a wider arc, moving forwards, following the sound.

She saw Abbi's back, her shirt soaked through and clinging to her tiny shoulders, her dark curls hanging straight in a curtain down to her waist. Even from this distance Lidan saw the girl's body tremble.

'Abbi?' Lidan asked, careful not to spook the girl and send her screaming into the bush like a frightened piglet. She took a step forwards, one hand reaching for Abbi's shoulder and the other hoisting the torch.

The growl came again and Lidan stopped cold.

Her stomach twisted to knots and her breath quickened. The ngaru was so close she could hear it sniffing and exhaling over the hiss of the rain. Her eyes followed the sound, rising from the crown of her sister's head to the darkness just beyond the light. It breathed again, preparing to pounce, waiting on her next move to decide its own.

'Abbi, it's Lidan,' she whispered, hardly daring to move her lips in case the creature snapped forward.

'Liddy?' came the shaking reply, Abbi's voice no more than a squeak of terror.

'When I tell you to run, you turn and run. Understand?'

She didn't answer.

The ngaru snarled again from the shadows.

'*Do you understand?*'

'Yes,' Abbi whispered, her tiny head twitching in agreement.

Lidan's free hand lowered slowly to her knife and settled on the bone handle. Once the weapon of a ngaru, now it would be turned against them. 'Abbi, *run!*'

Her sister spun and a clawed hand darted from the darkness. It snagged the girl and yanked her away by the back of the neck. Her scream ended in a hollow snap, and the creature launched itself at Lidan.

It hit her in the chest and knocked the torch away to sputter and die, driving her backwards in a tumble of flailing limbs, sticks, leaves, and cold steel. Somehow Lidan drew her knives and started slashing wildly, tangled with the creature and refusing to give an inch. She couldn't see the ngaru to plan her attack, she just cut and stabbed and screamed and punched, kicking and twisting whenever the thing got a hand on her for longer than a moment.

It faltered under the ferocity of her attack, fuelled by rage and pain and sadness. In the flashes of lightning, she saw the creature stagger as it tried to back away, and realised it was not nearly as large as the one that attacked Loge near the Caine. She launched at it, the knives bearing down on its back as it turned to crawl away.

Pus and mucus sprayed into the night as she stabbed. The ngaru wailed and screamed, thrashed and clawed, marking Lidan in a hundred places, yet she felt none of them. Driven by desperation and grief, she forced the ngaru against a tree in the raging storm, one of its arms hanging from threads of muscle while the other pawed aimlessly at Lidan's shoulder. Its strength faded, her cuts and slashes too much for its raw, rotting frame to handle.

Lightning flashed again and she saw its face. She jammed a knife under its chin, driving it through its mouth into its brain. It twitched and danced and Lidan yanked the blade free, swinging up with the other to stab the sharp steel through its neck and into its spine.

It fell, flopping to the wet ground and gasping like a dying fish. Its eyes found her for long enough to give one last, defiant snarl.

Lidan forgot her knives. She lifted her foot; then with all her anger, all her hate for the ngaru and Yorrell, all her fear of her mother and her desperation to please her father, she slammed her boot into the ngaru's face and crushed it like the insect it was.

Abbi wasn't far.

Her small frame lay at the foot of a huge ghost-bark tree, motionless and soaked by the drenching rain. Lidan found her in the flashes of lightning, following the sound of shallow breathing and the wheeze of exhalation. It became a desperate grunt as Lidan staggered to her side and pushed wet hair from her face. The darkness hid most of the horror, but in another flash of lightning, she saw blood coursing down from a grisly tear at the girl's temple.

One of Abbi's eyes swivelled to look up at her sister in the light of the storm, but the other remained fixed at an odd angle. Blood bubbled from her mouth as she tried to talk and a sob shuddered through Lidan.

Tears fell with the force of the rain, mingling with the water from the sky. Her small, favourite sister, gasped again for a breath and Lidan felt it rattle through her chest. Her ribs were shattered, and likely her spine fared little better. Lidan had seen enough rangers in the healing rooms to know what grunting breath and bubbling blood meant. Abbi was drowning and there was nothing she could do.

Shouts came from the trees. Torchlight glowed, and Lidan knew her sister's screams had raised the alarm.

'Too late, eh, little mouse?'

The one eye Abbi controlled levelled on her sister's face and her lips quivered. The pain must have been incredible. Lidan saw it in the shiver of her body and the twitch of her hands. She knew what her father did for his rangers when they lay broken beyond repair, too far gone for skilled hands to bring them back, yet not so damaged that death spared them suffering. He helped them with a small mercy, the last gift he could afford them after years of loyal service.

Abbi needed that mercy.

Lidan bit down on another sob as Abbi choked on her blood, her eye pleading for the pain to end. Lidan cradled her sister's head to her chest and wept. She kissed the little girl and held her close.

'I'm sorry, Abbi...'

It didn't take much.

Hardly any pressure at all and it was done.

Lidan looked down through her sobs at unseeing eyes, glazed and staring at the sky, unflinching in the rain. She gathered the broken little body into her arms and cried.

She found her family again as the storm passed to the north, the rain hammering down as the thunder retreated into the distance. The first person to see her was Kelill. The woman's hands went to her mouth and she screamed, turning to run, shouting for Erlon and the others to come. The sound was distant, across a great chasm of pain none of them could cross.

Rangers appeared with Lidan's father and stopped dead at the sight of her. Erlon hit the ground like a stone, staring at his eldest cradling the body of one of his babies. Siman waved and a pair of rangers pulled their daari to his feet and led him away, murmuring words Lidan could not decipher.

Siman appeared, his long, scarred arms reaching for Abbi and slipping the weight from Lidan's grasp with gentle ease. His eyes scanned Lidan's face in the driving rain but she didn't know what he was looking at, or searching for. He left her alone, surrounded by rangers who had no idea what to say or do except stare.

Sellan shoved them aside and ran to Lidan, for once a genuine expression of horror and sorrow on her face. She collected her daughter against her chest and sank with her to the ground, ignorant of the mud and dripping blood.

'I thought I'd lost you,' Sellan whispered in her daughter's ear. Lidan heard the breathless fear and knew it was the truth. She almost *had* lost her. If not for a pair of knives and the training of a young ranger with nothing better to do, Lidan would certainly be dead.

She listened to the beat of her mother's heart and let everything else fade; the rain, the thunder, the screams of Raeh realising one of her babies was gone. She let her father's roars and the distant howls of the ngaru vanish into the abyss of her sadness and heard nothing but the beat of the dana's heart.

There was one sound missing from the commotion of the camp, unheard among the groans of wounded rangers and crying children. There were no cries or grunts of birthing, no heaving efforts to push from the wagons.

'Mother?' Lidan asked in a hoarse croak.

Sellan rocked her daughter back and forth. 'Yes, petal?'

'Farah?' The name spilled from her lips to fall with the tears and rain. For a moment there was no reply, then her mother's hands squeezed a little tighter.

'It's a boy.'

EPILOGUE

The Hidden Keep, Southern Orthia

'You have to let me see her…' Ran protested in a barely audible whisper. His voice was broken and weak from lack of use, his head throbbed and he could hardly move his eyes without pain lancing across the front of his skull.

'I told you before, she is well, but you are in no state to see one another,' Collan replied from a table near the door where he stood busily grinding herbs. He moved to the hearth and swung the kettle off the fire.

'Is she awake?'

Collan shook his head but did not turn. 'Not yet. She stirs, but does not wake.'

'I need to see her,' Ran insisted. He tried to sit up, but the burns along his arms screamed with heat and he groaned, collapsing back against the bed. He surrendered and let the pain go, willing it to ease and soothe itself.

'Much better, Master Ran,' Collan nodded and approached with a pot of herbal tea and a clean towel. 'I felt the change that time. The more you turn your power inward, the sooner the wounds will heal.'

He held a cup of water to Ran's lips and let him drink—their usual ritual, before he was offered a pain-relieving tea and further rest. Collan wiped drops of water from Ran's chin and leaned back to check dressings and fuss over the cast on Ran's broken ankle—injuries all sustained in the explosion of his magic and taking what seemed an age to heal.

His power had only just begun to pool again, depleted and wounded in the effort to destroy the creatures that had chased them, and unable to heal his body as quickly as it had before. It left him languishing in a sickbed in one of the keep's towers, and at the mercy of Collan, the Keep Master, who appeared to moonlight as a nurse and teacher.

'You promised to tell me about Lackmah today,' Ran reminded him. He asked about it daily, and each day Collan found an excuse not to reveal any more than a few cryptic riddles.

'Did I?' He feigned surprise and moved to sit in a chair by the fire. 'I don't remember that.'

Collan cracked a walnut in his hand, the slight limp in his left leg belying the strength visible underneath the layers of his robes. Ran rolled his eyes. If this kept up, he'd be healed and a hundred years older by the time he got any answers.

'Yes, you did promise. You said you'd answer all my questions and then some—'

'When?'

'You said it the morning I woke up, after the attack!'

'No,' Collan corrected, tossing the broken nutshell in the fire. 'I said I *would* tell you, but did I happen to mention *when*?'

Ran searched his memory of the morning after his explosive arrival at the keep, Collan's face hovering over him as he demanded to see Sasha. He'd apparently screamed a few other things at his rescuers—an insistence on an explanation of the creatures and one repeated word.

Lackmah.

'You said you would tell me "all in good time".'

'You think now is a good time?' Collan eyed him, light brown eyes steadily watching for a reaction.

Ran looked at the ceiling instead and sighed. 'No. But—'

'The question runs through your head constantly, doesn't it?' Collan hadn't asked that before.

Ran swallowed and nodded. It did, haunting him through his dreams, his ghost asking day and night, more persistently than she'd ever asked about the scroll. He'd ignored her once, at his peril, and he wasn't about to do so again.

'And you think I know enough to end the confusion in your mind? Enough to put your questions to bed?'

'You have to! You're the Keep Master!'

'This is true,' Collan conceded with a nod, then looked at the fire. He steepled his fingers and sank into thought, leaving Ran to wonder if he would, just this once, give in to his pleas. 'Lackmah? You want to know about Lackmah?'

'Yes, I do!' If Ran could have opened his hands in supplication, he would have, but his burns and bandages held them still. All he could do was look at Collan and beg with his eyes. 'That name has followed me for more than half a year. Since the night I was cursed with this magic, it's all I've wanted to know.'

'And if I tell you, will you stop this infernal chatter? Will you leave it alone and submit to training here with the rest of the magic-weavers?'

Ran paused with his mouth open, unsure if the trade was worth the price. 'Yes...'

Collan narrowed his eyes and leaned towards Ran. 'If I tell you, here and now you must swear the oath and pledge yourself to the Keep. You will not leave, under your own power or that of another. You will commit to a life here, with your fellow magic-weavers, and you will train. You will learn to harness and control your power, and in time, you will become a teacher. Are you sure this is what you want?'

'Yes.'

'Right. In that case...' The man sighed and settled back in his chair. 'Lackmah and the creatures who hunted you are so closely linked, one story cannot be told without the other.'

'What?' Ran demanded. His heart began to pound and his mouth ran cotton-dry. He hadn't expected that.

Collan continued to speak to the fire, as if he drew the story from the flickering flames. 'Lackmah was a village near the Disputed Territory, mostly populated by farmers trading with passing army columns, supplying the front with fresh food and weapons. It became quite the hub of business over the summer, but in winter when the fighting ceased, the village returned to its quiet ways. One winter, about fifteen years ago, the village's population vanished. It wasn't until the thaw that the duke's vanguard found it empty, the livestock dead or missing, the crops abandoned. It took months to discover what had happened.'

Ran knew.

His stomach twisted at the memory of all those bones, the bodies piled in the cottage on the lonely road. He saw them in his mind—their white teeth and hollow eye sockets gaping from the depths of the house, some hidden in shadow and the rest illuminated by moonlight. His ghost's body lay prone across the doorway and he shuddered.

Collan continued in the silence, shaking his head. 'They found a place so foul and against the laws of humanity, the duke outlawed the mention of its name. The people of Lackmah were taken by witches, derramentis mages drunk on power, and murdered for the sake of experimentation. The witches killed them one by one, with each death fashioning a servant from the corpse.

'At first, they failed and the dead remained dead, hence the dusty bones piled high within the walls of the cottage. With practice and a steady supply of villagers, they perfected their magic. They tied the souls of the dead to theirs and held them trapped here, among the living, unable to pass through to the realm of the Black Rider. Lackmah is not the reason magic is despised in Orthia, but it is a powerful demonstration of the damage magic can inflict when allowed to run unchecked.'

He lifted a finger to Ran and their eyes met.

'One winter was all it took. One winter, to massacre an entire village. Men, women and children; house by house, farm by farm, until not one family remained to till the earth when the spring sun thawed the ice.'

'Fuck,' Ran breathed.

'Indeed.' Collan stood and slipped his hands up his sleeves, moving to the window and staring out at a view Ran could not see. 'The witches fled and evaded capture, but the legacy of their massacre remains.'

Ran's stomach flipped. 'The creatures on the road?'

Collan nodded slowly. 'The beasts are all that remain of the people of Lackmah. Their souls and lives, corrupted in death by an evil we have yet to comprehend.'

The image of his ghost girl, broken and alone in the cottage full of bones, rose again in Ran's mind. Then a flash of blackened teeth and spraying blood filled his vision and he flinched away.

It couldn't be true...

'When the witches fled, the creatures were left to wander. For the most part they keep to the caves and dark places of the world, but they do emerge to hunt. We often hear them, always moving south, but they've never tried to attack our walls.' He glanced at Ran. 'Until the night you arrived.'

Ran tried to swallow a hard lump from his throat but it wouldn't move. Collan's voice became distant, lost in the noise in Ran's head.

The creatures are the remains of the people of Lackmah...

'Ranoth, your power was triggered because you stumbled upon the site of the greatest magical massacre Orthia has ever witnessed. Had you never approached that house, you might have lived your life free of the curse that all in this Keep claim as their own. You are as much a victim of that place as those who died within its walls.' The Keep Master sighed and made his way to the door. 'I'll get your supper, Ran, and we can talk about it some more.'

He slipped out and left Ran alone, though he was never truly alone. His ghost stood at the end of the bed, pale and beautiful, unchanged from the first time he'd seen her in the house of bones. She watched him with sadness in her eyes but she did not flinch as he stared at her, almost gaping, rocked by the truth in Master Collan's words.

'Is it true?' he asked, not expecting an answer.

'Yes,' she whispered, her lips barely moving.

'And the creature from the Parry farm, the one who tracked us... The one who... The one who attacked Sasha?' Ran choked on the words. A tear slipped down his cheek and his hands shook with rage. 'That was *you?*'

Her ice-blue eyes locked onto his.

'Yes.'

To be continued...

ACKNOWLEDGEMENTS

I would like to take this opportunity to thank the people who have helped bring *Blood of Heirs* to the world. Without the care, love and support of those mentioned below, and likely dozens more I have encountered over the years, this book would never have seen the light of day.

My parents and grandparents—for supporting and enabling this obsession. You could not possibly have understood it or seen what it might become. I hope I have made you proud.

My husband, Josh—for paying the bills, wiping away the tears and making me laugh, for holding things together when the writing called me away and most of all, for loving me as I am.

My loyal beta readers—Bec Murton, Ben and Jess Dawson, Aiki Flinthart, Laura Hughes, Jeff Bryant and Graham Austin-King—for your encouragement, honesty, excitement and commitment to bringing this book to life. There are not enough words to thank you

My editor, Sarah Chorn and proofreader, Bethan Hindmarsh—you cannot know how much I value your hard work, critique and faith in the world I built.

My excellent cover artist, Pen Astridge—for taking this challenge with both hands and creating art so much better than I could have ever imagined.

My author-friends, literary colleagues and Fantasy Queens (you know who you are) — for welcoming me into a community of kindness, for your support, encouragement, genuine friendship and love, for being my cheer squad and pushing me through doors I did not know I could open.

All those who have read my work across the years (there are too many of you to name, so I must be content with thanking you as a collective)—for your thoughts, advice and critique. You taught me so much.

Finally, Dr Steve Andrews at Brisbane Private Hospital—for repairing my right hand halfway through the year I wrote *Blood of Heirs*, and again while I wrote *Legacy of Ghosts*. I couldn't have finished this book, or continued on writing more stories, without your expert care.

ABOUT THE AUTHOR

Living in outback Queensland, Australia, surrounded by coal mines, snakes, marsupials and a wide blue sky, Alicia is a writer, a mum, a cat-herder and a dog-whisperer. She began writing in her teens and never grew out of the phase, working in her spare time until the birth of her son allowed her to focus on writing full-time. She has also dabbled in editing and blogging while completing a Bachelor of Education and studying a Post Graduate Certificate in Ancient History.